THE
PANDORA
ROOM

Also by Christopher Golden

Ararat

Dead Ringers

Sons of Anarchy: BRATVA

Snowblind

Baltimore, or, The Steadfast Tin Soldier and the Vampire (with Mike Mignola)

Joe Golem and the Drowning City (with Mike Mignola)

Father Gaetano's Puppet Catechism (with Mike Mignola)

The Boys are Back in Town

Wildwood Road

The Ferryman

Strangewood

Straight On 'til Morning

Soulless

The Myth Hunters: Book One of The Veil

The Borderkind: Book Two of The Veil

The Lost Ones: Book Three of The Veil

The Ocean Dark (as Jack Rogan)

The Shadow Saga

Of Saints and Shadows

Angel Souls and Devil Hearts

Of Masques and Martyrs

The Gathering Dark

Walking Nightmares

The Graves of Saints

King of Hell

THE
PANDORA
ROOM

CHRISTOPHER GOLDEN

ST. MARTIN'S PRESS ☙ NEW YORK

THE PANDORA ROOM. Copyright © 2019 by Christopher Golden. All rights reserved. Printed in the United States of America. For information, address St. Martin's Press, 175 Fifth Avenue, New York, N.Y. 10010.

www.stmartins.com

The Library of Congress Cataloging-in-Publication Data is available upon request.

ISBN 978-1-250-19210-3 (hardcover)
ISBN 978-1-250-19211-0 (ebook)

Our books may be purchased in bulk for promotional, educational, or business use. Please contact your local bookseller or the Macmillan Corporate and Premium Sales Department at 1-800-221-7945, extension 5442, or by email at MacmillanSpecialMarkets@macmillan.com.

First Edition: April 2019

10 9 8 7 6 5 4 3 2 1

For Kristina Day.
A woman of courage and character.

ACKNOWLEDGMENTS

I'm deeply indebted to all of the folks who read and loved *Ararat*, who wanted to see more of Walker as much as I did. My profound thanks to my excellent editor, Michael Homler, as well as to Lauren Jablonski and the entire team at St. Martin's Press. Gratitude, as always, to my agent, Howard Morhaim, my manager, Peter Donaldson, and to all of the friends and family members who keep me sane when the world is not, or when I go down the creative rabbit hole. Special thanks to Dr. Maria Carlini and to Weston Ochse, for their advice and consultation. Finally, my love always to Connie, who is the reason for everything, and to the three excellent human beings who are our children.

THE
PANDORA
ROOM

ONE

Sophie Durand loved her work, but she didn't want to die for it. Today the two desires had come into conflict, which would have been unsettling enough on any day but was especially irritating given how otherwise perfect a morning it had been.

A gust of hot wind billowed the awnings of shops and rustled the linen dresses hung out for tourists to peruse as they navigated the narrow market street of Amadiya. Sophie felt beads of sweat run down the small of her back, but she ignored her discomfort, biting into a pear as she meandered, waiting for her colleagues to rejoin her. Despite the locals and a small handful of other tourists, she felt exposed and alone, and her gaze shifted left and right while she mentally calculated methods of self-defense that were close at hand.

She'd noticed the first of the two men twenty minutes earlier, watching her from in front of one of the stalls in the open-air fruit-and-vegetable market. He'd made a small bit of theater, getting the seller to weigh a cluster of grapes, but she'd noticed the way he looked at her. Not with benign curiosity or even lustful appraisal but with disinterest so carefully blank that it caught her attention immediately. There seemed something surreptitious about his lack of expression, and when she caught him looking again, she'd decided to move on from the stall laden with oranges and forego any further fruits and vegetables for this visit. What she'd already acquired would have to be enough.

Nearly ten minutes passed before she'd seen the second man. At first she'd assumed it to be the same person, but then she had realized there were two of these strange men with their mustaches and their sun-bleached linen shirts. They looked so alike they could have been twins whose mother had dressed them.

Tourists, she had told herself. Surely not locals. Their stiffness and their mode of dress set them apart, although something about that observation troubled Sophie. It niggled at the back of her mind, this assumption that they were tourists, but their glancing attentions bothered her more and so she moved on, never mentioning to her two colleagues that she suspected the three of them were being followed.

Paranoia, she thought, and she went about her business. She finished her pear, wrapped the core in a small cloth, and tucked it into the side pocket of her heavy rucksack before slinging it back over her shoulder.

Sophie liked pockets. Her coworkers tended to tease her about the capri-style cargo pants she wore on the job, but she always argued that male designers had historically deprived women of pockets in their clothing, and in her line of work, she wanted as many as she could get.

In one of those pockets, her phone vibrated against her thigh. Barely thinking, she drew it out and glanced at the message on the screen: *Are u really going to ignore me? Is that what it's come to?*

Sophie rolled her eyes. She didn't have time for this nonsense, but she did feel a flash of guilt. With a glance around her, she tapped a quick reply. *Just stop, for both our sakes. I'm not coming back to NYC anytime soon.*

She kept the phone in her hand for a half minute, expecting a response, but when she glanced at the screen again, there was not even the telltale ellipsis to indicate a reply might be incoming. Sophie felt frustrated for a moment and then realized that maybe she was getting precisely what she asked for.

Exhaling, she slipped her phone back into her pocket and kept moving.

The population of Amadiya consisted of fewer than five thousand souls. Tourists were as common a sight as birds flying overhead, but their numbers were smaller. A few dozen visited each day during the summer, no more than one hundred in the cooler months. It was early June now and getting warmer by the day.

Martin had gone off to the post office, and Lamar had stepped into a shop to see if he could find a little kit to fix his glasses. Sophie realized she'd nearly forgotten one of her vital errands for the day, and she ducked inside a shop to purchase several small jars of tahini that she had promised their cook.

After she'd browsed the little shop and the merchant tallied up the cost of the nuts and figs and bottles of tahini, she glanced up and saw one of the mustache twins standing in front of a rack of various dried, bottled herbs. The man had his back to her, but his hands were motionless. He gazed at the herbs as if trying to understand their purpose, with no evidence that he intended to buy anything at all.

Moments after Sophie exited the shop, the man followed. She glanced back down the market street and saw his partner. They'd done an awful lot of browsing, yet their hands were empty. They had no shopping bags, no backpacks, nothing at all. The first man had apparently not even bought the grapes he had fussed over at the fruit stall. In that moment, she knew she hadn't been paranoid at all. These men weren't here for grapes.

Sophie collided with a man on the street. She recoiled as he touched her arm, and her head struck a display of straw shoulder bags hanging beneath a shop awning. She whipped around to face the man, shifting into a defensive posture, right hand clenched into a fist, and only then did she see it was Lamar Curtis.

Lamar cocked his head. "Well, *you* seem distracted."

Sophie blinked, the words taking a moment to register. She mustered a polite smile—her business smile. "That's a good word for it." Her fist unclenched. "Sorry about that."

"You want to tell me what just happened?"

Sophie cast a look over her shoulder but now saw no sign of the mustache twins. She shrugged her rucksack to draw Lamar's attention to it.

"Figs and nuts. Tahini. A small portion of the truffles Dmitri wanted."

"A happy cook means our bellies will be that much happier," Lamar said, keeping it light, although he still studied her with cautious appraisal. He tapped his own bag, a heavily laden cloth sack he wore with its strap slung across his chest. "I've got apples and pears, a small watermelon, and those apricots you love so much."

She smiled. "I bought grapes. Some fresh greens and herbs."

"Oranges?"

Sophie frowned. "No oranges," she said quietly. "Where's Martin?"

"Probably off buying you roses," Lamar muttered.

Sophie shot him a hard look. "You know it's not like that. And now's not the time to have this conversation."

"You want to tell me what's got you so spooked?"

"When we're in motion," she said. "Go find Martin and meet me at the edge. No more shopping. I want to get to the car."

Lamar started to reply, but Sophie set off, leaving him near the awning-covered entrance to a tobacconist's shop. They were a block from the edge of town, and she crossed that distance as swiftly as she was able without appearing as if she wanted to flee. Her heart galloped along inside her chest, and she knew her face would be flushed—fear had that effect on her—but she did her best to keep her emotions hidden. Sophie had become good at that over the years, for better or worse. She'd had cancer as a child—acute myelogenous leukemia—and had quickly learned that if she put on a happy face, it meant she wouldn't have to help manage the emotional state of the adults around her. An ugly lesson, and she'd often pondered if that childhood self-preservation had turned her into a selfish adult, but there were days she still felt both the emotional and physical effects of her cancer, so she figured she could not be blamed for still protecting herself. Other people's emotions were messy and beautiful, but they could also be inconvenient and even dangerous.

Martin's, for instance. His infatuation with her felt nice, but she'd kept him at a distance. For now.

She willed Lamar to hurry. Martin had gone to get the mail. Normally, a courier would have brought any packages out to the dig later in the week, but the team had been complaining about a lack of fresh fruit for several days, and Sophie had spent so much time in the tunnels that she had decided to take Lamar and Martin with her to Amadiya. She'd needed to clear her head, shake off the psychological cobwebs that came from living a nomadic life, and at first it had worked.

Amadiya might have been something out of a storybook. Most Westerners would have appreciated its unique beauty but never guessed at its significance. Even now, with her pulse still racing, Sophie stood at a low rock wall and looked out across the valley and the mountain range around them, marveling at the tenacity of this little town. Sheer stone cliffs dropped off precipitously on the other side of the low wall, with vibrant green forest far below. The Assyrians had settled on top of this plateau nearly five thousand years before—*Five thousand years*, she thought—but Sophie and her colleagues believed there had been people here even before that. Never would she have imagined she would come to Amadiya to study something else, but her team wasn't here for the town. Archaeologists had been studying the place for generations and would continue to do so for generations more. Her job was elsewhere.

The town's isolation contributed to its beauty. A thousand meters long and half that in width, it had a gentle, integrated community of Muslim Kurds, Christians, and Jews, each of whom could lay claim to a portion of the local history. The minaret of the town's mosque towered overhead, a handful of tourists navigated narrow market streets, and otherwise people went on with their lives. They lived in Kurdish territory, in northern Iraq, only miles from the Turkish border, a region whose sovereignty was constantly being contested, but to its people, Amadiya was only Amadiya, far from such troubles, alone up on their mountain.

Sophie felt the sun on her face, let the wind blow her hair wild. To anyone passing, she'd look like an ordinary tourist, perhaps a bit weather-beaten and certainly not out to impress anyone with her outfit. Just a woman on vacation. She'd moved to the edge of town because others would be walking its perimeter, mostly locals but certainly the few tourists in town. Out here in the open, she'd be much more visible than in the narrow market street. If anyone were to come after her, there would be witnesses.

Minutes passed as she calmed the hammering of her heart into something like its normal rhythm. Just as she took a deep breath, a voice said her name. She turned, pushing her hair away from her eyes, to find Lamar standing with Martin Jungling. The contrast between the two men had never been starker. Short, often dour Lamar was as dark as tall, lanky Martin was pale, but their demeanor differentiated them even more than their appearance. At thirty-seven, Lamar had established a reputation as a serious historian and an expert on ancient languages. He taught classes at Columbia and the Sorbonne and had published two well-received books. Martin had energy and enthusiasm and a certain charm, but he was a twenty-four-year-old archaeology grad student eager to have his name on something—a discovery, a book, a professional paper, someday a college library.

Sophie liked them both a great deal, but right now Martin looked anxious as a hen in a foxhouse. She could rely on Lamar to stay cool, and that meant the world.

"Are we in danger?" Martin asked a little too loudly.

Sophie smiled, but not for their benefit. "We're leaving. Did you get the mail?"

Martin patted the leather satchel that hung at his hip. Unshaven, his hair unruly and his clothing rumpled, that satchel made him look as if he were still on a campus somewhere.

She stepped closer to them, looped her arm through Lamar's as if they were a couple, and smiled at both men. "We're not in any danger," she said, and she knew she might be lying. "But we've definitely been noticed by people whose attention we don't want. So we're—"

Martin started to turn to look back the way they'd come. Lamar patted him on the back with what most would view as an expression of bonhomie.

"Sophie's talking to you, pal. Keep your eyes on her."

Martin muttered an apology, struggling to keep himself from scanning their surroundings.

"We're leaving," Sophie said again. She and Lamar began walking along the edge of town. As Martin fell in behind them, Sophie glanced back at him. "Anything interesting in the mail?"

Martin looked nervous as hell. He stole a quick glimpse over his shoulder. Sophie and Lamar turned right and began to hurry closer to the center of town. The trio picked up their pace as they passed the end of the market street and moved along a wider road. She thought she caught a quick glimpse of a familiar mustache but tried to play it off as if she hadn't seen him, and she kept walking.

A bearded, wild-haired hiker flashed them a hang-loose hand signal in greeting as they passed him. His head bobbed as if he moved to music none of them could hear, and Sophie wondered if she imagined the pungent herbal aroma wafting off him. A local man hurried by them with a small hand truck burdened with wooden crates full of potatoes—late for the market.

"Sophie," Martin began.

"Not yet," she replied. "Tell me about the post office."

Martin swore under his breath, but he got the point. As he mentioned a package for the cook and something heavy he thought must be a book, as well as a few old-fashioned letters, the three of them moved quickly through the center of town. Once away from the market street, they encountered fewer and fewer locals. Sophie had no doubt that the two strange men would be following.

Her heart began to race again. As they walked past a shuttered home, lilting music coming from inside, Lamar tried to ask her if she was all right. Sophie kept her gaze fixed on the street ahead of them, ignoring the colorfully garbed generational trio of women who passed by, surrounding a man who might be husband to one, son to another, father to the third.

Finally, they arrived at the small, weedy parking lot where they'd left their dusty Jeep. The cracked and potholed pavement looked as if it had suffered a minor earthquake, and now that it occurred to her, she thought that might be true. This part of the world had done more than its share of suffering over the years. Hell, over the centuries.

Only when they were stowing their bags inside the Jeep did Sophie allow herself to look back the way they'd come.

The mustache twins were there. The two men had stopped a block and a half away to lean against the front of a building and smoke brown-leaf, home-rolled cigarettes. They seemed amused, as if they knew the fear they'd inspired and it gave them pleasure. Sophie had met such men before. They existed in every culture she'd experienced, and she wanted to run them over in the Jeep.

Instead, she slipped into the driver's seat, fired up the engine, and tore out of the parking lot before Lamar had even closed the passenger-side door. In the backseat, Martin let out a grunt as her acceleration bumped him about before he'd gotten his long legs settled.

"Sorry," she said. "But better this bumpy road than being back there with those assholes."

Martin turned on the rear seat and peered out the back. "Who the hell were those guys?" he asked, his Belgian accent thickening. "You were freaking me out!"

The phrase made her smile in spite of everything. Belgian by birth, American by education, Martin watched too much television whenever he could get a Wi-Fi signal on his laptop.

Sophie glanced in the rearview mirror, but she could only see the men's legs. At the corner, turning along the switchback road that made its way down the mountain, she looked out her window and saw the smug bastards smoking their nasty cigarettes. One of them raised a hand to wave to her.

Then they were out of sight, and Sophie exhaled.

The job had just gotten more complicated.

Martin had to be bursting at the seams, wanting to plead for answers, but he had learned to tamp down his enthusiasms around her. When he kept his cool, he could be charming as hell. His eyes were a sparkling blue so vivid they reminded her of the famed grotto in Capri, and he had a wonderful laugh, an insightful mind, and he tended to sing to himself while he worked as if he'd forgotten that anyone around him could hear. Some members of the team complained, but most of them found the habit entertaining, even joining in if they knew the lyrics. On days that felt more like drudgery than discovery, Martin made the hours more bearable. If he hadn't been so much younger, not to mention her subordinate, Sophie might have surprised him with a quick seduction, just for a night. But the way he often looked at her, the way he spoke to her, not flirting but yearning, she knew that if she ever crossed that line, he wouldn't want it to be a one-time thing, which was even more reason not to allow herself to be tempted.

Then there were days like this, when the novelty of being halfway around the world from his home made him jittery, even without the potentially real threat the day had brought them.

It would've been so much easier if it had just been Sophie and Lamar.

Her phone buzzed in her pocket. She kept her hands on the wheel and ignored it, though both men looked at her expectantly. Sophie steered around potholes on the road that wound down off the mountain and through the trees. The air conditioner had been cranked up full blast, but now she rolled down both her window and Lamar's. Hot air blasted in, but at least the air moved. The heat had been baking inside the Jeep the entire time they had been up in Amadiya. Now the shadows of the trees provided a bit of relief, though it would be short-lived.

Again, her phone buzzed, and again, she ignored it.

The Jeep emerged from the trees, and she turned west along a narrow road whose pavement was so dusty and faded that it seemed to merge with the land around it, as if one day the road might be erased altogether and the way out into the valley would be forgotten. The mountains loomed all around them, but down here in the hot, rocky basin, they seemed more ominous than beautiful.

"You really not going to look to see who's texting you?" Lamar asked.

"I know who it is."

In the backseat, Martin sniffed in disapproval. "It's Steven."

Sophie glanced in the rearview mirror, catching his eye. "Of course it's Steven. Mind your own business."

Martin threw up his hands as if to say he'd never intended to chime in, which of course was an unspoken lie. If anyone had opinions about the relationship she'd abandoned when she'd left her teaching post at New York University, it was Martin.

Her brows knitted. What if this time it wasn't Steven at all? For the first time, it occurred to her that it might be her mother calling . . . that it might be the call she had been dreading but expecting for the past two years. Sophie's parents had divorced a month after her high school graduation, and her father, French by birth and inclination, had moved back to Rennes. They'd made a strange couple, to be sure— he an Afro-French composer of motion picture soundtracks and she an American corporate lawyer. For years after their divorce, their only contact was through their daughter, but then Philip Durand had begun to slip, and that slippage became rapid early-onset Alzheimer's, and before Sophie even realized her parents had been in touch with each other, her mother, Imani, had announced plans to close her practice and move to France to care for her ex-husband.

The sweetest fucking story Sophie had ever heard, she had said at the time. And the saddest. There were other factors, of course, and Sophie focused on them, especially when talking to Steven . . . but really, once her mother had left New York for France, it had been only a matter of time before Sophie left, too.

Her pocket buzzed again. "Damn it," she muttered. What if it wasn't Steven?

Sophie glanced at Lamar, but he shook his head.

"We have more important things to worry about," he said as if she needed that reminder.

"So," Martin said, leaning forward between the two front seats. "You going to tell us what we were running from back there? I saw those two guys who were watching us when we got back to the Jeep."

"They followed me for at least twenty minutes. Probably longer. I overheard one of them speaking Turkish. Maybe they're government, maybe something else."

"Shit," Martin hissed.

Lamar shook his head. "Don't they realize we couldn't give a shit about politics?"

"I'd rather not get caught in an international incident out here," Sophie said quietly.

The Kurds were scattered across the entire region—nearly forty million of them, by some estimates, with at least six million in the autonomous region of northern Iraq now called Kurdistan. In late 2017, they'd voted for independence in overwhelming numbers, only to be pressured by the Iraqi government and military to call off any attempt to break away into their own independent state. The Turkish government was dealing with their own Kurdish insurgency and feared a truly independent Kurdistan would trigger a powder keg in an already volatile region. The Beneath Project—the archaeological dig Sophie had begun months ago—had been permitted by the Iraqi government, with supervision by their Office of Antiquities as well as a representative of the Kurdistan Regional Government. But given that the dig was only a handful of miles from the Turkish border, and many conservatives in the Turkish government were suspicious of any international activity in the area, the Turks had tried to insist they be allowed to send observers as well, and they'd been rebuffed.

"What did they think they'd accomplish by spying on us?" Martin asked.

Sophie glanced at him in the rearview mirror . . . and saw the plume of dust rising from the road a couple of miles behind them.

"Give it a few minutes," she replied, her chest tightening, "and you can probably ask them."

Lamar twisted around in his seat. "Fuck! Sophie, floor it!"

TWO

Sophie floored it. The Jeep bounced over the rutted, cracked pavement, but she was more worried about the road ahead than the road beneath them. In a mile or so, they would have to turn northwest on a narrow dirt road that led along a twisting path among the foothills of the mountains that separated this part of Kurdistan from Turkey.

"I don't want them following us." She glanced in the rearview mirror again, then had to swerve with the abrupt turn in the road. "Shit! We can't let these guys track us back to the dig."

Lamar held on to the dashboard with one hand, twisted around in his seat and looked out the back window. "Why would they do it like this? I don't get it. We've got Beyza at the dig every day. If these guys are Turkish, they could get anything they need from her bosses."

Sophie blinked. Her heartbeat thrummed in her ears, and she kept glancing at the road and the rearview, at Lamar and at Martin, trying to decide what to do. She couldn't think about who might be chasing them now. Turkish spies made sense to her, but Lamar was right. Beyza Solak was a professor from Atatürk University whom the Iraqis had allowed to take part in the dig at the request of UNESCO.

Martin unbuckled his seat belt and turned onto his knees, peering out the rear windshield. "Who the hell are those guys?"

They hit a pothole so deep it made the whole car drop and then slam upward. Martin smashed his head into the hardtop and sprawled across the rear seat in a daze. He swore, rubbing his head, and started to buckle himself in again without Sophie having to bark at him to do so.

Seconds passed by with Sophie and Lamar staring out at the road ahead of them. They rounded a bend and started down the dusty slope between two low hills. A stretch of woods awaited at the bottom of the slope, and Sophie wondered if she could hide the Jeep in there, let their pursuers pass, then turn around and hightail it back to Amadiya, where there were people who would bear witness if their pursuers tried anything.

But the vehicle behind them seemed closer now. Whatever engine it had under its hood had more power than the Jeep's. Her heart thrummed in her chest like the engine racing under the hood. She worried about her heart. Sometimes she had trouble catching her breath and her chest hurt, and she thought of all the warnings her childhood doctors had given her about adult complications from radiation and chemotherapy.

You're fine, she thought. *Drive!*

"They're closing on us," Lamar said calmly as if he'd resigned himself to a fight.

"Shit," Martin muttered in the backseat, wincing in pain as he clutched at his skull. "What is wrong with these people?" He snapped his head up, catching Sophie's eye in the rearview mirror. "Hold on—do you think they're going to kill us?"

The question went unanswered. The Jeep's engine roared, and Sophie wondered how it had come to this. They were archaeologists, researchers, teachers. Martin was still a graduate student, but here they were on a stretch of road in the middle of nowhere with men chasing them—men full of menace and malice and the presumption that they could do anything to anyone and get away with it.

Sophie feared they might be right.

In her pocket, her phone buzzed again. *Damn it, Steven!*

She hoped it was Steven. Told herself it wasn't her mother, that today wasn't the day her father would leave the world.

Sophie's hands hurt from gripping the wheel so tightly. Her knuckles had turned white. Nothing in her life had prepared her for this. She had been in danger before, been face-to-face with indigenous people or local militia who didn't want an archaeology dig to continue. She'd been robbed at knifepoint on the New York subway by a man who'd put his hands on her in ways that still made her seek out crowds on public transit. She'd nearly died when an airline pilot decided to try to land in the middle of a blizzard that had turned away dozens of flights already at an airport that should have been closed. She'd endured the ominous physical encroachments of racist assholes just looking for a reason.

You don't know these men intend to kill you, she thought. *Don't be stupid.*

In truth, all she knew was that the mustache twins wanted to talk to them, question them where nobody else could hear, perhaps follow them to the dig. There were guards there—a unit made up of both American and Kurdish soldiers—but they would never make it to the camp before their pursuers caught up. For a moment, Sophie considered pulling over and getting out, forcing the men to reveal their intentions, but then it occurred to her that even if they fell short of murder, abduction might be on the table.

Sophie had slowed to skid around the bend in the road. Now she floored it again. The Jeep roared down the hill, lost in the shade of the trees looming up on either side. Fifty yards later, the trees thinned out and they were out of the woods. Something buzzed overhead, dipping so low that she nearly swerved, thinking a bird might crash into the windshield.

"Did you see it?" Lamar asked, twisting around again.

"What was—" Martin began.

"A drone," Lamar said. "Someone's following us with a goddamn drone. This is out of hand, Sophie. These crazy fuckers are going to start an international incident. What do they think—"

"They're not following us," Martin said. He'd craned his neck to look behind them.

Sophie hit the brakes. The Jeep skidded, dust flying up around them, and she brought the vehicle to a juddering halt before she flung the door open, undid her seat belt, and jumped out. Lamar and Martin piled out seconds later, and the three of them stood and stared back the way they'd come.

The mustache twins had stopped their car. More accurately, they'd been stopped by a pair of unmarked Humvees that even now were disgorging half a dozen soldiers. Reality seemed to bend and flex for a moment, and Sophie felt as if she might be dreaming. Where the hell had they come from?

"They weren't there two minutes ago," she said aloud, hot wind whipping around her. "We'd have seen them on the road."

The drone that had buzzed overhead now hovered back there at the edge of the woods, likely getting the entire scene on a live feed, but who was watching it? And where?

"The trees," Martin said. He walked toward the back of the Jeep, one hand rubbing at his aching skull. "They were hidden in the woods."

Sophie narrowed her eyes. These soldiers weren't from the Beneath Project's camp at Derveyî, but she saw U.S. Army markings on several of the soldiers, while others seemed to be Kurdish. The two militaries were working in tandem out of a base in Erbil, but that was intended to be a continuing struggle against ISIS remnants, the Americans ostensibly helping the Kurds to root out terrorist factions. So what were these other soldiers doing, staking out the road to her dig?

"They were waiting," Lamar said. "So they knew these guys would be coming after us?"

"Well," Sophie said, exhaling loudly as her heart began to calm. "Better they know than not know."

Lamar shot her a hard look. "You're okay with them spying on us?"

Martin laughed. "If men who mean us harm are going to spy on us, and there's nothing we can do about it, I'm with Sophie. Let the ones who want to keep us safe watch all they like. Besides, they're probably in contact with Ellison."

Sophie realized that must be true—that whatever these troops were up to, the commander of the unit guarding her dig, Major Ellison, had to know about it. She watched as the soldiers bundled the handcuffed mustache twins into the back of one of their vehicles, hoping this didn't lead to further trouble. The whole region was in conflict, every moment of peace tenuous, and any spark of violence might set it all aflame. It had been a miracle that the European Union's Alliance

Européenne pour l'Exploration Scientifique had managed to persuade all the governments involved to allow the dig to proceed, even with sponsorship from UNESCO.

"Let's just hope whatever happens now, they do it quietly," she said. "If we're perceived as a potential problem, the U.S. and the Iraqis will kick us out of here without a second thought, no matter how loudly anyone complains."

In her pocket, her phone buzzed again, but this wasn't a text message. Someone was calling. A flutter of fear went through her as she pulled the phone out, and she found herself hoping it was Steven. She recognized the irony, but that would be better than an unexpected call from her mother. As it turned out, it was neither of them.

"Beyza?" Sophie said into her phone. "What's going on?"

Lamar and Martin turned their attention her way, but Sophie ignored them as she listened.

"When will you be back, Dr. Durand?" Professor Beyza Solak asked. "You need to be here."

"Is something wrong? Has there been an accident?"

Martin started asking questions, but Sophie shushed him with a raised hand.

"A happy accident," Beyza replied. "In the lowest level. The wall of the worship chamber—Alton cracked the wall."

Sophie's heart jumped. She stared at Lamar as she spoke. "What do you mean he *cracked the wall?*"

"It's cracked. More than that," Beyza said. "There's a hole in it. And Sophie . . . there's another room beyond it. With writing on the walls. Some kind of cuneiform, but nothing I've seen before. Nothing like we've found. We've only got a few inches cleared. The wall is unstable, so we must be very careful, but Sophie . . ."

"Wow," Sophie breathed. "Yeah, Beyza. I'm coming. Be there in fifteen minutes. Don't let anyone in that room before I get there."

Beyza laughed. "No chance of that. The team's more afraid of the wall collapsing on them than they are of you."

Sophie ended the call and slipped the phone into her pocket, texts from Steven forgotten. She glanced at Martin and Lamar, who were talking to her, though she couldn't really process their questions. Her mind had already begun examining the information Beyza had given her, turning it all over, wondering what it might mean.

The soldiers had climbed back into their vehicles. One of them was driving the mustache twins' car. One of the Humvees rolled toward her, but Sophie had no time to deal with soldiers now. The excitement of this new mystery lit up inside her like a bonfire catching its first spark. This sort of thing was the very reason she'd given up academia, the taste of discovery, the thrill of the unknown past.

"Lamar," she said. "Stay and tell the soldiers whatever they want to know. Find out what you can. I'm taking Martin back to the dig, and then I'll send someone out to pick you up."

"Are you kidding me?"

Sophie cocked her head. "You heard at least part of that conversation. Do you think I'm kidding?"

Lamar rolled his eyes. He'd known her long enough to realize when there was no point in arguing. He reached back into the Jeep and grabbed a bottle of water, then started walking back to meet the Humvee.

Martin grinned and climbed into the passenger seat. Sophie got behind the wheel, fired up the engine, and turned the Jeep around. She felt bad leaving Lamar in a cloud of dust, but when she pulled up adjacent to the Humvee and pointed back at Lamar, one of the soldiers nodded, and that was all the permission she needed.

Later, Lamar would be pissed. She hoped whatever they found in this secret chamber would be enough to make him forgive her.

THREE

"This isn't just crazy," Beyza said. "It's foolish, and it calls your leadership into question."

Sophie bristled, but she forced herself to remain calm. With Beyza voicing doubts about her leadership, snapping at her where others could hear was a terrible idea. What would she do, call out Beyza in front of the staff for the affair she'd been having for months with Elio Cortez, who was a graduate student? That would only make things worse.

"Question all you like, but I'm project director," Sophie replied calmly. "Your presence has been helpful, Professor, and your knowledge of the region's history invaluable, but no one is insisting you stay."

A hush fell over the worship chamber. Sophie and Beyza had shifted their conversation into the most private corner of the room, an elevated stone platform they'd identified as an altar, and they tried to keep their voices down. Apparently, the acoustics were not helping.

The worship chamber had an oblong design, perhaps fifty feet in length, half that in width, and a dozen feet high. The symbols on the walls and the altar had been well documented by now. At the height of its activity, the Beneath Project had employed eighty-seven people, not including the military guard unit in the aboveground camp, which they typically referred to as *topside*. By now, much of the work had begun to wrap up, and the numbers belowground had dwindled to fifty-one, with another dozen scheduled to depart in less than a week.

Alton Carr had been tasked with making final notes before they officially closed the book on the worship chamber—at least for the purposes of their project. But then he'd noticed the crack the team had made in the wall while doing rubbings of the carvings there, and beyond the crack—a gap. Heavy stones had been piled up and sealed with a crude mortar, then covered over in an effort to obscure the presence of something on the other side. A farther chamber, perhaps an entire network of them.

Now there were seven people in the worship chamber, including Sophie, Beyza, Alton, and four other members of the team. Ostensibly, Alton and the others were photographing, marking, and taking notes as they attempted to carefully excavate the wall, but thus far they had made only a narrow hole through it. Enough to know that the mortared rock went about six feet deep before opening into another room.

Sophie intended to go in. Beyza thought her irresponsible.

"Dr. Durand," Beyza said now, returning Sophie's chilly formality. "If you need me to make an official protest—"

Sophie shifted closer to her, almost nose to nose. They were similar in height and build, not to mention determination.

"Your protest has been noted." She gestured to the others in the room. "And you've made certain everyone here is aware of it."

Beyza looked as if she might argue further. Her eyes were aflame in a way that Sophie had never seen before. The two women had gotten along quite well, beginning on the very first day. Even up to this morning, they had been friends—it had been Beyza who'd asked her to bring back some tahini for the cook—and Sophie hoped they would still be friends after this. But she had made up her mind.

With a sigh, Beyza threw up her hands. Sophie nodded and shifted past her, walking toward the hole in the wall, where Alton and the others were cataloging everything and shifting away the stone that they removed. Sophie had sent Martin to lie down, worried he had a concussion, but three of those present were his fellow graduate students. The other two, Alton and Marissa, were archaeologists employed by the Alliance Européenne, and Sophie had a great deal of respect for her team. She had chosen most of them herself. Marissa, in particular, had been the silent and reliable backbone of her team.

"Hey, Soph," Alton said, stepping in to bar her path. "Can I ask you something?"

Sophie smiled, closed her eyes a moment, and shook her head. "Not you, too?"

Alton gave her a sheepish grin. "I have to ask. What's the hurry?"

Sophie expected to feel herself bristle, but it didn't happen. Smart, quiet, savvy Alton had charm and a smile so amiable that he'd earned a reputation as the peacemaker of the group. He came from a little village in the north of England, from a family whose identity remained profoundly entwined with their forefathers' history as coal miners. The first of them to attend university, the first to live outside the country, Alton missed them fiercely, but he had family anywhere he went, by virtue of his genial nature.

"Alton," she began.

Then she saw his gaze shift past her, and she realized he was looking to Beyza for guidance. Sophie rolled her eyes and moved around him. No matter how charming he could be, and though she knew he meant well, Alton still had a bit to learn about diplomacy and being someone's employee.

"All I'm saying," he added, walking beside her, "is that I think if Lamar were here, he might be able to talk you out of this. And if I'm permitted an opinion, I think it'd be wise for us to wait for him to try talking you out of it before anyone goes through that hole."

Sophie stood in front of the hole in the wall. She put her hand on the crumbling edge of the hole and peered at the large rocks that had been used to construct the barrier. With her back to the team, she inhaled deeply of the dust and age of the earthen chamber around her.

How many conversations had they had about the sort of worship that had gone on in this room? A hundred, at least. The world around them existed in a constant state of crisis, a global turmoil that seemed only to worsen by the day, but down here, in this subterranean warren, a place where people had lived and thrived and loved and prayed—all underground—secrets of the past had been unveiled. Further mysteries awaited them, but what Sophie loved the most about those mysteries was that they were—in this case quite literally—set in stone.

The past awaited their discovery, but it held no dangers. No peril, only fascination.

Yes, it might still surprise them. But it wouldn't disappoint them, and it couldn't kill them. Only the present-day world could do that.

Sophie had left her life as an archaeology professor behind. It had begun at a charity event at New York's Museum of Natural History, where the museum had given some award or other to Alex Jarota, the director of the Alliance Européenne. Alex had sought her out afterward and confessed that one of the reasons he'd attended the event had been to meet her. By the end of the evening, over a great deal of wine, he'd nearly convinced her to cast aside her academic career and come work for him. Sophie had been solo that night—Steven had been out of town, at a conference—otherwise, Alex might not even have gotten that far.

At first, she had turned the offer down. But the more she had thought about the unique position of the Alliance, the louder the little voice in the back of her mind grew. The one that said, *Don't be a fool. It's all you've ever wanted.* Financed by the European Union, the Alliance would enable her to do her work without constantly having to bow and scrape for funding. As a child, Sophie had been quiet and dedicated, and that trend had largely continued into adulthood. She'd worked hard, trying to make the most of a life that had once almost been stolen from her, but she had also been hesitant to make the big moves, always wary of upsetting the stability she'd built. When her father had begun to fail and her mother had moved to France to be with him, that stability had vanished. The idea of seizing the life she truly wanted had been frightening, but now that it lay right in front of her—and all she had to do was reach out and grasp it—she could not refuse.

Her employers at NYU had been understanding, if disappointed. Steven had been far less of the former, and far more of the latter. But Sophie had only ever dreamed of dusting off bits of history, unraveling the past, and sharing it with the world—even if most of the world might be profoundly disinterested. Her work would go unnoticed by most people, and that was just fine with her. Filling in the blank spaces in archaeological textbooks seemed like a wonderful way to spend her life.

Sophie blamed Alex Jarota for all of it. The Frenchman admired her, but he admired many people, and no one more than himself. An ambitious man, he wanted to further his own career by furthering the fame and reach of his organization. To do that, he needed all his project managers—people like Sophie—to share his ambition. He'd wanted her for her expertise, yes, but he also wanted to forge her into someone who cared about publicity and status. Neither of those things interested her very much . . . but she was trying to learn.

Marissa walked over to Sophie, ignoring the others, and handed over her flashlight. "You're going to need this."

Sophie grinned. With her ginger hair clipped short and her black-rimmed granny glasses, Marissa looked more like a punk bass player than an archaeologist, and her attitude matched.

"Someone's on my side, at least," Sophie said.

"Don't get excited," Alton replied. "Marissa just wants to know what's on the other side and doesn't mind if you get crushed to death finding out."

"This is more or less true," Marissa said with a shrug. "No offense."

"None taken," Sophie replied.

She hadn't even gotten a look through the hole yet. She hadn't wanted to interfere with the work that was going on, but now that the hole had been widened enough—or nearly enough—for someone slim to shimmy through, she had made up her mind. She clicked on the high-intensity flashlight and shone the narrow beam through the hole. It took a few seconds to get the angle she wanted, but as she peered through, she got a small glimpse of the far wall inside the secret chamber. Heat flushed the back of her neck, but this time it wasn't out of embarrassment or anger.

"Cuneiform," she said. "But Beyza's right—not like anything I've seen."

"Thanks for confirming what I've already told you," Beyza replied, the voice floating through the worship chamber. She had stayed over near the altar, miffed by the way Sophie had pulled rank.

One of the grad students had gone pale and begun whispering to another.

"Something on your mind, Rachel?" Sophie asked sharply.

The young woman, Rachel, took a deep breath. "Nothing, Dr. Durand. It's just . . ." She glanced around. "Did anyone else hear that?"

"Hear what?" Alton asked.

Rachel frowned, glanced into the shadowed corner of the chamber behind the lighting rig, and shook her head. "I don't know." She glanced up. "I'm actually not feeling well. Do you mind if I . . ."

The question trailed off. Sophie frowned, wondering what was up with her, but she waved the young woman away. "Go and lie down. Check on Martin before you do."

With a grateful nod and a pale, nervous glance at that dark corner, Rachel hurried out of the worship chamber.

"All right," Sophie said. "Let's quit stalling."

Beyza scowled halfheartedly, but Sophie ignored her. What little she could make out of the cuneiform visible through the narrow opening might indeed be different from what she'd encountered before, but her mind began interpreting the symbols regardless. A slash here, a slant there, a series of crescents and splayed figures . . . they might be unusual, but Sophie already thought she could make out the meaning of some of that writing. Was that phrase *the glories of* . . . no. The *blessings* of Zeus.

Zeus. In northern Iraq.

Not long ago, archaeologists had found heavy Greek influence, including astonishingly preserved mosaics depicting Greek mythological figures, in the ancient Turkish city of Perga. But what she saw were not mosaics.

"What is this?" she muttered.

Alton leaned against the wall beside her, arms crossed, that roguish grin on his face. "That's what we'd all like to know. But we don't want to die finding out."

Sophie pushed away the temptation to keep arguing. She clicked off the flashlight and turned to face them. Across the worship chamber, she could see a couple of silhouettes beyond the entrance—more workers on the dig, wondering what the hell their project manager was thinking. Word had begun to spread.

"Beyza, come closer," she said.

Her friend—if Beyza remained her friend—kept her face free of expression, but she did approach the rest of the small gathering. Sophie glanced around at them, faces cast in golden light and odd shadows by the lights that had been strung throughout the chamber. Alton had a scar through his left eyebrow that seemed much deeper at this angle, furrowed with shadow. The strange light gave them all a sort of antique cast, as if they'd emerged from an old sepia-tone photograph. With her shortish black hair tucked behind her ears and her eyes narrowed with doubt, Beyza looked decades older than her thirty-five years. The others had a ghostly cast to them, but they were her team, and she'd been unfair to them.

"I'm going through, and I'm doing it now," she said.

Alton started talking again, but Sophie held up her hand.

"I know the risks, and I'm going, anyway. You all know what happened earlier. You know that whoever those men were, they were taken into custody—but for how long? And how long before others like them come to see what we've discovered? We've been fortunate that we've been able to work on this project for so long with very little interruption. Out here, we're not bothering anyone. But where, exactly, are we? Kurdistan, yes. Iraq, yes. But there are disagreements over that, aren't there?"

Beyza clucked her tongue. "Don't demonize my government."

Sophie sighed. "I'm not. At least not more than any other government. But as progressive as Atatürk University might be in comparison, you can't say there aren't factions in the Turkish government who might want to lay claim to anything we might find here. We're officially in Iraq, but this territory has changed hands over the course of millennia, so an argument could be made that whatever we discover might not belong to the Kurds, or the Iraqis, and certainly not to the Alliance Européenne."

Beyza exhaled. "All right. Go on."

"I'm only saying that we have worked very hard here, and I intend that our work be treated properly, that any antiquities are handled as

UNESCO has outlined." Sophie turned and clicked on the flashlight again, shining its beam at the hole in the wall. "Whatever's beyond this chamber, it's something new. I heard the way your voice trembled when you called to tell me about it, Beyza, so I know you agree. The skin's prickling on the back of my neck. No ancient civilization made secret chambers without a reason. I want to know what's in there, and I damn well do not want some spies snatching it—whether it's information or antiquities—before we've done our job."

"Lamar—" Alton began.

Sophie rolled her eyes. "Lamar works for me, not the other way around. Yes, he's my conscience sometimes. Right now, he's dealing with the military . . . or he's on the way back here with whichever one of the diggers we sent out to fetch him. But I'll tell you this much about Lamar . . ."

She let the unfinished sentence hang in the air for a few seconds, and then she pulled a rubber band off her wrist and began tying back her hair.

"He wouldn't fit through the hole." Lamar might be short, but his shoulders were wide. He was well acquainted with the gym.

Sophie turned and walked to the hole. She shone the light through the narrow opening again, then clicked it off and slipped it into her pocket. For a moment, she hesitated. Alex Jarota wanted her to be ambitious, to strive for the glory of publicity to further her own career as well as his. Beyza and the others thought she would get stuck or that the rocks would collapse and she'd die or be trapped, and she couldn't deny there was risk involved. What she was about to do was stupid. Sophie told herself she was doing it for the thrill of the discovery and to protect their work, just as she'd said.

She took a moment to consider whether that was the truth, and she realized she didn't know.

A deep breath, and she glanced back at Alton.

"Give me a boost," she said. "And if I die, don't let Beyza write 'I told you so' on my tombstone."

FOUR

Sophie's courage failed her halfway through the wall. It pressed all around her, rocks scraping against the thin cloth protecting her back and chest and hips and thighs. A curve of stone bulged against her abdomen, and she knew if she'd attempted this weeks ago, she'd never have slithered this far into the hole. Every time she went into the field, she began to lose weight instantly. But slim as she'd become, she still found herself wedged across her hips.

Whispering profanity that would have horrified her mother, Sophie stretched her arms forward, scraping her fingers on the rocks and crumbling mortar. Every time she pushed herself an inch ahead, she hoped that her fingers would find the other side of the wall and she'd be better positioned to pull. But her team could still reach in and grab hold of her feet, and she knew she hadn't made it yet.

"Be careful," Beyza called to her. "If you shift too hard—"

"I know."

"If you dislodge part of the wall above you—"

"I fucking know."

Alton tapped her ankle. She knew it was Alton because he'd been the one on her left as she had first inserted her upper body into the hole and begun to drag herself in. Alton and Joe Bonetti had helped to hoist her and slide her in as if she were a torpedo being loaded into a tube.

"We can pull you out," Alton said.

Sophie shuddered. "No," she whispered, unsure if it was loud enough for him to hear. She could smell the dust of age, the rich earthen aroma of history all around her. Breathing it in, she soothed her fear. She laid her cheek against the sharp stone edge below her and took another long, deep breath, and then expelled it from her lungs and pressed her lips tightly together.

Eyes closed, she felt the stone and mortar around her. It had looked as if there was enough room, and she told herself that hadn't been an illusion. She might have gotten lodged in that spot, but they had been able to reach in with digging tools and widen the hole somewhat, and a visual examination had suggested to her that it she could make it.

Never assume, she thought, remembering the old adage about making an ass out of you and me, which was funny considering it was her ass causing all this trouble. She'd never thought her butt had much shape to it, but here she was, a prisoner of her hips and ass.

She inhaled and exhaled again, and her lungs ached. She wondered how much damage they'd sustained from radiation and chemo, wondered how much stress her heart could take. Sophie never talked about these fears with anyone. Unless someone had been through it, unless they shared her memories of being in the clinic surrounded by other children who were sick, some of them dying . . . no one could understand. As strong as she felt, those memories were ghosts haunting the corridors of her mind, and she knew they would be there forever.

"Okay," she whispered. Inhale, exhale, emptying her lungs to make herself as small as she could be.

She couldn't buck upward. Instead, she shifted her hips to the left and then the right. In her mind, she imagined using her hip bones to crawl. Arms reaching, shoulders stretching, she dug her fingers into the space between the rocks that had been used to build the wall. She tucked her butt, shifted her hips again, left and right, dragged herself an inch and felt a spark of triumph, before mortar showered down from above her. Dirt and dust sifted into her mouth.

Sophie drew a sharp breath and felt something shift above her, a sharp bit of rock, one brick in this wall, things moving against one another. *Stupid. So stupid*, she thought, knowing she might have fucked up for the last time.

Her thoughts went to her cell phone and all the text messages from Steven that she hadn't really answered. Messages she might never answer, and though she did not regret her decision, Steven deserved better than that.

Back where she'd begun, her team gathered in the worship chamber and urged her forward, or pleaded with her to let them draw her back, but Sophie thought going backward might be just as dangerous as going forward. Either way, she could disturb the thousands of tons of stone above her. What kind of example had she set for them, doing something so foolhardy? The question came into her mind unbidden, but immediately she had an answer. *An ambitious one. A determined woman.* Sophie heard the response in the voice of her boss, Alex Jarota. He'd ignited that fire of ambition in her . . .

No. That was bullshit. Sophie could lie to herself, but not in this moment. Here and now, she had to admit that all Alex had done was unleash the ambition in her, as if she had been waiting her whole life for permission to pursue her dreams.

Of course, her dreams would die with her if she couldn't get out of this.

Trembling, breath catching in her throat, she fought away despair and refused the tears that wanted to come to her eyes. Instead, she dug down beneath her fear to the iron core inside her. Her life had been in peril before. She'd broken bones and suffered at least one concussion doing her work, and she'd been many places where she wasn't welcome. Her life hadn't ended on those days, and it wouldn't end today. Not yet. Not without the answers for which she had risked herself.

With one enormous huff of exhalation, she stretched her arms out farther, dug her fingers in, and twisted her hips to the left, much harder than before. To the right. To the left. Stone scraped her back as she inched and dragged herself forward, her hips coming free.

Back in the worship chamber, someone shining a flashlight at her feet cheered for her.

That sharp, low-hanging rock scraped against her ass, pressing down. Stone dug in, something shifted overhead, and mortar rained down again. This time she heard rocks moving, a quiet rumble, like something shifting chairs in the room next door.

But her right hand found open air. She waggled her fingers, reached around to see, and knew she had made it to the secret room. Or her hands had. Only that low rock, pressed against her sacrum, held her back.

"You're beyond our reach now," Alton said from behind her.

Sophie inhaled. He had no idea.

She exhaled. Grasped the outside edge of the hole with both hands, tucked her hips down as low as she could manage, and then dragged herself forward. The rock dug into her tailbone, scraped hard, and shifted with a groan and the cracking of mortar. Her arms floated free, dangling at the elbow, but only for a fraction of a second. The whole wall above her seemed to bulge, and she whipped her arms out, pressed against the interior of the secret room, and thrust herself in. She heard the rock thunk down in the tunnel as she slid free.

Stone cracked and collapsed, even as Sophie tumbled out of the hole and onto the dusty floor of the secret chamber. A wan shaft of light came through from that hole, but as she scrambled to her feet, more rocks dropped down to block the passage, and in seconds she found herself in near darkness, only the dimmest bit of illumination still showing through.

"Sophie!" muffled voices called from beyond that hole. From the other side of a wall that had let her slip through, but would now not let her out.

"I'm okay!" she called back.

Shouts of alarm continued, so she put her mouth to the opening in the wall and called through to them again. "I'm fine! I'm not hurt!"

Someone shushed the others, and she was shocked, standing there in the mostly dark, to hear the one voice she did not expect.

"What the hell have you done? Are you insane?"

Lamar, she thought with a smile. He worked for her, but she couldn't help feeling that she had made it into this room just in time, that as her dear friend and her colleague—maybe her one real friend at the dig—Lamar would have had a much better chance of talking her out of this than any of the others.

"I think that is a very distinct possibility," she called back to him. "But I'm in here now, which means your job has just become trying to figure out how to get me out before I starve to death."

At first there came no reply. Sophie frowned, thinking that more of the wall might have blocked the hole, but then she realized she'd heard no more rumbling. Narrow shafts of light still streamed through, illuminating bits of mortar that floated like motes of dust. Sophie drank up those bits of light, thirsty for something other than the darkness that embraced her all around.

"You can live without food for weeks," Lamar called through to her, his voice somehow sounding farther away. "You can go without water for maybe six days, but it won't be fun. I'm worried about something else."

Sophie frowned. She inhaled the dust of age, tasted it on her tongue and teeth. She peered at those thin beams of light, and then she froze. Oxygen. Lamar was worried about oxygen. If this part of the underground city had the same sorts of ventilation shafts they'd found elsewhere, and they were unblocked, she would be okay, but now the worry settled heavily on her.

"You've got to excavate the wall without letting it collapse completely," she said, speaking loudly as if to someone hard of hearing.

"We're on it!" Alton called to her. "Don't be afraid."

"I'll do my best."

Sophie rested her forehead against the cool stone on the inside of the wall. No strange mortar here, no effort to make this wall look like anything other than a pile of rocks. She spread her arms out to either side and found the place where the false wall became smooth, ancient rock, the soft volcanic stone—tuff in English, *tuffeau* in French—that had allowed these caves and tunnels to be easily carved but which slowly hardened after exposure to air. In the Cappadocia region of Turkey, there were well over one hundred such warrens, dating back to the Bronze Age and earlier. During a period where villages were constantly under attack, locals had been forced to create entire subterranean cities, with markets, living quarters, and religious centers going many levels deep into the earth below their aboveground settlements.

The most remarkable thing about their dig, about this subterranean

city—which she had named Derveyî, the Kurdish word for *beneath*—
was that it had been discovered a thousand kilometers from Cappadocia. Derveyî might be part of Kurdistan, it might belong to the Iraqi
government and fall under the auspices of UNESCO, and even of her
own employers, but as far as Sophie Durand was concerned, Derveyî
was hers. Her project. Her home for the past year.

Now, she began to wonder if it might also be her grave.

A chill went through her. She felt unsettled, her skin clammy and
damp. A twinge of nausea hit her gut, and she shook herself. What
the hell was wrong with her? It felt as if she'd developed a sudden fever.
Sophie blinked and shivered and wrapped her arms around herself,
and for ten or fifteen seconds she felt panic seizing her as she wondered what she would do if something happened to her in here, in the
dark, before the others could dig through the wall.

Then the moment passed. Her thoughts seemed to clear. In her
peripheral vision, she thought she saw the shadows shift, like something silver moved there in the cave with her.

Get ahold of yourself, woman, she thought. And she forced herself to
smile at the darkness.

Sipping at the air around her, wondering if she would be able to
tell if oxygen grew short, she reached into her right-hand pocket and
withdrew the slim but powerful flashlight Marissa had given her. It
was the only thing she'd brought, the one thing she had known that
she could not do without, thinking that she would want to be able to
investigate the secret room immediately. What she hadn't counted on
was it being her only source of light.

Sophie clicked the flashlight on. Its narrow beam illuminated
enough that she felt some of the nervousness dissipate. Inhaling deeply,
she reassured herself that she could breathe, that her paranoia would
not be enough to deprive her of oxygen.

"You're okay," she quietly assured herself as she had so many times
over the years.

Then she began to look around. The narrow beam of the flashlight
moved smoothly, slowly, as she took note of her surroundings. Other
than the false wall, the rest looked much like they'd found elsewhere
in Derveyî, smooth, as if it had been carved from soap instead of stone.

The writing, though, that was different. The chambers and corridors were filled with symbols and ancient writing, but not like this. The cuneiform language seemed different, as she'd observed from outside the room, but now she saw that it had been painted and carved throughout the chamber. Words leaped out at her. Lamar was the expert, but she figured she would try her hand at translating some of it while her team excavated the wall.

She swept her flashlight around in a slow circle. The secret room felt larger than it was. Perhaps eighteen feet square, it had nothing that suggested it had been furnished, save for a raised area and what appeared to be some sort of altar or table carved from the same stuff as the room itself. The beam of the flashlight continued to move, and Sophie noticed a recession off to the left of the altar, a place where the flashlight's illumination did not seem to reach.

Around that recession, the language on the wall changed. In fact, the cuneiform scrawling stopped several feet from the shadows, and there stretched a gap of nine or ten inches before other writing began—this one much more familiar to her. Stepping closer, eyes narrowed, heart racing now from the urgency of discovery instead of from fear, Sophie picked out text in a distinct Doric Greek idiom and recognized it immediately. She had spent a great deal of time in graduate school studying the Pella curse tablet, a lead scroll discovered in the ancient capital of Macedonia in the 1980s. For long moments, she stared at this writing, wondering what it could signify.

A warning, yes. Sophie had no doubt about that. But unlike the Pella tablet, this held no curse. Instead, it reminded her of the cautionary scrawl in Dante's *Inferno*, "Abandon hope, all ye who enter here." The Doric script seemed less dire, but the wariness came through loud and clear. *This is a secret place, the city beneath the city, and none may enter except with the authority of the king of Asia.*

"The king of Asia?" she asked the dust and the shadows.

Then it dawned on her, and she smiled. "No fucking way."

Only then did she realize she had moved much closer to the wall and that her flashlight beam had strayed toward that black recession and that the blackness felt so deep because instead of stone wall, a tunnel waited there, yawning and dark.

A tunnel. And stairs, carved into the stone, descending into the se-cret place, the city beneath the city, where none might enter without the authority of the king of Asia. A ripple of unreality passed through Sophie, and her breath grew shallow, not because she lacked oxygen but because she had entered her dream, an archaeological find that would be talked about, written about, and taught in schools for gen-erations to come.

Numb, Sophie backtracked to the collapsed hole through which she'd entered. "Lamar? Beyza?"

"We're here!" Beyza called back. "Are you all right?"

"Fine!" Sophie shouted, maybe too loud, giddiness overtaking her. "I'm going for a walk. Don't panic if you call and I don't respond!"

"A walk?" Lamar said. "What the hell do you mean, a walk?"

"Trust me!" was all she said.

Then her feet were moving again, and she surrendered to the dream, and the smile on her face, and the way her thoughts spun drunkenly around one another, no single ponderance able to nest long enough to take root before the next one shoved it away.

Only one. As she passed the warning outside the entrance to the steps that led into the city beneath the city, she whispered to herself.

"Sorry, king of Asia," she said as she disobeyed his orders.

After all, there was nothing he could do to her now. Alexander the Great had been dead for more than two thousand years.

As she descended into Derveyî's heart, Sophie knew the city's great-est secrets waited below, yet with every step, she chided herself for not turning back. Her team would be furious, and rightly so. Had any one of them done something so reckless, she would have raised hell. But presently she had nothing to do but sit in the dark and await rescue . . . or explore a mystery labeled with warnings from two sep-arate historical eras, including one seemingly from Alexander the Great himself.

They're just stairs, she told herself. *I'm just walking down some stairs.*

Again, a shiver went through her. She wet her lips with her tongue and wiped at her forehead. With a deep breath, she continued to descend.

Sophie tried not to think about what it would feel like if her flashlight battery died, how dark it would become. At the bottom of the steps—she ought to have counted, why hadn't she counted?—she entered a circular chamber perhaps fifty feet wide. There were niches carved in the walls around the room where oil lamps and other goods might once have been placed. A quintet of columns created deeper shadows when she shone her flashlight beam upon them, as if something old might lurk behind them. As Sophie crossed the floor, holding her breath, an errant breeze whispered past her, caressing the back of her neck, and she let out a small noise of fear that would have shamed her if she hadn't been so entirely alone.

Something rustled in the darkness between columns, and she went still. Her breath caught in her throat. A scuffing noise, not like scuttle of vermin but more like a footfall. Her mind tried to make sense of it, to configure some way for another person to be down here with her, in the vacant heart of Derveyî, but there was no way. Sophie listened for the sound to come again and then smiled to herself. The dark beyond the light of her flashlight grew deeper, somehow, but she heard nothing more, and she knew she had to be alone.

She stepped around the column, swung the light back and forth. For a moment, she thought she saw a figure dart out of the reach of her flashlight, a pale gray curtain of fabric swaying like something undersea, but she blinked and found nothing there. As she searched with her light, she confirmed it. *Nothing*. Her anxiousness had her seeing things.

Her heart still pounded, and her face felt flush with something not quite relief and not quite disappointment but a mixture of the two.

Taking another calming breath, she surveyed the room. Nothing waited in the shadows. The columns were only that—carved from the same soft stone as the rest of this subterranean city—though one of them, in the center of the chamber, doubled as a fireplace. Broad and softly moaning with a breeze that drifted up its flue, the fireplace seemed larger than most they'd found. There were ventilation shafts all through Derveyî, some long since clogged or collapsed or covered by some change in the land aboveground. Sophie shone her beam into the fireplace and saw gray ash and bone there, and a flutter of excitement touched her heart. She looked inside and upward, but although it was clear that at least some air moved through, no light reached her from above.

Two tables had been carved as well, a part of the stone around them just as the columns and the walls were. Some kind of communal space, then, likely to take meals. She paused to take stock and felt a tremor of guilt, knowing her team would be working hard to free her and would be worried if she remained out of communication for too long, but she made a quick circuit of what she had already begun to think of as the column room.

Throughout Derveyî, there were tunnels and passages, some right on top of one another. There were stairs and ramps, water tanks and stables, family dwellings and places of worship. The architecture had not been constructed but burrowed and carved, and the design seemed all the more remarkable because of it. Outsiders tended to be most astonished by the moving stone doors. In the era when Derveyî had been created—*built* seemed the wrong word—threats from above had been a near constant. The weather posed certain perils, as did those who might want to take the settlement by force. In the event of attack, they could not only survive below . . . they could live well.

The doors were few, but they were remarkable feats. Round like millstones, they were balanced perfectly and could be turned into place in the event of an attack. Better still, once the doors were closed, they could only be opened from the inside.

As she walked the perimeter of the chamber, Sophie's flashlight beam found three other, smaller rooms and a corridor leading away into narrow, claustrophobic darkness. But it was the other set of steps that interested her most. Opposite the stairs she'd descended to reach this place was an exit, beyond which were thirteen steps down to a doorway.

Closed.

It couldn't be closed, of course. Not unless someone had remained on the other side.

"What in the hell is this?" she whispered, running her hands over the smooth stone of the door.

Her flashlight beam found symbols carved into the stone, both in cuneiform and in the language of Alexander. Sophie put both hands on the door, sighing and quietly cursing. She leaned her forehead against the stone as the almost narcotic buzz of discovery began to seep out of her. Lamar would be waiting for word. The whole team would be desperate to hear from her. Slithering through the hole they'd dug had been one level of irresponsibility, but staying too long down here and making them worry . . . that was another level entirely.

An image rose in her mind of soldiers standing in this very spot, men in the uniform of Alexander's army. *Alexander the Not-So-Great*, she thought.

But a frown creased her forehead, and she stepped back from the door. With her flashlight, she began to investigate the edges. The Doric Greek writing in the altar room she'd found had been a clear warning, a decree from the emperor not to descend those stairs. Not to enter this portion of Derveyî, which they'd endeavored to hide from anyone who might discover the city.

Which meant that Alexander's men had gotten to see what was on the other side of this door.

Sophie set the flashlight on the floor. Carefully, she ran her fingers along the edge and gave a gentle push every few inches, trying to nudge it aside or to find some kind of leverage. When her fingers found a thin gap, she exhaled loudly and her heart began to pound. Fearful of what might happen if the gap closed instead of widened, she worked her fingers inward until she felt the stone door shift.

Her mouth went dry. Digging in, she put her weight into it. The doors were supposed to open smoothly, but someone had tried to force this one off balance. With a grunt, Sophie shoved, and the door turned on its balance point. She scraped her knuckles raw as she stumbled forward. Her boot tapped her flashlight, and it skittered through the opening. For a moment, her heart forgot to beat. The light spun, the beam flashing around the circumference of this new, small room. She thought it would go out, but it kept spinning as she inhaled the dust of long centuries. She started coughing, and for several seconds, she bent, rasping, trying to clear her throat.

The flashlight slowed its spin. She heard the grit of small stones beneath the hard plastic and watched the flashlight beam come to rest. The room was much smaller than the one she'd just left, no more than eighteen feet wide, nothing more than a rectangular box. It felt like a crypt instead of any space for the living, and where the beam came to rest, it illuminated the base of another altar, again smaller than the one in the room above her.

Sophie whistled in appreciation of the odd cuneiform writing that covered the altar. Tiny engraving, ancient lines close and tight, like some long-ago lunatic had scrawled them there. She bent to pick up the flashlight and raised it, noting for a single moment that the wall behind the altar had also been engraved with that tiny writing.

Upon the altar rested a single object, a stone jar perhaps sixteen inches high, pale yellow and red, fat-bellied and with its cap tightly sealed. The writing on it seemed done in a clearer, less manic hand, and for the first time since entering the room, Sophie paused to try to translate a little of what she read there. Lamar had far more knowledge of ancient languages, but she'd studied enough in her time.

"Oh, my God," she said softly.

Her hand wavered, and all the breath went out of her. A numbness spread through her. The excitement of discovery, the thrill of ancient secrets, had driven her until this moment, reminding her of the spark that had ignited her interest in archaeology when she'd been just a girl. Now all that adrenaline left her in a rush, for this wasn't just a secret. This was a myth. This was impossible.

"Holy shit."

The dust and shadows made no reply.

Sophie sank to the floor, took a breath, and began trying to read what little of that writing she could make out. Upstairs, her team would be worried for her, working to free her, but in those moments— and for an hour or two more—she had forgotten that they, and the rest of the world, even existed.

At first, she found what little she could translate very hard to believe.

Slowly, she became filled with wonder.

In time, that wonder turned to fear.

FIVE

Ben Walker thought the low hills stretched out before him would have been beautiful in the right light. The distant mountains were covered with ice, and the tundra of Greenland glistened with frost that coated miles of green-and-yellow scrub grass. Of course, to Walker, *the right light* would be in the middle of July, with the sun high in the sky, not this frigid early spring, with gray clouds slung low. The raw, almost primeval landscape looked as if it might have gone unchanged for thousands of years, when in reality it had folded and warped, heaved into mounds and caved in. The tundra was changing fast, and that change had the potential to unbalance the global ecosystem.

Tony Shen stepped up beside him, hands buried deep inside the pockets of his Canada Goose parka. Shen had to have the best gear, always new, always absurdly expensive. Walker had no idea where he got the money—it certainly didn't come from his government job.

"It's fucking cold," Shen muttered.

Walker sniffed. Not quite a laugh, but he rolled his eyes to make sure Shen got the point. "You're in the Arctic, man. Get used to it."

"You telling me you're used to it?"

The question reminded Walker of the pain in his fused vertebrae and the ache around the pins in his right leg, old injuries he tried to ignore but of which the cold in this part of the world made constant reminders. He had scars that were visible evidence of difficult past missions, but the ones people couldn't see brought him pain.

The wind kicked up. Walker tugged his hat down farther over his ears and flipped up his collar. "You think this is bad? You should've been here in January."

"So . . . at least it's getting warmer?"

Walker shot him a dark look. "Is that meant to be a joke?"

Shen didn't waver. "You think I'm going to make a climate change joke? Here?"

Walker glanced over at the stretch of ground where the research team had been digging this week. Over the course of months, they had moved from place to place and taken samples of the frozen soil. About three miles to the north—yellow flags flying high enough to be seen from this distance—a secondary team operated a drilling rig that dug deeper and deeper, taking samples from depths that stunned Walker. Other operations had measured carbon dioxide levels, but Walker's team wasn't interested in duplicating the work of those scientists. They were searching for killers.

As recently as the 1980s, the temperature of the permafrost in this part of the world had averaged eighteen degrees Fahrenheit. The average had gone up ten degrees since then. The permafrost was already softening, releasing carbon dioxide that had been frozen in the earth for more than forty thousand years. By 2040, the Arctic Council expected at least 20 percent of the permafrost near the surface to melt, regurgitating massive amounts of carbon into the atmosphere.

Walker's mission focused elsewhere.

"You going to tell me where we stand?" Shen asked. "Or am I going to just hang out and freeze my balls off?"

"It's your first day. Sure you don't want to ease in?"

"I don't even know what we're doing here."

Walker smirked. He ran a thinly gloved hand over the dark beard he'd been growing in the months he'd been here. "David didn't tell you?"

Shen huffed. "Dr. Boudreau doesn't tell me shit."

"Comes from being the new guy."

"I've been working for DARPA nine years," Shen said.

Walker nodded. "But you've only been working for the National Science Foundation since October."

The National Science Foundation barely existed as anything more than a name stenciled on a frosted glass door in the halls of a building in Washington, D.C., a decades-long façade for use when the U.S. Department of Defense didn't want anyone to know that DARPA was involved with a research project or an unfolding crisis. The Defense Advanced Research Projects Agency had a fancy name but a relatively simple job—look into emerging science and unexplained phenomena and make absolutely certain that if it was possible someone could make a weapon out of it, the United States would be the first to do so.

Walker had never really liked working for DARPA—he didn't appreciate weaponized science—but he had a lifelong fascination with mysteries both natural and unnatural, a thirst for explanation that would not be quenched. And when those things turned out to be potentially dangerous, he did prefer they be in his own government's hands instead of someone else's. Not that he trusted his superiors. It was simply a case of better-the-devil-you-know.

There were members of the team from Greenland, as well as the Arctic Council and the United Nations Commission on Science and Technology for Development. Walker had been point man for months, but when he had accepted the assignment, he had been emphatic about not staying away from home for too long. He had made promises to his son, Charlie, and he intended to keep them. Now Dr. Boudreau had sent Shen to replace him, and Walker wanted to cheer. Not that he minded the work, but he had spent the first eight years of Charlie's life putting his son last, and he had made a private vow to change that.

The Greenland Initiative wasn't like any other project he'd been involved with. The National Science Foundation's director, David Boudreau, had been persuaded to take an interest thanks to pressure from his superiors in Defense and the deputy director of the Centers for Disease Control and Prevention. Down in the permafrost, there were things other than carbon and the methane from plant life that had been frozen for so many thousands of years. But it wasn't the poisoning of the atmosphere that worried them the most. People with more doctorates than Walker had were already working on technology to try to filter the poisons from the air or expel them somehow. They knew what they were working with, and toward.

The microbes were another issue.

"We've found eleven," Walker said.

Shen gave him a sidelong scowl, then walked half a dozen steps away from the camp. "All this time and you've classified eleven different microbes? It hardly seems worth all the time and money. There must be hundreds—"

"Killers," Walker interrupted. "Eleven previously unknown killer microbes. Eleven deadly diseases. Eleven new illnesses for which there is no cure."

Shen widened his eyes. "Well, fuck."

Walker nodded. "Yeah."

In his career, he had seen things that would have given anyone a lifetime's worth of nightmares. He'd survived storms and terrors that had killed nearly everyone else around him, discovered the existence of creatures that the world's governments pretended did not exist, and he had been in the presence of tangible evil. Breathed the same air as that evil, bled on the same patch of soil, and lived to tell of it.

Or not to tell, because that was the job, after all. Face the kind of thing that would make any ordinary person shit themselves, find ways the United States could utilize those things for its benefit, make goddamn sure no enemy nation could do the same . . . and never tell a soul.

His current mission held all the secrecy of past assignments, but this was new. This was different. And it scared the hell out of him.

"You must be glad to be getting out of here, then," Shen said.

Walker shivered from the wind. "You can say that again, brother."

Shen tugged off a glove, stuffed it into his pocket, and reached inside his bulky coat to withdraw a cream-colored envelope. "From Boudreau. You know he likes the old-fashioned formalities."

"He gets it from his grandmother," Walker said, taking the envelope. "Alena used to be the best investigator we had."

"His *grandmother?*"

Walker ignored the question, lifting the envelope. "It's not sealed."

"It wasn't sealed when he gave it to me. I didn't read it, if that's what you're worried about." Shen smiled. "But he did mention you were headed to Iraq. I'm not sure which assignment is worse."

Walker frowned. "That's not funny."

Shen looked genuinely confused, and Walker felt a twist in his gut. "You're not joking."

"Why would I—"

"Fuck!" Walker shouted, the word echoing out across the landscape. "I'm supposed to be going home."

"Man, I'm sorry," Shen said. "I didn't know."

Walker felt a tremor in his gut. Iraq sat nestled in a part of the world he had never wanted to visit again. The last time he'd been in the region, it had been in Turkey, but Iraq was close enough to make him shudder.

He studied the envelope. "Boudreau didn't say what the assignment was?"

"I'm sure he spells it out for you." Shen gestured to the envelope. "All he told me was that it was Iraq and it was weird shit, and that nobody's better with the weird shit than you."

Walker laughed, but there was nothing funny. Dr. Boudreau apparently thought surviving so much horror, time and again, made him the perfect person to throw into another bizarre assignment. When this was over, he and Boudreau were going to need to have a talk.

"All right," he said, tucking the envelope into his pocket for later reading. "Let me introduce you to the team. If you don't touch anything without asking, you probably won't get a virus that'll liquefy your bones and make your blood leak out every orifice."

"Oh," Shen replied. "I love the Arctic already."

By then, Walker had tuned him out. He would make the introductions, then pack his gear as quickly as possible. Whatever might be waiting for him inside that envelope, it would be sensitive, dangerous, and the sort of thing the average person would dismiss as lunacy. For better or worse, that was the job.

Iraq, he thought as he strode across the tundra.
Shit.

A hand shook Walker awake. His right fist clenched, and he sucked in a breath, belly tightening, ready to fight. He'd been having a nightmare about almost drowning in Guatemala, and the things in the depths of that awful lake, the glow of their eyes and the sharpness of their teeth, and he had woken from that dream in the midst of defending himself.

The corporal who had unknowingly risked a beating flinched backward, hands coming up to defend himself if necessary.

Walker exhaled. Tried on a smile that didn't really fit. "Sorry, soldier."

"No worries, Dr. Walker. Just wanted to let you know we'll touch down in Mosul in about fifteen minutes."

"I'm surprised there's anywhere to safely land in Mosul, based on some of the pictures I've seen."

The corporal did not smile. "Recovery is slow, but it's happening. Our runway will be safe."

"I don't doubt it," Walker replied, surprised the man had taken the comment personally. Much of Mosul had been reduced to rubble by ISIS and the battle to take the city back from them. Success there had been costly.

The corporal made his way forward and strapped himself back into the jump seat he'd been slotted into throughout the flight from Germany. The small military jet would make a short stop in Mosul to let him off before reaching its final destination in Baghdad. It carried supplies meant for Iraqi military use—and one passenger who wouldn't be listed on any manifest.

Walker didn't like traveling this way. If anyone attempted to track backward from his arrival, it would seem like he'd just magically appeared in the country. If David Boudreau and his DARPA taskmasters wanted the National Science Foundation to appear a benevolent civilian operation, it would have been better for Walker to travel on commercial flights instead of risk tipping their hand.

Which told Walker exactly how troubled Boudreau and the rest were by whatever this archaeologist, Sophie Durand, had found in Kurdistan.

He sat up, groaned quietly as his spine popped, and rotated his head to get the stiffness out of his neck. Walker had several doctorates and a set of skills he'd picked up through a much rarer sort of education, but the talent for which he felt most grateful was his ability to sleep anywhere, at any time. He had old injuries—acquired under circumstances that still gave him nightmares—and there were some very strong pills that went along with those injuries. But sleep . . . that was a drug he could administer to himself. A five-minute nap, or one lasting five hours, it restored him.

His ex-wife, Amanda, had always envied that. And cursed his name when their boy, Charlie, had been born and he'd been able to sneak in enough sleep to avoid falling apart.

Walker frowned. Charlie would be turning eleven this year, and Walker had promised to be home for his birthday, which was less than a month away.

As long as you come home, Charlie had said the last time Walker had left, less worried about his birthday than he was about his father's safety, which made it all the harder for Walker to contemplate disappointing him.

The plane rumbled and then banked left. The pilot hit an air pocket that dropped them for a solid three count before the wind buoyed them up again. Once upon a time, it would have scared the crap out of Walker, but he had a different threshold for fear than he'd had as a younger man.

When they were safely on the ground and the engine began to whine as it cooled down, Walker stood and grabbed his gear—a scuffed blue canvas duffel and a jacket that nearly matched—and then he exited the plane by way of metal steps that had been rolled up to the door. The sun baked down on the back of his neck as he reached the tarmac, and he headed toward a U.S. Army sergeant who was trotting in his direction.

"Dr. Walker?" the man said.

"That's right," Walker said, shaking his hand.

"Sergeant Peter Dunlap. Please come with me."

He didn't wait for an answer, just headed off in another direction and expected Walker to follow. Strong and tanned and too weathered for his age, the sergeant seemed like the hard-eyed sort of soldier the military thrived on finding young and forging into loyal fighters.

Walker had never been to Mosul International Airport before, but he felt confident this wasn't it. Iraqi military vehicles were parked in various defensive positions, and he could see a high fence in the distance, topped by barbed wire. Towers were spaced at intervals with guards on sentry duty. The United States had relinquished control of the country years ago, but there were American soldiers as well, working in cooperation with local forces. ISIS might have been driven out, but its scattered components still existed, dreaming of an ascendant and oppressive Islamic state. To Walker, it felt as if every person he saw was holding their breath, waiting for fresh violence to erupt.

Dunlap marched him across the tarmac, where the helicopter sat waiting, one of its doors already open. The pilot turned to watch them, anonymous with his sunglasses and headgear, but only when Walker climbed into the chopper did he realize two other passengers were already on board. Both were women, and one was a friend. More than a friend.

"Welcome to Mosul," Kim Seong said as Walker stowed his duffel and slid into a seat. She smiled, and Walker couldn't help but smiling in return.

"It's good to see you," he said loudly as the helicopter's rotors began to turn, the noise growing by the second. "I wasn't sure you'd come."

Kim smiled uncertainly. "You weren't sure I'd come? We're here under the auspices of the U.N., Walker. Which means that this time, you're on *my* team."

Walker smiled. "I've always been on your team."

"Dr. Walker," Kim said, her Korean accent barely noticeable, "meet Erika Tang. She'll be joining us at Derveyî."

Walker paused in the midst of belting himself in to reach out and shake hands with the other woman.

"Dr. Tang is a biological anthropologist and epidemiologist," Kim said loudly. "My superiors felt she'd be invaluable to our efforts."

Walker cocked his head. "What efforts are those? They've told me almost nothing."

Given her specialties, Erika Tang would have been very welcome on the Greenland Project he'd just left behind, but the U.N. had sent her here to join him and Kim for whatever mysterious bullshit was unfolding.

Dr. Tang crossed her arms. She seemed uncomfortable meeting anyone's eyes. "You mean to say, Dr. Walker—"

"Just 'Walker.'"

"—that your government has sent you here without informing you of what you're expected to do?"

He studied Dr. Tang. "Judging by your credentials, I think I can guess."

Dr. Tang glanced at him, then at her feet, then away. "I very much doubt that." She took out her cell phone and began to scroll through messages or photos or something, behaving as if the others had become invisible to her.

As Walker fastened his seat belt, he turned to Kim for an explanation of Dr. Tang's remarks, but she shook her head. He understood. Whatever Tang was talking about, the U.N. had given Kim instructions not to speak about it in public, even in front of the pilot.

Just when Walker was about to ask the pilot what they were waiting for, Sergeant Dunlap reappeared at the open door with a go-bag. He climbed inside, stowed his bag, slid the door closed and latched it, then belted himself into a seat beside Walker.

"Time to go," he called to the pilot.

Walker glanced at him. "You're coming with us?"

"Apparently, I've been promoted to babysitter," Dunlap replied. "First I'd heard of it was about twenty minutes ago."

"You don't seem happy about it," Dr. Tang said.

"I have my orders. Captain says I should think of it like a vacation." Dunlap's grin showed his teeth. "But this ain't the Bahamas."

The helicopter lifted off, and in moments, they were tearing across the sky above Mosul. In the distance, Walker could see plumes of smoke rising. They might have come from anything—fire, a roadside bomb, or combat—but he was relieved the chopper wasn't headed in that direction.

Exhaling, he turned to Kim. "It's good to see you."

They had met under circumstances that echoed their present assignment. Archaeologists in an unstable region of the world had found something that made people nervous. Kim had been born and raised in South Korea but worked for the United Nations in New York. It had bothered her for years, she had once told him, that so many Westerners failed to understand that Kim was her family name, and that Seong was her given name. One of the things she had liked about Walker when they'd first met was that he went only by his last name. If he could be just "Walker," then she could certainly just be "Kim."

Strong, she'd said. *It makes me feel strong.* But he remembered other times with her, times when she wanted very much for him to use her given name, to call her *Seong*. Quiet times, just between the two of them.

The earlier part of their story—their first adventure together—had started with a helicopter, too. Even a flicker of memory from that time made Walker shudder, but the two of them had made it out alive and salvaged something from the horror. Kim had moved to D.C., continuing her work as an advisor and observer for the U.N., and she and Walker had pursued a relationship unmarred by crisis or adventure.

When the U.N. wanted to relocate her to Brussels—the capital of the European Union—she had taken a week to think it over, and then she had agreed. Kim had told him that she would be in New York every few weeks, just an hour by plane from Walker's home in D.C., and that if they wanted to make it work, their relationship could survive the distance.

So far, so good. It wasn't a fairy-tale romance, but they didn't lead the sort of lives that allowed for a lot of exotic holidays or moonlit strolls, so they took their time together when they could.

"So you requested me for this?" Walker said, thinking about his promise to his son, trying not to be upset with her for unknowingly interfering with his plans.

"I did," Kim replied. "And I'm happy you're here."

"Me, too. But I will be very angry if you get me killed."

SIX

Walker liked Dr. Tang instantly, though he doubted she had that effect on most people. The lean, ponytailed woman had a gravity that
he appreciated, although he could tell there was more to her severity
than simple focus. She had a jittery nature, glancing sharply here and
there like a nervous bird. Given her dry delivery and her reluctance
to make eye contact, Walker suspected an autism spectrum disorder.

"Is this your first time on a chopper?" he asked her as they sped
over low mountains.

Dr. Tang frowned and leaned toward him. "I'm an epidemiologist,
Walker. I teach, I research, and in cases like this—when they pay my
fee and it's not too out of the way for me—I sometimes advise the
U.N. on global health concerns. Occasionally, that means racing to
the site of an epidemic to save lives in some of the most inhospitable
places imaginable. Does it sound like this is my first time on a helicopter?"

Walker raised his eyebrows. "Just making conversation."

"If that's your best attempt to get to know me," Dr. Tang said, "I'd
prefer you use Google."

Blinking, Walker paused, and then gave the woman a nod. "Fair
enough."

Neuro-diverse individuals made some people uncomfortable, but
Walker felt at ease. Dr. Tang might be brusque, but she would be absolutely reliable.

"Okay, folks!" the pilot called as the helicopter began to descend. "Special delivery to the middle of fucking nowhere."

Walker settled back into his seat. "Thank God."

They peered out of the chopper at the camp below. In its way, the terrain shared similarities with the tundra in Greenland, even the hills and mountains in the distance, but he could feel the heat baking through the helicopter's windows and knew there would be no ice and snow here. His old injuries would be glad of the warmth.

From above, it was easy to see there had once been an ancient town here, but all that remained were the rough outlines of dwellings and the nubs of walls. It appeared that the archaeologists were not there to excavate this town, although their camp sat on the outskirts of the ruins. Walker spotted half a dozen trailers and two prefab buildings that had likely been brought in on flatbeds. A series of military tents were being erected even as the chopper circled for landing. Dunlap had mentioned that the Beneath Project had been going on for most of a year, but with all the people crawling around, it showed no sign of petering out. More than a dozen vehicles, mostly Jeeps and Humvees, some of them military, were parked here and there.

At the edge of the camp, almost growing up from the lines that suggested the foundations of the ancient town, a stone ridge rose from the earth. The stone was like nothing he'd seen before, reminding him of the drip sandcastles he'd made with his father on the beach as a child, or of the terrifying wasp's nest he had discovered in the mulch of his mother's flower bed the summer he'd turned nine years old. Like the wasp's nest, the ridge had a single dark hole in its face, and as the helicopter settled to the ground in the whirlwind of dust kicked up by its rotors, Walker saw the soldiers who were guarding that hole, the entrance into the nest.

"All ashore that's going ashore," the pilot said, glancing over his shoulder.

Walker undid his seat belt, grabbed his duffel, and cranked the door latch, jumping down from the chopper before turning to offer a hand to Kim. She took it and dropped to the ground beside him, narrowing her eyes against the swirling dust.

"Kurdish and U.S. forces," she said, studying the sentries.

"Coalition," Walker replied. "If that's still what we are."

"Whatever they are, they're not archaeologists."

Sergeant Dunlap exited the chopper from the other side. Walker turned to offer a hand to Dr. Tang, but she ignored him, jumping down unaided. The four of them set out toward the camp and hadn't walked twenty feet before a tall, lanky guy jogged from one of the trailers to meet them. The helicopter's rotors churned back up to speed, the chop of air and sound thumping the ground as it lifted off again. Walker tasted dirt and pulled his shirt up to cover his nose and mouth as he and the others picked up their pace.

The slim, scruffy guy looked to be in his midtwenties, tanned, with pink spots showing through on his forehead where burned skin had begun to flake away. Walker figured he was the kind of white guy who turned remarkably pale in the winter or any time he wasn't spending months in the sun in northern Iraq.

"Martin Jungling!" he shouted over the noise of the departing chopper, not bothering to shake anyone's hand. "I'm the site supervisor. Follow me."

Then he turned and trotted off toward the wasp's nest in the side of the hill. Walker shifted his duffel and turned to the others.

"Hell of a welcome," he said.

Dr. Tang hoisted a heavy-looking backpack about half her size onto her shoulders and started walking. "He seems in a hurry," she said, glancing at Dunlap. "I was under the impression I was here to consult, not take action. Should we be worried?"

"There are men with guns," Kim noted. "I always worry when there are men with guns."

Martin Jungling led them to the entrance. A stack of metal crates with numbers stenciled on the side drew Walker's attention along the way—supplies coming in, or artifacts going out?

The two American sentries at the entrance watched them with narrow-eyed suspicion, but they saluted Sergeant Dunlap, and the action alone seemed to relax them.

Martin showed his ID badge. "This is the group from the U.N. that Sophie told you guys about."

"ID?" said one of the sentries.

"They're earlier than expected," Martin replied. "The IDs are in a box inside. Alton has—"

"You know the deal, Martin," one of the soldiers sniffed, casually holding his weapon as if it were an umbrella he'd taken out with him just in case of rain. "No ID, no entry. All parties agreed on that."

The burned patches on Martin's forehead flushed a bit darker. "Look, Taejon, I know the rules. But it's not like you didn't know they were coming. I'll bring them in on my authority—"

"What authority?" asked Taejon, a corporal.

The other sentry smiled. Walker didn't know Martin Jungling, but he felt embarrassed for the guy and angry on his behalf.

"Mr. Jungling, we can wait," Kim said. "Go on and get the IDs."

Martin looked as if he might argue, then he ran a hand across the back of his neck and marched, huffing, through the hole in the hillside. Walker shot Corporal Taejon a hard look, but the soldier only smiled.

Sergeant Dunlap started to speak, but Dr. Tang cut him off.

"Corporal, this is a crisis situation—"

"Ma'am, there's no crisis here."

Dr. Tang stepped up to within inches of him, her ponytail bouncing innocently as if to suggest there was nothing about her that should be feared. The look in her eyes said differently. Apparently, Dr. Tang could make very effective eye contact when she had the right motivation.

"I don't get invited to anything but a crisis," she said quietly, shrinking him with the ferocity of her gaze. "And it's 'Doctor.'"

After that, they stood in silence until Martin returned and handed out lanyards with their badges on them. There were no credentials for Sergeant Dunlap, as he'd been a last-minute addition, but this time, when Martin began to explain to the sentries, neither of them seemed to feel like delaying their entrance any further.

Martin led the way inside, and they stepped into the strange, yellowish gloom of a small chamber that Walker could only think of as the cave's foyer. He heard a chuffing sound beside him, and it took him a moment to realize it came from Dunlap, who'd been laughing quietly to himself.

"Sergeant?"

"Sorry. I just enjoyed that a little," he said, glancing at Dr. Tang. "Were you ever in the military?"

"Never. But I've been around a great many soldiers in my time."

"You'd have made a hell of a commanding officer."

Walker had never seen anything like it. When he'd heard the words *underground city*, he had imagined architecture like something from a 1950s science-fiction movie. But the moment they began to follow Martin through an enormous atrium, along tunnels, and down circling stairways, he felt the presence of the real people who had once worked and slept and cooked and borne children here. He glanced into well-lit rooms where members of the archaeological team seemed to be dismantling their own camp, preparing to depart. They had been here a while, but like him, they were visitors. The original inhabitants had been gone a very long time.

They passed through junctions where they could look across an open space and see more levels above and below, tunnels branching off. In some places, the walls were totally bare—just that yellowed rock—but in others there were ancient mosaics, cracked but still vividly colorful. Walker noticed benches and fireplaces, as well as a system of ordinary vents. All of it looked as if it had been carved from beige stone, stained yellow by the industrial lighting rigs that the archaeologists had set up throughout the place, although strategically placed openings brought sunlight down in narrow shafts—an ingenious element of the original design.

Walker could almost hear the sounds of those original inhabitants, or hear their footfalls. A similar sort of frisson had passed through him several times in the past, in catacombs and cathedrals and in a Civil War fort on a Boston Harbor island, where men had waited for a conflict that never reached them. It felt strange to breathe history.

"This place . . . ," Sergeant Dunlap said, but he let his words trail off.

"Yes," Kim said as they turned a corner, following Martin down a ramp.

They passed men carrying sealed plastic boxes and another with a ladder on his shoulder, and then they reached a larger room, where another pair of armed sentries flanked a doorway that had been barred by a sawhorse and a sign that had been posted in four languages. Simple, clear words. NO UNAUTHORIZED ADMITTANCE.

Martin flashed his ID. One of the soldiers picked up the sawhorse and moved it.

Then Martin turned toward them. "I'm sorry, Sergeant Dunlap. You haven't yet been cleared by Dr. Durand. You'll need to stay here."

Dunlap's forehead creased with irritation, but then he glanced at the sentries and nodded. "All right. Don't all gossip about me while you're gone."

Walker saw Kim smile, and for a moment, he didn't like Dunlap quite so much. He had changed a lot as he grew older, and it surprised him to know that jealous part of him still remained, down inside, waiting for a trigger. It made him feel faintly ridiculous.

"Ready?" Martin asked as if they were about to step into some amusement park ride.

Visibly disappointed at their lack of enthusiasm, he led them down another level, and they turned right into a large circular chamber, its ceiling supported by five columns. Across the room was another stairwell, this one short, with one of the round stone doors at the bottom. Voices came from beyond the door.

"Only six people have been allowed inside the Pandora Room. The three of you make it nine," Martin informed them as they descended.

Walker frowned. "What the hell is the Pandora Room?"

A woman stepped out through the door. She held a thick notebook in one hand and had a pencil balanced atop her left ear.

"The Pandora Room, Dr. Walker," she said, "is the reason you're here."

"You're Dr. Durand?"

She smiled thinly, glancing at the group gathered on the stairs. "You mean you haven't done your homework?"

"I mostly slept on the flight."

She stepped aside and gestured for him to pass through the hole in the wall. "Well, you're well rested for the tour, then. Best we get to work."

The woman had an aura of certainty about her, a confidence that spoke of expertise and authority. He'd seen a file with her credentials, but no photograph. Perhaps five foot nine, Dr. Durand seemed fit, but nothing about her height explained how physically formidable she seemed. Perhaps it sprang from her obvious desire to skip the pleasantries and get to work. Walker admired that quality. With her hair collected in a tangle of thick braids, rich brown eyes, and strong, angular face, she would have been attractive regardless, but her presence had very little to do with her looks. Sophie Durand was in charge.

"I couldn't agree more," Walker said as he stepped through the door and into a small chamber.

"Hold on a moment, please," Dr. Tang called after him.

Walker turned to see that she'd set her backpack down on the steps and unzipped it. Now she drew out a thick black filtration mask made to cover nose and mouth. Dr. Tang slipped the mask over her own face. It amplified the sound of her breathing slightly, but not to Darth Vader proportions.

"Military grade," she said. "Just a precaution."

Then she dug into the backpack and pulled out two more, handing one through the entrance to Walker and one to Kim. "Put them on. No arguments." She glanced at Sophie. "I have another, if you'd like."

Sophie stood on the threshold and smiled. "I've been in this room off and on for days. I think I'm fine."

Dr. Tang pulled on a pair of latex gloves. Walker wondered if she was being paranoid or if he simply wasn't worried enough. The thought made the back of his neck prickle with heat, but he slid on the mask, adjusted the strap, and wondered what it was supposed to keep out.

Behind him, he heard Kim and Dr. Tang introducing themselves to Dr. Durand. "*Sophie* is fine," she told them, and he smiled to himself. Sophie hadn't been so informal with him, but he wasn't bothered. This dig belonged to her, as did the project. Her staff might not be able to keep whatever they had found, but she didn't want any government, not even her own, to hijack her work.

Two other people were in the small chamber. They were working in tomb-like silence, and neither looked up to greet him as Sophie led Kim and Dr. Tang into the room. With the lighting rigs and six of them now crowded inside, Walker fought a sense of claustrophobia he had combatted in the past, fought the memories of Guatemala and the cave on Mount Ararat.

"Dr. Walker, Ms. Kim, Dr. Tang," Sophie said, "meet Lamar Curtis and Professor Beyza Solak. Sometimes I think they're the only people on this dig who know what they're doing, myself included. Lamar and Beyza, meet our new arrivals."

Lamar wore dusty spectacles. When he gripped Walker's hand, he held on firmly and gave a sharp nod of acknowledgment.

"Welcome to the land of conjecture and disbelief," he said.

Beyza had been shifting a light fixture, presumably to better illuminate the writing on the wall. A camera hung from a strap around her neck, and Walker put two and two together. They were making a full record of what was written here, in case they had to leave faster than they hoped. Now she lifted the camera and took a photo of the new arrivals.

"Tight quarters, I know," Beyza said, seeming to sense their discomfort. Then she glanced at Sophie. "How much have you told them?"

"Getting to that," Sophie replied.

She gestured to Lamar, who shifted out of the way, and for the first time, Walker caught sight of the small altar engraved with a tight scrawl of writing quite like what they'd seen upstairs. And upon the altar, a squat jar covered with dusty paint and ancient scribbling. The whole chamber seemed to pulse, as if this underground city had taken a breath and held it.

"You know the story of Pandora's box?" Sophie asked.

For a moment, Walker felt the temptation to turn on his heel and leave that place—to take Kim with him and exit as quickly as possible. Whatever proceeded from this moment, it felt to him that it could only bring them misery. The instinct made him feel foolish, and he would never have abandoned his duties, but a fresh ripple of anxiety went through him.

"Of course," Kim said. "It's central to Greek mythology. Zeus gave it to Pandora. It contained all the evils of the world—"

"Actually, no," Beyza put in. "It's come into pop culture that way, but as usual, it's all about the men."

Sophie tapped her nose and pointed to Beyza as if to say she'd gotten the point just right. "According to the tale as recounted by Hesiod in the eighth century B.C.E., the gods created Pandora themselves, built her up from earth and clay—"

"The original Wonder Woman," Walker suggested.

"If you like," Sophie replied. "According to the myth, Hephaestus and Athena made her, and all the gods contributed some element of her nature. She was presented to Prometheus's brother to be his wife. Zeus was angry that Prometheus had stolen fire from the gods, and this was his scheme. He knew that Pandora's curiosity would be too great and that she would open the box."

She glanced around to make sure they were following her, then forged ahead. "The word *box* was a mistranslation. You see, the original text referred to a ceremonial jar."

Sophie shot Walker a meaningful look, then glanced at the altar.

He scoffed, but then he saw the grave expressions on the faces of Dr. Durand and her team and remembered that he had been summoned here in the first place.

"You're telling us Pandora's box was a jar," he said. "And it's sitting on that altar right now?"

Dr. Tang approached the altar the way Walker had seen soldiers approach roadside bombs. A chill went through him, watching her, and suddenly he didn't feel like scoffing anymore. A haunted look had touched her eyes, which were all he could see of her face above the filtration mask. She seemed more jittery than ever, glancing toward the corners of the room as if afraid they were not alone. When Walker followed her gaze, for half a moment he almost thought he caught a glimpse of something himself, the suggestion of a figure in the dark between two lighting rigs, but then he blinked and knew it had just been the power of suggestion.

Kim took a step nearer to the altar, but not too near. "In the myth of Pandora, the box—the jar—is emptied. But this appears to be sealed."

Walker understood. He and Kim had experienced outrageous claims before. They would hold off on judgment for now but weren't inclined to immediately disbelieve the way most people would.

Sophie went down on one knee beside the altar, startling Dr. Tang.

"The story is written here and on the walls and on the altar itself, but it's not the same as in Hesiod's *Theogony* and *Works and Days*. There are numerous other versions as well—"

"But none of them like this," Lamar added.

Sophie seemed almost entranced by the jar now. "Some mention Anesidora. Historians translate this as an alternative name for Pandora, but what's written in this room corrects that assumption. Pandora had a sister."

Walker studied the altar. "Anesidora."

"Pandora's jar contained all the evils that might plague mankind, including pain and disease and monstrosity," Sophie said. "But only in some versions. In others, the jar contained not evils but all the goodness and blessings of the earth. As written here in this room, the story suggests a reason for this confusion."

"Two jars," Kim said.

"Two sisters," Sophie replied. "A jar for each."

"But there's only one here," Dr. Tang said, glancing up sharply. "So which one is it?"

Sophie rose to her feet. For the first time, Walker noticed the gray circles beneath her eyes and wondered how little sleep she had been getting in recent days.

"That's the question, isn't it?" she said.

Lamar crossed his arms. "We're not suggesting the gods of Olympus existed or that they made women out of clay. That only happens in comic books."

"Whether they were forged by gods or just the daughters of some minor king," Sophie went on, gesturing around the room, "if all of this is true, we have a dilemma in front of us. Or a mystery, if you want to approach it that way."

She let the words hang in the room, lingering like the smell of age and the ancient dust that floated beneath the glow of the electric lights. Walker let out a long breath and moved past Kim, then slid between

Beyza and Lamar. He stared at the scrawl of abandoned language on the altar and the jar, wishing he could read it.

"I know it sounds like just a legend," Beyza said.

"We've encountered legends before," Kim replied, her voice quiet and as dry as those swirling motes. "A lot of people died. So trust me when I say we will take this seriously until there is evidence that such caution is unnecessary."

Walker bent toward the jar, staring not at the scrawl now but at the seal between lid and lip.

"Please don't touch it," Lamar said.

Walker rested on his haunches and glanced up at him. "I have no interest in touching this thing without proper containment protocol."

Dr. Tang nodded slowly. "A good choice." She turned to Sophie. "In fact, Dr. Durand, I'm surprised you're taking the risks that you're already taking. Keeping exposure limited to a handful of the dig's staff is smart, but you need—"

Sophie held up one finger to halt her. "Let me stop you there. Regardless of what's in the jar, the Pandora Room, as we're calling it, is a massively important discovery that will echo across many disciplines. From what we've already translated, these writings will help establish a tangible measure to begin to gauge the veracity of Greek mythology, to disentangle metaphor from reality in early Greek culture. My boss is thrilled. As soon as we evacuate this space, he wants me as his show pony. He wants to go public with conclusions about this site that my team and I are not ready to make. Not without a hell of a lot more research."

Beyza leaned against the wall, arms crossed. "We have more imminent concerns, however."

"You certainly do," Dr. Tang said. "I honestly doubt there's anything dangerous inside that jar, but I can't promise you that, and I absolutely disagree with any action moving forward until this room can be sealed and the jar properly contained or removed."

"Sealed?" Lamar asked. "You can't do that."

Walker stepped in. "Can we focus on the story for a second? It sounds like some kind of ancient conspiracy theory. How are we supposed to believe any of this?"

"Let's proceed from the assumption that there were no gods on Olympus," Sophie said.

"Define 'gods,'" Walker replied.

"Fair enough," Sophie said, "but humor me. We may determine all of this is just a story, but given the potential for truth, let's examine it. Picture the scientists of the era deciding to create microcosms of their research, or what they knew of their world, either for future study or for posterity, or in case something happened to whatever space they used as their de facto laboratories."

"A data backup," Lamar added.

"Or something like a miniature version of the Svalbard Global Seed Vault," Dr. Tang said. "It might contain seeds and grains to plant the best crops from that era. Cures for a hundred diseases."

Walker studied the jar again. "One jar with blessings, the other with curses. If one had seeds and medicines, the other could be full of samples of the diseases and viruses of the ancient world."

"Sealed for study at a later time, when people of the future—meaning us—would have a better chance of learning how to treat them," Dr. Tang replied. "But we've cured most of the ills of the ancient world."

"The ones we're familiar with, yes," Beyza replied. "This is your field, Dr. Tang. If there are influenza strains the population hasn't encountered in thousands of years, or ever encountered on a wide scale, isn't that a problem? The Plague of Athens hit in the fifth century B.C.E., during the second year of the Peloponnesian War. There are dozens of theories about what caused it, including a hemorrhagic fever like Ebola, but nobody really knows what caused it. So you tell me. Should we be afraid?"

Walker shuddered. He'd just come from Greenland, where the melting permafrost had already uncovered eleven potentially deadly prehistoric bacteria. There was no telling what might be in this jar.

They all stared at Dr. Tang, who shifted uncomfortably. "I can't speak for the rest of you, but I'm absolutely terrified."

Dr. Tang dug back into her backpack and pulled out three more filtration masks, handing them to Sophie, Beyza, and Lamar. "I don't intend to prevent those who have already been in the room from entering, only to reinforce the rule you already have in place. Nobody else should enter, and everyone who has spent time in this room needs to be masked from now on. That includes the sentries who've been guarding the room."

"When you say 'from now on . . . ,'" Beyza began.

"I mean from now on. At all times, until the jar has been removed from the premises and we can all undergo a thorough medical examination under quarantine. Most, if not all, of the staff will have to do the same."

Lamar put the mask on with no further questions.

Beyza turned to Sophie. "Is this really necessary? It's a four-thousand–year-old jar."

"Maybe older than that," Sophie replied, slipping her own mask on. "But this is the reason Dr. Tang is here, so we'll follow her lead."

"If we've been exposed to something in here, it's already too late," Beyza argued.

"For you, maybe," Dr. Tang replied. "But on the off chance you have been exposed to something, do you really want to share it with your coworkers?"

Beyza glanced back and forth between Sophie and Lamar and then reluctantly put on her own mask. "I feel ridiculous."

"Let's talk about the next step. There are already too many people who have at least an inkling of what's going on here. How do we get the jar out of here safely, and how soon can it be done?"

Sophie Durand thought Kim and her team had come to help them, and Walker would contribute to that if he could. But regardless of what might really be in the jar, his mission was very clear—his superiors at DARPA would expect him to acquire it.

"Actually," Kim said, studying him as if reading his mind. "The most important question isn't how you get the jar out. It's whose hands the jar will end up in. The United Nations will have an opinion on the subject."

Walker kept his expression neutral. Kim understood his dilemma and had made her position clear, though nobody else in that tiny room would have understood the undercurrent of her words, but Walker figured they had to feel the tension.

"My boss wants us to extract the jar ourselves and film the whole thing," Sophie said. "The Iraqis and the Kurds also have opinions. As will the Turks, if they don't already know about it."

"They do," Kim replied, taking a step toward the jar. "I'm sure the whisperers are at work everywhere. It will take time for them to determine how much of what we're discussing is true."

"You think they'll wait to verify any of this?" Sophie asked.

"No," Kim replied, her voice muffled behind the mask. "Of course they won't. Which is why I'm here."

Walker nodded. "If you can persuade the U.N. to step in as more than observers, that may be the only way to untangle this."

"Agreed," Sophie said. "If the U.N. will mediate, I'm confident we'll find a resolution to the question of custody. Until then, nobody enters this room without my permission."

"You said you were preparing to evacuate," Walker said, glancing from her to Lamar, to Beyza, and back again. "Which means you're expecting someone to try to enter this room without your permission, and probably with guns."

Dr. Tang made a low humming sound, unsettled and perhaps unaware they could hear her. She rocked slightly on her feet.

Sophie shot Walker an appraising glance. "Lamar and Martin and I were followed by Turkish spies the other day. Those men may have meant us harm or just been curious, but either way, coalition soldiers stopped them. A drone had been following us as well. A lot of people were interested in laying claim to whatever we found here even before they knew about the jar. If people who think they have a claim learn what we've found, they're going to come for it."

Not just people who think they have a claim, Walker thought. Anyone who suspected there might be ancient diseases in that jar that could be used as biological weapons—or long-forgotten cures—would want to get their hands on it, including his own employers. Some who wanted those ancient diseases would have monstrous intentions, and those people would do absolutely anything to see them through.

"Consider us part of the team," Kim said, with a warning glance at Walker.

Of those in Derveyî, only she knew who he really worked for, and she would have known it was a risk to bring him into this if there was any truth to what Sophie suspected about the jar. He told himself Kim had wanted him here in spite of his loyalties because they had survived trouble together before and she trusted his priorities if danger arose. But he had to wonder if it was a test. She hadn't asked the Americans to send him because she missed his face. Unless it seemed clear the jar was a fake or that there was nothing of potential use to DARPA inside it, he and Kim would definitely be at odds over its possession eventually.

He wished he'd stayed in Greenland.

"We'll do whatever we can to help," Walker said. "But whatever it is, let's do it fast."

Sophie glanced at Beyza and Lamar. "You two get back to work. Ms. Kim and I have some phone calls to make."

Walker watched as Sophie and Kim struck up a conversation and quickly left the room together, focused entirely on the task ahead. He took no offense at being ignored. After all, he had his own phone calls to make, and he didn't want anyone else around to hear them.

He hesitated, not wanting to abandon Dr. Tang. She stood between two lighting rigs, staring at the jar from as much distance as she could manage in the small room. Beyza had gone back to photographing the writing on the walls. Lamar picked up a thick journal-style notebook, studying the jar, and began to make notations on a page already filled with ink.

"Dr. Tang, why don't we rejoin Sergeant Dunlap and see if we can figure out where we're supposed to bunk?" Walker suggested.

She cocked her head again, tilted it left, and then upright, but all the while her gaze remained on the jar. With the mask obscuring her facial expression, her eyes were impossible to read.

"Dr. Tang? Are you all right?"

She turned her head so swiftly that Walker flinched. Her eyes reflected the industrial lighting, giving them an unnatural gleam.

"All right?" she said. "No, Dr. Walker. I'm not the slightest bit all right."

Dr. Tang turned and hurried from the Pandora Room so swiftly that he wondered if she might actually be fleeing from the jar. Walker thought of canaries in coal mines and wished he were anywhere but Derveyî. Anywhere but down there with the curses of the ancients.

Or the blessings, he reminded himself as he left the Pandora Room.

But the room carried silent echoes of age within it, resonated with the potential of that jar and the warnings of Alexander. The walls seemed almost to whisper the stories that were written there, although Walker couldn't read them. All he knew was that whatever power breathed inside that room, it sure as hell didn't feel like a blessing.

SEVEN

Kim lay in the dark, trying not to scream.

It had been so foolish of her to come here, but in the moment when the assignment had come to her, she had felt a powerful serendipity. Nearly two years before, she had met Walker in Turkey on the way to Mount Ararat. A pair of young adventurers had found what they believed might be the historical root of the tale of Noah's Ark. It had seemed so exciting to her then—a landslide revealing a mountainside cave, the ark in the cave, this kind man who had been broken more than once and put himself back together—but in the back of the ark had been something else.

She didn't like to use the word *demon*, even now.

Nearly everyone had died. Most of those deaths had been chalked up to a murderer among the archaeological team—a very different, less professional group than this one—and the rest had been blamed on the blizzard through which they'd descended to escape the cave.

But Kim remembered. The things she'd seen had scarred her deeply, invisibly, and she had been asked not to speak of them to anyone but Walker or a therapist. Her coworkers, even her direct superiors, had no idea about what really happened on that mountain. How could she tell them when so many would think her mind had unraveled? Even if those within the U.N. who knew the truth stood up for her—and she knew they would not—so many would never believe her.

So she kept the memories to herself, and the less she talked about them, the more they festered inside her.

Tight places frightened her. Airless spaces, windowless rooms made her heart race and her gut churn. Deep darkness gave her chills, made her want to weep. Worst yet, an unexpected grin from friend or stranger made her want to scream. There were no demons behind such grins, nothing hidden in the dark. The private therapist she had seen for the first year had promised her that, but the woman clearly had not believed anything Kim had told her. Which meant she couldn't know those unexpected grins hid nothing sinister. She simply couldn't know.

Now she lay in the dark, in a windowless room—a cave underground—with the utter certainty that something malign breathed and pulsed inside the Pandora Room, and the urge to scream built up steam in her chest. The filtration mask lay on a small desk in the corner of the room.

The jar might be nothing. She knew that. Odds were it was empty or contained dust or some sort of time capsule that would make the world's archaeological community reach an earthshaking collective orgasm. No curses, no blessings, no evils. But in the dark, with nearly all the Beneath Project's personnel asleep in various chambers throughout Derveyî, she felt small and suffocated and helpless.

Kim exhaled. Eyes wide in the dark, she glanced at the doorway, comforted by the illumination glowing beyond the privacy curtain but afraid, each time she glanced at it, that a silhouette would appear. Her heart fluttered, and she pulled her gaze away, turned on her side, and stared at the sleeping form of Dr. Tang on the next bunk. Dr. Tang twitched and muttered in her sleep as if she were fighting her own subconscious battles. Beyond her were three other bunks, only one of them occupied—a grad student named Rachel shared the space with them. Many members of the staff of the Beneath Project had already finished their work and departed. The dig had been winding down before the Pandora Room had been discovered, so there were open beds for Kim and her team.

Her team. She smiled weakly at the thought, although she had been disappointed that Walker hadn't bristled at being under her thumb.

His egalitarian nature had impressed her early on, strange traits for a man with so secretive a life. She hadn't expected him to be troubled by a woman telling him what to do but by *anyone* telling him what to do when it came to a field assignment. Kim knew better than to be fooled by his quiet acceptance. If push came to shove, he would do whatever he thought was necessary to protect the people around him. It was the reason she would have wanted him on this assignment regardless of their personal connection.

The thought of Walker—sharing quarters with Dunlap two rooms down the corridor—eased her mind a little. Yes, she'd have asked for him in spite of the personal connection, but it certainly helped. When she'd heard that Derveyî was a subterranean city, a network of caves and tunnels, it had triggered a fear response that she'd barely been able to hide behind a thin smile and too much nodding. When she'd heard what Sophie Durand thought she'd found, she'd had to excuse herself from the room and compose herself before returning.

Even now she wondered why she had accepted the assignment. She'd read enough about PTSD and spoken to enough veterans and survivors of violence and catastrophe that she knew she needed more help than she was getting. But a part of her—the part nurtured in the care of her perfectionist mother—needed to keep up the unflappable mask of normalcy. The rest of her was just stubborn, like her father, who had taught her to face her fears head-on.

But she didn't have to face them alone. If she'd learned anything from her time with Walker, it was that. Kim wasn't sure she could have said they were in love, but they were certainly intimate. He had lived through Ararat with her and understood the person that experience had made her better than anyone, even though she had never told him about the nightmares. Never told him that even now, when she closed her eyes, she could still see the horned thing in the coffin . . .

Kim saw it now. While her thoughts had been drifting, her eyelids had lowered. Without being aware of it, she had slid toward the edge of sleep, nearly there, and now the memory of that dry, desiccated thing surfaced and her pulse began a familiar, dreadful gallop.

With a sigh, yearning for real, restorative sleep, she opened her eyes and saw a silhouetted figure beyond the privacy curtain. Staring, she realized the figure was not behind the curtain after all but in front of it, there in the room with her and yet dark and featureless as a shadow. Kim's breath quickened, heart racing as she tried to tell herself she must be asleep after all. She could feel malice in the room, taste it.

Beside her, Dr. Tang whimpered. With a gasp of relief, so happy not to be alone in this moment, Kim turned to find the woman had not woken and seen the shadow but made yet another strange muttering in her sleep. Dr. Tang rustled beneath her sheets, grumbled, and turned to face the other direction in her bed.

When Kim glanced toward the privacy curtain again, the silhouette had gone, as if it had never been there at all. Her breathing began to slow, but her heart took time to quiet as she wondered if she had imagined it. Was her psyche so broken that she'd conjured something terrifying out of thin air? She had come here to face her fear, to challenge her trauma, not to relive it. Or so she hoped.

Being in Derveyî had frightened her, but she'd forged on regardless of fear. Now she thought she might've been foolish instead of brave, that being underground might make her unravel. She had an assignment here—a few days at most and she could leave, just as soon as the jar had been removed.

A few days.

At most.

If she told Walker what she was enduring, would that make him less likely to fulfill his duties to his employers, or more so? Kim thought he might try to take more decisive action, thinking he was helping her by allowing her to go home sooner. She would have to keep a close eye on him, but she knew he would comfort her if she needed it, and he would fight at her side if it came to that. They'd proven themselves to each other already.

As for Sophie Durand, she seemed smart and competent. If tonight became too difficult for Kim, she'd find Sergeant Dunlap and ask him to see if there might be a bunk available with the military unit outside Derveyî. She was sure Sophie wouldn't mind. Sleeping in a tent would be better than this, by far.

Just the thought soothed her. A tent sounded like a fantastic idea.

A few days, she thought again.

When she fell asleep, she did so facing away from the privacy curtain. If there were more shadows out there, Kim did not want to see them. Better for them to take her unaware, she believed, than to feel the terror of their coming.

A few days.

Beyza could often be found walking in the tunnels late at night. Members of the staff sometimes went up for air or gathered in one of the common rooms where work had already been completed. They might put on some music and drink whiskey or play a card game. She had walked past the entrance to the lower-level baths one night and spotted half a dozen staffers playing strip poker like a bunch of horny teenagers, but who was she to judge?

The staff of the Beneath Project had become a family, and over the long months they had learned one another's habits and peccadillos. Alton smoked the cigarillos he had grown up seeing in old Western movies. Marissa did late-night yoga and occasionally guilted others to join her. Kevin Ruiz had a guitar and a harmonica, and he liked to play but didn't really like to have an audience, so he would often explore the remotest tunnels, venturing into areas that had not borne archaeological fruit or where the team's work had been completed. Depending where he set up, his music might reach one part of the tunnel system or another. He would play and sing quietly, and most of the time nobody mentioned they could hear him for fear that he would turn shy and the late-night concerts would stop. He played beautifully, and they had all been down there in the subterranean world long enough to appreciate such things.

Tonight, all seemed quiet in the world underneath. If there were people blasting music, or if Ruiz had taken his guitar into one of those private places, not a single note reached her. Beyza found herself humming as she made her way through the tunnels and down curving staircases, then through a door most of the staff had never noticed. She avoided the atrium, which had become the intersection and public square for the project. Few knew the curves and passages the way she did. Some had never seen the tiled mosaics in what she thought of as the Sun Room because it received more natural light than almost anywhere else in the city. The ventilation shafts brought in slivers of daylight that checkered the stone floor when the sun shone, and even on moonlit nights the room seemed to glow.

The room had been one of the first they had explored. It had been photographed, the mosaics cleaned, several artifacts had been discovered, and one ancient altar had been removed in its entirety and sent to her employers at Atatürk University. It would eventually be part of a traveling museum display cosponsored by the dig's sponsors and the Iraqi and Kurdish governments.

Of course, the Pandora Room had changed everything. No one cared about mosaics or altars or even that traveling museum display now. The focus would shift, even if they found the jar to be empty. The writing on the altar, the walls, and the jar created the perfect twenty-first-century narrative. So much of the world's population didn't bother to read, but there were still stories that would fire the imagination, and Beyza knew this would do it. An ancient myth come true, the promise of one jar and the threat of the other. It had romance and danger and politics all bound up together. She thought that perhaps, for at least a news cycle or two, the Beneath Project would make the world interested in archaeology and history, but she had earned enough wisdom to know it wouldn't last.

Still, in the community of people who loved knowledge and learning, it would be the revelation of a lifetime, and she was proud to be a part of that. Soon, it would come to an end, and although part of her yearned to go home, there was another part of her as well.

She stood in the moonlight, thinking how ironic it was that she called it the Sun Room but came here so often at night. The shafts of light seemed as always to make the shadows around them even darker. Something shifted off to her right, the outline of a figure in the dark, the scuff of a boot, and a smile touched Beyza's lips. She was a serious woman, dedicated to her work, but her visits to the Sun Room released her from that gravity, allowed her to float, unveiled the core of her.

"You were early for once," she whispered.

In the shadows between shafts of moonlight, the darkness coalesced and Beyza smiled, her heartbeat quickening. She wished someone, somewhere would play music so that it could drift to them through the vents and drafty corridors. Music helped ease her tension, and it let her tell herself that the sounds of their lovemaking would not be heard elsewhere in the labyrinth. Tonight she would try to be silent, although she rarely succeeded in the moment, crying out even after she'd bitten her lip bloody.

Hands touched her sides, began to slide around her abdomen, a body pressing against her from behind. Beyza shouted and threw herself forward, out of reach. She turned, mouthing a stream of profanity that would have shocked most of her colleagues, but none so much as Elio Cortez.

He stood staring at her, frozen between apology and amusement.

"Just saying hello," he said.

Beyza took two strides and punched him in the chest harder than she'd meant to. "Don't sneak up on a woman like that! You scared the hell out of me!"

Cortez chuckled quietly, raised a hand to try to hide it, and then burst out laughing. "I'm sorry. I just . . . you should have seen the look on your face."

"It's not funny!"

"Well, it is a little bit funny. From my point of view." He massaged his chest where she had struck him. "A little bit painful, too. Were you expecting someone else?"

Beyza could not keep herself from smiling, though her heart continued to thunder in her chest. "I haven't invited anyone else, if that's what you mean. I don't make a habit of this sort of thing."

Cortez moved closer to her, took her hands, and kissed them. "This sort of thing. You make it sound forbidden."

"You know it is." She didn't like to talk about this part, about what it would do to her reputation among her colleagues if it became public knowledge that she had carried on an extramarital affair with a graduate student under her supervision. She could lose her job. Her husband might divorce her, but that conflict had been developing for years and was only a matter of time.

"I like that it's forbidden," Cortez said, sliding his fingers into her hair, tilting her head back to kiss her.

The kiss deepened, and her pulse raced even faster. His hands stroked her back, then held her firmly as he kissed her neck. Gently, he kissed her forehead and her temples as he began to undress her.

"Did I really frighten you?"

Beyza smiled. "Yes," she whispered.

"You were speaking to me. I thought you knew I was here."

She had been unbuttoning his shirt, but her hands faltered. He kissed her neck again, rolled his thumbs across her now bare nipples and kissed them. Beyza's body responded, her fingers tangling in his hair, wanting his mouth lower. He obliged, laying her down on her own discarded shirt, but as he parted her legs, Beyza felt the powerful lure of that space between shafts of moonlight, that shadowed corner where she had felt sure Cortez had been waiting for her. All she saw there now was darkness within darkness, no suggestion of a human figure.

Cortez's tongue found its mark, and suddenly all fears and worries were forgotten.

"Elio," she whispered.

And if something in shadows beyond the moonlight whispered back, Beyza could not hear it.

EIGHT

Night had passed, and the day, and now sunset approached again.

Sophie couldn't breathe. In the year she'd spent in the haunting, ethereal chambers and corridors of Derveyî, she had never felt claustrophobic. All that had changed. Even out here, aboveground, with the sun warming her and the breeze tugging at her clothes and her hair—even here, where she could see miles around her—she felt as if the walls of the world were closing in.

Get it together, she thought. *You're in charge.*

She wanted to laugh at the idea, but instead she felt a twist of nausea in her gut. Not long ago, the only vehicles around the dig were a handful of dusty Jeeps and a truck bearing the UNESCO logo. Other cars had come and gone. A general supply delivery had arrived twice a week. She'd spoken on her phone and via video conferencing with her boss, Alex, every few days, but other than that, she had been the woman in authority. Even the handful of U.S. and Kurdish soldiers who had been posted at the dig for the duration tended to look to her for guidance.

All that was over now.

The number of vehicles had more than quadrupled. Most were military. The coalition between American and Kurdish forces held, but the Kurds were prickly as hell now that rumors had begun to spread. Most of them knew something major had been discovered, and that had only been amplified in the twenty-four hours since Walker, Kim, and Dr. Tang had arrived. According to Lamar, the whispers about Pandora's box had begun with diggers and soldiers, and by now those rumors would be out in the world. Any version of that story, truth or fiction, would lead to a great deal of attention, much sooner than she wanted.

Now a new truck had arrived. Dr. Tang had spoken to Major Bernstein, the CO of the coalition troops on-site, just so that she wouldn't step on his toes. Then she had called a friend with USAMRIID, the United States Army Medical Research Institute of Infectious Diseases. Under ordinary circumstances, Dr. Tang had explained, she would have been content to wait for whatever the army's red tape might do, but given that they wanted to move the jar to a safer location as soon as possible, Dr. Tang had recommended they get a small USAMRIID team out of Baghdad immediately to properly pack up and move the jar.

Sophie knew Alex Jarota would hate the idea, but she was thrilled. When she had heard the United Nations might intervene, she had been anxious, but Dr. Tang had the contacts and the sense of urgency to move things forward.

The white box truck, its wheels outfitted for the rutted roads, had pulled into the compound an hour earlier. Sophie had watched as the techs from USAMRIID climbed out. If anyone still doubted they had a crisis on their hands, that doubt would have been erased the moment the techs had opened the back of the truck and began to step into pale blue hazmat suits.

"Shit," Sophie sighed, glancing over at the box truck.

The back had been locked up by now. The techs had carried a plastic crate inside, presumably with whatever materials they needed to examine the Pandora Room—maybe even to remove the jar. They'd met Beyza at the entrance to Derveyî, shown their credentials, and been led downstairs.

Sophie didn't feel like the boss anymore.

She didn't think she wanted to be the boss of this.

Her eyes grew damp, but she blinked it away. *What if?* She'd asked herself that question a hundred times in the past couple of days. What if the whole thing were real? What if Pandora and Anesidora had been historical figures instead of creatures of myth? And what if instead of curses, the jar contained blessings? What if it contained *cures*?

In France, right now, her father deteriorated by the day, Alzheimer's thieving every memory that made him the man he was. She'd survived her own childhood leukemia, but there were kids dying right that very minute. Sophie felt the breeze and the warmth of the sun, and though her body remembered sickness, she could still run. She could have turned, in that moment, chosen a direction and just started to move. Her body would carry her to the mountains, carry her to Amadiya. If she found a lake or a river, she could swim. She had spent her adult life making herself strong, because she remembered what it had felt like to be weak, and to feel death so near, just over her shoulder, whispering in her ear.

She watched the soldiers at their posts. Watched them walk the perimeter. Watched a Jeep kick up dust as it sped away from Derveyî. Down below, her team continued to dismantle and pack up the dig, prematurely concluding a year's worth of work. Somewhere, if Kim Seong had done her job, U.N. diplomats would be negotiating possession of the most important archaeological find of the twenty-first century, and Sophie had no say in the matter. What happened to that jar and its contents had ceased to be her concern, even if she wanted it to be.

Maybe that was for the best.

She told herself that. *It's for the best. Your father is dying. What happens to the jar, whether it will ever be opened, is not for you to decide.*

For the best.

Her phone vibrated in her pocket, but for once it didn't startle her. Sophie had been expecting this call. Not from Alex Jarota or from one of her own contacts at UNESCO or even from her mother. As she slipped the phone from her pocket, the name on its screen only confirmed what she'd somehow already known. How long could she hold Steven at bay? How long before even she thought it was unfair?

Sophie answered. "Hello, Steven. I'm here. I'm alive. I'm sorry."

A breath. A hesitation. "Jesus, Soph. You couldn't text me back? Even if you couldn't call, you could at least have—"

"I know. I do."

"—texted me."

"Steven, I promise you, when I tell you the story of the past few days, your jaw will drop. And it's only going to get more interesting from here."

The pause that followed went on a second too long and made Sophie wonder if her ex had hung up or if the call had dropped.

"Hello?"

"I'm here," Steven said, his voice tight as if he'd forgotten all the things he'd meant to say, all the times he had called to talk to Sophie. "Just tell me this. Is it dangerous, this 'interesting' thing that's happening?"

Sophie wanted to lie, but she'd promised herself not to do that anymore. "Probably. That's the best answer I can give you. Even if what we've found isn't dangerous itself, it's getting a lot of people with guns very nervous."

"Marvelous," Steven said. "I'd tell you to come home, but you don't live here anymore."

"That's true."

"I guess I should ask what kept you from calling all the other times, before whatever is happening now. Before things turned 'probably' dangerous."

Sophie couldn't help smiling. Despite the dig and the soldiers and the hazmat suits, despite it all spinning out of her control, Steven's voice made her happy and made her remember sweet and simple times. The memories let her exhale, and when she took another breath, she no longer felt like the walls of the world were closing in.

"I'm sorry," she said again. "I've just been focused on the work here, and I didn't want to call if I couldn't commit to a real conversation. No jokes about me and long-term commitment, please. I just mean I didn't want to get on the phone and then brush you off."

"Better to do that by not answering at all?"

Sophie's smile vanished, and yet she still felt she could breathe again. Steven knew her, knew who she really was, and nobody within a thousand miles could have said the same.

"I'm an ass," Sophie said.

"On that, we agree. But there's another reason I've been calling. Something I need to tell you."

A chill passed through her. "You're okay? You're not . . . are you sick? Is everything—"

"I'm not sick. Nothing like that. It's something good, Soph. But I wanted you to hear it from me. I've met someone. Her name is Annabeth."

"Steven, that's fantastic," Sophie said, though she felt a twinge of regret. "That's wonderful."

"We're . . . actually, we're getting married in the spring. Next May," Steven said. "I wanted you to know, from me."

"Wow. That's . . . Congratulations, Steven. I guess you really *are* okay."

Dead air. That long pause again.

"Steven?"

"You left, Sophie."

"I know that."

"I want you to be happy for me."

Sophie exhaled again. "I can do that. You deserve this, Steven. You deserve someone who makes you happy, who can be there with you. You deserve that kind of love."

There were other things she wanted to say, but she would only have been repeating herself. Loving Steven had never been a problem. Sophie had never strayed while they were together. When she had left New York, she would have preferred to bring Steven with her, but it wasn't to be.

"Thank you," Steven said. And then, very quietly, "So do you, Sophie. You deserve it, too."

"I've got to go, love. When this is all over, I'll call you and tell you the whole story. If you haven't seen it on the news first."

"Stay safe, Sophie."

Sophie promised that she would. They said good-bye, and when she slid the phone back into her pocket, she breathed deeply. The situation with the jar had already given her a sense of urgency, but now she wanted to get out of Iraq more than ever. Derveyî had been her greatest professional joy, and now she couldn't wait for it to be a memory, to move on to the next thing and start fresh.

Alex Jarota wasn't going to allow that, of course. He needed her to be the face of this discovery. Sophie knew she would have to go along with that, at least for a while, but she looked forward to the time when she had a new dig, a new project, a new place to feel like she belonged. For a while, Derveyî had felt like home. Now she felt cast adrift. Whatever Derveyî had been, it didn't belong to her anymore. It belonged to the world, to the U.N., to the inevitable media dissection.

With a huff, she stood and looked up at the mountains. Afternoon had begun to darken toward evening, and she still had work to do.

A scuff of footsteps made her turn, and she saw Martin trekking across the camp toward her, his own filtration mask firmly in place. Her mood brightened just a bit. With all these new arrivals, she had begun to feel isolated, but seeing Martin reminded her that she still had her own team here, people she liked and trusted. People who were counting on her to get them out of here safely.

"Sophie," Martin said.

"That's *Dr. Durand* to you."

He blinked, slightly taken aback. That innocence and gullibility was one of the things she liked best about him. Martin was smart and dedicated. Yes, his crush on her remained obvious, but he had a purity of spirit that she admired. It made him an easy target for teasing, but mostly she envied him.

"I'm kidding, Martin."

He gave her the small, self-conscious laugh that seemed to be his trademark. "I know that," he lied. "Anyway, you asked for a team meeting. Beyza and Lamar wanted you to know everyone's going to gather in about twenty minutes in the atrium."

Sophie studied him, searched his eyes. "Everyone except you and Lamar. I want you with the guards, making sure nobody gets into the Pandora Room who doesn't belong there."

Martin stood a bit straighter, visibly heartened by her faith in him. "Of course."

She had been wearing her own filtration mask down around her neck like a cowl. Now she pulled it up to cover her nose and mouth and started away from him, her boots scuffing on the dusty slope. A Jeep trundled by on the rutted dirt road thirty yards away, and she caught sight of one of her colleagues, a professor from the Sorbonne, in the passenger seat. There would be files in that Jeep—computers and records and photographs, not to mention personal gear. The team would be gathering, but some of them were already departing.

Sophie thought about Steven and felt happy for him. But happiness sometimes had a bitter aftertaste.

She halted. The horizon wavered in the light of the setting sun, and she turned to face Martin.

"Is something wrong?" he asked, worry lines creasing his forehead.

Sophie put a hand on his arm. "You're a good man, Martin. Scruffy, but good. I've got a lot of . . . turmoil in my head right now. Later on, that may manifest in me snapping and shouting at people, or it may manifest in me getting drunk and taking you to bed."

His startled expression made her want to either hug him or lead him into the tunnels and seduce him. The dichotomy of the man was attractive, even when she'd lost her patience with his awkwardness. But now they were leaving. The job was over, and she had nowhere to go and no one to go home to, even if she wanted to go home. A door had closed.

"I think the shouting is more likely," Martin managed, reaching up to tuck his curly hair behind his ears, which also served to break the contact she'd initiated.

"So do I," she agreed. "But I thought I should warn you, either way."

He cocked an eyebrow. "It's appreciated." Not taking her seriously.

Sophie sought his gaze, made sure he wouldn't look away. "You've been passive-aggressively flirting with me for most of the time we've been here."

"That's not . . . Okay, that's a little true. But I—"

She shrugged. "I just wanted you to know. If anything happens before we leave here, I'd just be using you to drown my sorrows. No different from getting myself wrecked on a bottle of one of Lamar's fancy whiskeys."

"So I'd be fancy whiskey, then? Not the crappy stuff."

"You're not listening to me."

Martin slipped his hands into his pockets as if he were afraid of what he might do with them. "I'm listening. But like you said, you're in turmoil. We've all got a lot on our plates right now. On the other hand, I'm an adult. I've been someone's drunken mistake before."

"You're sure I wouldn't break you?" she asked, teasing now. Flirting with him in a way she never had. It felt irresponsible and stupid, but she had to keep her shit together in every other way, so maybe this was harmless. Maybe.

"My heart would be fine," he assured her.

"Oh, sweet boy," Sophie said, eyes widening. "I wasn't talking about your heart."

With that, she turned and continued down the slope, a grin on her face. It took a few steps before she heard the stunned Martin following, and she liked that. She had no intention of sleeping with him—at least, she didn't think so—but she'd been so professional and focused for so long, it felt good to be bad.

The whiskey, though . . . that part had been the truth.

"Can I ask you a question?"

Walker glanced toward the privacy curtain that hung across the entrance to his quarters and saw Kim standing there, curtain drawn back, filtration mask in place. The room had most recently housed members of the archaeological dig—grad students and professors who had already departed—but the echoes of its ancient residents remained. Carved into the soft yellow stone, the room had no doors or windows. Anyone could come and go as they wished.

Which was how Kim had arrived without him hearing her approach.

Walker studied her. "Of course you can."

She gave him a sheepish look. "I'd have knocked, but . . ."

"But there's no door to knock on."

"Exactly. Anyway, it seems to me we are overdue for a conversation."

Walker frowned. To him, their roles in this place seemed clearly defined. Kim had her job to do, and she had already begun to do it. Calls had been made and the United Nations had put plans in motion. In many ways, although this was Sophie's project and although they were within the jurisdiction of the Iraqi government and the Kurdish autonomous district, Kim had become the de facto authority on the site, and that suited him very well.

"I'm not sure what we need to discuss," Walker said. His voice sounded muffled behind his mask.

Kim laughed softly. Shaking her head, she let the curtain fall and crossed to one of the empty cots, where she perched on the edge.

"You're a spy," she said quietly, her voice a soft rasp.

Walker scoffed. "Seong, come on. You know that's not what I do."

"It's close enough," she whispered, eyes narrowing. "I am the only person here who knows who you really work for. I'm the only one who knows that you lie about your mission objectives."

He spread his hands wide. "You know those things because I trust you."

"I know them because of what we went through together," Kim replied. "Not because of what happened with us afterward."

Walker decided to sit after all. He took a spot on the cot across from her and searched her eyes. "You talk about it as if we gave one another some kind of virus."

"Your job won't allow me to trust you completely," Kim said. "And it's not fair of you to ask or expect it."

That quieted him.

"Just promise me this," she went on. "Promise you won't make a move regarding the jar without telling me about it. If something happens, if you have to act, be honest with me about it."

Walker regarded her carefully. If he did as she asked, especially if it compromised his goals, he could be fired, even brought up on charges.

"I can do that," he said.

A moment passed between them. The room grew strangely warm, and he felt her nearness. Only a few feet away, hair framing her face so that her eyes seemed veiled in shadow. He wanted to touch her.

Instead, he laughed quietly. "Can you believe this?"

"Believe what?"

Walker gestured to the walls around them. "This. Underground city. Pandora's fucking box. Countries ready to kill for it."

"Jar," she corrected.

"Pandora's fucking jar."

"Yes," Kim said quietly, glancing at the door, apparently to make sure no one overheard them. "Humans have been digging up terrifying things since the first time we buried something dangerous. We fight over such things the way dogs fight over a bone. This is only the latest bone."

Walker stood and went to the entrance, glanced out at the empty corridor, and then turned to face her again. "My first responsibility is to make sure the wrong dog doesn't get that bone."

Kim opened her hands. "The question then becomes, who is the 'right' dog?"

"That's going to be up to the U.N."

She stood, smoothing her shirt. "Dr. Tang's phone calls turned up results faster than mine. Techs are on the premises from USAMRIID." She spoke the acronym like a word—*you-sam-rid*—but Walker knew the army institute well. He'd dealt with them before.

"Good to know. I'll breathe a little easier knowing steps are being taken to isolate the jar. Just in case."

"They're in hazmat suits," Kim said. "It's a little unsettling, to be honest. I wonder if we should be topside with the soldiers instead of down here with the jar."

Walker smiled, though he knew she couldn't see it. "I don't have a choice. I need to stay down here, make sure the jar is safe. My guess is that it's all for nothing, that there's nothing but dust in that jar, but better safe than sorry."

"That's sort of the motto of both our employers," Kim said.

Walker nodded. "Speaking of your employer, any word from them on a decision?"

"A day or two before they decide about the disposition of the jar," she replied. "The sooner the better."

Walker did not tell her that he had spoken to his own superiors as well or that David Boudreau had told him that he should stand ready to claim the jar should the U.N.'s decision be what DARPA would consider unwise. She would assume it.

"Dr. Durand has called a meeting of all personnel," Kim went on. "I'm not sure if that includes us, but I thought it would be polite to attend."

"That's starting now?"

"A few minutes ago. Probably already under way."

Walker gestured for her to precede him out of the chamber. The unearthly quality of the city struck him as they made their way down a curved staircase and then along a narrow switchback corridor that descended three levels before opening into a balcony that overlooked the so-called grand foyer.

Perhaps a hundred feet from the entrance into the underground city, reached through a twisting corridor that barely hinted at the space inside, the grand foyer rose into a four-level atrium, the junction of many stairways, ramps, and corridors. It was a marvel of architecture, carved by hand, and as Walker gazed around at the dozens of people gathered to hear what Sophie had to say, the tension with Kim was momentarily forgotten.

"It's so beautiful," she said quietly as if reading his mind.

"You don't think it's a little creepy?" he whispered.

Kim gave a nod. "Maybe a little."

They fell silent then, because Sophie had begun to address the personnel gathered below. She thanked them for their efforts and announced the arrival of the techs from USAMRIID, as well as the steps that would be taken over the next twenty-four hours. Walker glanced around at the project staff, identifying the few faces he already knew and wondering about the others. Then he noticed a conspicuous absence and furrowed his brow.

"Why isn't Dr. Tang here?"

Kim replied with a shrug. "She'd been talking to many of the staff today, general medical inquiry, but I haven't seen her in a couple of hours."

Walker leaned closer to her, dropping his voice even lower. "This all seems to have unsettled her more than I'd have expected. Do you think—"

A tap on his shoulder made him turn, and he saw Sergeant Dunlap had come up behind them. With his filtration mask on, his face was difficult to read.

"Is something wrong?" Kim whispered.

Dunlap glanced at her for a moment, then seemed to make up his mind and focused on Walker. "Can we step outside? There's something we need to discuss."

Walker frowned. Had Dunlap discovered who he really worked for, or was this about something else? Only one way to find out.

"Let's go," he said and then turned to Kim. "We'll talk later."

Kim gave him a curious look, but then her attention returned to Sophie and the gathering below, and Walker followed Dunlap down another corridor, wondering how long he would have to live down in this stone labyrinth before he had the map of it in his head. Dunlap seemed already to have learned to navigate the place.

You're not going to be here long enough to need to know, Walker told himself.

But he paid attention, anyway. It felt unsafe somehow. Unsettled. If there was anything he'd learned in working for the government, it was that he always needed to have an escape plan, just in case.

NINE

Dr. Tang rarely found herself curious about the minds and thoughts of others. She typically observed human interactions as if she had landed on another planet whose customs were inscrutable. Large groups made her nervous, and small groups made her more nervous still. One on one, or with just a few other people, she felt functional, but even then she rarely considered what lay beneath the superficiality of words and emotions that were plainly expressed. So when she began to wonder what the dig personnel thought about the Pandora Room—what they believed, what they knew, how it felt to be forbidden from viewing the jar—she surprised herself. But this was a time of surprises for her.

The greatest surprise of all was that she felt afraid.

The staff was gathering upstairs, but that was too large a crowd for her. From the moment she had first entered the Pandora Room and felt the ominous weight of the air in there, Dr. Tang had wanted to be by herself. Over the past day, there had been conversations and small meetings and phone calls where her expertise had been requested, but everything she had said was pure conjecture. If they were fortunate, nobody would ever know if they had anything to fear from the jar.

Yet here she was, standing outside the thirteen steps that led down to the Pandora Room. There were two sentries outside the entrance.

Dr. Tang had been here when the USAMRIID techs came through—two men, both wearing hazmat suits. She'd asked them if they had a spare for her and had been told that they had brought several additional suits. That news comforted her. Her filtration mask was probably sufficient, but if she wanted a hazmat suit, she could have one.

Ebola she could handle. What frightened her was the unknown.

She didn't want to be among those crowded into the atrium, but neither did she want to be alone in the west wing quarters that had been assigned to her and Kim. She had decided to explore more of the underground city, but she had not meant to find her way here. Her feet had led her, and now she discovered that those same feet were reluctant to lead her away.

Even there in what she'd heard referred to as the column chamber, she could hear voices coming up the steps from the Pandora Room. Lamar Curtis had been there on his own at first, doing his best to translate the writings on the walls and the altar. Then he'd been joined by the USAMRIID techs. Their words were muffled, but she could make out enough to understand they were discussing the precautions necessary to move the jar. First they would drape it in plastic, then clear the area before lifting it just enough to place it into a transport crate—what one of them called the *contagion box*. Dr. Tang had seen similar precautions taken many times. They would pack the box carefully to make sure the jar didn't shift much when the time came to transport it.

Just get it out of here, she thought. *Stop wasting time.*

"Ma'am?" one of the guards said, staring at her. "Are you all right?"

Dr. Tang laughed softly, her voice shaking. She had put on a hooded sweatshirt, the one with the striped Princeton *P* on the chest that reminded her of Riverdale High School in the old *Archie* comics.

The scuff of a footfall made her flinch, and she glanced over to see Martin coming through the chamber, moving past the shadowed columns toward her.

"I'm sorry if I startled you," he said.

"Not at all. I'm a bit jumpy on a good day." Dr. Tang decided she wanted to be anywhere but here. "I'll speak with you later, Martin."

He gave her a strange look as she moved past him but did not try to engage her any further, and she was glad. Dr. Tang had never been good at small talk, and she discouraged it whenever possible.

Hurrying up the corridor, Dr. Tang moved away from the column chamber with a sense of both relief and deeper anxiety. This section of hallway seemed rougher than much of the labyrinthine city, strangely isolated from the rest. Somewhere ahead were the stairs that led up to the room Dr. Durand's team had discovered by breaking through a false wall, so it made sense that it felt quiet and disconnected down here.

She paused and exhaled, leaning against the wall. Her nerves were frayed, and she needed a moment for herself. With a glance in each direction, she pulled down her filtration mask—against her own explicit instructions—and breathed a bit easier. Aware of the irony, Dr. Tang snaked her hand into the pocket of her sweatshirt and pulled out a package of Parliaments and a lighter.

Dr. Tang tapped out a cigarette, tipped it between her lips, and fired up her lighter. The first inhalation of nicotine flooded her with relief. Delicious carcinogens. The guard had asked if she was all right, and what kind of question was that, anyway? Of course she wasn't all right. She was in a part of the world where people tended to violently disagree about things like borders, part of a team tasked with delivering a potential biohazard into safe hands, and there was something about this place, this subterranean city, and that damned room.

A shiver went through her, and she took another drag on her cigarette to dispel the chill. What had she felt yesterday when she'd entered the Pandora Room? Not fear . . . at least, not fear of contagion. The room had felt impossibly full, almost alert, though such a thing was impossible. It had felt to her as if somehow the room sensed her presence and *objected*.

Or had it been the room? Might it not, instead, have been the jar?

Fucking madness. She knew it. After the long journey and so much exposure to new people, she had just been tired and claustrophobic, perhaps having a new sort of anxiety attack, or simply fearful of what unknown diseases might be sealed inside that jar. Anything else, any other explanation, was just idiocy or lunacy, and Dr. Tang could not decide which she would have preferred.

One thing she did know, however, was that she had zero interest in going back inside that room, but she knew that she would have to do so eventually.

When she took her next drag on the cigarette, her hand shook.

She heard footsteps and looked up to see Martin coming back from the Pandora Room.

"You caught me," she said.

Martin gestured toward her cigarette. "Seems counterintuitive, if you don't mind me saying. Someone in your line of work smoking."

She smiled thinly. "I've worked in a lot of places where there are diseased corpses putrefying around me because people are too busy trying not to join them to remove them. Cigarette smoke helps mask the stink, and it kills my own sense of smell. I'm afraid I've gotten into the habit."

Martin blanched. "Shit, Doc, I guess you've earned it. Have another one."

Dr. Tang saluted him with her cigarette. "I'm sure I will. I don't like it down here."

"I'll see you upstairs? Sophie's talking to the whole team."

"I'll be along soon," she told him.

Martin waved and carried on along the corridor. Dr. Tang continued smoking and listened as the sounds of his passing had faded to silence again. She took a long draw on her cigarette and exhaled a thin puff of gray smoke, watching the smoke dance and waver in a swirling breeze that seemed to come from nowhere.

Drawing in another lungful of smoke, she blew a billowing ring and watched the same thing happen. Closing her eyes, she felt the draft moving around her and turned to examine the wall several feet back along the corridor. A thin line ran down the rock face like some kind of seam, and at knee height she found an actual crack. When she put her hand in front of it, she could feel cold air whispering past her fingers, and she shivered. Despite the meticulous architecture of the place, it was still made of stone that had settled over many long centuries. The hollow behind the wall must have been a ventilation shaft.

Dr. Tang took another drag on her cigarette. The tip flared orange in the gloom of the corridor, and she wondered what the hell she was doing here.

Your job. You are doing your job.

She had been at a conference in Tel Aviv when the call had come in. She had consulted for the U.N. before, and this had seemed like another job like that—good money to visit a site of concern, not an active outbreak of any kind. Dr. Tang had done plenty of fieldwork, but teaching was a hell of a lot safer. Not for the first time, she wished she had stuck to teaching.

A sound made her look up, squinting into the interplay of light and darkness back along the tunnel in the direction of the Pandora Room. What had it been? A cry, she thought. A shout, but muffled by distance and the soft curves of yellow stone. There came an echoing crack, and another, and she froze.

Dr. Tang dropped her cigarette and ground it out with the heel of her boot. She slipped her filtration mask into place and began to retrace her steps, knowing that she should listen to the wise cowardice of her heart and head the other direction but unable to resist the urge to investigate and to help if she could.

Her steps quickened along with her pulse.

The crack in the corridor wall had been forgotten.

Evening had set in when Walker and Sergeant Dunlap stepped outside. The sun had vanished below the horizon, but the western sky remained the vivid shade of indigo that always seemed to hint at the night's unspoken promise. Walker glanced in that direction, and the sight gave him a moment's respite before the trouble he knew was to come. Dunlap hadn't asked him out here for a romantic stroll.

"What's on your mind, Sergeant?" he asked, tugging down his filtration mask. Unlike Sophie and her inner circle, he hadn't been inside the Pandora Room without it on, so he felt it was safe out in the fresh air.

Dunlap pulled down his own mask and glanced around.

"Come with me," the sergeant said, leading him on a diagonal path away from the sentries who stood at the dig's entrance.

Nightfall had dropped a blanket of quiet over the camp. No truck engines growled, and the shouts of soldiers had ceased. Guards were posted around the camp, men and women were moving from one tent to another, and from a distance there came the deep bass thump of old-school hip-hop. A ripple of laughter rose from another direction, but for now those aboveground were doing much the same as those below—waiting.

"Pretty sure we're alone," Walker said, growing irritated.

Dunlap stood a bit straighter, lifted his chin. "Dr. Walker, my CO told me I was to keep you in the loop, treat you like you're the man in charge—at least in charge of me. I find that strange, sir, but I'm in the army and I know how to follow an order. So I'm making this report to you."

Walker made sure his face betrayed nothing, but he knew the sergeant had to be wondering why he was supposed to treat a civilian scientist like a ranking officer.

"Go on, Sergeant. What's troubling you?"

"I'm hearing chatter. One of the Kurdish sentries was talking—maybe he figured I didn't speak the language, but I know it well enough. From what he's saying, word of this is everywhere."

Walker swore quietly. "Exactly what we figured would happen."

"This Kurdish sentry . . . he heard about it from his brother, who called him to ask what was going on here."

"The brother's a soldier, too?"

Dunlap shook his head. "No, sir. That's what I'm saying. The brother's a fucking grocer up in Amadiya. A Turkish woman came in—a journalist—and apparently she'd been asking a number of other merchants and businesspeople in town. Man-on-the-street interviews, that sort of thing, to find out what people thought about Pandora's fucking box being found nearby."

Walker stared at him, but all he could think about was the world they lived in now. He'd anticipated the Turkish government learning about the Pandora Room, but if it had already filtered down to journalists in the neighboring country, then the whole populace would know about it soon enough. Many would already know.

"We've got a unit of U.N. peacekeepers on the way to accompany the transportation of the jar, wherever it goes from here," Dunlap went on. "But there are hundreds of American soldiers in this area and thousands of Kurdish fighters. Most of them are deployed where they're needed, but we're only going to be here for a couple of days, maybe three at most. Not enough time for us to get any significant backup."

"You think someone's going to make a move?" Walker asked.

Dunlap exhaled. "This part of the world, someone is always going to make a move." He glanced across the camp, seemed to hesitate, and then beckoned for Walker to follow. "Come with me."

For the second time that night, Walker let the sergeant take the lead. He found that he liked Dunlap. The guy had an air of zero bullshit around him. Solid and intent on doing his job. As they crossed the camp, Walker listened to the noises of the people and the land around them. He wished whoever had their music playing would shut it off. This region went through periods when it was a powder keg. Tensions were not unusual. But the last thing anyone wanted to do was to give the conflicting powers in Kurdistan something else to argue about.

They reached a line of military tents, things large enough to sleep twenty soldiers. Parked in the midst of them was a Humvee with a passenger door open. As they neared the vehicle, Walker realized this was the source of the hip-hop pumping out across the camp. Across the front seat of the vehicle, a lone officer lay propped on a stained pillow with a reading lamp, a book open on his chest. Walker caught a glimpse of the cover—*Lonesome Dove* by Larry McMurtry.

Dunlap rapped on the side of the Humvee. "Lieutenant Cobb?"

The lieutenant didn't startle. He glanced up over the top of his book as if he'd known they were coming, and maybe he had. With a sigh, he dog-eared the book and set it aside, then slid himself over to the open door and settled there with his long legs dangling. Lieutenant Cobb had to be at least six foot three, and if he intended to sleep across the front seat, he'd be folded up in a fetal position for the night, but maybe he felt safest that way, inside the armored vehicle. Or maybe he was just a weird son of a bitch. He had shaved his head bald, but dark stubble had grown in. The deep tan of deployment in this part of the world couldn't hide the dark circles under his eyes.

"You must be Walker," he said, with a head-to-toe glance.

"Lieutenant," Walker said. "Maybe you could turn the music down?"

His nostrils flared as if he'd smelled something dead, but the lieutenant obliged—a little. The thumping bass line still resonated across the camp. Walker could feel it in his chest, punching him in the rib cage with every beat.

"You want to tell him what you told me?" Dunlap said.

Lieutenant Cobb studied Walker again. Obviously, the two men had discussed this in advance, but he gave another few moments over to the evaluation.

"Who do you work for again?" the lieutenant asked.

"National Science Foundation. But it's all the same government, Lieutenant. I'm just not one of the folks with the guns."

Dunlap leaned against the Humvee and crossed his arms. "Whoever he works for, he's the guy they sent to make sure shit doesn't get out of control down below."

"I thought that was Major Bernstein," Lieutenant Cobb replied.

"Up top, that's the major, sir," Dunlap said. "Down below, Walker's the one someone back in D.C. is listening to."

"I'm here as part of the U.N. observation team," Walker corrected him. "Kim Seong's in charge of that."

Dunlap smiled. "This isn't a coalition conversation or a U.N. conversation. This is us figuring shit out."

"Fair enough," Cobb said, reaching back into the vehicle and turning the music down a bit more. He ran a hand over the stubble on his head. "Short version. Sergeant Dunlap shared his concerns with me, and I have my own. We have two men in custody—twin brothers who were stalking Dr. Durand and her team in Amadiya some days ago. These two assholes didn't know a thing about the Pandora Room.

They just wanted to know what Indiana Joan and her crew had found down there, because whatever it was, there are factions in the Turkish government who might have made an argument over where it belonged."

"This isn't news," Walker told him. "The Turks have lodged complaints throughout the process."

"These two guys won't say exactly who they were working for," Lieutenant Cobb went on. "But they were willing to tell us who else was paying attention to the dig."

"Kurds. Shia. Who else?" Walker asked, because he saw now that this really was heading somewhere. "ISIS?"

"Do you even know what that means?" the lieutenant said, frowning at Dunlap as if he was to blame for the simplicity of Walker's answer.

"I know they're unraveling."

"They were never that raveled to begin with," Lieutenant Cobb explained. "Or not for long, anyway. Look, there are dozens of Salafi jihadist movements in the Middle East. I'm not going to give you a local history lesson, but when ISIS came together, it included a lot of smaller groups. One of the most popular in this neighborhood was Ansar al-Islam, or AAI, a Sunni Muslim jihadi group. Some of them fragmented off—they didn't want to join ISIS—and our Turkish friends are telling us they're coalescing a new alliance with some of the others that have fragmented from ISIS. In English, they call themselves New Caliphate, basically picking up ISIS's dream but with even less rational behavior."

"Less rational than ISIS?" Dunlap said. Apparently, the lieutenant hadn't shared that observation with him before.

"Rumor has it we've got people embedded inside New Caliphate, and the word I've heard is that they watched what happened with ISIS. You're talking about a jihadi group that looked, briefly, like they might be able to conquer the Middle East. They came together so fast and in such numbers and did so much damage that they scared the shit out of everyone, but then they fell apart. Apparently, the lesson New Caliphate took from that is that the old Al Queda model works better—hit hard, sharp, and nasty, strike vulnerable targets, terrorize and demoralize, murder people's hope, don't win hearts and minds—take them."

"And your Turkish twins?" Walker said. "They're telling you New Caliphate's interested in the dig?"

"The twins say New Caliphate have been interested all along. Anything that comes out of there that emphasizes any history but the version they want to teach, they'll want to destroy it."

Dunlap sniffed derisively. "So these spies that were following Dr. Durand . . . they claim they were trying to help her?"

"I wouldn't go that far," the lieutenant replied. "They have their own angle here, but letting New Caliphate destroy artifacts is definitely not on their agenda. There's one other thing the twins told me. According to the whispers they've heard, New Caliphate has someone inside the dig already. On Dr. Durand's team."

Walker exhaled a quiet profanity, letting his thoughts flicker through images of the members of Sophie's staff that he'd met, trying to figure out who among them might be on the payroll of jihadi terrorists.

"What a mess," he said, glancing back toward the entrance to the dig. "How much of this have you told Sophie?"

Lieutenant Cobb stood straighter, emphasizing his true size. Walker thought of the Frankenstein monster.

"I'm taking my own initiative to tell you," the lieutenant said. "I figure someone underground ought to know. But Dr. Durand doesn't work for the U.S. government, and neither does Ms. Kim. You do. If you want to lay it out for them, that's up to you. I've done my part here. Everyone here knows Dr. Durand is wrapping this up quickly. If anyone's going to make a move, it will have to be soon. So watch your ass."

Walker swore again. For the first time, he was grateful for the thumping rhythm of the hip-hop pumping out of the Humvee. Anyone who wanted to listen to their conversation would have had to get damned close to do so. It occurred to him that this might be why the lieutenant had the music up loud in the first place, and he looked at the stubble-scalped giant with new perspective.

"Thanks, Lieutenant," Sergeant Dunlap said.

"Double from me," Walker added.

Lieutenant Cobb waved them off as if he'd nearly forgotten them already. He crawled back across the Humvee's front seat and plumped his pillow, turned the volume up further, and adjusted his reading lamp. By the time he'd picked up his copy of *Lonesome Dove*, he seemed as if he hadn't a care in the world, but Walker understood how far that was from the truth.

He's waiting, Walker thought. *Not for orders to clear out but for the shit to hit the fan.*

TEN

Walker and Dunlap strode back the way they'd come. The camp remained quiet save for Cobb's music, but Walker could feel the tension in the air now. American and Kurdish soldiers alike were on edge, as if a fuse had already been lit but they didn't know how much time they had until the boom.

The breeze that kicked up in that moment felt strangely warm, as if the sun had not already vanished over the horizon. Walker tugged at the collar of his T-shirt. His skin prickled, and when his thoughts tried to flicker back through a slideshow of past dangers, he pushed the images away. Whatever bad intentions anyone might have, he had no reason to think that he and Kim and everyone else here wouldn't be long gone before trouble could start.

"Mask on," Walker said, adjusting his filtration mask to cover the lower half of his face once more.

"You all right?" Dunlap asked, following suit.

"I don't look all right?"

"You want the truth? You look like you just found out your house is haunted."

Walker laughed quietly, nodding. "Feels a bit like that."

Just that bit of humor had worked out some of the tension in his back, cooled some of the heat inside his chest.

"What are you going to tell Sophie?" Dunlap asked.

"Aside from hurry the hell up, you mean?"

A voice barked loudly, not far ahead. One word. "Hey!"

Walker and Dunlap glanced at each other.

Someone replied to the first voice in a stream of Arabic, and the two men picked up their pace, striding past the last of the tents. From there, they could make out the hole in the face of the hill, the entrance into Derveyî.

"Look," an American soldier snapped, moving in front of the entrance, blocking two men in civilian clothing. "I don't care who you're supposed to be. You don't have the right credentials, you don't get inside."

There were three other soldiers guarding Derveyî. Two Kurds and a second American. One of the Kurds muttered something to the two civilians, his lips twisted into a sneer that made his dismissal of the men clear.

"I have the credentials!" the older of the two civilians said. He must have been around fifty, with thinning hair and at least a little black left in his gray beard. "You see this! I am a professor at Atatürk University. I have been sent as an advisor. Summoned here. If you men have only your clipboard for a brain, that is not my doing."

The second civilian was younger. Clean-shaven, fresh haircut, but when he glanced back and saw Walker and Dunlap approaching, there were dark bags under his eyes and he looked twitchy.

"Professor, please," he said, taking the older man by the elbow. "We must—"

"No!" the professor shouted. "I will not endure such rudeness. I must see Sophie Durand, and I will see her. Now."

The professor wore an expensive-looking suit with a red tie and round spectacles that perched on the bridge of his nose. His assistant might have been a grad student, in a loose windbreaker, wrinkled khaki pants, and a canvas rucksack on his back. But Walker didn't like the nervous glance the man had given them or the way his hands hung at his sides as if he might be about to bolt or throw a punch.

But it was the boots that made Walker's hackles rise. Dirty, battered, and scuffed—they weren't the boots of anyone's assistant, and they weren't the boots of a student. The man's right hand hovered, open, as if he might perform a magic trick for the soldiers around him. The professor kept arguing, kept insisting as Walker and Dunlap moved toward the entrance to Derveyî.

"Dunlap," Walker said quietly when they were forty feet away.

"Yeah," Dunlap replied as if that said it all.

A voice shouted from the darkness at the edge of the camp. American. "Perimeter! Check the perimeter! I've got movement—"

The crack of a rifle silenced him. One shot, and for a heartbeat or two, all was quiet except for the damned music thumping from Lieutenant Cobb's Humvee.

Then the camp lit up with gunfire. Voices shouted. Soldiers burst from within tents as if they'd been on edge, crouched and ready to spring. A ripple of gunshots, automatic weapons fire, dropped three men in the moment before Walker tore his gaze away and turned back toward the entrance.

The noise seemed to cancel itself out. Even the music receded. Walker saw the professor's assistant draw his gun and shoot one of the Kurdish soldiers in the face. The professor hurled himself into the two American soldiers before they could raise their guns, slammed them both into the crack in the face of the hill, the entrance to the dig. One soldier stumbled and fell, and the professor grabbed the other by the face and smashed his skull against the stone, ripped his gun out of his hands, and killed them both.

Dunlap had drawn his sidearm by then, the filtration mask making him look like some kind of bandit. He paused and took two shots at the professor, but both went wide, taking chips out of the hole in the wall. Walker ran harder. Weaponless, he sprinted toward the assistant even as the younger man struggled with the remaining Kurdish soldier. The two of them shouted at each other in words Walker didn't understand, but the meaning was clear, especially when the assistant wrested his gun hand free, kicked the Kurd backward, and shot him three times in the chest.

Behind him, the whole camp had come alive with gunfire and emergency lights that flared. Alarms blared. The sounds had receded in his mind for a few seconds, but now they came roaring back, drowning out even Lieutenant Cobb's hip-hop. Under attack, bullets flying, jihadi militants invading the camp, there was no way anyone would have noticed the gunfire at the entrance to Derveyî. Even if some of the gathered forces had seen the skirmish, they were busy defending the camp from dozens of attackers. Two fuckers with guns were not a large enough threat to distract from that, even when those two fuckers with guns were headed inside a subterranean city where dozens of civilians were gathered and where a potentially deadly biohazard might be waiting.

Walker twisted around, saw Dunlap catching up. "We've got to keep them away from the jar. No matter what!"

"I'm on it!"

Walker didn't waste time on more words. He had the jar on his mind, but the people inside were closer than the jar, and they were his first priority. One in particular. Kim would have been furious at him for thinking of her safety. Once upon a time, he would have been furious with himself for the same reason, but experience had changed him. There was no route out of Derveyî except through this door, which meant he could try to save the lives of the people below before he worried about what the jar might do.

"Go!" Walker barked, and Dunlap raced through the entrance.

Walker stopped to snatch up a pair of guns the Kurdish soldier had dropped. One was a sidearm, an M17, but the other was an HK416 assault rifle issued by Joint Special Operations Command.

He didn't care how the Kurds had gotten them, only that he had them in his hands. But three steps into the tunnel, he turned and threw the HK416 back outside. There were two jihadis inside and dozens of civilians. The assault rifle was not the right tool for this job.

M17 gripped tightly in his right hand, Walker hustled after Dunlap. He heard the sergeant's footfalls ahead, heard the grunts as Dunlap rushed down the entry ramp and then the curving staircase that would take them into the grand foyer atrium.

They heard the screaming a moment later.

Gunshots echoed up from below.

Walker felt his heart go cold, and that was for the best. He needed that coldness right now. Up ahead, the stairs ended in a narrow corridor, only fifteen feet long. Dunlap raced headlong for the atrium, and Walker swore and called his name. The so-called professor might not have seen them coming, but the assistant knew they were there. He had to be ready.

He was.

Walker could see the mouth of the corridor, where it opened into the brighter light of the atrium. He saw the assistant appear there, silhouetted, backlit by that yellow illumination. The man raised his weapon, aimed it at Dunlap's chest. Walker threw himself to the left, steadied himself against the corridor wall, and pulled the trigger. The angle was shit, but he caught the assistant in the shoulder. The bullet backed the man up, buying Dunlap's life and a few precious seconds during which the sergeant tackled the asshole to the ground.

The two men struggled. The assistant's windbreaker had a blood-stain spreading on the shoulder, and Dunlap punched the wound. The jihadi cried out, and Dunlap wrested the gun from his hand. The guy tried to reach back and dig into his rucksack, but Dunlap denied him that as well.

More gunfire erupted ahead. People screamed. Walker barely heard any of it as he raced past Dunlap and the jihadi and darted into the atrium. He scanned faces, saw the terror in them. People up on the balconies had crouched to hide themselves, but here in the main area, the sloping ramp at the center of the atrium, he spotted Sophie Durand immediately. No sign of Kim or Dr. Tang, and maybe that was for the best. He recognized a few other faces, but they weren't his focus.

The professor had his gun aimed at Sophie's face. He shouted angrily, demanding she take him to the Pandora Room. Walker absorbed the words but paid them little attention. All he saw was the gun, and the fear, and the back of the man's head. The dignified man in his shiny gray suit and round spectacles and red tie. That too-expensive suit. Walker chided himself for not noticing immediately that the suit was too nice to be the wardrobe of a college professor, but at least he'd noticed the assistant's boots.

Sophie noticed Walker then.

The professor saw her notice. He had to. When a man aimed a gun at someone's face and that person abruptly stopped focusing on the imminent threat of death, the gunman was bound to notice.

He started to turn, to see what had diverted Sophie's attention.

From twenty yards away, with dozens of people around him on their knees or with their hands laced behind their heads, shouting for mercy, Walker shot the professor through the left eye, shattering his little round spectacles. Blood and brain matter spattered Sophie's face and clothes as the man twisted and crumpled to the stone floor.

Someone screamed, and then silence enveloped the atrium, leaving only the echo of the gunshot.

"Oh, my God," Sophie whispered, staring at the professor.

Walker glanced back at Dunlap, who sat astride the assistant. The man might have been dead or unconscious, but either way, Dunlap's fists were the reason.

"Well, now, Dr. Walker," Dunlap said. "I'm going to guess that's not the first time you've fired a gun."

Walker glanced around at the many faces now giving him a much closer look than they had before. Very curious faces, all of them wondering the same thing. Who the hell was this guy?

It was going to be hard to convince them he was just a scientist.

The first artillery shell destroyed one of the housing trailers and blew another one off its moorings. Screaming came from within the one that had suffered a direct hit, but Lieutenant Cobb did not stop to listen or to help. He heard the whistle of another artillery shell and felt the momentary urge to throw his arms wide and try to catch it. Then it hit the northern perimeter of the camp and snapped him out of that flicker of madness.

Soldiers were in motion, men and women flying past him as fast as their feet could carry them. Cobb began barking orders, no idea where Major Bernstein might have been in that moment. His unit wouldn't need much encouragement. Nearly all of them had been under fire before—hard to spend time in this part of the world, and in this uniform, and avoid it for very long. They knew their jobs.

A drone soared overhead, paused a moment, and then it zeroed in on him and began to zip toward him out of the night sky, nothing but a blinking red light and the buzz of its rotors to indicate its presence in the dark.

"Lieutenant!" a voice shouted.

A woman came barreling out from between two tents, took aim, and blasted the drone. It exploded, the makeshift bomb it carried going off in the air instead of on impact as planned.

Corporal McHugh had the best marksmanship in his unit, and Cobb was grateful to her, but there would be time for thanks later—if they were lucky.

"Get some elevation, McHugh," he said. "Watch the skies. Take out anything you see."

Even as she barked a "yes, sir," the soldier was in motion. Cobb left her to her work and wove through the tents as another artillery shell exploded, this one missing the camp by fifty yards, still to the north, away from the strangely shaped hills of the Beneath Project. New Caliphate had been coalescing for a while, but not long enough to have amassed the kind of weaponry ISIS had used in the field. Most of the so-called Islamic state's tanks, aircraft, and artillery had been stolen, bought, or captured in Syria and Iraq, a hodgepodge of armaments from the American, Russian, Syrian, Iraqi, and Turkish armies. In dismantling ISIS, coalition forces had destroyed or recaptured most of those weapons, so the question of what arms New Caliphate had at its disposal had been lingering.

Now the forces around Derveyî were getting an answer.

Mobile artillery, probably on the back of a flatbed truck, civilian drones repurposed with bombs, as well as handheld rocket launchers from the sound of things. They would never commit all their resources to this one attack, this one location, for fear of losing them, so Cobb hoped what they were seeing now would be the extent of what New Caliphate could throw at them.

We can survive this, he told himself as he burst from among the tents and ran for a trench they had dug at the perimeter of the camp. Bullets erupted from the darkness, tore up the dirt around him, and punched through a Humvee behind him and shattered its windows, but he leaped into the trench, shouldered his weapon, and began returning fire.

We can survive this.

ELEVEN

Kim pushed away from the balcony the moment the shooting started in the atrium, darting past others who were ducking for cover. Her heart raced, and she saw the fear around her as gunshots and shouting echoed off the walls, but she stayed in motion. Walker was down there, in the midst of it, and she wouldn't run the other way. She nudged people aside as she hurried down stone steps while others were rushing up. One man collided with her and nearly picked her up off her feet with his desire to reverse her direction, warning her to run. Kim knocked his hands aside and slipped past him, then rushed out onto the floor of the atrium as the last reverberations died out.

People had thrown themselves to the floor or dived for cover in doorways, but now they helped each other stand. Archaeologists and grad students and a handful of hired laborers glanced around in fear, comforted one another, and looked to their leadership for help.

"It's over," Sophie Durand announced, turning in a full circle. "Whatever that was, it's done."

Kim exhaled and began to scan the atrium for Walker, and in that same moment, the whole underground city shook with an explosion overhead, and people screamed and swore and began to chatter while dirt sifted down from the ceiling.

It's not over, Kim thought, staring up at the stone dozens of feet overhead.

Like the buzz of a mosquito, barely heard, she sensed the staccato crack of gunfire from outside, but the sound seemed to come and go as if only the twist and gust of the night wind decided whether or not the noise would reach inside Derveyî.

Observer, she thought. *That's the job. Just observe.*

Frightened people surrounded her. Her claustrophobia seemed distant and compartmentalized in that moment, but traumatic memories echoed like the gunshots that had rung through the atrium only moments ago. In those memories, in the midst of fear, she had fought to survive—and she'd do so again.

She spotted Sophie and Beyza calling to those around them to calm down, to back away. Marissa and Cortez, Alton and Rachel, so many people who had been diligent about their work, even to the point of boredom, only yesterday.

"Give Sergeant Dunlap room, please," Sophie said.

Dunlap marched away from the body he'd left on the stone floor of the atrium. The bearded man had a bloodied face and a gunshot wound to the shoulder, and he lay sprawled on his back. Kim watched his chest for a second, wondering if he was alive, but the man did not seem to be breathing.

She hurried up to Dunlap. "Who are they?"

The atrium shook with another thump from overhead. More dirt sifted down onto them. Dunlap glanced up, then turned to look up the slope toward the exit. He held his weapon loosely but ready, tensed as if anticipating an incursion at any moment.

"Sergeant—" she began again.

"These two were spies, trying to get in to see Sophie. Maybe kill her or take the jar or both," he said, gesturing to the man he'd just killed. "Considering our friends topside are under attack, I'm assuming a terrorist cell. Jihadists. We were just telling Walker about a group that calls itself New Caliphate, and my money's on them. No way would any local government sanction something like this."

Staff members listened in, breathless and frozen. Someone had crouched by the dead man. Kim called to the woman to step back from the body, and now she turned toward the other part of this gruesome tableau, the corpse of an older man that lay splayed on the floor. Ten feet from that second corpse, Walker loomed in partial shadow, strangely isolated from the rest of them as if he were a ghost none could see but whose presence they all felt and avoided. The gun in his hand had something to do with it, she was sure, although he held it down at his side.

Walker went to kneel by the old man and check his pulse. "Dunlap," he called. "Check the backpack on the other guy. He went for it. Maybe more weapons?"

Dunlap did as Walker had asked, and Kim saw his face go pale as he glanced around at them. "Explosives."

"Shit," Kim muttered. "They were going to blow us up?"

"Not us," Walker said. "The jar."

Dunlap shook his head. "No, sir. If that was all they wanted, they didn't need to come in after it. They could have found another way. Maybe the explosives were a backup plan, in case they were able to sneak in but couldn't get the jar out. But you'll never convince me these guys didn't want to leave here with the jar if they could manage it. The prospect of something that might be deadly and contagious would be too tempting."

"Either way, they weren't here for a friendly visit," Sophie said.

Dunlap put the rucksack full of explosives over one shoulder. "I'll take charge of this for now and bring it topside later."

He shot Walker an appraising glance, then strode over and relieved the other man of his gun.

"Hang on, Sergeant," Kim said.

"Stay back, Kim," Sophie warned.

Kim ignored her. *Stay back from what?* she wondered. Men with guns? The blood pooling beneath the dead jihadis? She had faced so much worse.

The lighting inside the atrium flickered, and the yellow hue deepened as if the industrial illumination had begun to blend and blur with the shadows. A sense of unreality came over Kim, and the desire to flee flared at the base of her brain. She pushed the flickers of memory away.

"Sergeant," she said, approaching Dunlap. "Did that gun come off the terrorist or one of the coalition soldiers?"

Dunlap glanced at her. "It belonged to a Kurdish sentry."

"When the fighting is over, we'll ask the Kurds if they object to him keeping it. For now, return it to Dr. Walker, please."

"Ms. Kim," Dunlap said, "I'm not sure what you think you're doing, but—"

"If I'm not mistaken," she interrupted, "Walker shot that man. He's proven his marksmanship. We don't know what happens next, but I'm more comfortable with that gun in his hands than as anyone's backup weapon. If the fighting upstairs spills down here, we will be in serious trouble."

"Kim," Walker began.

She turned to him. "The sentries outside the entrance. They'll be fighting now, right? Protecting the camp?"

"The sentries who were on duty are dead," Dunlap replied.

Kim nodded. This was what she had feared. She turned to Sophie. "Dr. Durand, please post two of your people—volunteers, obviously—at the entrance. We need someone up there to monitor the situation and come running if it looks like our defenders are losing. We're blind down here."

Two women had appeared with blankets and were covering the corpses. Sophie had been talking quietly with them but turned now to stare at Kim.

"Down here, I make the decisions."

Kim glanced at her in surprise. "We're under attack," she said sharply. "Do you really want to argue about who's in charge?"

Sophie glanced around at her people, but everyone had kept a respectful distance.

"Everyone's terrified," she said quietly, shifting her gaze from Walker to Dunlap to Kim. "They need to feel safe. They have to know I'm looking out for them."

Barely aware she was doing it, Kim moved nearer to the other woman. Walker and Dunlap closed in as well, tightening the circle, keeping the conversation private.

"You asked me to secure help from the U.N.," Kim said. "The techs from the USAMRIID are already down in the Pandora Room. The U.N. is playing the role you want us to play. Peacemaker. The

Grown-Up in the Room. But U.N. peacekeepers won't be here until at least sunrise, and that's many hours from now."

The atrium trembled again, but whatever had exploded this time felt farther away. It gave Kim some hope.

"Sophie," Walker said, "it's still your project and your team. But Kim is right, and she's good in a crisis."

The argument could have gone further. Kim saw it glinting in Sophie's eyes. But then the other woman gave a quick nod and turned to call for volunteers. At first there was an air of reluctance, but as soon as one woman stepped forward, a pair of men raised their hands high, perhaps abashed that they had hesitated. Sophie had gone pale and her forehead had a sheen of sweat, and it occurred to Kim that she looked more than tired and scared; she looked ill.

She moved off to the side of the atrium to talk quietly with her three volunteer lookouts.

"Just one thing," Walker said, coming up beside Kim. "We have to get the dead guys out of here."

Kim nodded, but the way her heart thundered, her temples pulsing, she could not focus. The artillery shelling had ceased for the moment, but the draft, or the ventilation system, still brought the muffled staccato of gunfire. The battle went on up there, and she thought it would continue for a while.

Members of the dig team milled about in frightened clusters, talking nervously among themselves, waiting for someone to tell them who their attackers were and what to do next. There were forty or so people in the atrium, most of whom seemed on the verge of bolting. Kim did not blame them. They would all be thinking now about where they might hide if the jihadis made it into Derveyî. All of them would know a niche or two where they might go undiscovered for a time in the sprawling warren, but the only exit from this place led right into the midst of the gunfire, and so for the moment they had no way out.

Kim saw Lamar emerge from a tunnel at the back of the atrium, a worried look in his eyes. He spotted them all and started moving, though several people delayed him, engaging him in anxious conversation.

Walker caught her attention. He guided her a few steps away into the shadows between two lighting rigs.

"Okay, boss," he said quietly. "We need a plan. If they get down here, what do we do about the jar?"

Kim shuddered. She studied his eyes, wishing she could read his mind. What were his plans for the jar? If they ever got out of here, she supposed she would find out.

"For now, we should probably hide it. We'll talk to Sophie, figure out the best place."

"Nobody can know but the three of us," Walker said. "The fewer people who can answer their questions under duress, the better chance of the jar staying safe until help arrives."

Kim felt nausea roiling in her gut. "Do you think it will come to that? How many soldiers do you think they have? Enough to take the camp? Enough to kill everyone topside?"

Walker brushed a hand against her arm, a small gesture of comfort. "I wish I knew."

He slid his newly acquired gun into the rear waistband of his pants and untucked his shirt, letting it hang down to hide the gun. People wouldn't forget he had it, but Kim knew this strategy. Most would stop being nervous about the weapon if they couldn't see it.

Kim turned to scan the atrium again. Some of the staff had dispersed, off to gather weapons or lie low. Beyza stood with a handful of others, men and women who had never imagined themselves in the path of jihadi killers, never imagined waiting in breathless terror in a cave underground, wondering if they would ever get home again. Kim had never imagined it, either, even after all she had been through.

She realized she had made an error in trying to wrest control from Sophie. Her people needed her, needed a chain of command. They trusted Sophie, and they didn't know Kim at all.

Sophie was still talking to the volunteer lookouts, and Walker and Dunlap seemed to be discussing what to do with the dead men, so Kim started toward Beyza and Lamar and the cluster around them. Lamar took a step away from that group, and for the first time, she noticed the fat camera bag slung across his chest. With the techs working downstairs, he'd apparently been unwilling to leave his camera equipment with them, perhaps worried they would damage it.

As Kim approached the group, Lamar laughed at something Beyza had said and then turned to walk up toward the exit. He glanced at Kim as he passed, and from his sour expression, it seemed he disliked her taking charge as much as Sophie did. Also like Sophie, Lamar had a sheen that made him look ill, and Kim realized the toll this was taking on the entire team.

"Sophie," Walker said, interrupting her conversation with Beyza. "Can we have a moment?"

Kim found herself distracted by the sound of someone stumbling into the atrium, far at the back, where the corridor led to the stairs that descended to the worship chamber and down into the Pandora Room.

It was Dr. Tang. She looked frantic and bedraggled. Even at thirty yards, Kim could see there was blood on her face and her filtration mask. She swore in Korean as she started walking toward Dr. Tang, mind awhirl with confusion. What the hell had happened to her? The jihadis hadn't gotten that deep into the atrium. There had been two men—she had seen them from the balcony—and Walker and Dunlap had brought them down.

"Dr. Tang?" she called. "Erika?"

Walker called after Kim, but she quickened her pace. Dr. Tang stumbled a bit. A couple of graduate students caught her and kept her from falling, and then she lifted her bloody face and looked at Kim.

No. Not at me, Kim thought. *Past me.*

She turned, trying to see where Dr. Tang was looking, just as the woman shouted a name. "Lamar!"

Kim stared at Lamar's back. He'd nearly reached the opening to the corridor that would take him outside, but with the acoustics in the atrium and the hushed, somber silence in the aftermath of the attack, there was no way Lamar hadn't heard her call out to him, and yet he didn't turn. He kept going, with the camera bag clutched tightly against his hip.

It made no sense.

Then it dawned on her what was happening, and it made absolute, total, horrifying sense indeed.

Walker saw it instantly. The epiphany on Kim's face, the blood on Dr. Tang's filtration mask, and the way Lamar stiffened without turning and clutched the camera bag too close. The distant sound of gunfire still filtered down from the surface. Nobody in their right mind would go up there right now unless they intended to join the fight, and Walker knew Lamar had no intention of entering combat.

The gun stayed tucked at the small of his back, but he started toward the exit.

"What are you doing?" Sophie asked, her voice tight.

"Lamar?" Walker called, picking up his pace.

"What's going on?" Sophie asked, beginning to follow.

Lamar was only two steps from the exit. He kept going, despite the danger aboveground.

Walker drew his gun. "Lamar, stop where you are! Do not make me shoot you!"

Sophie shouted at him, but her voice cut off midsentence when Lamar bolted from the atrium. Running for the exit.

Walker grimaced as he pursued, cursing Lamar under his breath. His old injuries shot fresh pain up his spine and along his left leg, but he gritted his teeth and kept running. Sophie shouted right behind him, and Walker didn't want her to catch up, didn't want to negotiate the gulf between her feelings of friendship and trust for Lamar and the reality unfolding in that moment.

As he reached the exit, her fingers brushed his jacket, nearly snagged him as she tried to get his attention.

"Damn it, Walker, stop!"

He threw himself against the wall, just inside the short corridor, gun at the ready. Walker doubted Lamar had paused to ambush him, but he wouldn't have guessed the man would betray his team, so he would not underestimate him now.

The corridor was short and mostly straight and empty.

"You don't really think Lamar—" she began.

Walker shot her a dark look. "I do, and so do you. Keep your people back. Keep them safe."

Stricken, she shook her head in frustration, but when Walker rushed along the corridor, Sophie didn't follow. It relieved him of having to worry about her safety, which quickened his pace. If Lamar had a gun, if Walker had to take a bullet, it wouldn't matter as long as he didn't get out of Derveyî with that damned camera bag.

This guy. I never would've called it.

When he reached the bottom of the curving stairs, he could hear huffing in the stairwell overhead, punctuated by the thump of boots. Lamar might have been sauntering before, taking his time, trying to make his escape seem ordinary, but now he was running for his life. A traitor to his country, to his employer, and to the world.

Walker thundered up the stairs. He didn't bother trying to stay quiet. Focused as he was on ignoring his pain and how badly he wanted his pills in that moment, silence was the furthest thing on his mind.

The ground shook again. The sounds of combat grew louder. He heard soldiers shouting to one another, but there would be no sentries at the entrance now. Nobody would notice Lamar making a run for it. Even if he got to a vehicle, he was more likely to be killed by the jihadis or in a cross fire than by anyone trying to stop him.

A terrible thought occurred to Walker. This timing could not be coincidental. The terrorists trying to infiltrate Derveyî, the attack on the camp, and Lamar betraying his team. Which meant the New Caliphate attacking the camp might have been cover for Lamar, and if he could get out of the camp, they might not shoot him at all. They might welcome him with open arms.

Above, a turn or two around the curving stairwell, he heard Lamar swear. The gun felt light in his hand, almost weightless, as if it wanted to be used, but Walker wanted answers from Lamar, and answers required that the son of a bitch keep his blood on the inside.

Two more steps and he saw Lamar's shadow bouncing off the wall in that garish industrial lighting. An explosion outside made him flinch, raining dust and debris onto him, but he kept moving.

"I see you, motherfucker, and I will put a bullet in your back!" Walker shouted over the sounds of war from outside. "Stop now and you can tell me the whole story."

"I can't!" Lamar replied, the words an anguished wail.

Walker heard fear in the man's voice, human terror and regret, and a part of him just wanted to understand why Lamar had done this. Money or threats or promises—what had been the trigger for his betrayal? But then the staircase ended, and he found himself in the long, ramping entry tunnel that led to the exit. The staccato bursts of gunfire and the scream of rocket launchers seemed impossibly loud there in the gullet of the cave.

A moment later, Walker saw that he'd been wrong. Two sentries had been left behind, dark silhouettes of men guarding the entrance, preventing anyone else from getting inside but not ready for someone trying to get out. Lamar ran toward them, calling for help.

Smart son of a bitch, Walker thought even as the sentries turned toward the sound of his shouting. They knew Lamar a hell of a lot better than they knew Walker. Dunlap would have known who to shoot, but the sergeant was back inside the cave, restoring order underground.

"He's one of them!" Lamar shouted. "He's gonna kill me!"

Walker had been shot before. He didn't want to die, but more importantly, he couldn't take the risk of letting Lamar outside. The jar might be empty, but even the chance that it could be deadly meant he had no choice.

He went down on one knee, took aim, pulled the trigger. Two gunshots echoed off the stone walls. One bullet punched through Lamar's thigh, and the other hit him in the lower back, just to the left of his spine. He stumbled, but momentum carried him forward, and he crashed to the tunnel floor with the camera case still strapped across his chest. Both Lamar and the cushioned case bounced once and then went still.

The sentries shouted. With the weird play of light and shadow from the lighting in the tunnel, they might not know what they were looking at, but they took cover on either side of the exit, thinking more gunshots were on the way. One of the sentries ducked in and squeezed off a barrage. Bullets chipped the wall, even as Walker threw his gun away. It skittered along the stone floor, and he went down on his chest, hands stretched out in front of him.

"Don't shoot! I tossed the gun. Get Lieutenant Cobb!"

That gave them pause. "Who the fuck are you?" one of them barked.

"Ben Walker. I'm unarmed." His voice echoed, despite being muffled by his filtration mask and because he lay on his chest.

The two sentries hustled down into the tunnel, both covering him with their weapons, ready to put a dozen holes in him. One crouched to check Lamar's pulse, and Walker craned his neck to watch them. He saw the pool of blood spreading around Lamar.

"Weak pulse," the crouching sentry said. His name tag read RUIZ.

The other one reached for the camera case.

"No!" Walker shouted. "Don't touch it. Just get Cobb and Dr. Durand. Whatever the hell you do, do not open that case."

TWELVE

Martin had spent his life blending in. He had always had a way with a joke, but he had rarely been the funniest guy in the room. In school, he had quietly excelled, never quite earning the same approbation from his instructors that the more outspoken students had. In a club, he would wait until his friends had all gone off to dance before asking a woman to dance with him. Working for Sophie on the Beneath Project had changed him, changed his life. She had made him site supervisor three months earlier, when the person who'd held the job had finished up work in the east wing and gone home. The courage he'd mustered up to flirt with Sophie, even obliquely, had come from some hidden reserve within him. It had been idiotic and inappropriate, but she had always seemed amused, and somehow—though he had known the flirtation meant nothing—it had given him new confidence.

But Martin still loathed being the center of attention. And that had never been truer than now.

"Martin, brother," Elio Cortez said, "you want to tell us what's going on here?"

Alton asked if that had been gunfire that they'd heard, which Martin thought had to be the stupidest question he had ever heard. He and Alton had become friends, and he respected the man as an archaeologist, even hoped to be half as good at his job as Alton was, once he received his doctorate. But they had all seen Dunlap and

Walker kill the two jihadis—or whoever they were—who had infiltrated Derveyî. They had all seen Lamar running for the exit with Kim shouting after him and with Walker and Sophie giving chase.

The atrium shook with the impact of another explosion aboveground. Dozens were gathered in that space and some of them shouted, even screamed. Rachel and a historian named Mursal held on to each other and went down on their knees, heads bent almost as if they were in prayer, but Martin thought it was just a strange attempt to protect themselves if the ceiling should cave in. They were brilliant people, but of course kneeling and covering their heads would not save them.

The sound of gunfire—of war, really—echoed down through the entryway of Derveyî all the way to the atrium.

"Martin?" Cortez prodded.

"Lamar is dead. Someone's going to have to—"

Dr. Tang caught up with him from behind, making Martin realize how slowly he was walking.

"I need volunteers to move Lamar and the two intruders," Dr. Tang said, glancing around at the gathered staff members as she walked beside Martin through the atrium. "If there's a space away from everyone, isolated, that I can use temporarily as an examination room, that would be helpful."

So cold, Martin thought. *Clinical*. People would not love her for it, but they responded to that sense of authority and practicality.

Several hands went up.

Beyza stood in the midst of those gathered in the atrium. "The first chamber on the left as you enter the east wing," she said, glancing at the volunteers. "There's still lighting rigged in there, still connected to the generator. Nobody goes in there from now on without Sophie, myself, or Dr. Tang giving you the okay."

Dmitri the cook separated himself out from the others. "Can someone please tell us what the hell is going on here?" he snapped. He wore an angry expression, but his voice cracked with fear as he pointed at the camera case, which hung from Martin's shoulder. "And what the fuck is that supposed to be?"

People milled around, but now they fell silent, staring at Martin, making him the unwilling center of attention again.

"It's . . . it's Lamar's camera case," he said.

Dmitri started toward him, and several others also began to approach. Bastien and Mursal, Rachel and Cortez . . . they all drifted nearer, frustration and fear on their faces. The cave shook, and everyone took a collective breath, listening to the crackle of gunfire from outside, hoping Derveyî did not collapse around them.

"I know it's Lamar's camera case," Dmitri said after a moment. "What I want to know is, what's in it? Lamar ran for the exit. I figure he was stealing something or Walker wouldn't have shot him."

Cortez laughed. "Are you stupid, chef?"

Beyza shot him a dark look. "Elio, don't."

In that moment, Martin realized the rumors about Beyza and Cortez were true, but that thought vanished in an instant as Dmitri and Bastien came toward him. Dmitri spoke, angry and afraid, but it was Bastien who grabbed the strap of the camera case and tried to tug it off Martin, even though he had slung it across his shoulder.

"No! Don't!" he called.

Cortez moved in, grabbed Bastien, and shoved him back. The camera case jostled and bumped against Martin, and he held his breath inside his filtration mask, hoping Lamar had thought to cushion the stolen artifact well. Pandora and Anesidora did not seem like myths to him in that moment, and neither did the curses of the gods.

"Please!" he said. "Don't do that!"

Beyza put a hand on Dmitri's arm. "Are you stupid? Don't touch that!"

They all went silent, staring at her instead of Martin. He understood. Beyza might be serious about her work, but she had never shouted at any of them before.

"You fool," Cortez said quietly to Dmitri. "It's the jar. Lamar tried to steal the jar."

They all shifted, some just a few steps and others much farther, and suddenly a path opened right down the middle of the atrium. Nobody wanted to get in Martin's way now.

"Are . . . Martin, are we in danger?" Marissa asked.

He looked at her, this hardworking woman who had taught him as much as he had learned from Sophie and Lamar combined, because he had learned from them by observation, while Marissa had gently corrected and instructed him for months, making him better at his job every day.

Martin smiled. "Do you hear gunfire? We are under attack."

"You know what I mean."

Dr. Tang took his arm and gave him a soft push, getting his legs moving again. "The answer to your question is that we do not know, but I am going to do everything in my power to find out."

"In the meantime," Beyza said, "it's best you all return to your quarters and stay there until we know more."

Some of them nodded in relief and began to move off immediately. Others milled about in clusters, talking among themselves. Dmitri stood with Rachel and Bastien and several others.

When the cook began to cough, hardly anyone took notice.

Everything had changed. Sophie and Kim had taken a few minutes to bring order to chaos, but they had left the atrium before the others had come down from topside. Beyza, Dr. Tang, and Martin had gone to join Walker there, to help with the jar and with Lamar's body.

The thought sent a tremor through Sophie. *Lamar's body.* The phrase broke something inside her.

Now she stood in the column chamber and listened carefully. The explosions had ceased, but the sound of gunfire still filtered down through ventilation shafts. At first she had thought this was a good sign, that it meant the jihadis would not just overwhelm them, sweep through the camp, and invade Derveyî to kill them all and take the jar. Upstairs, while Sophie had stood staring at Lamar's bleeding corpse, Walker had explained that he would have expected the New Caliphate to hit and run, that an ongoing fight would mean they believed they had superior numbers and could take the camp.

Sophie did not share Walker's opinion with anyone else, but with every minute the combat raged on, her disquiet and sense of urgency grew. Dread slithered through her with the thoroughness of the best drugs and the worst. She stood in the column chamber, at the top of the steps that led down into the Pandora Room, and stared at the dead soldier on the floor, facing away from her. The way he had fallen, he might have been sleeping if not for the pool of blood around him, and the wicked knife that lay like a stained, gleaming island in the midst of that pool.

"Sophie?" Kim said. The woman stood a few feet behind her, awaiting instructions.

If Beyza had followed orders, the staff had been instructed to seek shelter in their quarters, to gather any weapons they could find, and to stay in groups. It seemed far too little, but as soon as reality began to settle in, they would all realize the hard truth that Sophie had confronted the moment the attack topside had begun—they had no way out of here, no way to escape if the New Caliphate made it into the tunnels. The original layout of the place had included at least two other doors that they knew of, but they had not gone to the trouble of excavating those entrances, thinking it would only make the dig harder to protect.

"Just . . . give me a minute," she said now. Her throat felt dry and raspy, and her chest ached. It would be so easy to attribute that to Lamar . . . to the sting of his betrayal and her grief at losing him.

Dead. Lamar's dead. The concept felt so difficult, like trying to tell herself the world had indeed been flat all along.

How did I not see it? How did I not know?

She told herself there would be answers. His bank accounts would be researched, his whole life autopsied in the quest for an explanation for his behavior. It had to be leverage, she felt sure. Whoever had done this had some kind of pressure to use against him. He'd known the risks—even if he had never really believed the jar might contain curses or disease, he'd known the possibility was there.

"Asshole," she whispered. If only he'd talked to her. If only . . .

The worst words in the English language. *If only.*

"I'm sorry," Kim said quietly. "I didn't mean—"

"Not you, Ms. Kim." She gave the other woman a weak smile. "Not you."

The dead guard had fallen to the left of the stairwell entrance. His blood had pooled and run into cracks and runnels in the stone floor, but it wasn't the only blood up here in the column chamber. They had passed a smattering of red on the floor a dozen feet back, red turned black by the glare of the industrial lighting. Dr. Tang had said this was where Lamar had assaulted her. She had come back down, wanting another look at the jar, wanting to talk to the USAMRIID techs. They were her colleagues, and she wanted their input.

According to Dr. Tang, she had been nearly to the worship chamber and she'd turned around, come back down to speak with those techs. She had not yet reached the stairs when she heard the scuffle. She saw the guard, bleeding and dying, but from down those thirteen steps she'd heard a gunshot, a fight, something shattering.

Now Sophie descended the stairs herself and entered the Pandora Room, leaving Kim waiting in the column chamber.

One of the techs lay off to the right, the clear plastic face shield of his hazmat suit completely painted with gore from the inside. The bullet seemed to have gone through the back of his head, the results spraying out the front. The other had been beaten with one of the lighting rigs. The gun had somehow landed in the far corner of the room, in the shadows born of having a quarter of its illumination used to commit murder. The tech had grabbed for the gun. Sophie didn't need to be a forensic scientist to work it out. She had unearthed enough death sites as an archaeologist to see it in her mind's eye. The tech had gone for the gun and they'd struggled, but the tech had won possession of the weapon. Lamar had grabbed the only thing nearby, the metal lighting rig, and smashed the gun from the man's grip, and then kept smashing.

Lamar. Her friend had done this. Sophie thought she ought to be crying, but no tears came to her eyes. The Pandora Room had never felt so small, so suffocating. The copper stink of blood filled the air, and she felt nauseous. She coughed through her filtration mask, and it hurt like hell. A little bile rose in her throat, but she swallowed it down.

She stared at the altar, at the empty space where the jar ought to have been, and she jumped a little when she saw movement out of the corner of her eye, but it was only Dr. Tang entering the room.

"I didn't mean to startle you."

"It's fine," Sophie told her.

"Martin will be here in a moment. He's being very careful with the camera case."

"I have no doubt," Sophie replied. "You gave the soldiers filtration masks."

"All of the soldiers down here with us, yes," Dr. Tang replied. "We'll need them to guard this room, so they received masks. I think I only have one other."

"It doesn't feel right," Sophie said. "Us with masks on, and most of the staff without them."

"You know why that is," Dr. Tang replied. "We've had exposure to the Pandora Room. To the jar—"

"They've all had exposure to the jar now," Sophie said.

Dr. Tang hesitated. Even with the mask covering the lower half of her face, her eyes revealed her disquiet. "It was inside the camera case, and the atrium is an enormous space. I think they're safe."

We don't even know if there's anything for them to be safe from, Sophie thought. This woman was the expert, but they were in uncharted territory here, and the world had no experts for this.

"Since we can't know if Lamar's behavior resulted from desperation, outside pressure, or something more . . . some illness or episode," Dr. Tang said, "we must be even more vigilant with our masks. I think it's best we separate those who've spent time in the room from the rest of the staff."

Sophie turned toward her. "So we're segregating the team? You know there's a war going on over our heads, right? The only thing we need to worry about is whether or not jihadi-fucking-terrorists get in here and kill us all."

Dr. Tang regarded her calmly. "That is, unfortunately, not our only concern. Lamar spent more time in this room than anyone. We can't ignore the possibility that his behavior might have been affected. I intend to examine his remains, and the others as well."

Sophie shuddered and tightened her mask a bit more. "Do what you need to do."

Dr. Tang went to the doorway and called up the steps. "Bring it down. Let's do it right this time."

Corporal Taejon was the first one down the stairs. He had been part of the coalition unit assigned to the site before the discovery of the Pandora Room. He'd rotated into the assignment five months earlier, and Sophie felt sure he was regretting it now. Some members of his unit must be dead now, up on the surface. Others would die before sunrise. But Taejon was a professional. He and Private Ruiz had been on sentry duty when Walker had shot Lamar, and they had helped bring Lamar's body back underground, even after Dr. Tang had told them they might not be able to leave until she cleared them.

Quarantine, Sophie thought. That was where Dr. Tang was headed, she had no doubt. It was premature, but at the moment it didn't matter. With the battle still going on, they were all stuck down here for now, anyway.

She wondered how fast reinforcements could be sent, or an airstrike. How far away were the forces that could help them? Sophie had no idea. It was the sort of question that had never interested her before, and now she wished she knew.

Sunrise, she thought. By then it would be over, the jar would be removed to wherever the U.N. wanted to send it, and soon afterward, they could all go home.

Except you don't have a home, she thought, and perhaps for the first time, she regretted having left New York. Regretted having left the soon-to-be-married Steven. Regretted leaving her teaching position.

She'd go to France and visit her father, who would not remember her, and her mother, who had given up her daily life in an act of kindness and sacrifice Sophie felt shamed by. She could never have done that for another person. *You just haven't met the right person*, Lamar had told her when she'd voiced her self-doubt.

Martin came down the steps next, his scruffy face strangely distorted by his mask. He carried the camera bag in front of him, the strap over one shoulder.

"You all right?" Sophie asked him.

Martin smiled. "Not my best night."

Dr. Tang called for him to join her at the altar. Martin set the case on the floor, where Dr. Tang unzipped it, pulled back the cover, and revealed the vibrant aqua blue of Lamar's Miami Dolphins sweatshirt.

"Jesus," Martin whispered. "He really did it."

Dr. Tang looked confused, but Sophie understood. They had seen Lamar trying to leave with the jar, but the presence of that sweatshirt meant it had not been completely spur of the moment. He had gone back to his quarters to fetch the sweatshirt to cushion the jar.

Dr. Tang shifted backward and glanced at Sophie. Thus far, only Lamar had actually touched the jar, and the doctor was no archaeologist. It would be up to Sophie to move the artifact.

Martin went to the plastic crate that Dr. Tang had called a contagion box. He opened the lid, reached inside and arranged the padding there, then looked expectantly at Sophie.

"Here," Dr. Tang said, taking a pair of latex gloves from the pocket of her hoodie. "Put these on."

Sophie exhaled. Her breath felt warm inside the mask, but her skin had gone cold. She tugged on the gloves, reached into the case, and unwrapped the jar, pushing aside the soft sweatshirt. Gently, she lifted the jar out, glad to have the gloves separating her skin from contact with the ceramic.

"Well?" Dr. Tang prodded.

Sophie lifted it to look at the base, turned it in her hands, satisfying herself that it was intact. They were dealing with legends here, but they only needed a single germ of reality for legend to become threat.

"It's okay," she said.

Martin released a muffled sigh of relief inside his mask.

Sophie crossed the few feet to Martin and knelt beside the contagion box. She set the jar carefully inside, but it sat unevenly on the padding, so she rotated it slightly. Only then did she notice the jagged black line along the seam between lid and jar, where the gray crust of ancient sealant had cracked.

Frozen, her breathing amplified inside her filtration mask, Sophie stared at that crack. Martin said her name, but his voice seemed very far away.

Air would have seeped in through the crack, potentially damaging anything that might be inside the jar. But Sophie didn't care about air getting in.

She was far more concerned about what might have seeped out.

Walker crouched just inside the entrance to Derveyî. The battle continued, but it had quieted down. No artillery shells had fallen for fifteen minutes or so. A drone bomb had flown overhead and been blown out of the sky by two quick-thinking Kurdish soldiers. Other than that, the night alternated between deathly quiet and quick eruptions of gunfire. The coalition forces in the camp had hunkered down in trenches and behind vehicles. Some had scrambled up onto the hill that rose above Derveyî, snipers with night scopes, ready to put a bullet in any jihadi asshole stupid enough to reveal himself within range.

It felt like a stalemate, but Walker knew better, and he was sure Major Bernstein knew better, too. The enemy was out there in the night. The quick bursts of gunfire were sparks in the dark, just a reminder from each side to announce they were still there. But the New Caliphate would not wait until dawn. They wouldn't even wait very long, not when they had no idea when air support might arrive. Maybe they had been working with Lamar, maybe they had expected to have the jar already, but if they had not yet retreated, that meant they still intended to get their hands on it before they went home.

Meanwhile, Derveyî was under unofficial quarantine. Dr. Tang was a strange woman, but her response to the attempted theft of the jar had been swift and precise. The sentries on duty had been brought inside. The bodies of the dead had been moved to a room in the otherwise empty east wing, where the Beneath Project had wrapped up their work months ago. Most of the staff had been confined to quarters, despite their fear, and told to be prepared to defend themselves. For the moment, they seemed to be cooperating, but Walker did not know how long that would last. He had come topside to evaluate their situation, thinking that if the attack had come from the west, they could flee east toward Amadiya, but the camp seemed to be surrounded. Until reinforcements arrived or the jihadis were driven off, there would be no escape for those underground.

Another sustained gunfight began off to his left. Shots came from high on the hill over his head and from the roof of one of the prefab barracks buildings across from the cave entrance. Walker's hands tensed at his sides, tempted to go out there and help, but he knew the people in Derveyî needed him more than Major Bernstein needed one more gun.

Footsteps echoed up through the tunnel. Walker turned to see Kim and Martin emerge from the top of the circular steps at the back of the tunnel, both still masked. He knew from her eyes alone that the news wasn't good.

"What's going on?"

Martin was young and looked fit, but he heaved and huffed and bent to put his hands on his knees to catch his breath. It might have been the illumination, but Walker thought his skin had taken on a yellowish tinge.

"The . . . the jar . . . ," he managed.

Kim halted him with a gesture. "I've been on the phone to my superiors at the U.N. Our unofficial quarantine just became official. If the fighting ends, we can't let anyone enter Derveyî."

A flicker of fear went through Walker, but not for himself. Once upon a time, he had been almost fearless. Now he worried about his son. He felt angry with himself for allowing his work to put him into this position again, to know he might leave Charlie without a father, leave his ex-wife to tell the boy his dad had died.

"What happened?" he asked. "Did Tang find something? Is there contagion?"

Martin coughed and wheezed, still partly bent over but starting to catch his breath. "The seal on the jar . . ." He started coughing again, and then he put a hand on his abdomen and looked up, an edge of despair in his eyes. "Oh . . ."

"It's cracked," Kim said. "Dr. Tang has sealed it into a sterile box that the techs brought, but the seal is cracked. If there's anything contagious in there, it's virtually certain that some of us have breathed it in."

Martin turned away from them, retched twice as he yanked back his filtration mask, and then vomited with a splash and the most pitifully anguished roar Walker had ever heard. He put his hands on his hips and held up a finger, taking slow breaths to steady himself.

"I'm fine," Martin insisted with a wan smile, wiping the back of his hand across his mouth. "It's not . . . I mean it's just, with everything going on . . ."

They all stared at him. Walker saw the fear in his eyes.

"I'm fine," he repeated, less certain now.

Walker heard shouting, then a whistling, and something exploded out in the camp. A fresh volley of gunfire erupted, and suddenly it seemed like every soldier on both sides began to shoot at once. He shouted at Martin and Kim to get back into the tunnels, and then he followed them, wondering who was in more danger—the soldiers out in the open . . .

Or the people trapped below.

THIRTEEN

Sophie hurried back to the west wing, trying to ignore the new tremor in the hill overhead. The fighting continued, and all they could do was wait and hope. With the filtration mask on, her breath seemed too loud, as if someone stood just behind her, always just beyond the edges of her vision, breathing warm and eager against the back of her neck. The feeling kept her unsettled and anxious, but at least it distracted her from the pressure in her head and the raw tightness of her throat.

She coughed lightly, and a bright flare of pain pulsed in her throat. She put a hand on the wall. The rock felt strangely soft and malleable, as if the tuffeau had returned to its original state, something they could carve and shape as they saw fit.

Frowning, Sophie stared at the wall. Pushed her fingers into it. The stone did not give or shift, seemed as unyielding as ever, and she knew it had been her imagination or a hallucination. She swallowed, and her throat gave another bright flare. There were medicines back in her quarters—lozenges and ibuprofen and all sorts of other things that had been sent in the monthly supplies the dig staff received—but she had more imminent concerns.

Her room in the west wing was small, but it was hers alone, as the director of the project. A heavy curtain hung across the entrance to the room, and as she slipped past the curtain, she worried for the first time about eavesdroppers. There was nothing she could really do to prevent it if someone wanted to listen out in the corridor.

She went to the small desk in the corner and opened her laptop. Tapping in her password and opening her video conference software, she saw that Alex Jarota had already logged in. He had been waiting for her, and Alex didn't like to be kept waiting. Still, she risked further ire by taking a moment to plug in her headphones. She wouldn't be able to keep anyone from overhearing her end of the conversation, but his words would be for her ears only.

Sophie moved the cursor and clicked to begin the conference. Alex's face appeared on the screen almost immediately. He settled himself into the chair in his office on Rue Monge, just a few blocks from the Sorbonne, where he lectured as a visiting professor to make himself feel as if he were still an archaeologist.

Such bitterness, she chided herself. The man had given her the job of her dreams, but she could not deny that his approach to the work and his general demeanor had been sapping her love of her job for some time. And now this.

"Sophie! What in the name of God is happening there?" he asked in a French accent thinned and warped by decades doing business with foreigners and watching too many American films.

The only question that mattered, really. And so she answered it, as briefly as she could, and in spite of his expressions of disbelief. Alex Jarota looked like a nineteenth-century duke with a proper, well-groomed mustache and thinning gray hair whose every wisp had been tamed by gel and comb. He wore a three-piece suit, and even alone in his office, he kept jacket and vest on, and his tie cinched up tightly as if to strangle himself.

"Lamar Curtis is dead?" Alex asked, incredulous. "And the jar . . . the jar is cracked?"

"Well, the substance used to seal the jar, but yes to both."

Alex's scowl might have been silent, but it came through loud and clear. Sophie felt queasy. She coughed slightly, ignored the pain, and watched Alex's face to see if her coughing alarmed him, but he was either too self-involved or too foolish to notice or to worry.

"The U.N. . . . I've been calling my contacts there, but no one will speak with me," Alex said. "This is a disaster."

Thinking of himself, not of his employees or what kind of danger they were in.

"The coalition soldiers will hold off the jihadis," Sophie replied, more to comfort herself than to comfort Alex. "Kim Seong says the U.N. has promised her a decision on possession of the jar by the time the peacekeepers arrive. For now, it's in a containment box, ready for transport. Dr. Tang will put on a hazmat suit and transport it herself once it's secured and we know where it's going."

Alex nearly snarled. "It doesn't matter where it's going now, don't you get it? The Americans will take possession. Or the fucking Russians. Someone who isn't us. Tests will be run. The jar will be opened. Before Lamar decided to get himself killed trying to team up with fucking jihadi terrorists—"

She winced.

"—we might have had a chance at controlling this, making sure we were a part of whatever team examines it, and making sure we could get it back at the end. Now all of that is finished. We will be shunted aside as if all our work means nothing."

Sophie heard a whisper and glanced at the curtain over the doorway. Was someone eavesdropping after all? Her throat tightened and pain flared again, and she wanted only to finish this conversation so that she could take some medicine. She needed to rest, but she doubted this night would provide an opportunity.

"Are you even listening?" Alex snapped.

"Yes, I'm fucking listening!" She lifted a hand to her throat, wincing. Raising her voice had been a bad idea for so many reasons.

Alex leaned closer to his computer, his face looming larger on the laptop screen. "Who are you shouting at like that? Swearing like that? Me?"

"I'm . . . It's been a long night, and it's not over," she replied, knowing it was not an apology.

Alex sat back in his chair, looking down his nose and mustache at her as if she had shrunken down to a miniature version of herself.

"My dear Sophie, you were to be my shining star," he said. "This project was to be your ticket to greater things, and when you discovered the Pandora Room . . . well, it felt like serendipity, did it not? It should have been our crowning glory. Both of us. Now you have made it an albatross around both our necks."

"Me? What have I—"

"Well, what is to be done now?" Alex asked, shaking his head. "Nothing. You are there, on-site, and so whatever decisions must be made about the staff and the jar and the United Nations, I leave it to you."

Sophie felt her upper lip curl into a sneer. "This is the time you decide to let me make decisions about my project?"

"Yes, well, I am not there, am I? I cannot be responsible for—"

Sophie laughed. She couldn't help herself. "Okay, Alex. Thanks so much for your support. I understand completely."

Alex's eyes narrowed. He sat a bit straighter in his chair. "I thought you might."

He had shifted all responsibility for what happened next to her. Whatever came of the Pandora Room now, of the jar, Lamar's betrayal, all of it . . . he would lay it at her feet. He wanted to be able to wash his hands of it all, in case things became even worse.

Sophie said *adieu* and ended the conference. She hung her head, pain in her throat flaring. With a sigh, she got up and began to rummage around in her medications, glancing up when she heard a rustle at her door.

Beyza poked her head around the curtain. "Are you done with Alex?"

Sophie sighed. "You have no idea how done I am."

"Good, because there's something else you ought to know," Beyza said, glancing back out into the corridor before letting the curtain fall into place.

"I'm not going to like this, am I?" Sophie asked.

"I doubt it," Beyza said. "It's about Ben Walker. I'm not entirely sure he's on our side."

At its height, Derveyî had housed well over a thousand people. Martin had always thought calling it a city seemed to be overstating its importance, but he'd never dared say such a thing to Sophie or Beyza.

Among his fellow grad students, the place was sometimes referred to as *the warren*, but he tried to avoid the term because it made him think about the novel *Watership Down*, and he knew that life in the warren hadn't ended well for them.

Still, whether it had housed one hundred, one thousand, or ten thousand, Derveyî had felt magical to him from the beginning. Just as he found himself fascinated with Sophie, whom it had taken him months to stop calling *Dr. Durand*, he felt a constant sense of wonder about this underground world. He liked to sit quietly in its more remote corners, to ponder by himself, but he'd had the tendency to do such things ever since he could wander from his childhood home on his own. He'd grown up on a small dairy farm in Belgium, where his exhausted father had run out of curse words to hurl his way for forgetting his chores and rambling off to the river or climbing the highest trees just to sit and absorb the world.

Even at that young age, he had liked his quiet places, especially the oldest places, where traces of earlier families and farms and peoples remained. His deeper fascination had begun when a neighboring farm had expanded and discovered a battle site from the First World War. Watching the excavation that resulted, seeing archaeologists at work, he had realized he would never be a dairy farmer.

But he still retreated to the quiet places, still cherished isolation.

In Derveyî, his favorite place to be alone was the kitchen, which made it sound much smaller and less dramatic than the reality. He'd pushed for Sophie to call it *the oven*, but the name had never stuck. There were smaller ovens in various wings and levels of the city, but this had been the central food preparation space. Columns made the vast chamber look more like a primitive church, but there were six large stone ovens, and the room had the best ventilation in Derveyî. When the ovens had all been in use, the kitchen would have been infernally hot, but without fires burning down there, the ventilation— even after thousands of years—made the room cold and drafty. It had been one of the first spaces the Beneath Project had studied, yielding dozens of minor artifacts. Since then, hardly anyone came down here. They had nowhere near the numbers, so Dmitri used a smaller, more central space with only a single oven.

Which left the kitchen to wanderers like Martin.

In better days, he'd come here to let his mind drift, to wonder, to read or scribble in a notebook. Tonight he had come because he knew of nowhere else he might hide his shame and fear. Down here, the muffled, insistent punch of gunfire couldn't reach his ears, and any explosion outside registered only as a faint thump.

"Coward," he whispered.

Inside the mask, it sounded like someone else talking. Alone in the vast kitchen, he stripped it off his face.

People were dead. Shot and stabbed. One of those people had been a friend and mentor to him, and Martin did not know how to process that. His mother would have spit on Lamar, maybe even on Lamar's corpse, but Martin only wanted to shout at the shadows. More than anything, he wanted to get on the next helicopter or into the next vehicle leaving this place, but of course nobody would be going anywhere tonight. There were wolves out in the dark, hunting them, a pack of terrorists who wanted the soldiers in the camp dead and wanted to take the most important archaeological find of the century out of the hands of the team who'd discovered it.

I'd just give it to them.

The thought shocked him. The moment it entered his mind, he fought against it. For its historical value alone, the jar could not be allowed to fall into the hands of those who would destroy or bury it. But if one believed it held wonders, or horrors that might put people in danger, handing it over to the New Caliphate would be the most grievous of sins.

If one believed.

Martin's gut still roiled with a remnant of the nausea he'd felt topside. He vomited in front of Walker and Kim, but at least Sophie hadn't been there to see it. She wasn't just the boss, she was just about the most impressive person Martin had ever met, and he had gotten used to his infatuation being the source of amusement for some members of the Beneath Project. Sophie had flirted with him from time to time over the past year, but he'd never sensed any real intent or interest in her until today.

But that had been *before*. Any hope that might have been sparked

by her comments had now been extinguished. Catastrophe had inter-
vened. Murder and fear had killed that flicker of hope that she might
see him as something more than a student with a crush on his teacher.

He knew it ought not to matter anymore, but it did.

"What is wrong with you?" he whispered, hanging his head. The
taste of bile remained in his mouth, and he spit onto the stone floor.

His face felt flush with embarrassment. Once upon a time, by the
river or in a tree, he'd enjoyed isolation for its own sake. For the quiet.
But tonight he just wanted to be invisible, to hide from a year's worth
of being the butt of jokes that would only get worse now that word
would spread of his vomiting.

Martin lifted a hand to his mouth, intending to wipe his lips.

Oh, you asshole.

He looked at the spit on the ground, tasted bile again, and then
looked at his hand—still halfway to his mouth. He let his arm fall
weakly to his side.

What had he been thinking? His colleagues would not be amused
by the story of him throwing up; they'd be terrified. Martin shuddered, more unnerved by this dissonance of thought than he'd been
by anything else thus far. Sickness . . . sickness was the problem, the
fear. If he'd contracted some illness, there was no shame in that.

Another shudder. He'd felt warm before, but now he trembled from
the chill in the kitchen. The ventilation shafts breathed, drafts swirling, and he could hear their voices like a conversation on the wind.

He squeezed his eyes closed and opened them wide, realizing how
drowsy he'd become. His skin felt clammy, his forehead damp.

Fever. Oh, you fool. You have a fever.

Again, Martin looked at the little spot of drying spit on the floor,
and another shiver passed through him. He told himself it couldn't
be possible, that any contagion inside the Pandora jar could never have
survived for thousands of years—nothing could live that long, not
even microbial bacteria. But what did he know? He was no biologist.

His eyes felt heavy, and he rested his back against one of the stoves
and exhaled. Perhaps he ought to just stay here, to hide until it was all
over. Shame rushed through him again, but this time he embraced it.

"Coward," he said again.

Something in the kitchen repeated it back to him.

Martin froze. Only his eyes moved as he glanced around, then at last he turned his head. Could it have been just the ebb and flow of the drafts through the ventilation shafts? Just the whisper of air coming through one of the ancient stovepipes?

He stood, filtration mask gripped in his left hand. After a moment, he slipped it on. If someone had come down here, either to follow him or—like him—to find some isolation, he did not want to risk exposing them to whatever might be wrong with him.

Nothing. There's nothing wrong.

But there was. It might have been an ordinary virus—he certainly hoped so—but to suggest there had been no effect at all would be foolish.

"Hello?"

The team's lighting fixtures had been left in place, but most were no longer connected. Martin had been sitting in the shadows at the edges of the pool of light, but now he moved into the gloom. He narrowed his eyes but couldn't seem to focus on the darkness.

"It's all right," he said. "I'm wearing a mask. No chance of exposure. But don't just . . . don't just . . ."

His words trailed off. The echo of his own voice was the only sound in the kitchen. Martin felt like an idiot. If someone had come in from the opposite entrance, he'd have heard footsteps, so unless there had been somebody hiding down here when he'd arrived, the whole chamber had to be empty. It could only have been noises filtering through the ventilation shafts from some other room.

Martin turned to leave. Sophie would need help. It had been a foolish indulgence to come down here.

Another whisper in the dark.

But more than a whisper this time. Before, it had seemed an echo of his voice. Now he heard a shuffling sound and a grunting, followed by a whimper. Sounds of a struggle.

His hands tightened into fists as he turned. It had never occurred to him that there might be other traitors beyond Lamar, but now he fought the urge to run. Something terrible had begun, and if he only ran for help, it would continue. Someone else might die, and he couldn't live with that.

"*Coward,*" someone whispered in the dark, behind one of the columns, near the fourth oven. The scuffling continued, and a muffled, pleading groan.

Martin strode into shadows at the edge of the lights' reach, where the soft illumination frosted the stone with a diffuse blue glow, and then he took one more step so that he could see behind the column, beyond the fourth oven.

Inside the filtration mask, his gasp sounded like a hiss. Two men struggled in the darkness, cast in that same diffuse blue glow. Bearded and clad in only loincloths and rough cloaks, one man had the other from behind, a crude dagger at his throat. Martin knew he had to act, but something about the blue light made him stop. The light seemed too much, the substance of the men too little. For a moment, it seemed like only an image in the dark, a scene projected into the dust motes swirling in the air, and he was merely the audience. The struggling men didn't even know he was there.

The victim twisted his head to gaze at Martin. His eyes were pleading, and he spoke words in an utterly unfamiliar tongue. His voice seemed to come from the base of Martin's brain instead of across the dark space between them.

The other man grinned and hacked open the victim's throat with that dull blade.

When the first man fell, the wan blue light of him began to dim and fade, erasing murderer and victim as if they hadn't ever been there at all. Except for a spot on Martin's left eye, a dark spot—a blind spot—that hadn't been there a moment ago.

He blinked, and a spike of pain stabbed his head. Martin cried out, the sound trapped with him inside the mask, and he staggered back into the light. He fell to his knees, took deep breaths, waiting for the pain to ebb. When at last it began to subside, he struggled to his feet and toward the exit, thinking only of company. Of Sophie and the others. He had always cherished isolation, but no longer.

Martin glanced back the way he'd come, but he saw nothing and no one there. No dagger, no struggle, no murder. Yet the shadows seemed pensive, heavy with intent, and the blind spot in his left eye did not go away.

His heart hammered in his chest, and there were words bubbling up inside him. He knew what he'd seen, but did he dare to tell anyone? Nausea. Fever. Now hallucination? If he told the truth, he'd have all the isolation he could stand, a quarantine within a quarantine.

Back in the kitchen, the ovens and ventilation shafts continued to breathe and whisper.

FOURTEEN

Dr. Tang felt a clock ticking inside her, keenly aware of the hours remaining until dawn and of every minute the battle aboveground continued to wear on. At this rate, it could go on all night, with jihadis out in the dark, waiting for an opportunity and then launching a fresh attack. She told herself it couldn't possibly last all night, that air cover would arrive soon and the jihadis would be decimated. It had been over an hour since the assault had begun. How long would it last? How long before Black Hawk helicopters arrived? How long could the coalition soldiers in camp hold out?

She had two choices—she could sit in her quarters and wait for the battle to be decided one way or another, or she could do the work that needed doing. Lamar Curtis had murdered four people before being shot to death himself, and she wondered if she could learn anything about why he had done so by examining those remains. No way would she be able to sleep, and curling into a terrified fetal ball seemed pointless, so she decided to go to work.

The bodies of the dead had been placed in a room in the east wing that still had a lighting rig set up. Much of the wing had been dismantled already, as the workers who had lived there had departed in the previous couple of months, so the corridor and the rooms branching off from it were quiet and only sparsely lit. Dr. Tang appreciated the isolation. Being alone in the quiet helped her to think and helped her to forget the danger overhead.

She stood in the room and gazed down at the bodies, which had been laid out respectfully, blankets covering them. The weight of the hill above her seemed to grow, and the air in the room to grow thin. It was not like her to be frightened, but she shuddered at the way the blankets lay across the faces of the dead, at the pools of shadow in the depressions where their eyes would be. The fabric seemed to flow there like the darkest water, and the illusion made her blink and shake her head.

For this task, she had dragged on one of the hazmat suits the USAMRIID techs had brought with them. There were only three. In the ten minutes she'd been wearing this one, it had already become stiflingly warm inside, and sweat trickled down the small of her back. The headpiece provided filtration similar to the masks she had handed out, but still it would be difficult to stay inside the suit for more than an hour, so she knew she had best get to work.

Inside the suit, she began to sing quietly. The song was "Chicago" by Sufjan Stevens. In medical school, she'd had only a few real friends. None of them had liked Sufjan, or none had admitted it, but this song had that refrain that always haunted her, a strange sort of lullaby. "All things go."

She might not have the easiest time getting along with other people, but her heart responded to music. In the car or in the shower, when she knew she was alone, she often sang softly to herself. It lifted her, eased the troubles from her brow and the tension from her shoulders.

To her knowledge, only her parents had ever heard her sing. If either of them had ever had an opinion about her voice, they'd never mentioned it. They had been flawed creatures, as all parents were— as all people were—but they had loved her, taught her how to live in the world, and if they had not often laughed, they had smiled every day. Her mother had enjoyed whatever might be on the radio, and her father had put classical music on in the background whenever he might be working around the house or fixing the family a meal. But they never sang.

Dr. Tang's mother had died young, only forty-two. She'd been feeling unwell for days, had made an appointment to see her doctor, then had a massive heart attack while walking Cookie, their truculent

French bulldog. Cookie had wandered home trailing his leash, and twelve-year-old Erika had tutted the naughty beast and backtracked the usual route to meet her mother, a smile on her face. By the time she'd reached the corner of School Street, the EMTs were already there and her mother had died.

Erika sang more quietly after that, and never when her father was home.

Now, with only the dead to hear, Dr. Tang sang in a muffled voice while she got down to work. She began with the USAMRIID techs. Methodically, she removed their clothing. The cause of death didn't concern her—there was no mystery involved in that. She had neither the facilities nor the tools to conduct a proper autopsy. Someone else would do that, eventually.

The bodies revealed the violence Lamar had perpetrated against them, but Dr. Tang ignored those fatal injuries. What she sought instead was any evidence of unusual illness, signs of infection, though these men hadn't been exposed to the jar after the seal had cracked— as far as she knew.

She used a penlight to check inside their mouths, ears, and nostrils, then pressed her fingers into their armpits and groins in search of buboes, although she felt foolish doing it, as any disease she sought would not have been passed by animal bite. If there were plague here, it would have been pneumonic, and given that the men were dead, a simple physical examination would not tell her whether they'd had fever or headache or difficulty breathing. She tried not to let it frustrate her, but it would be extremely difficult to tell Sophie or Kim that they were in no peril without knowing what it was she might be looking for.

Using her left hand, she forced the younger tech's jaw open and shone her light within. A shudder of dread touched her as she saw a small wad of bloody phlegm at the back of his mouth. Lamar had attacked the tech, and it was possible the blood originated with that violence. The consistency and color of the fluid troubled her, but all she could do at the moment was make a mental note and move on.

Dr. Tang left off that Sufjan song in the middle of a verse.

It took a moment, staring at the dead man, before she realized the singing had not stopped completely. Her breath caught in her throat and she froze, listening. The song continued, but not from her lips.

Dr. Tang turned. The crinkle of her hazmat suit seemed to disrupt the singer, and the words ceased abruptly. She frowned, staring around the room. There were seven bodies here—two jihadi terrorists, two techs, two sentries, and Lamar Curtis. The room might be fifteen feet by twenty, and it was made quite cold by the depth and the draft that slipped up through the ventilation shaft. She couldn't feel the draft in her suit, but the temperature seemed to have dropped since she had entered the room.

She walked to the door and into the corridor. A gently sloping staircase went up to the next level, just twenty feet away, where another hallway led back toward the atrium. Sergeant Dunlap had recruited one of the grad students, outfitted her with a filtration mask, and posted her as a guard up there to make sure nobody else was exposed to the bodies, but that hadn't been her voice.

The singing had ceased, but a strange sensation gnawed at her. Sometimes, after her mother's death, when she had been singing while doing homework in her bedroom, she would get the sudden inescapable feeling that her father stood outside the door, listening to her.

Dr. Tang had that feeling now, as if someone had been out there in the corridor just a moment before, listening to her sing. She stared into the barely lit corridor and up the stairs, then turned the other direction and gazed into the real darkness of the east wing, certain she was being observed. That she was not alone.

Nothing moved or breathed in the corridor, so after a moment, she reentered her makeshift morgue. This deep, no light from above filtered through the ventilation shaft. It carried air through carved stone, up into another chamber or through a curve somewhere, but the draft shifted and moved and whispered.

Someone upstairs, she thought. That was the only explanation.

A drop of sweat slid down the small of her back, inside her shirt and the hazmat suit. Cold as it was, she could feel it beading on her forehead. Her lips felt dry, and she wet them with her tongue, ignoring the ache in her throat.

The feeling of being observed remained, but she had a job to do, and so she returned to it.

The sentries and the jihadis could wait. The corpses of the techs had been her baseline. Now she moved on to Lamar and began to remove his clothing. She found a wallet, two pens, a small tin of breath mints, and—secreted in the inside pocket of his zippered sweatshirt—a small black journal bound in three rubber bands. Dr. Tang set all of this aside as she continued to undress him. She had known Lamar only briefly, but now the intimacy unsettled her . . . until she recalled that this man had risked all their lives by buckling to whatever pressure or promise the New Caliphate had employed.

She saw the rash when she removed his shirt. Angry red, raised blisters ran from the center of his chest along his left side. There were some on his left arm as well. Even with the hazmat suit protecting her, she wanted to rush from the room. Dr. Tang had seen disease and plague, viruses of all kinds, but nobody in her field enjoyed being in the presence of the unknown. It was their job, of course, figuring out what it was and what it might do, but the sight of that rash was enough to make her forget the singing she'd heard, at least for a time.

His groin and thighs also showed the rash, and there were bruises on his legs that she could not explain, but it was when she pulled up his right eyelid that Dr. Tang felt the deepest dread. Both eyes had a red hue, and a bit of blood had pooled in the corner of the right one. She'd helped to fight the spread of Ebola in West Africa, and memories of those nightmarish days surged in her mind now. This wasn't the same, but the rash and the red eyes were familiar enough to haunt her.

This woman with a fever. This woman who found herself hearing things, even seeing things. Hallucinating. There were many symptoms at play here, and if the damned jar actually contained a virus, it was certainly possible that there could be more than one. The myth suggested it.

Whatever had infected Lamar, it hadn't been a myth.

She wondered if that had been part of his calculus, one of the reasons he had betrayed them. His eyes hadn't been that hue when she'd first met him, so that symptom would have had to develop immediately before or after his death. But the rash, at least, wasn't new, and it would have terrified him.

Dr. Tang found herself singing that Sufjan song again.

"All things go."

Dr. Tang had been on her knees. Now she sat back on her haunches and stared at Lamar's corpse. Whatever else might be going on above- or belowground, there could no longer be any question—there was some kind of contagion in Derveyî.

She glanced at Lamar's belongings. Without a lab, without proper equipment, she wasn't going to be able to get much by way of solid answers—only guesswork, and she had never liked guesswork. But the little book with its multicolored rubber bands might contain some clues if Lamar had made any notes about his illness. Dr. Tang picked up the book, considered looking at it herself, then realized this was something Sophie would want to do. Lamar had been her friend and part of her team. Dr. Tang had never been very good at considering the feelings of others, but once in a while she surprised herself.

The USAMRIID tech kit had included sterile sample bags. Dr. Tang opened one, inserted Lamar's wallet, pens, mints, and the journal, then resealed the bag. It felt somehow heavier than it ought to.

As she stood, she heard a cry out in the corridor. Without thinking, she ran toward the sound. Only as she left the room did she realize how foolish she'd been, that this might be another attack and that she had no weapon and no protection other than an unarmed grad student named Zehra.

But when she ran into the hall, she saw it wasn't Zehra who had cried out.

A man stood a dozen feet to her left, in the shadows of the east wing. Long-bearded, draped in cloth, he held a child by the arm as he beat her. The child cried out again, raising her other arm to defend herself, which infuriated the man even more. He clutched her arm, twisted it behind her. The snap of bone echoed through the stone corridor, and yet her scream seemed only a whisper.

The man hurled her to the ground and kicked her, but suddenly no sound came from either of them. Not even the sound of flesh upon flesh. The girl turned to look at Dr. Tang as if pleading with her, and though they had felt so tangible in the gloom of the barely lit corridor a moment ago, the girl now seemed a phantom. A specter with pain and terror in her eyes.

Dr. Tang found herself as soundless as these phantoms, for she thought she recognized the girl, though she hadn't seen her in many years, and even then only in a mirror.

Then they were gone, as if they had never been there at all.

Soon, Walker thought. The firefight aboveground would end soon. No way could some upstart jihadi army get the better of the hundred or so American and Kurdish fighters in the camp. Even if the odds were against the coalition fighters, air support would show up soon enough. It couldn't take much more than two hours for them to scramble a couple of combat helicopters and get them here . . . unless they were engaged elsewhere. That last part was his fear. Had the New Caliphate started trouble elsewhere, drawn away the most likely air support to some other conflict? If someone needed to cut through red tape to get the support they needed, how long would that take? An extra hour? Two?

Walker told himself not to worry. The coalition forces topside could take care of themselves. But the courageous volunteer Sergeant Dunlap had assigned to monitor the situation at the mouth of Derveyî had yet to come running down with good news, and in this case, no news was bad news.

He told himself it would be over by sunrise. The U.N. peacekeepers would arrive shortly after that. USAMRIID had been informed of the murders of their techs, and a full emergency response team was en route. The jar would be taken away, and a mobile lab would be installed in the camp. Derveyî's staff would be examined, starting with those not suspected of exposure to the jar, and if they seemed healthy they would be transported to a secure facility where they would undergo a period of observation, just to be certain. The others—those who'd been inside the Pandora Room or who'd been near the jar after the camera bag had fallen—would take a little longer to get cleared, but they would be all right.

Walker told himself that.

The problem was the jar. He doubted very much that the U.N. would decide to put the jar into American hands, but he thought it highly likely that USAMRIID would be tasked with transporting it. If he had to guess, Walker suspected it would be remanded to a special research lab in Switzerland. In his tenure with the National Science Foundation, other potentially dangerous items had vanished inside that lab for study by the U.N. science council and never seen again. In this case, Walker's job was to make sure that did not happen. It would have been impossible for him to get the jar out of Derveyî now, with the firefight raging aboveground, and just as impossible once USAMRIID came and really clamped down on the quarantine. Walker would be stuck here while the jar was spirited away.

Somehow, he had to make sure that didn't happen, but there were other obstacles to contend with first, all of which focused on keeping himself and Kim alive—and the others in Derveyî as well, if at all possible.

What troubled him the most was Charlie. His son had grown up accustomed to him being away for long periods, but Walker had been trying to change that. At first the boy had not wanted to depend on him, but Walker had promised to call him every week when he was traveling for work. Tomorrow, he and Charlie were due to have their weekly phone call, but he had a feeling he was going to disappoint his son, one way or another.

For the moment, he was glad to have a task on which to focus, to distract him from everything else. Dr. Tang had caught him as he returned from the surface, drawn him aside, and told him she thought there were people in the abandoned east wing who were not a part of the Beneath Project. Not jihadis, she said, or at least she did not think so. One of them had been a little girl.

The story sounded crazy, but Walker had not wanted to share that observation with Dr. Tang and he did not mind the diversion, so he had told her he would do a little exploring of his own.

Much of the underground labyrinth was empty, abandoned. Some spaces still had lighting rigs and power cords, but others were as dark as the darkest places he had ever been. As dark as the sea caves in Guatemala, where hungry things with sharp teeth and fish tails had come out of the water and trapped his team. Killed most of them.

This darkness meant nothing to him. He'd survived so much worse. But he still kept his filtration mask on, just in case.

Whatever work the Beneath Project had done in the east wing had been halted. Some evidence of their activity remained, including several sawhorses blocking passages and a few lighting rigs that had been left in place but disconnected from the dig's generators. He passed the room Dr. Tang had converted to a temporary morgue and moved deeper into the eastern part of the warren of tunnels and caves and stairs until he came to utter darkness.

Slipping a small but powerful flashlight from his pocket, he clicked it on, moved around a sawhorse, and strode carefully into the dark. The flashlight beam turned the corridors and abandoned rooms into eerie, yawning holes. Walker felt as if he were diving in some nameless depth, the beam of light his only illumination in this strange and silent ocean.

Then a cry broke the silence. He froze, listening intently to discern the source of the cry and for any further sounds. He heard panicked voices, speaking in hushed tones, and then another startled cry. Rapid footfalls echoed along the corridor, rushing toward him, but even with his flashlight piercing the darkness he saw nothing until a cold blue light began to glow. One of the voices rose to a shout, a woman, on the edge of panic.

Walker switched the flashlight to his left hand and drew his acquired gun with his right, hurrying up the tunnel. To the left, a passageway opened to a ramp, and he saw two figures rushing up toward him, little more than silhouettes behind the sphere of blue light.

"Just go!" a man's voice urged. "Move!"

"It's following."

"You don't know—"

"It's following!"

Walker took a defensive posture, aimed the flashlight and the gun at the same time.

"Stop where you are and identify yourselves!" he barked.

The man cried out in alarm.

"Jesus," the woman said from the darkness behind that blue light, "you scared the shit out of me."

The blue light had stopped moving, and now Walker could see it came from a handheld lantern. The silhouettes had taken shape, their faces in strange blue shadows in the tunnel.

"Identify yourselves," he said again, less urgently.

"Fuck that, masked man. We work here. Who the hell are you?" the man said.

Walker took two steps forward. "My name is Walker. I'm armed, and I'm asking for your names."

The man had been carrying the lantern. Now he lifted it up so that their faces were better illuminated. "I'm Dmitri Koines."

"You're the cook."

"Rachel Porter," said the woman, her face twisted up in a mix of emotions—anger and something else. "Can you put the gun away, please? We don't want to be here right now."

She glanced back over her shoulder as Walker processed what she'd said and what he'd heard.

"You were shouting." He slid the gun back into his rear waistband. "What was that about?"

Dmitri lowered the lantern now, and those blue shadows enveloped their faces again. As Walker flashed the beam of his own flashlight at them, he saw them exchange a hesitant look, and then Rachel glanced over her shoulder.

"Look," he said, "with all that's going on here, you need to tell me what just happened. You're walking around in the dark in a part of the dig that's been basically blocked off, I hear shouting, and I'd like to know what the shouting's about. I'm not the only one who's going to ask that question, so you might as well—"

"Ghosts," Dmitri said, locking eyes with Walker. "We saw ghosts."

"Jesus, Dmitri," Rachel hissed.

"Well, what else would you call them?"

"It just sounds so stupid saying it out loud."

Dmitri nodded in agreement, then glanced at Walker. "It sounds stupid. We're going to look like assholes when you talk to Dr. Durand, but I don't know how to say it differently. Apparitions. We were down by one of the blocked exits—the ceiling caved in centuries ago, and there's no way past it."

"Why would you two . . ." Walker started to ask, but he saw them exchange a different sort of glance, and he realized why they'd wanted to be alone together. "Okay, go on."

"They were fighting," Rachel said. "Two of them, but one had the upper hand. The one kept smashing the other's head into the ground, and I heard the noises, even grunting. The smack of his skull—"

Dmitri stared at her. "That's not what I saw."

Walker moved nearer to them as they began to argue. They were both sweating and skittish in the light of his flashlight, irritated by his closeness.

"One was a woman. She straddled his chest and strangled him. They were in among the rubble, so I couldn't see very well, but—"

"What are you . . . that's not right," Rachel argued. "It was two men. They were in the alcove there on the left, just before the rockfall area."

The two of them stared at each other, and their expressions seemed to slacken with confusion.

Walker used his flashlight beam to examine them more closely. They were visibly exhausted and pale, despite Dmitri's Greek complexion. Their eyes were wide, with dark circles beneath, and he could not deny they looked unhealthy. But it was when Dmitri turned to address Rachel again that Walker felt a tremor of fear. A bruise-purple lesion marred the side of Dmitri's neck. It could have been some kind of love bite, a hickey from whatever the two had been up to down in that tunnel, but that was not at all what it looked like.

"I feel so stupid," Rachel said. "Saying it out loud makes it sound ridiculous, but I know what I saw."

Walker wasn't sure about that. "I'll walk you back to the atrium, but I don't want you going to your quarters yet. I'll go see Sophie—Dr. Durand—and explain the situation, but I want you to wait in the atrium for Dr. Tang. She needs to take a look at the two of you."

"Who the hell is Dr. Tang?" Rachel asked.

"Just do it, please," Walker said. "I promise I'll bring Sophie to you. There'll be nobody in the atrium at this hour, I don't think. I'll find you a place to wait, and I'll bring them to you."

Both still rattled, they followed him. Walker kept up a brisk pace but still wished they could move faster. Alarm bells were going off in his head that had nothing to do with ghosts. Behind him, Rachel began to complain that she felt unwell. Dmitri admitted to feeling slightly queasy.

"It's hot in here," he added. "It's usually cold at night."

They had almost made it back to the atrium when the cook asked for a rest. Walker turned, prepared to urge him on, but saw that his olive skin had turned ashen. They had a small stairwell to descend and they would be in a tunnel that fed into the atrium, but Dmitri looked like he might pass out.

"I need to sit for a minute," Dmitri said, but it seemed as if he might be talking to the air rather than to Rachel or Walker. "Just a minute, okay?"

Rachel nodded and voiced her agreement, but she seemed distracted by an itch on her scalp. She glanced back the way they'd come, but they had moved beyond the sawhorses now, and there were lights strung along this part of the tunnel that were still attached to the generator. Not all the lighting rigs were on, but enough so that the shadows back the way they'd come seemed less ominous now. Less full of ghosts.

Walker made a decision. "Sit. I'll bring Sophie and Dr. Tang here."

"I'm sick, aren't I?" Dmitri said, his voice cracking. His hand went to the side of his neck, and he used a fingernail to pick at the lesion there.

"Don't—" Walker started.

"I knew it," Dmitri went on. "I saw this in the mirror an hour ago and tried to tell myself it was nothing. I thought, *No, not me.* I don't know what happened to the jar, but I know we're fucking quarantined and you people are in those damned masks, saying you're protecting us when you're just protecting yourselves."

"That's not true," Walker argued, but Dmitri's eyes had gone glassy and he wasn't listening.

Rachel slid down the wall, slumping to the ground. She stared at Dmitri, tilted her head, trying to get a glimpse of the side of his neck. "You thought you were . . . infected or something? And you still brought me down there? We still . . ."

She didn't finish the thought, but Walker didn't need elaboration.

"I'm coming with you," she said, struggling to stand. "I can't stay with him. If he's sick, I'm not staying here."

"You have to, Rachel. If he has anything contagious, you've already got it and we can't risk transmitting it to others. You look pale. Maybe feverish. And I can't help thinking these ghosts might be hallucinations."

Rachel laughed darkly. "Well, at least there's a bright side."

"What bright side?" Dmitri said, an edge of sorrow in his voice. His eyes had filled with unshed tears. "I'd rather it be ghosts."

Walker thought that, on the whole, he would also have preferred ghosts.

"Sit tight," he said. "I'll get Sophie and we'll decide what to do."

"Take your time," Dmitri said. "We're under quarantine and trapped in a man-made cave system. It isn't like we're going anywhere."

FIFTEEN

Sophie couldn't help wishing she had never left New York, or that she'd moved to Paris with her mother. Her irritation with her boss had grown into venom. Alex Jarota had planned to exploit her for his personal glory, and now he had abdicated any responsibility for what happened next. The old adage insisted that a captain go down with his ship, but Alex had been the first to abandon the boat.

Walker, she thought angrily.

She'd had it with men who weren't what they appeared to be. Steven's face flashed through her mind, and she allowed a moment of resentment before firmly reminding herself that in that case, she was the one who had abandoned ship. But that didn't make her less disdainful of Alex's attitude, and it didn't mean she was willing to put up with being deceived.

"What are you going to say when you find Walker?" Beyza asked, hurrying to keep up with her.

Sophie reached the narrow, curving stairwell that led from the west wing down to one of the balconies overlooking the atrium.

"Don't worry about what I'll say," she said, descending swiftly, her footfalls echoing off the walls below. "Worry about what I'll do. I'm in the mood to punch someone in the throat, and it might as well be Ben Walker."

She came around the corner and nearly collided with him. Beyza swore, bumping into Sophie from behind. If Walker hadn't grabbed her shoulders, she would have stumbled into his arms like they were in some old romantic comedy.

Glad as she was to be saved that embarrassment, she pushed him away.

"Watch the hands," she said.

"Just saving us from smashing heads," he replied. "I was on my way to see you."

"Coincidence. I was looking for you."

The yellow industrial light of the bulbs strung along the stairwell made his eyes look black instead of brown, like they were nothing but dark pits in his skull.

"So I heard. Though I'd prefer you not punch me in the throat."

"What if you've got it coming?"

Walker glanced past her. "What about it, Beyza? Do I have it coming? You clearly know what this is about."

They both turned to look at the other woman. Beyza narrowed her eyes. "I'm sure you can guess, Walker. You're not who you say you are."

Sophie studied his face. At first he seemed ready to argue, and the good-natured confusion in his expression had a rough charm to it, but then he exhaled and his face changed entirely.

"You know what? We've got bigger problems than this, so I'm going to give you the short version, if that's all right?"

"Try me," Sophie said. "I'll even help out. You work for a different agency than the one you claim. I just don't know which one."

Walker raised his hands, palms facing her as if surrendering. "Succinct. I like that. I can't say much, except that I do work for the American government and my job includes making sure the jar doesn't fall into the wrong hands. Under present circumstances, it also includes trying to keep the people down here alive."

"So you're a professional liar," Beyza said, her tone frosty.

"It's part of the job, yes."

Sophie narrowed her eyes. "Kim knows this. That's why she made sure you kept that gun."

"Yes."

"I'm glad to hear it," Sophie said. "I don't like being lied to, Walker.

If there are things you can't tell me, be honest about it. As for the rest, when we're no longer under attack or under quarantine, I'll decide if I like you or hate you. Until then, do your job."

"Yes, ma'am," he replied. "Only that might be harder than I'd thought an hour ago. I'm happy you think me having useful secrets is good news, but I'm sorry to say there's some bad news to go along with it."

Sophie didn't want to ask the question.

Beyza did it for her. "How bad?"

"Follow me," Walker replied, turning back the way he'd come. It wasn't an answer, but the expression on his face had been answer enough.

Dr. Tang felt words on her tongue and pressed her lips together to keep them from coming out. She had waited for Walker in the atrium, but it had been Beyza who had come to find her, instructing her to seek Walker and Sophie in the south wing. A nervous Beyza had gone off to her own quarters and left Dr. Tang to fend for herself.

Now she stood sweating in her hazmat suit and listened to the cook and his girlfriend talk about everything except the ghosts they had supposedly seen, and she wanted details. They had to be hallucinations, Dr. Tang felt certain of that, but how strange that all three of them had interpreted those hallucinations as something spectral.

They were in Dmitri's room. Rachel apparently normally shared her quarters with someone named Marissa, but she'd been sleeping with the cook for months, ever since Dmitri's former roommate—the original site manager—had been dismissed due to behavioral issues, including being high on whatever drugs he might get his hands on while in town. These were more details than Dr. Tang required, but once she'd begun talking, a frightened Rachel seemed unable to stop.

Walker had left on other errands, and Sophie had instructed the others living in the south wing to remain in their rooms. The nervous, frightened Rachel continued to babble, revealing her deep respect for Sophie along with her belief that Sophie had never really noticed her, and generally thought the grad students were extensions of her own identity instead of people in their own right. While Sophie stared at her in astonishment, Rachel also went on to confess that she had been fucking Dmitri mostly out of boredom.

The cook's head did a slow swivel, and he stared at her. "Did you just say that out loud?" he asked, seeming as amused as he was insulted.

Rachel started to cry. "I did, didn't I? Oh, my God. What is wrong with me?" She sat down on the edge of the cot and stared up at Sophie. "Do something."

Dr. Tang glanced at Dmitri. "Is she not usually like this?"

"Not that I've seen," he said, reaching up to scratch at his arm but then lowering his hand, self-conscious about the rash. "She's just freaking out. She's afraid."

"I am," Rachel agreed. "I'm freaking out. I'd try to sneak out right after you leave, but I'm afraid the soldiers will shoot me. Jesus, I need a sedative." She buried her face in her hands. "Seriously, Doc, do you have anything?"

Dr. Tang sat next to her on the cot, the hazmat suit crinkling conspicuously. "I wish I did, Rachel. I could use one myself. We're getting some supplies from camp, so if I get something, I'll bring it for you."

The woman glanced up hopefully. "Really?"

"I promise. Now—"

Voices in the corridor made Sophie snap her head around. She swore under her breath and stepped from the room.

"Marissa. Bastien, listen, get back into your rooms, please," she said out in the hall, the words seeming to slither through the doorway, whispering along the stone walls. "I know you're worried. We all are. But please try to get some rest. We're going to have a long day tomorrow."

The voices argued with her, politely but urgently, judging by their tone, and the conversation moved farther down the hallway. Dr. Tang shifted her attention back to Rachel and Dmitri, alone with them now.

"Walker told Sophie that you saw ghosts."

Rachel laughed softly. "Wow, you just threw that out there."

Dr. Tang shrugged inside the plastic suit. "Seems like the best approach. It's not every day you hear a good ghost story."

Dmitri sat on the cot opposite them and hung his head. "I don't know what I saw now. What does it matter? That guy Walker thinks we were hallucinating, anyway."

"Sure didn't feel like a hallucination," Rachel said.

"Have you had a lot of those?" Dr. Tang asked, smiling behind the clear plastic mask of her headpiece.

"One time, on mushrooms in college, I thought my hand could paint the sky." Rachel's eyes were deeply earnest. "And when I was six, I thought my dolls were having a party without me and cried all day. My mom told me it was a dream, but I could have sworn I heard them right before I opened my eyes."

Despite the things she had said about their sex life, Dmitri leaned toward her, eyes narrowed with concern. "Love, are you all right?"

Rachel snickered at that. "Of course not. Neither of us is all right. Probably none of us."

"The ghosts," Dr. Tang prodded.

She didn't want to seem too eager, didn't want them to suspect she had a personal interest in this question of ghosts, but she needn't have worried. Both of them were too focused on their circumstances to pay much attention to her. Dr. Tang listened as they recounted what they'd seen, shuddering as she recalled her own experience. Rachel had witnessed an act of brutality, but it seemed Dmitri's ghosts had been engaged in violent sex or some kind of sacrificial rite.

If these were mere hallucinations, they certainly shared a theme. The knowledge sent a spider of dread scuttling along her spine.

"So what do you think?" Rachel asked.

Dr. Tang tilted the woman's head back, studying the dark spots under her chin. The gloves of her hazmat suit weren't as thin as she'd have liked, but she felt for Rachel's lymph nodes and they did seem swollen.

"I think you're both ill."

"Obviously," Dmitri said. "But the ghosts?"

"I've never encountered evidence of their existence," Dr. Tang replied. "I'd prefer a natural explanation."

"So we're ill," Rachel said. "That's the best you can do? Aren't you supposed to be the expert?"

Smiles did not come naturally to Dr. Tang, but she smiled then, as best she could. Best not to tell them their symptoms reminded her of not one but several viruses but still mystified her. Had they been exposed to some unknown microbial bacteria? It certainly seemed that way.

"I'll need more to go on than a cursory physical examination," Dr. Tang said. "In a hospital environment, with the right tests and labs and equipment."

She stood, aware of Rachel and Dmitri watching her closely, stunned that she would just walk out without giving them more answers—answers she didn't have, though they seemed to believe otherwise.

"For now, I have to insist that you stay in this room. The others on this corridor may already be exposed to whatever's causing your rash, but we can't take any risks. Sit tight here. Get some rest. Try to sleep."

"Not likely," Dmitri muttered.

"Try," Dr. Tang said, walking to the curtained doorway. "Whatever's going on, rest will help. Meanwhile, I'll be back to check on you in a couple of hours, and then again at sunrise." She lifted the curtain and held it open as she stepped out, turning back toward them. "If you develop any other symptoms or things worsen considerably, give a shout and someone will come find me."

"And if we see more ghosts?"

Dr. Tang did not smile this time. "Say hello for me. Trust me, they're a product of fever, triggered by the virus."

Ghosts did not exist. Of course not.

She let the curtain fall and paused a moment to breathe and think. When she glanced up, she saw Sophie emerging from another of the staff rooms on the corridor.

"Anything?" Sophie asked.

Dr. Tang approached her, wary of being overheard. "Not here."

"Do you have any sign of rash?" Sophie said, eyes narrowing.

"Not that I'm aware of. No itching, anyway." Dr. Tang had experienced some symptoms that indicated illness, including chills and shortness of breath—and the ghosts, she couldn't forget those—but exhaustion and being inside the suit could contribute to some of that. Now wasn't the time for that conversation.

Sophie nodded. "No itch for me, either." She gestured toward the room she'd just left. "At least a couple of others have the beginnings of a rash. And one didn't want to let either of us examine him, so I don't know what to make of that."

Dr. Tang gestured for Sophie to precede her, and the two of them headed down the corridor. The lights flickered. Her heart jumped a bit at the idea that the generator might shut down, but it lasted only a moment. Surely they had a backup generator. *Nothing to worry about*, she told herself. There were plenty of things to be afraid of down in Derveyî besides the dark.

"Doctor?" a voice called behind her.

She turned just as a woman came into the corridor, coughing loudly.

"Marissa, go back into your room," Sophie said.

Instead, someone else pushed through a curtain. The man had a thin golden beard, the sort of thing that resulted from shaving every few weeks and then not bothering in between. His cheeks were flushed pink, his expression deeply anguished.

"Dr. Durand," he said, "you gotta give me one."

"Sean, I told you—"

"You gotta," Sean wheedled. "Not for me, for my mom."

Dr. Tang backed up a step as the man came toward her, hands outstretched and pleading.

"I'm the only one who takes care of her," he said, tears at the corners of his eyes. "Something happens to me, she's got no real income. Nobody'll look out for her. Don't you get it? I need one of those goddamn suits!"

His voice rose to a shout.

Marissa coughed again, erupting in a jag of wheezing, choking coughs that bent her over in the corridor, blocking Sean from advancing any farther. Sophie took Dr. Tang by the arm, and it took a moment for her to realize Sophie wanted her to keep moving, to leave these people alone.

Dr. Tang slipped by her and started for the door. One of the soldiers would be out there now. Walker had said he would get Corporal Taejon to come up or Dunlap to assign someone. A quarantine within a quarantine. It seemed absurd, but also the very least they could do.

"Give me a fucking suit," Sean demanded. "I'm not kidding, Sophie. I swear to God—"

Marissa's cough turned wet. She cried out in pain. At the door, Dr. Tang turned to see the woman doubled over. The lights flickered, and for a moment the dust eddying in that light seemed to form a figure. But then that wet, violent rattle came again, and Marissa coughed a wad of something thick and dark onto the stone floor. It might've been red, darkened by the strange lights, but it didn't look like blood to Dr. Tang. Just black sludge.

"What the hell—" Sophie began.

"Doc, you're not listening!" Sean screamed, spittle flying from his mouth. He shoved Marissa aside. "*I want* a fucking suit!"

Sophie shifted into a defensive posture, ready for a fight. Dr. Tang took another step back, feeling vulnerable although she was the only one in a hazmat suit. Sophie wore only a filtration mask, and if Sean ripped off the mask it would leave her exposed.

"Okay," she said, her voice cracking. She would give Sean a hazmat suit, or at least lie to him to calm him if that meant avoiding violence now. "I'll get you a—"

Then Sean lifted his head and she saw his eyes clearly for the first time, saw how bloodshot they'd become, so red that only blotches of white remained. Blood ran from his nose, onto his lips. He reached for Sophie.

Gasping for breath, Marissa managed to grab his shirt.

Sophie punched him as he turned, caught him hard in the temple. Sean staggered backward, and in that moment two others came out of their rooms. From the back of the corridor, Dmitri pushed out through his curtain.

"Dmitri, I told you—" Dr. Tang said.

But then Dmitri and the others were on Sean. He roared and bucked against them as they dragged him to the floor. Behind and above them, the lights flickered, and again something formed in the dust in the air, a silhouette, a figure reaching its hands up toward the ceiling.

Dr. Tang saw its face, saw pure avarice, as if it reached for its darkest heart's desire. The lights winked, and it was gone. Voices shouted, but Dr. Tang glanced around and realized none of the others had seen it.

Marissa wheezed as she knelt by Sean, whom the others kept pinned to the floor. She lifted the bottom of her shirt to cover her mouth as she shouted at him.

"Be still, Sean! Be still! This is not helping your mother."

He bucked once more and then began to cry, lolling his head to one side in shame. Between whimpers, he gritted his teeth and raged for a moment or two and then surrendered anew.

"You're sick," Marissa said, more gently this time.

Dmitri glanced around at them. "By now we're all sick."

They looked up at Sophie for confirmation. She was their leader after all, but there she stood in her filtration mask, and Dr. Tang in a hazmat suit. Sophie had first put on that mask for their protection, but they wouldn't see it that way now, Dr. Tang knew.

"Go," Dmitri said. "Figure this out. I don't want to die here."

"Nobody's died from this," Sophie replied.

She didn't say the word *yet*, but Dr. Tang felt sure they'd all heard it implied.

Marissa coughed again, and all but Sean turned toward her. Dr. Tang thought it was a good thing they hadn't seen her cough up that black sludge or seen the figure swirling in the flickering lights. They were frightened now, but not terrified. Terror would make things so much worse.

"We'll do all we can," Sophie said. "I'm going to get Kim and tell her we need evac to a hospital immediately. U.N. peacekeepers aren't going to do us any good. They need to get us out of here."

"What about the jar?" Marissa rasped.

Dr. Tang stood behind Sophie, so she couldn't see the other woman's face, but the tone of her reply said it all.

"Fuck the jar."

SIXTEEN

Beyza nearly jumped out of her skin when she drew back the curtain to enter her room and saw Cortez sitting on the end of her bed in the dark. Only the slash of light from the corridor cast any illumination, and she held the curtain open so she could get a look at him.

"What are you doing in here?" she said quietly, urgently, voice muffled by her mask. "Are you okay?"

Cortez made a sort of huff that reminded her of her father's favorite dog. "You're joking, right?"

Beyza let the curtain drop behind her and reached out to grab the power cord that hung from overhead. She clicked on the lights, a rack of three that had been arrayed along the left side of the chamber. Cortez shied away from the brightness, but when he glanced up, she saw the sadness in his eyes.

"Perhaps *okay* is the wrong word," she admitted. The tension and anxiety caught up with her, then, and she swore under her breath.

"I'm not going to ask how you are," Cortez said. "Just come over here."

Beyza smiled wearily and went to join him. It felt strange to be in such a quiet place with this man with whom she shared such intimacy, when so much horror had been unfolding around them.

"You're not supposed to be in here," she told him. "I thought this thing between us was meant to be a secret."

"I needed to see you. To be with you," Cortez said, pushing her hair away from her eyes. "You still look silly with that mask on."

"You're still silly looking." Beyza turned her back to him. "Massage my shoulders? I'm all knotted up."

He obliged, softly at first and then more forcefully, kneading her neck and shoulders before he leaned in to kiss her in those tender places. Beyza shivered with pleasure and pain and the release of tension.

"This isn't really the time," she told him, face flushing. She took his hand and put a little distance between them, but she stayed on the bed. "Something is going on. Dmitri and Rachel are sick. Hallucinating, too."

Cortez paled. "Were you with them?"

"I didn't touch them, if that's what you're asking. I'm not stupid. Nobody coughed on me, either, but we really need to be careful. You are supposed to be confined to your quarters, for instance."

"I could be confined to *your* quarters."

He gave her that smile that always destroyed her, the one that had persuaded her into bed with him in the first place. Well, not *bed*. The first time they'd made love, it had been up on the rocky hill on top of Derveyî, on a moonless night but with an ocean of stars across the sky. And it hadn't been making love then; it had been pure fucking. Beyza could not have said if they had ever really made love, but whenever she was with Cortez, she forgot her husband, forgot how unhappy her life had been before coming onto this project. This kind, handsome, playful man was not the source of her happiness—he did not get credit for that—but he had been instrumental in her unlocking the prison of depression she'd kept herself in for years.

The idea of being quarantined in here with him was not so terrible at all. Together they could forget the people dying aboveground, and the danger they were in, and the uncertainty of what the night and the following day would bring.

"Take off your clothes," she whispered to him.

Cortez grinned.

Beyza struck him halfheartedly. "I want to make sure you don't have a rash or something."

"I'll have to inspect you, too," he said.

She smiled. "Of course."

He peeled off his shirt. Beyza started with her pants. Both of them half-naked, Cortez went to her, stroked her hair, and untied the mask from the back of her head. Beyza reached up to stop him, but then he kissed her and more of the tension left her shoulders and neck. She wanted to forget her fears and to help Cortez forget his own.

"Elio," she said when his hands began to explore.

Something moved behind the curtain, out in the hallway.

Beyza jumped, both of them turning to stare at the dark cloth over the doorway.

"Hello?" she called.

A figure shifted, just beyond the curtain, a darker silhouette.

"Professor Solak?" the figure said. "It's Sergeant Dunlap. Dr. Durand is gathering anyone who's been in the Pandora Room. She'd like you to join us in the worship chamber."

Cheeks burning, Beyza covered her mouth with both hands to stifle a cry of embarrassment or a peal of laughter, she wasn't sure which. Cortez was halfway bent over, wearing an enormous grin.

"I'm changing," Beyza said. "I'll be along as quickly as I can, Sergeant. Thank you."

Dunlap returned her thanks, and then the silhouette vanished from the hallway. They both stared at the curtain for twenty or so seconds before Cortez exhaled.

"Okay," he said, grabbing his shirt. "I guess I'll just wait here."

Beyza ripped the shirt from his hand and tossed it on the floor. "Yes, you will. You're officially quarantined to this room." She slipped her hands into the waistband of his pants and tugged them down. "But I haven't finished examining you yet."

Sophie could wait a few minutes. After all, none of them were going anywhere.

As it turned out, though Beyza had not been feeling well, Cortez proved himself to be feeling very fine indeed.

Sophie wondered how long her pulse could race so quickly without giving her a heart attack. She felt like an animal backed into a corner, a wolf trapped in its den while the hunter waits outside. At least a half hour had passed since the last loud explosion aboveground, but in the quiet of the worship chamber, she could still hear the staccato punch of gunfire ripping up the night. The sound drifted down the ventilation shafts so quietly that she could almost have imagined it, but then it would grow louder, or fall silent, and it could not be denied.

She watched as they entered, one by one—all those who had spent time in the Pandora Room. Sophie had asked Sergeant Dunlap to gather them in the worship chamber for a private meeting. Dr. Tang, Walker, Beyza, Kim, and Dunlap himself came in, found stone seats or leaned against the wall. There were a total of twelve filtration masks, and they were all accounted for. Sophie ticked them off as she glanced around the room—counting herself, there were six in the room. The sentries each had one, and that made ten. There was the grad student, Zehra, who'd volunteered and received a mask in order to be posted to watch over their makeshift morgue.

Dr. Tang had been wearing a hazmat suit but had removed it and opted for her own filtration mask again. The suits were not meant for long-term wear, but Sophie had made certain Dr. Tang kept her suit and the others close by, worried they might still be needed. The rest of the staff were confined to their quarters, so there was little chance they would be spied upon.

Someone was missing.

A shudder went through Sophie as she glanced at Beyza. "Where's Martin?"

An exhausted Beyza looked up. "I don't know." Perched on the edge of a stone bench, she glanced around the room as if to confirm he wasn't there.

"I looked for him," Dunlap said. "But I didn't have time to search everywhere."

Sophie felt a tremor in her chest. Her throat still hurt, but that seemed the least of their troubles now. The sight of what had happened to Marissa and Sean and the others had shaken her deeply. As the others waited on her to speak, all she could do was imagine herself locked inside a plague ward.

"Okay," she said, glancing around. "Let's make this quick, and when we're done here, someone needs to find Martin and make sure he's all right."

"I'll go," Beyza said.

"I'll cover your back," Dunlap replied.

Sophie nodded her thanks, then turned to Dr. Tang. "Doc, go ahead."

Dr. Tang sat unusually still. "Some of the staff are suffering from an ugly rash, along with raised lymph nodes, dark-colored lesions, and other symptoms."

"Shit," Dunlap whispered.

"Have any of you noticed a rash or sores?" Dr. Tang went on.

Sophie exhaled slowly as a chorus of negative replies went around the circle.

"We're being honest here, right?" Dunlap said.

"We have to be," Walker replied.

"My throat's killing me." The sergeant shrugged. "That's really it, other than a headache, but I'm so tired I hoped that was the reason."

"It might be," Sophie said, "but my throat is also very sore."

The others began to chime in with symptoms from headaches to minor coughs to dizziness.

"But no rash?" Sophie asked. "Nothing like that?"

"Under my jaw. There's some pain," Walker said hesitantly.

Dr. Tang went to him and used a penlight to examine him, careful not to disturb his filtration mask.

"I don't see anything, but the glands may be swollen," she said.

A quiet descended on them all as she moved from person to person, shining that light beneath their chins and into their eyes.

"So the crack in the jar released something," Walker said.

"I guess there are other ways to explain this," Dunlap replied, "but I can't think of any logical ones."

"I was sick before the jar cracked," Sophie told them.

"Lamar had the rash," Dr. Tang said. "Badly. He had other symptoms, too, including eyes so bloodshot they'd gone totally red by the time he was shot, or maybe while he was dying."

Sophie winced, but Dr. Tang didn't seem to notice her grief. The woman didn't mean to be callous, she knew, but the thought of Lamar cut her deeply.

Beyza spoke up. "Lamar spent three times as much time in the Pandora Room as any of us. Even when he was just working on translating, he'd sit in there. He said he'd rather look at the original than the photos while he was trying to puzzle it all out. Maybe we were all exposed to something in there, even before the crack, but Lamar just had more of it."

"What about the others? The rash?" Walker asked. "None of them were in the Pandora Room."

Kim crossed her arms. "Let's go through the steps. Lamar stashes the jar in his camera bag, wrapped in his sweatshirt. When he was shot, he fell on top of it. Assuming that impact cracked the seal, it's possible the first bit of whatever came out of the jar got into his system then, in the moments when he was dying."

Sophie frowned. "Unless the crack happened earlier, in the Pandora Room. It's hard for me to imagine him attacking the sentries and those techs, but he did. He . . . Lamar killed those people. Maybe in the middle of that, the jar was knocked over, and the seal cracked then. He wraps it up in the sweatshirt, stashes it in the camera case, and whatever microbes are released are trapped there until . . ."

She buried her face in her hands, mask and all. "Fuck," she said. And then shouted. "Fuck!"

"Until we took it out of the case," Dr. Tang said, "and packed it into the contagion box."

"We all started wearing masks before that," Walker reminded them. "We thought we'd been exposed, but—"

"I'm lost," Sergeant Dunlap said. "We're talking before and after the crack, right? Two different effects?"

Sophie nodded slowly. "At least two. Remember the legend? 'All the curses of humanity.'"

"Or all the blessings," Beyza said.

Dr. Tang whipped her head around. "I think we can rule out the blessings at this point. But I'd like to point out that Dmitri was very close to Martin when he carried the camera case through the atrium.

Giving him a hard time. There were several others there, but you'll have to identify them. If we're trying to establish a contagion model and we begin with the jar—"

"Cortez," Beyza said, burying her face in her hands.

"What's that?" Sophie said.

Beyza glanced up. "Cortez was there. He grabbed Dmitri or something."

"We need to have a look at him," Dr. Tang said.

"I . . . I just did," Beyza said, glancing sheepishly around the room. "About ten minutes ago."

"What do you mean?" Dr. Tang asked. "He's supposed to be confined to his quarters."

Sophie stared at Beyza, surprised she would share that bit of information. Beyza was both very private and very married.

"You and Cortez?" Kim asked.

The worship chamber went very quiet. Even the gunfire seemed to have paused.

Dr. Tang leaned toward Beyza. "You took your mask off?"

Kim gave a nervous laugh. "Of course she had her mask off, Erika. Let's move on, shall we?"

Dr. Tang flashed an irritated look at the entire group. "Don't do that again. Any of you. Whatever this is, it is moving very quickly. If Cortez is in Professor Solak's quarters, he should remain there until I can examine him. We'll need to track this from person to person."

Walker stood, pacing, staring at the floor as he walked as if he could see through to the center of the world. "I'm still not sure how this works, with the jar causing some effects before and some after."

"Maybe the mortar used for the seal is porous," Dunlap offered.

Walker nodded and pointed at him. "Okay, yeah. It wasn't meant to be, but thousands of years pass and it dries out enough that some kind of contagion gets through, enough to have . . . some effect on everyone who spends any length of time in that room."

"But when Lamar steals it, he cracks the seal," Dunlap added. "Now something else is coming out."

"I didn't believe in the danger," Beyza said. "It's a myth."

Kim glanced at her. "Walker and I have met myths before."

Dr. Tang cocked her head. "What does that mean?"

"There's something more going on here," Kim replied. "There's natural science, and then there is what I cannot help thinking of as unnatural science."

"Kim—" Walker began.

But Kim would not be halted. She leaned back against the wall and crossed her arms as though to give herself warmth. Above her mask, her eyes were wide, pupils fully dilated in search of brighter light.

"I'm talking about evil," she said. "All the curses of humanity."

Sergeant Dunlap scoffed, smiled as if he thought she must have been kidding. Sophie could see from her expression that she wasn't.

"That's ridiculous," Beyza said, studying her as if she'd appeared out of thin air.

Dr. Tang coughed lightly. "Well, perhaps not." She glanced around as they all turned to stare at her. "Dmitri and Rachel said they'd seen ghosts. I've seen them as well, and I'm willing to bet some of you have, too."

Sophie stared at her. She didn't seem like the kind of woman to joke about this—or anything else, for that matter. Dr. Tang looked around the circle, trying to get a glimpse of their expressions despite the masks eclipsing the lower halves of their faces.

"Or maybe it's just me," Dr. Tang said, cocking her head in her quirky fashion.

"I might've seen something," Walker said. "Just a glimpse. Corner of my eye. I thought someone was there."

"That's happened to me in my apartment," Dunlap replied.

"It happens more here," Beyza said quietly.

Sophie stared at her. "Something you want to say, Professor?"

Beyza narrowed her eyes as if she'd been wounded, and she looked up at Sophie. "You really haven't seen anything?"

Sophie sighed. "Like Walker. Maybe a glimpse. I chalked it up to exhaustion. I still think that's what it was."

"Not me," Beyza said. "What I saw was . . . it was awful."

She went no further, and it seemed clear she would not say more, so Sophie decided not to push her. Instead, she turned to Dr. Tang.

"Ghosts," she said aloud, just to taste the word on her tongue. The flavor was ridiculous. "I'm sorry, but I have trouble with that. What's happening here is some kind of virus. Contagion. Like we said, maybe more than one kind, but—"

Dr. Tang pointed at her. "You just said it. Maybe more than one kind. These hallucinations are manifesting in specific ways, but with apologies to Kim, I'm not willing to assume there's anything supernatural about them. I will admit they scared the hell out of me."

"You may be right, Doctor," Kim said, her tone crisp and cold. "But if you had been on Mount Ararat with Walker and me, you would know there are things in the world science cannot yet explain."

"Or doesn't want to explain," Walker added.

Sophie glanced back and forth between them and made the connection she ought to have made before. "Mount Ararat," she said. "You were part of the Ark Project."

Kim nodded slowly. Her eyes closed, and she muttered something too quietly, the words lost behind her mask.

Sergeant Dunlap threw up his hands. "What's 'the Ark Project'?"

Beyza turned to him. "A couple of years ago? They thought they'd found Noah's Ark?"

Dunlap shrugged. "I've been in Iraq a long time."

Sophie kept her gaze on Kim and Walker, shifting from one to the other. "A lot of people died, including nearly all the archaeologists involved."

"Suddenly, I don't feel as comforted by the impending reinforcements," Beyza said.

It was an offhand comment, but Walker shot her a withering glance.

"We did all we could," he said. "It's a miracle we got off the mountain."

Kim shuddered again. She took a series of deep breaths, her whole body shifting with each lungful of air. "You don't understand."

"There was a storm," Sophie said, recalling the news reports. "And someone on the team lost it, started killing people."

"That's the story the media told," Walker said, his eyes turning cold. "They found more than timber in that cave. Ark or not, there was something else inside it."

The sorrow in his voice was unmistakable, but Sophie heard more than sorrow. This time, she heard fear.

"You understand how hard it is to believe, don't you?" she asked.

"Of course we do," Kim said. "It wasn't easy for us, either. Maybe Dr. Tang is right. What she saw, what the others saw, might have some other explanation. I'm just saying don't assume. Don't . . ."

Walker put a hand on her back. "You okay?"

Her voice cracked when she spoke again, fighting tears. "I've been struggling with the trauma of that since we came down off the mountain. Some days I can almost forget. But now here we are, in another cave, and I'd do anything to get out of here. I'm the one who had to order the quarantine. Trust me, the irony is not lost on me."

"We're all claustrophobic after a while. You've been fine till now," Walker began, trying to soothe her.

Kim rounded on him, eyes flaring. "I haven't been fine! I've been crawling out of my skin since we got here. That's the whole reason I wanted you with me!"

Silence enveloped the worship chamber. The others stared at Walker and Kim, but then as if at some unspoken cue, they all looked away. Walker said something too softly for the rest to hear, and when Sophie glanced up, he was shifting to be nearer to Kim, taking her hand. In that moment, Sophie hated the Pandora Room and everything about the work they'd done.

She wanted to go home.

"Evil exists," Kim said with a hitching breath. "Trust us. Whatever's here with us, I feel it. I can practically taste it, whatever it is."

The words sank in. The people in the worship chamber grew uneasy, glancing at shadows, and it became clear the conversation had ended. They had only conjecture now. What they needed was sleep—and sunrise.

Walker glanced at Sophie. "You don't have to believe in evil, but you have to believe there are things science doesn't understand. And that those things can kill us."

Dr. Tang stood up. "I'd like to hear the story of what happened on Mount Ararat sometime, when we're out of this. When we can all breathe easier."

It surprised Sophie to hear such hopeful talk coming from the ever-serious Dr. Tang, but it lifted her spirits a little nevertheless. Under their present circumstances, a little was all she could ask for.

Sophie stood and glanced around at the others. "We're all a wreck. I don't know if any of you will be able to sleep knowing the fighting is still going on above us—"

"I'd like to try," Dunlap said.

"Fair enough," Sophie replied. "But it might be a smart idea to take turns so whoever is awake can rouse an alarm if something goes wrong. If the USAMRIID team hasn't arrived by sunup, Dr. Tang will examine everyone showing symptoms—"

"I'm going to check on them tonight and then again at dawn," the doctor interrupted.

"Fair enough," Sophie said. "The rest of us are going to get some rest. If we're showing no further symptoms ourselves in the morning, that'll be a good sign. We'll have learned something, anyway. If anybody has any ghost stories in the morning, we'll talk about that then, too."

Beyza glanced at Dunlap. "The sergeant and I are going to try to locate Martin first. He had his mask on, but he was the one who carried the camera case back down to the Pandora Room. I'm worried about him."

Sophie felt badly. She had forgotten all about Martin for a few minutes. "Thank you. But don't stay up all night. Give it half an hour and then turn in. Sergeant, tell the sentries we need them to stay up. Tomorrow we'll find a way to let them rest, even if we need to guard the Pandora Room and the cadavers ourselves. I'm sure the fighting upstairs will be over by morning."

"Let's just hope our side wins, or we're going to have some very ugly company," Walker said.

They began to disperse, Beyza and Dunlap on their mission, Dr. Tang to check on her new patients, and Walker and Kim last of all.

"I'm sorry," Sophie said to Kim before they left the worship chamber.

Kim frowned. "For what?"

"I shouldn't be the one telling the sergeant what to do. It's your show down here."

Kim reached out and took her hand. "You're a good leader, and so far you're keeping your head when a lot of people would be out of their minds. This was your show to start with, and it's easy to see why. But we're in this together now, whatever happens."

Sophie squeezed her hand and thanked her, and then she stood in the entrance to the worship chamber and watched Kim and Walker head back toward their temporary quarters.

Only when they'd gone did she lean against the wall and lift a shaking hand to her mouth to stifle the cry she'd been wanting to unleash for hours.

God, she needed sleep.

In the quiet of the worship chamber, gunfire drifted down through the ventilation shafts again. It occurred to Sophie that if they were not very lucky, she and her team might be the next generation of ghosts haunting Derveyî.

SEVENTEEN

Walker and Kim lay facing one another on a pair of cots. He felt torn in half, part of him certain he ought to stay with Kim even as the other part was drawn to the conflict aboveground. He hated how vulnerable it made him feel to be out of the fight and to be ignorant of the situation. He had gone up to the entrance and spoken to the volunteers who were monitoring things. Major Bernstein had apparently sent a young soldier over some time earlier with a message for everyone in Derveyî.

Tell them to keep their heads down, Bernstein had said. *We'll let you folks know when we're done with these fuckers.*

Walker liked the major's confidence, but it was difficult to share it when a different sort of battle was raging underground.

"I'm not going to be able to sleep," Kim said. "It's insane to think any of us can."

Walker studied her, all thoughts of the battle overhead forgotten. "I wish you'd told me how panicked you were. About your claustrophobia."

Kim gave a small nod, her face brushing against the pillow. "I had to face it. Just you being here helped me more than spending a lot of time talking about it would have."

Walker reached across the space between them, and their fingers latched together for a few seconds before she released him.

"Are we going to get out of this?" she asked.

Walker sat up and fixed her with a hard look. "We've been through worse than this and survived. Whatever happens, we'll take one crisis at a time. Let's try to rest awhile. I know you said you can't sleep—"

"I'm *afraid* to sleep," she said quietly. "I'm so tired, but I feel like the second I close my eyes, something worse will happen."

"We have to try if we're going to be any use to anyone in the morning."

"I know," Kim replied. "I just . . . I still have nightmares about the mountain. About the ark. When I'm home, I wake up and it's okay; I can catch my breath and know that I'm safe. But it's different here. I know you have them, too. Sometimes you wake up and you're panicked and pale, and one night you were shouting. I don't know if you remember."

Walker had been having nightmares for a very long time.

"I don't remember that specifically," he said. "But as awful as Ararat was, my nightmares aren't usually about that. The worst ones, the ones that wake me up like that, are about Guatemala."

Kim said nothing. Walker glanced into the darkest corner of the room and tried not to think about the worst night in Guatemala. Another night in a cave. The first time he'd survived a horror that had ended with most of his team dead. He'd fucked up that night, and it had cost him a great deal, but not as much as the people he'd let down. What were nightmares and a lifetime of chronic pain in his back and his leg compared to what had happened to them on his watch? Dr. Tang had talked about ghosts, but Walker believed it was the things inside people that haunted them the most.

A low whistling noise drew his attention, and he glanced over to see that despite her reluctance, Kim had fallen asleep and begun to snore lightly. He knew he had to try to do the same and was just about to lie down when the curtain drew back and Dr. Tang entered.

He raised a hand and gestured to Kim. Dr. Tang nodded tiredly and walked toward the third cot in the room.

"You don't mind if I sleep in here?" Walker said quietly.

"I'm barely on my feet," Dr. Tang rasped. "Sleep wherever you like."

Walker felt relieved. He wanted to stick close to them—to Kim, especially.

"How were they?" he whispered. "Rachel and Dmitri and the others?"

Dr. Tang kept her back to him, standing for a moment in thought. "They're worse. The whole south wing has symptoms. Nobody in the north wing admitted to having a rash or much more than cold symptoms, but some of them might have been lying. Regardless, they're all confined to their rooms until we get more medical staff here. The infected are going to need treatment as soon as possible."

"But how do you know how to treat them?"

"I *don't* know yet. USAMRIID will have a mobile lab. We'll run some quick tests on things that seem likely. Whatever this is, it probably at least shares roots with something we're familiar with. There will be medications we can try once we know more."

"And if you're wrong?" Walker asked.

Dr. Tang tilted her head as if she hadn't understood the question. Or as if she'd thought he ought to know the answer.

Walker thought he did know, after all, and the answer chilled him.

Sophie lay alone with her fear. How had it come to this, some sort of blind chess match against one illness or another? Talk of ghosts? She knew she ought to have asked Dr. Tang precisely how sick her staff were and their prognoses, but she didn't want to know. All her life she had been haunted by disease, by the memory of hospitals and the smell of the sick. There on the cot, alone in her quarters, she could remember the torrent of emotions she'd gone through during cancer treatment. She had made friends with Caryssa, a girl whose birthday had been a year and a day before Sophie's and whose chemo schedule tended to match up with hers. Their mothers had become friendly through the shared fear and the courage of their daughters.

Then Caryssa's schedule seemed to change. Sophie had asked her mother about it several times before, at last, she admitted that Caryssa's chemo had not been as successful as Sophie's. Months later, her mother had told her that Caryssa had died. By then, Sophie had been in complete remission, and she couldn't help but wonder why she had been spared and Caryssa taken. In a secret place inside her, a place where she put all the feelings that made her ashamed, she felt glad that if it had to be one of them, it hadn't been her. The feeling tortured her, but she could never make it go away. She remembered the sparkle in her friend's eyes, even when she had been at her sickest, and always wondered whether Death had chosen wisely.

After that, she had found it harder to make friends, harder to get close to people. It hadn't helped that she had felt so isolated during treatment. Some people came to see her—family, a few friends with their parents, even her teacher, Mrs. Campos—but most stayed away. Her mother told her people felt awkward, they didn't know what to say, and Sophie knew that must be true because even the ones who did come to see her seemed as if they would rather have been anywhere else.

Human connection seemed like too much effort, too much pain.

And now her father didn't even know her anymore. Disease had taken him away, and he wasn't even dead yet.

She wanted to reach out now, which seemed so surreal to her. All those years trying to avoid becoming too dependent on friends and lovers, trying to prevent herself from loving anyone too much to lose them, and now she yearned for contact. Lamar had been her friend, and he had betrayed her. He had been the closest to her among the staff, and now who could she turn to? Not Martin, wherever he was. Their rapport had been defined by his crush on her. She prayed he was all right.

Sophie knew she could talk to Beyza or even Alton, but they were both trapped in here with her, and it would be unfair—even foolish, or cruel—to look to them for comfort. Alton did not even have a filtration mask.

Her gaze shifted to her laptop, and she considered trying to get Alex Jarota on Skype. The thought gave her stomach a sick twist. How desperate did she have to be in order to think of Alex?

On the small table between her cot and the next one, her cell phone sat, quiet and dark. Selfishly, she wished she could call Steven, but after she had left him confused and angry in New York, it had taken him over a year to find a new beginning. To phone him now when she needed solace would be wrong, and she would never get a signal this far underground, anyway. For that, she needed her laptop.

Anyway, it wasn't Steven's voice she really wanted to hear.

Sophie opened her laptop and started up a phone app, then called her mother. Somewhere in France, her mom's cell phone began to buzz. On the fifth ring, a sleepy voice picked up.

"Whoever this is, do you know it's the middle of the night and decent people are sleeping?" her mother said.

At first, Sophie had difficulty speaking. The sound of her mother's voice had unraveled something in her, and now she wanted to scream or cry.

"Hello? I'm hanging up in three seconds," her mother snapped. "Middle of the goddamn—"

"Mom, it's me."

"Sophie. Honey, what's the matter? Are you okay?"

She took a breath and grinned, thinking the smile—fake as it was— might translate into her voice. "I'm fine. I just miss you. Both of you. I wish I was there."

"Well, you're nearly done, aren't you? That's what you said. You should come and see us as soon as you've wrapped up your project. You should see your father soon."

The message came through loud and clear. *You should see your father soon.* The way her mother had said it, Sophie understood that if she did not see him soon, she might never see him again.

"How are you, Mom?"

"Tired," she said with a little laugh. "But I'm glad to hear your voice. You sound strange, though. Are you sick?"

Sophie nearly burst out laughing with the bubble of hysteria that rose in her chest at that moment. "I think I am," she said, shaking. "But I'll be all right."

"You have to take care of yourself, Sophie."

"I'm working on it."

The line went quiet for a moment, both of them sleepy enough to let the conversation lag, neither apparently knowing what to say next until, at last, her mother spoke again.

"He had a good day today, Sophie. For a few hours, he knew exactly who he was and who I was. He asked for you."

A knife to her heart. For all the mixed emotions she had about her father, to know that he had asked for her in a moment of lucidity and must have been disappointed that she hadn't been there . . . it stabbed deeply.

"What did you . . . I mean, he really knew who I was? He wanted to see me?" Sophie asked.

"I told him he would see you soon. That I would call you tomorrow and he could talk to you on the phone if he was feeling up to it. I think he knew then that he'd be fading soon, but he said . . . he said, 'When you talk to her, tell her I love her, and I'm sorry.'"

Sophie shook and began to cry silently. Tears rarely flowed easily with her, but tonight was different.

"I asked him what he was sorry for," her mother said. "And he told me, 'For missing my chance to be better.' He really does love you, Sophie. Down inside, the part of him that hasn't been erased . . . he loves you so much, and so do I."

"Thanks, Mom," she managed. "I've . . . I've gotta go. I'm sorry I woke you. We both need some sleep."

Her mother started to go on, but Sophie ended the call and then closed the laptop. Head hung, she let herself cry for another minute or two, and then she took several deep breaths and wrested control of her emotions.

Whatever happened next, tears would not help them.

She lay down, thinking about her father and his disease and the jar sitting even now inside that contagion box in the Pandora Room. She would never have believed the myth of Pandora might be true, but there seemed no other explanation. But why couldn't it have been the jar of blessings? The jar of cures?

Somehow it seemed only natural that the only true legends would be the awful ones.

Beyza unclipped a flashlight from her belt and shone its light down a narrow, sloping corridor the Beneath Project had lost interest in several months earlier. The corridor led to a series of chambers that were virtually identical to one another, the dwellings of some of the people who had lived in what they now called Derveyî. The lighting rigs had been removed from here a while back and repurposed elsewhere.

"Where's the light switch?" Sergeant Dunlap muttered, voice low.

"There isn't one."

"I can see that. It's a joke," he said, taking out his own flashlight. He clicked it on and held it with his left hand, pistol in his right. "Why don't you let me go first?"

Beyza ignored him and started down the corridor, hating the awareness of the gun at her back but not interested in letting Dunlap precede her. If they did run into Martin down there in the dark, she thought there might be a fifty-fifty chance Dunlap would accidentally shoot him.

She thought about Cortez, waiting back in her room. He would be wondering what had become of her, worrying. Or perhaps he had fallen asleep. She hoped he had, for his sake, and hoped he had not, for her own.

"You always this quiet, or was it something I said?" Dunlap asked, his voice seeming to fill the darkness around them.

"I am focused on the task at hand," Beyza replied.

"Okay, let's focus. No sign of Martin so far. Why are we headed this way? You have a reason to think he's down here?"

She bristled at his presumption that she should explain herself. "If you have a more efficient plan, by all means, suggest it."

"I didn't mean—"

"We've checked the obvious places," Beyza replied. "Now there are a few I'd like to check that aren't quite so obvious. Martin likes to wander when he's upset."

"He get upset a lot?"

"He's not good at hiding his emotions, so when he's depressed or upset, he vanishes." She glanced at Dunlap, wondering why she felt she could be so open with him. "Martin has had a crush on Sophie for months. Maybe ever since he met her."

"Can you still call it a crush if it lasts that long?" Dunlap asked.

Beyza said nothing. They reached the end of the corridor, where she shone her flashlight left and right. It appeared to be a dead end at first, but there were doors in both directions that led to staircases. To

the right, if they'd shifted the door, they would have found stairs leading upward. She held up a hand to halt Dunlap, then reached out and
gave the outer edge of the round door a gentle push. It turned as if
weightless, a bit of architectural magic Beyza had never failed to find
magnificent.

"Secret passages?" Dunlap asked.

"Related more to privacy than secrecy, we believe," Beyza replied.

She slipped sideways through the door, entering a section of narrower tunnels, rougher-hewn chambers, and smaller rooms. In silence,
she led the sergeant around corners, down short ramps, and up
staircases comprised of as few as three steps.

"What are these, servants' quarters?" Dunlap asked several minutes into this strange labyrinth.

"We don't think so, but certainly the rooms of those less fortunate.
There are several small worship chambers here, and workshops as
well. Animals were kept here, too, presumably prior to slaughter."

"That's a pleasant thought."

Beyza paused and directed her flashlight beam into one small room
after another, then up a narrow staircase that led into a strangely isolated room they believed had been used as a quiet place for meditation,
or perhaps a nursery.

Dunlap stepped past her. Gun in one hand and flashlight in the
other, he turned toward her, and she saw the furrow of his brow above
his filtration mask.

"What's that noise?" he asked.

Beyza stiffened. She had not wanted to admit to herself how much
it unnerved her to walk through this darkness. Without Dunlap, she
would never have come here looking for Martin, no matter what she'd
promised Sophie. A flashlight made zero difference, and a dozen of
them wouldn't have helped much. But at least she wasn't alone.

"I don't hear anything," she said, though that wasn't strictly true.

"Come here. Closer to the wall," Dunlap said.

The wall had a rough quality to it as if, unlike the rest of Derveyî,
these rooms and passages had been carved and hollowed in haste.
Beyza had long wondered if the work had remained unfinished, if one

of the dead-end corridors had been meant to lead to a new entrance. The city had still been growing when its people had abandoned it.

"There. You hear that?" Dunlap asked.

"I do," she admitted. A shushing noise, a whisper from below them, perhaps far below.

She trained her flashlight beam on the wall and saw the two small open holes where the wall met the floor, and the grooves in the wall that led up to similar holes above their heads.

"You spooked me," she said. "They're just air vents. No ghosts here."

Even as she said it, though, it occurred to her that the flowing air sounded stronger here than elsewhere in Derveyî. Louder and layered as if there might be another susurrus of noise beneath the gusting drafts.

Dunlap took a step away from her. "I wasn't suggesting ghosts."

Beyza smiled behind her mask. "If you start seeing things, do let me know."

She tore herself away from the wall and the vent and continued through the maze of smaller, more claustrophobic rooms. Less than a minute later, they found themselves at the top of what she'd always thought of as the back stairs. When she swung her flashlight beam back and forth, she saw that the strings of lights still hung there, but then she remembered they were no longer connected to the generator.

Quietly, she swore.

"What's wrong?"

"Nothing," she insisted and started down.

"Anyone ever tell you that your communication skills leave a lot to be desired? Or do you just not like me?"

Beyza glanced back at him, flinching when Dunlap lifted his flashlight. "I don't know you. But I'm uncomfortable around guns and have had little reason to trust American soldiers in my life. So you'll forgive me if I focus on finding Martin?"

"Guess there's no arguing with that," the sergeant replied.

Beyza started down. This was the longest continuous staircase in Derveyî, a lazy spiral of seventy-two steps that led to the deepest part of the subterranean city, including the space they believed had been used for grain storage, as well as the main kitchen for the entire population.

The whistle of the wind through the vents seemed to have grown louder. For a moment, she could hear Dunlap's footsteps on the stairs behind her, but not her own. She felt outside of herself somehow, and then her heartbeat grew louder and she heard the scuff of her footfalls. For a moment she was light-headed, and her clothes clung to her, her body sheened with perspiration despite the chill.

Her flashlight wavered from the trembling of her hand, and then she lowered it, leaning against the staircase wall.

"Professor?" Dunlap said, jostling up beside her, braced to catch her if she collapsed.

In the moment before she would have replied, she heard someone else speaking. The voice came from below her, around the curving of the spiral stairs, a laughing whisper.

"So easy," the voice said. "No hesitation. The lion or the lamb, that's the question. Always the question."

The whisper became a quiet chuckle, and something about it made her realize she knew that voice. Exhausted as she was, in the darkness, with all the talk about ghosts, she had been quick to let fear creep in, but now she knew better.

Beyza hurried down the stairs, once around the spiral and halfway again, and then her flashlight found the figure seated on the steps with his back to her. Martin's filtration mask hung uselessly around his throat. She thought about Cortez back in her room, about him removing her mask and everything that came afterward, and found she could not chide Martin for a foolishness she shared.

She crouched beside him, trying to work his mask back into place.

"You have to put this back on, Martin. I'll help—"

Martin grabbed her wrist tightly enough so that the bones hurt. She began to wrest herself free, but he only shoved her arm away. Beyza leaned against the opposite wall.

"Put it on, Martin," Dunlap said above them, shining his own flashlight down on them, casting strange shadows and too bright a light.

"Lion or the lamb," Martin replied, shaking his head.

When he turned, Beyza saw that he held a stone shard in his hands. He'd been cradling it, and now he reached out to her and grabbed her wrist again. He yanked her close, and he raised the stone. Her flashlight fell out of her grasp and tumbled down several steps, the lens cracking though the light continued to shine.

Dunlap shouted at him, raised his gun, and took aim.

Beyza roared one word. "No!" But she wasn't sure which one the word had been meant for.

Martin hesitated, then tossed the stone down the stairs, where it ricocheted off the turn in the spiral and bounced out of sight.

The drafty vents moaned.

Beyza wished herself into the arms of her mother or the wine-soaked company of her dearest friends, or even back in her quarters with Cortez. Even being home with her dreadful husband would have been better than this. Instead, she remained there on the stairs, for her wishes had never had much power.

Again, she said his name. Again, she lifted the mask and tried to put it on him.

"Let me help you," she said, too many questions in her head. All she knew in that moment was that Martin had been broken.

"What's the point?" he said quietly. He turned toward her, and in the light from Dunlap's flashlight, she saw the first blemishes beneath his jaw, dark spots that would become lesions.

"Oh, Martin," she said.

He shrugged. "No point at all, Bey. We're never getting out of here."

EIGHTEEN

Taejon could barely keep his eyes open. He leaned against the wall at the top of the steps leading down to the Pandora Room, weapon cradled across his chest. Private Carson had jumped up and down quite a bit, trying to wake himself up, whining a lot because nobody had told them how much longer they would be on duty before someone would relieve them and they could get some sleep. Taejon figured it must be past two in the morning by now, hopefully even later.

"No reason we both need to be standing," Carson said. "Maybe we take turns. If I could lie down on the floor for twenty minutes, that'd be enough."

Taejon glanced at him. "You're gonna be able to sleep with that mask on, lying on a stone floor?"

Carson laughed. "Brother, I can sleep any damn place. Comes to it, I could sleep standing up, but I don't want to start snoring and piss you off."

"A person can't sleep standing up."

"Cows do it," Carson said. "Seen 'em on my family's farm a million times. As kids we'd go over to the neighbors' farms and sneak up behind the cows and tip 'em over while they're sleeping."

"That strikes me as pretty mean," Taejon said.

Carson cocked his head. "They're cows, Tay. They're dumb as shit."

Taejon kept his own counsel. If cows could sleep on their feet because they were so stupid, he figured Carson might be able to sleep standing up after all. If dumb was all it took, the guy had the credentials for it.

"You want to lie down, go on and do it," Taejon said.

"You outrank me, Corporal, so if you're ordering me to lie down, I might just do that."

The only emotion Taejon felt at this pronouncement was envy. If Carson wanted to close his eyes for twenty minutes, he didn't see the harm, but no way would he risk it himself. He might only be a corporal, but Carson had been right—he had rank down here. And someone had to stay awake and pay attention with all the weird, hinky shit that had been going on. Bad enough he had to stand at the top of the stairs with the jar down there in that room, maybe giving off some kind of contagion despite the special box they'd locked it in. People had been getting sick in the south wing, or so he'd been told. Taejon felt okay, but the idea still creeped him out.

Carson made a big show of yawning behind his filtration mask and then sat down. He lay on his side and drew his weapon up to his chest like a kid cuddling with his new puppy.

"You serious?" Taejon asked.

"Ten minutes, man."

They'd had way worse duties than this and gone far longer without sleep in much worse conditions. That was the nature of the army, especially out in the middle of nowhere. They'd both had posts in the desert where it was hot as the devil's taint in the daytime and cold as Frosty's balls at night, and Carson would never have dreamed of taking a nap or even closing his eyes for more than a minute.

"Carson, you feeling all right?"

With a sigh, Carson sat up and leaned against the wall. "I knew it was too good to be true."

Taejon couldn't see his face at this angle. "That's not an answer. You okay?"

"Naw, man. I feel like crap. Kinda queasy, sore throat, hard to keep my eyes open. You?"

"Yeah, my throat, too," Taejon admitted. He swallowed uncomfortably. "Head hurts. But I figure it's mostly just exhaustion. I've felt worse."

They both knew what they were worried about, but they talked around it, never mentioning the jar. Not while discussing whether or not they felt the symptoms of any unusual sickness. Carson didn't lie back down, but neither did he stand up. Instead, he sat with his weapon on his lap, and when Taejon glanced over at him, he saw the other man's head had drooped a bit. A few minutes later, a soft snoring noise came from Carson.

Son of a bitch really can sleep anywhere, Taejon thought.

A sound made him jump. Cursing quietly, Taejon lifted his weapon and aimed into the darkness, watching the five columns in the large room. There were lighting rigs in here, but not enough to dispel the shadows, especially near those columns. What the hell had the sound been? A slap or a crack, or a single clap of someone's hands?

The noise came again, and this time he recognized it as the sound of flesh on flesh, the sound of pain. A desperate cry followed it, a voice raised in desperation, a plea for mercy in a language he did not understand.

Taejon glanced at Carson, but the private remained fast asleep, slumped against the wall. A whimper arose, followed by rasping whispers, and then a series of moans that sounded more like pleasure than pain. All of them came not from the shadows around the columns but from the Pandora Room.

He stood at the top of the stairs and peered down at the stone door, which stood sideways on its axis. Even from here, he could see shadows playing across the floor of the half-lit room, and his heart went cold.

Taejon shook himself. *No, uh-uh,* he thought. Not a chance anyone could be down there, of course, because the room had been empty when he and Carson had taken up their posts—he had cleared it himself—and they had never left the spot at the top of the stairs. His eyes had been heavy, but he had not fallen asleep on his feet—he wasn't a cow and he wasn't Carson.

Quietly, listening to the grunting and a cry of pain down below, Taejon went to Carson and gave him a light kick in the ribs. Jostled, Carson flapped his hands as if he might be drowning and then looked up at him.

"What the fu—" Carson began.

"Hush," Taejon said, holding up a hand. "You hear that? Am I passed out on the floor and dreaming this shit?"

Carson paused, head cocked. His expression shifted first to mild disgust and then to incomprehension. "Who's down there?"

Taejon shook his head. "Nobody. You were sleeping for about four minutes."

"Funny," Carson said, climbing sleepily to his feet. "Try again."

"Unless there's another way into that room," Taejon said quietly, and that made him feel a little better. The Pandora Room was small, and he couldn't see how a secret entrance would have escaped discovery by Dr. Durand's team, but how else could people have gotten in?

Secret entrance. It seemed like a stupid idea, but he held on to it, because otherwise he must actually be dreaming or have lost time somehow. The world felt uncertain beneath his feet as he held up his hand again, instructing Carson to stay put, and then started down the steps.

The noises weren't loud. Even that first slap had only startled him so much because any sound down there had been amplified by the relative quiet around it. Now, in the isolation of the staircase, the sounds seemed to swirl and eddy around him as he made that brief descent. His footsteps were quiet but not inaudible, so Taejon felt certain whoever had managed to get inside the Pandora Room would hear him coming, but the moans and whimpers and the pounding of flesh did not cease.

"Tay," Carson called quietly from the top of the steps.

Taejon set one hand on the round stone door, careful not to put any weight on it. The architects had balanced it so perfectly that it turned effortlessly. Starting forward again, he put both hands on his weapon and stepped through the door, sweeping the gun barrel left to right.

He felt a prickling at the back of his neck as he stood staring, unable at first to comprehend what he saw. A tall woman draped in rough cloth beat a young girl, grabbed her hair, pulled out a crude dagger, and began to carve lines in her skin. The girl cried out, shrieking in anguish and fear, and yet her voice sounded muffled and far away.

Only a few feet from them, a robed man held a woman's face against the wall, forearm across the back of her neck, as if he meant to take her against her will. On the other side of the room, a couple made urgent love while another man watched, fury engraved on his face, while nearby two younger men did their best to beat each other to death with stones.

All of those noises blended into a terrible chorus, a muted, almost strangled sound, just as the people themselves were muted and distant. In the glow from the lighting rigs that still worked, they cast no shadows. Instead, shadows fell through them, as did the light—they were transparent. If they had ever been in that room at all, they were gone now, just the spectral echoes of the past. Only ghosts.

"Holy motherfucking—" Taejon began.

At the sound of his voice, one by one, the ghosts all turned to look at him. Taejon let out a small whimper, which he would later deny. His insides turned to jelly and he crossed himself—something he hadn't done in years—and began to back out of the room with the ghosts tracking his exit with their eyes. The ghost of the little girl, the one with the cuts all over her flesh, grinned at him as he went.

Back on the bottom two steps, he began breathing too fast, nearly hyperventilating inside his mask. The sounds had muffled even further, as if the ghosts were fading, and he prayed that was the case, prayed he could pretend he had not just seen what he knew he had seen.

"Taejon," Carson called down at him in a tone that suggested it wasn't the first time. Then the younger man barked at him. "*Corporal!*"

Gun trained on the light and shadow inside the Pandora Room, Taejon stumbled backward up several more steps before he finally managed to twist around and look blankly up at Carson.

"What?"

"You better get up here," Carson said. "There's people."

Taejon glanced at the entrance to the Pandora Room again, the doorway split in two by the big stone door, still open. He wanted to close it, but he didn't want to get any closer to the room, and now the sounds had ceased and the shadows had stopped moving down there, at least as far as he could see.

"People down here, too," he muttered, the words so muffled inside his mask that they sounded as if someone else had spoken them.

Carson called for him again. Taejon turned his back on the Pandora Room and hurried up the last half dozen steps, emerging into the column chamber ready to snap at Carson for his sense of drama. Then he saw the figures in the shadows near the columns, and he whipped his gun up and nearly pulled the trigger, thinking there were more ghosts, more specters doing unspeakably evil things in the darkness of Derveyî.

One of them stepped into the light, and Taejon recognized the face if not the name—a short, broad-shouldered guy who came out of the underground at least three times a day for a smoke break. Sophie didn't allow anyone to smoke down below. Smoke Break was some kind of engineer, the guy who strung the lights and was responsible for the generator. He had three other people with him, maybe others in the darkness behind the columns. These were north wing people, which made him feel a little better. He hadn't heard anything about the north wing—although they were all supposed to be confined to quarters.

"Corporal, I'm only gonna say this once," Smoke Break announced, stepping out of the shadows. There were welts on his face, but Taejon realized quickly they weren't just welts. He had some kind of rash, purple-black sores that were weeping something grotesque. His eyes were narrowed and puffy, and his neck looked puffy, too, and dark with bruising.

So much for the north wing being uninfected.

Taejon raised his weapon, not quite taking aim at the man.

"You folks stay back," he said. "You know we have instructions here. The last thing you want to do is start some trouble and end up getting hurt over it."

Smoke Break didn't seem to hear him, only took another step forward, gaze locked on Taejon. "You're gonna take off those masks and give 'em over. It's not right that you fellas got some protection and the rest of us are out here, sick with whatever's leaked out of the damn jar. Then you're gonna go down there and get that thing, take it outta here."

Carson laughed. "Buddy, there's hundreds of people shooting at each other up there. We're not going anywhere, and neither are you."

"Sir," Taejon said, eyes narrowing. "I'm gonna ask you to back away."

Carson shifted, aiming first at Smoke Break and then at the other three—two other men and a woman. It was hard to tell with the other two men, but the woman had the same visible symptoms as Smoke Break. Taejon recognized her immediately, had admired her from the day of her arrival about four months ago. She was an American historian named April Riordan, a quiet woman who'd always had a smile for him when he was on sentry duty.

Tonight April Riordan had a knife. She stepped forward.

"Boys, here's the story. I'm sick, and I'm not the only one. They've got a guard on the south wing, and word is everyone's sick in there," she said. "Sophie told us the people getting the masks had been the ones exposed, that her and you fellows and the rest wearing those masks was to protect the rest of us from contagion, but now we've got this rash, and worse, and it's spreading, so it seems Sophie is either a liar or she made a mistake that might be killing us."

Taejon and Carson spread a bit farther apart, forcing the four to pick a target if they intended any violence.

"That's something you'll have to take up with her," Taejon said. "If she's sleeping and you want to wake her, that's not my business. But I'll need that knife, Miss Riordan."

"Careful or you'll get it," April replied, calmly as could be. When she scowled, one of the rash blisters on her cheek burst, and black, bloody sludge dripped down her face and ran along her jawline.

Smoke Break cleared his throat and spat onto the floor. In the yellow light, it looked the same black and red as what had seeped from April's face.

"Stand aside, soldier. Both of you," Smoke Break drawled. "We're taking those masks if we have to strip 'em off ourselves. And then I guess we're going down into that room and smashing that fucking jar."

Carson lifted his weapon and took aim at Smoke Break's head. "Jesus, you are stupid. If whatever's wrong with you came from the jar, how is smashing it going to do anything but infect more people?"

April hefted her knife. "Everyone in Derveyî is already infected, at least the way I figure it. Except maybe you people in your masks. Frankly, I think it's only a matter of time for you, masks or no masks. They're gonna keep this place quarantined. People are going to start dying, and they're going to end up building a fence around Derveyî and treating it like Chernobyl or that nuclear plant in Japan. They're not going to let anyone within miles of this place. But if the jar gets out of here, who knows how many people will get sick?"

Smoke Break took another step. The two other guys moved forward with him, fanning out to right and left as if they might try to attack.

"That's not up to you to decide," Taejon said. "It's above your pay grade—and mine, too."

"Oh, but dying isn't?" asked one of the other men, his throat thick and rasping. He burst into a fit of coughing.

April rubbed at her eyes. Taejon thought she might be crying, but then he saw that what trickled down from her eyes was blood instead of tears.

"The rest of you can fight over the masks," she said, voice rasping as she tried to clear her throat. "I don't care as much about that. I figure I'm already sick, but I'm not leaving that jar intact. Get out of my way, Corporal."

She started forward.

Taejon shifted closer to the open stairwell door, raised his weapon to his shoulder, and aimed at the center of her chest. "Ma'am, do not take another step."

April did. Just one more. Taejon shifted his weapon to the right and fired into the shadows of the column room, beyond the reach of the lighting rig. The gunshots echoed back to him, and he thought of the ghosts in the Pandora Room and the fact that he'd been feeling feverish, and then he pushed all such thoughts away. A woman with a knife was easier to handle than the question of madness, the question of ghosts.

"Fuck this," Smoke Break said. "You're not gonna shoot her, or any of us. And we want those goddamn masks."

April raised her hands as if to surrender herself and started walking toward Taejon, who shouted at her to stop, aimed again at her chest, and hesitated. The blackish blood still seeped down her cheek, and now he saw the deep purple bruising on her throat and the festering sores there. Her eyes had gone fiercely bloodshot.

"No, damn it, listen to me!" Taejon shouted. "I don't wanna—"

She burst out coughing. Bloody black phlegm sprayed from her mouth and spattered the floor just inches from his boots, and he pulled the trigger by reflex, stitching bullets across her body from left thigh to right shoulder as she staggered backward and then slumped to the floor with a wet slap, even as the echo of gunfire slithered again into the shadows.

Carson turned toward Taejon. "Oh, shit! Oh, Jesus, Tay, what did you—"

Smoke Break roared something unintelligible as fear finally broke him. He and the other men rushed at Taejon. Carson tried to get between them, and two of them broke off attacking Taejon to take him down. Smoke Break got a hand on Taejon's weapon, and they were wrestling for it, Taejon taller but Smoke Break so much stronger. But the son of a bitch started coughing, great racking brays that sounded like they were tearing his throat and lungs apart. Still he fought, yanked, tried to rip Taejon's weapon from his grasp, and Taejon pulled the trigger, shot him in the gut and groin, then kicked him away and shot him through the head.

To his left, Carson struggled with the other two. One man had ripped his gun from his grasp, and the other used both hands to tear off Carson's filtration mask. Carson fought back, trying to hold on to the mask, but they were yanking at his arms and hair, screaming and coughing, and they tripped him up. Carson hit the floor hard. One of them tugged up his own shirt to show the hideous rash on his side and abdomen, kicked Carson twice, then picked up Carson's weapon and took aim.

Taejon shot the guy once through the chest, center mass, and he dropped. The other man took three bullets before he went down.

Carson fell to his knees, staring at the dead men and the signs of their disease, then picking up the torn filtration mask, trying to figure out a way to mend it. They both knew there weren't any spares.

Taejon had stopped the men attacking him, maybe even saved his life, at least for now. But these had been ordinary people, mostly kind and intelligent and hardworking, and he'd just had to kill them all.

He turned away from Carson, stomach churning, bile rushing up the back of his throat. His hands flew to his mask, and then he thought of the sores and the blood and the coughing and he choked back down his revulsion and horror.

Down in the Pandora Room, the ghosts had gone quiet. But Taejon couldn't help thinking that up here in this place, he had created more.

Sophie came awake with a start, lost in darkness, head pounding and throat aching. Her eyes felt like she'd had a visit from the sandman, and she rubbed at the grit, careful not to push aside her filtration mask. She ought to be safe alone in her room, with nobody there to pass along the contagion, but she wanted to take no chances. Moaning quietly, she squinted at the shadowed figure shaking her awake.

"Okay. You got me," she rasped, knocking the offending hand away.

The person backed off, and in the low light coming from the softly glowing lantern in the corner, Sophie saw it was Dr. Tang.

"What the hell's wrong now?" Sophie asked. "If I'm gonna die before morning, you could have had the decency to let me sleep through it."

"I'm sorry," Dr. Tang said, reaching over to the adjacent bed and picking up a clear, sealed plastic bag. "With all that's going on, I'd forgotten about this, but I think it could be important. If we have any chance of learning more, I realized that chance might be here."

"What is that stuff?"

Dr. Tang unsealed the bag, reached inside. "The things I took from Lamar's pockets when I examined his remains." She withdrew a small journal bound with rubber bands and resealed the bag before tossing it back on the empty bed. "This is his."

"Of course it is," Sophie said. "He wrote in it constantly while he was . . ." She swung her legs off the bed, taking the journal from Dr. Tang's hand. "While he was translating. Of course. If he found something about hallucinations, or the symptoms, he might not have told me. Not if he was working with the New Caliphate."

She held the journal, wishing she had latex gloves or something. What she wanted more than anything from this book was the one thing she doubted she would find inside—understanding. Lamar had been loyal to her. They had trusted each other. She allowed very few into the intimate space around her, had been hurt too much by sickness and loss and so kept the world at arm's length, but Lamar had been an exception. If she could just understand why he'd done what he had done, she might begin to, if not forgive him, at least hate him a little less.

"Thank you," she said, slipping off the rubber bands.

Dr. Tang sat on the spare bed in silence while Sophie began to flip pages. The early pages were no surprise, as Lamar had given her highlights throughout the days he'd spent translating. She found herself skimming through the tale of Pandora and Anesidora and the two jars given to them by the gods. Lamar's neat, slanted writing began with large, looping letters, but as she turned the pages, the entries grew less legible, the writing smaller and sharper, until she had to decipher a scribble.

"Whatever was going on with him, it didn't happen suddenly," she said, glancing up at Dr. Tang.

"You think he was sick earlier than we thought?" the doctor asked.

"Sick, or under a lot of pressure, which would make sense if the jihadis were threatening him somehow."

Dr. Tang tilted her head in the birdlike way she had, but she said nothing. Sophie knew the woman must have already made up her mind about Lamar's betrayal, but for her it did not seem so clear. The more she turned it over in her head, the more she tried to swallow that Lamar had been a spy and a traitor, the more she believed she had been too quick to just accept that theory. He had betrayed her, yes. But there had to be a reason.

In the quiet chill underground, she turned her attention back to the book, deciphering not just translations but little notes and questions that Lamar had jotted to himself.

She turned the page and saw a break, a slash of white space about a third of the way down the page. Written there were three emphatic words, the second one underlined. *What's* this *now?*

Exhausted, head aching, she had to focus on the scrawl. Lamar had given up recording a direct translation, instead marking some lines and phrases and summing up his revelations in bursts of confused, almost breathless writing. Sophie read two and a half pages in numb astonishment before flipping back and starting through them again. Before she went any further, she had to be sure she had interpreted Lamar's claims properly.

"My God," she rasped, sore throat stinging.

"What is it?" Dr. Tang asked.

Sophie glanced up at her, unable to keep herself from smiling. Lamar had betrayed her—had even kept all of this from her—but if she could confirm his translations and assumptions, the discovery of the Pandora Room had just become even more valuable.

"If this is true," she said, waving the journal, "it changes everything."

Dr. Tang sat up straighter, leaning forward. "Does it say what was in the jar? Any information might be vital to helping the people who are sick."

"Nothing like that," Sophie said. "Not that I've read so far." She saw Dr. Tang deflate a little, and felt she had to forge on to justify her own excitement. "What if I told you the Pandora myth has an older root? That the jar isn't Greek at all?"

Dr. Tang twitched her head. "Pandora is a Greek myth. You said yourself that there are variations, but—"

"Yes, it's a Greek myth. But we know there were no gods on Olympus. We have a jar, which had to come from somewhere. If it didn't come from Zeus, where did it come from?"

Dr. Tang raised her eyebrows. "From your tone, I presume you are about to tell me."

Again, Sophie waved the journal. "Lamar told us. Or at least he wrote down what he thought he'd translated from the altar and the jar. What do you know about the Thera eruption?"

"A little. Thera is the circle of Greek islands that includes Santorini. Once they were one big island. Most of it exploded, when, about 2000 B.C.E.?"

"Not bad. But let me back up," Sophie said, glancing again at the journal's pages while she spoke. "Minoan civilization sprawled across much of the Aegean during the Bronze Age. It's named after King Minos of Crete, he of the labyrinth and the minotaur in Greek myth. The Minoans predated the Mycenaeans, which is where we get the beginnings of Greek mythology, all of that. There were Minoan settlements all over the place, including at Akrotiri, on Thera."

"I've been there," Dr. Tang said. "Some archaeologists think the destruction of Akrotiri is the origin of the story of Atlantis."

Sophie rolled her eyes. They itched, and it made her head throb even harder, but she ignored the pain and forged onward. "Okay. I believe anything is possible after what we've found, but there are so many theories about the seed of the Atlantis myth." She flapped one hand. "Doesn't matter. The point is that the Minoan settlement at Akrotiri was obliterated in a volcanic eruption so enormous that Chinese and Egyptian records from the era—in the seventeenth century B.C.E.—note atmospheric and weather changes that almost certainly coincide."

Dr. Tang blinked tiredly. "Go on."

"Don't fall asleep on me. This is important."

"I'm awake."

Sophie didn't really need an audience, but it helped her to say this aloud, to make it real as she sorted it out in her brain. As she did, synapses began to fire, not just in her brain but between pieces of information in Lamar's journal.

"On second thought," she said, glancing back to the journal, "maybe the Atlantis seed was Akrotiri after all. Lamar translates a section of the writing that discusses a city he translated as *Locri*. The Minoan settlement on Thera became this place, Locri, whose people were viewed by the Mycenaeans as wise and just and peaceful neighbors. The city was considered a place of 'wondrous invention and music and art and magic.' Atlantis, El Dorado, Shangri-La . . . there are so many legends like this, and we can now add Locri to those. But the Locritians, or whatever we want to call them, started to fade. The bloom came off the rose, I guess. They stopped having children, stopped making art."

Dr. Tang gestured to the journal. "Does Lamar say why?"

Sophie felt a chill. The journal felt strangely warm. "What he says is that the Locritians traded with other islands, beyond the control of the Minoans, including some that would soon be absorbed by Mycenaean culture."

"I appreciate the history lesson, but I begin to regret waking you for this," Dr. Tang said. "If it won't help us determine what's in the jar—"

"I haven't gotten that far," Sophie said, forcing herself not to be curt.

"Perhaps you should."

"You're not hearing me. These people of Locri, they sound so wonderful, right? Capable of almost anything. Almost like gods."

Dr. Tang perked up. "You're saying Locri is Olympus."

"Not at all. But stories shift and change in the telling, passing down across centuries. Legends and myths especially grow and adapt to serve the people who need them, who cling to them. What I'm saying is that, according to Lamar, the writing on the wall down there says the people of Locri gave their Greek trading partners two jars and claimed one contained gifts they would not be prepared to use for . . ." She glanced at Lamar's notes in the journal and read aloud. "'Gifts they would not understand for three centuries.'"

Sophie glanced up again. "The other jar contained all the curses of humanity. Lamar wrote that phrase, but there's more." Her finger traced the line in the journal. "'The cruelties and frailties of all the hearts in Locri, and the plague of our bodies.'"

Dr. Tang leaned toward her, eyes flaring with uncharacteristic anger. "It's another version of the same story, Sophie. You're not thinking. So whoever wrote that on the wall told the earliest Greek iteration of the Pandora legend, and elsewhere they inscribed this one. Forgive me, I'll be fascinated later, when I'm sure we're not all going to die down here."

Sophie flinched. She nodded, taking even breaths.

"You may be right," she said, "but I don't think so. Yes, Lamar wrote that he thinks the language down there is influenced by Minoan language, might be the key to translating Minoan—a language that's never been deciphered. That jar might be the most priceless artifact in modern archaeological history."

"You're not listening—"

"Dr. Tang, please." Sophie held up the journal. "I am listening. And I'm going to keep reading. The story of the jar is in here. I don't know how far Lamar got, but we might get answers yet."

The two women stared at each other a moment, and then Dr. Tang lay back on the bed.

"Keep reading, then," the doctor said. "I don't need the background. Just an answer."

Sophie glared at her but knew Dr. Tang was right. She opened the journal and found her place, had to skip an urgently scribbled phrase or two, but kept working at it. As she read, she found herself missing Lamar, despite what he'd done. This journal felt like his last communication to her, but then she remembered that he'd experienced these epiphanies while working in the Pandora Room, sometimes with her and Beyza right there beside him, and never told her. It ought to have made her furious, she thought, but instead it just hurt. His handwriting showed his distress, but she wondered if she would ever know the true reasons for his betrayal, and if knowing would make her feel any better.

She paused, staring at a line on the page.

Her hand shook.

"Doctor," she said quietly.

Something in her voice must have excited or alarmed Dr. Tang, for the woman sat up abruptly.

"What did you find?"

"Ghosts," Sophie said, her sore throat tightening. She met Dr. Tang's gaze. "Lamar was seeing ghosts."

Before she could explain, they heard footfalls, and then Sergeant Dunlap shoved aside the curtain and entered Sophie's room without asking permission.

"Sergeant, what—" Sophie began.

"I'm sorry, but you both need to come with me right now," Dunlap said. "There's been trouble in the Pandora Room."

Sophie slipped rubber bands back onto the journal and stood, stuffing it into her back pocket.

"What happened?" she asked as Dr. Tang rose to join them.

Dunlap held the curtain back, and they all rushed into the corridor together.

"More of your team are sick than you thought, and worse than you thought," Dunlap said. "People are dead."

Dr. Tang grabbed his arm. "This sickness killed them?"

"No," Dunlap said, warily checking the shadowed tunnels with his weapon at the ready. "The bullets did that."

NINETEEN

Alton Carr had never missed his mother the way he did now, in these moments when he feared that the sickness growing in him—in so many of them—might be the thing that killed him. He came from a family whose men had often died young, or so his father had often told him. Both of his grandfathers had been coal miners in North-umberland, in the northeast of England, and both had died young, lungs black and clogged. His father's oldest brother had died in a cave-in, and though Alton's father had never been a miner himself, he had been raised in a family whose fabric was woven through with hard work, grim practicality, and whiskey. They'd accepted their lot, no matter how bleak, and he tried to remember that now as he weighed his own fate.

First in his family to attend university, he had been grateful to his parents, but particularly to his mum. As flinty as his father most days, she had nevertheless fought the battle for her son's future, arguing that the sorts of jobs earlier generations of Carrs had held were fad-ing and that he had the smarts to blaze a different trail. She had suc-ceeded in persuading his father, who had died while Alton was in his second year at Exeter. His mum had never been especially warm, and she had kept her grief well hidden, but she had comforted him as best she knew how.

Alton needed her now.

He lay on his cot, drifting in a fever-induced fog. His eyes fluttered open every few minutes, and he winced in pain. Every rattling cough seized his heart in a painful fist, chest muscles contracting. His throat ached and burned so badly that it hurt even to breathe. Inhaling through his nose would have made it better, but his sinuses were blocked, nostrils running with mucus.

How had this happened so fast? Just two hours ago, he had felt fine. Two hours.

In one of his more lucid moments, he wondered how contagious this virus might be and what would happen if it spread beyond these tunnels. Part of him didn't care at all—that part of him only wanted to be healed and didn't care who suffered for it. The urge to rise from his cot, to stagger out into the corridor and get past the sentry guarding them, even if he had to hurt the man, spread through him even faster than the sickness had. If he got outside, he told himself, he could get help. Who the fuck was Dr. Tang, anyway? She might not be able to help him, but surely the military topside could. Surely they would.

Had the fighting aboveground ended yet? Had the jihadis been driven back? Had reinforcements arrived?

The thoughts carried him down into darkness.

He blinked, rasped an agonizing breath, and realized he'd been unconscious again. Alton felt certain that for a few moments he had stopped breathing—that if he hadn't opened his eyes just then he would have died. How many times had he drifted off? How long had he been lying there? Alton had no idea. With no windows, and too weak to reach for his phone, he could not even check the time, had no idea if the sun had risen.

Mum, he thought. Despising himself for needing her. The kind of man she had raised would not be so pitiful, so yearning. The Carrs of the Northumberland Coalfield were not the sort of men who needed their mothers.

Images of her, and of his father, flickered through Alton's mind. Fading in and out, he spotted his phone on a little table just out of his reach, knew that if he could move himself, he could pick up the phone and call her. If he had a Wi-Fi signal, he could phone her through the app they all used down here. The call would wake her, but she would want to be woken. Solemn and proper as she was, Lydia Carr would want to know that her son might be near death, would want to hear his voice one last time.

His thoughts were shifting like sand underfoot. He coughed again, and the bright flare of pain gave him clarity for a moment. No, he would not call his mum. How cruel it would be, he thought, to put her through the panic of helplessness she would feel.

No.

Mum.

His thoughts drifted. His breath rattled. His vision blurred, and he heard something moving. A dim light glowed in the darkness of his room, a soft blue halo at the edge of his vision that eased his fear and pain ever so slightly. It seemed angelic, soothing and unearthly, but then the noises began—the hard slap of meat on stone—and the sounds so unnerved him with their wrongness that despite his weakness and pain, Alton managed to shift on the thin mattress and crane his neck to look down toward the foot of the cot.

Near the curtain that led into the corridor, one man straddled the chest of another, gripped him by the throat and slammed the back of his skull against the floor over and over. They were barely there, these men. Alton thought it must be him, that his blurring vision and drifting thoughts made them transparent, like afterimages left on the retina after his eyes were closed. That blue glow surrounded the men, but as he blinked his eyes, they were less and less substantial, both there and not there.

The man on top smashed the other's skull to the floor with one final, wet, bone-cracking impact, and then he stood abruptly and went to the wall, where he began to smash his own forehead against the stone. The blue glow dimmed, but somehow the sound seemed to grow louder. Another crack of bone and the murderer staggered, putting his hands against the wall as if waiting to die. Resting there, the see-through man threw back his head and howled. For the first time, Alton saw the tears sliding down his face, silver traces on thin air.

The ghost smashed his head again.

"Stop," Alton rasped, the pain in his throat causing his own tears to fall.

He'd spoken so quietly, and yet the silhouette of a man heard him. Stopped banging his head and turned to look directly at Alton with eyes that trailed a blue mist, eyes that were the only thing about the specter that seemed solid. The rest drifted, formless, barely visible.

Alton felt its attention on him like a fresh wave of fever, the flush of heat and panic and revulsion. Its eyes were wide as it flew at him, rushing with arms outstretched. He lifted his arms to ward it off, but when it touched him, the fever broke. A chill sank to his bones and raced along them, and Alton tried to scream. A hacking cough seized him. He lay on his side on the bed and choked up a little river of blood and viscous black bile.

The urge to scream built up, lodged in his chest. The pain abated, but a compulsion set its hook inside him, and he pushed himself up with trembling arms and rose from the bed with strength he hadn't possessed only moments before.

"No," he whispered.

Whimpered.

And oh, how ashamed his father and mother would have been at the pitiful, mewling sound that issued from his lips. His grandfather would have scowled and turned away. This wasn't how a Carr ought to behave.

Alton leaned against the stone wall near the door, in the spot where the ghost had stood. It felt comfortable, as if he'd been in the middle of a vital task and been interrupted, and now he could continue in peace.

No, a small voice said inside him. And the voice was his own. His true voice, lost now inside something else. Someone else.

Alton tensed, and he felt it coming, understood that his body would betray him.

He screamed so loudly it tore things inside him. His throat began to bleed, and he coughed loudly, chest seizing, racked with pain. He leaned against the wall, whipped his head back, and slammed his forehead against the stone.

Dazed, he stood for a moment with his head lolling to one side. His mouth opened, and again he screamed, that little voice inside him finding its way out, pleading for help.

Help arrived.

"Alton, what are you doing? We heard you—"

Though he tried to push away from the wall, to stop himself, Alton only managed to glance toward the doorway, where Dmitri stood holding back the curtain. Rachel pushed in behind him. The rash had spread, and sores had formed and split on their necks and arms and one whole side of Rachel's face.

"Get out," Alton managed.

The urge came over him. The dreadful urge.

Dmitri held up both hands. "I know, my friend. We look awful. But surely we are all sick now, and we heard you scream. What have you done to your head?"

The urge stifled what remained of Alton.

It lunged at Dmitri, grabbed him by the throat, twisted and tripped and forced him down on the ground and then began to smack his head into the stone floor again and again, just as the see-through man had done to his victim. Surrendering to the urge, Alton smashed Dmitri's head against the floor while Rachel screamed, and then Dmitri's skull gave way with a wet crack. Dmitri's legs jerked and danced and then went still.

Alton stood. He turned toward Rachel, but she had stopped screaming. The whites of her eyes were a dark, bloody red, and she stared at him.

"Do it," she said.

She might have been asking him to kill her, just like he had killed Dmitri. But the urge understood her words differently.

Alton turned back to the wall and resumed smacking his head against the stone. Rachel watched and did not interfere. Out in the hall, he heard others crying out, heard the voice of the sentry shouting into the corridor, demanding to know what had transpired. Rachel kept mostly silent, but in the moment when Alton struck his forehead against the wall hard enough for his skull to cave in, he heard her make a single sound.

She laughed.

After that, he heard nothing at all.

At first, Walker thought the screams were just the wind whispering through the ventilation shafts. He had slept for a short time, then snapped awake as if his body knew that this night was not going to allow for rest. When he'd opened his eyes, his breath warm inside his filtration mask, he had seen Kim looking back at him. She had tried to sleep, even drifted off for a few minutes, but had been lying there beside him the whole time. *Waiting for morning*, she'd said.

After that, they had waited for morning together.

Now the screaming had started, and morning had yet to arrive.

Walker grabbed his gun from the side table.

"Where's it coming from?" Kim asked.

"Let's find out." Walker tugged back the curtain and stepped into the hall. He glanced in both directions, but nobody else was stirring in the west wing.

Kim followed him into the corridor. "You go first. You're the one with the gun."

"You're the boss."

They moved swiftly and quietly, falling back on the trust they had established and their shared memory of survival. When they reached the short steps that led into a wider hallway, and toward the atrium beyond that, Walker hesitated.

"What is it?" Kim whispered.

The screaming had stopped. He heard muffled shouts, but they were only quiet echoes of something happening elsewhere.

"I promised Charlie," he said.

He didn't have to explain further. Kim knew his son, knew Walker had not always been a good father, that he had been trying to grow into the role. He did not have to explain what his promise had been.

"You're going to get home to him," she said, giving him a gentle shove. "Come on. I'm counting on you to keep us both alive. Charlie likes me, too. Don't disappoint him."

Walker gave a quiet laugh. "He likes you more than he likes me."

"Most people do."

They raced down the steps, Walker leading with the gun, passed through the hall, and then hurried out to the balcony overlooking the atrium. The shouting had died down, but the sounds still seemed to slither along the walls and ceiling. There in that vast space, the sounds of gunfire aboveground were clearer, more insistent, almost as if the shooters were inside with them instead of topside.

He took a few steps toward the exit, wondering about Cobb and the other coalition soldiers. How long until sunrise? How many of them were dead by now?

"South wing," Kim said, breaking his train of thought as she started in that direction.

"You sure?" Walker asked.

She glanced back at him. "Where else?"

As the shouts rose to a new crescendo, they broke into a run. Walker passed Kim again just as they came around a turn in the hall and nearly collided with an armed man in a filtration mask. Walker dropped into a firing stance and took aim, even as the other man lifted his gun.

"Hold your fire," Walker snapped. "Is that you, Ruiz?"

The sentry hesitated. In the ugly yellow industrial light in the corridor, Walker got a glimpse of his fear and desperation. It was Ruiz.

"Walker?" the soldier said. "I almost killed you guys."

"I haven't heard any gunshots yet. Which means whatever you're running away from, you haven't killed anyone."

Ruiz glanced over his shoulder. "They're all infected, man. Some turned violent. Others are just sitting in the corridor, crying. One woman started ripping open those blisters on her face with her fingernails, and I figured that's it. They're all losing their minds, which means if I stick around, I'm gonna have to shoot some people. I need to talk to Dunlap."

"Where's Sophie?" Kim asked. "Have you seen her?"

Ruiz gestured past them. "Dunlap came to get her a little while ago, right before all this shit started up here. He swung by to check on me, said there was some trouble down in the Pandora Room, but didn't explain."

Walker didn't like the sound of that. "And Sophie went with him?"

"I assume so."

A long, keening wail of despair came from down the corridor—from the south wing. Walker stared down the hallway, feeling the lure of that despair, knowing those people needed help. But what help they needed, he could not provide.

"Come on," he said, turning back the way he and Kim had come.

"What about them?" Kim asked.

Walker glanced at her but didn't slow down. "Charlie wants to see you again, remember?"

Ruiz followed, and in moments, the three of them were running along the ramp that led into the atrium, from which they could reach the stairs to the lower level and the worship chamber and beyond.

Ruiz had just started to ask a question when he was interrupted by a thunderous boom. The whole cavern shook, and dust rained down from the ceiling of the atrium. Distant gunfire still popped and echoed, but it was that explosion that pushed Walker into motion again. Whatever they were going to do to defend themselves in the worst-case scenario couldn't wait.

Shrieks carried through the tunnel, back the way they had come. The infected had felt that explosion, much more powerful than those that had shaken them earlier. Closer, almost on top of them. Whatever fear and madness had embraced the staff, they would be in a frenzy now. Ruiz whipped around, aiming his gun in that direction, ready to kill those who had succumbed to the sickness leaking out of the jar.

Walker grabbed his arm. "Save your ammo. We may need it."

Ruiz nodded, and then the three of them were running for the stairs that led down into the dark heart of Derveyî. Whatever happened now, the jihadis could not be allowed to get their hands on the jar, but Walker didn't have the first clue how to prevent it. The only thing he knew for certain was that a lot of people were going to die before the sunrise.

Sophie swayed on her feet. She had to lean against one of the columns and catch her breath. Suffocating, aching, she wanted to tear off the filtration mask just so she could scream and hear it echo off the walls.

You should be crying, she thought. *Why aren't you crying?*

Yet there were no tears now. No more recriminations about having left New York or worries about Alex Jarota or yearning to be with her parents. She loved both her mother and father, but they were far from here and safe from the horror unfolding in Derveyî, so although her father's condition deteriorated every day and would continue to do so until Alzheimer's took his life, at least her mother understood the darkness they faced. As terrified as her dad must have been, the course of his destruction could be predicted.

Sophie's hand rose to cover her masked mouth. *Jesus*, she thought. *When you start thinking Alzheimer's is the bright side, you've gone pretty dark.*

Mentally, she took it back. Of course she wouldn't want to trade places with him. Her father lived in a nightmare of constant unknowing, and she could not think of anything worse. Even dying from whatever contagion had escaped the jar would be better. *Had* to be better.

But she wouldn't want him to trade places with her, either, because the people splayed on the floor in the column chamber were dead because of her. Not directly, of course. She had not killed them, but the Beneath Project had been her baby. Some of the dead, their blood spattered and puddled all around her, had joined the dig because they wanted to work with her, and others had come specifically at her request. Lou Redfearn, for instance. Sophie had actively recruited Lou, and now he had weeping black sores all over his body and a bullet hole in the side of his skull.

Why can't I cry?

She told herself she must be in shock, that she would grieve later when the rest of them had survived this. Her throat felt raw and ragged, but she fought the urge to cough.

Sophie blinked as if coming awake. Someone had been talking to her, and she glanced around the column chamber. Dr. Tang sat against the far wall, reading Lamar's journal, which she had taken from Sophie at some point while they were following Sergeant Dunlap down here. Beyza and Martin—*They found him, where had he gone?*—stood together at the top of the thirteen steps, talking quietly.

But it had been Corporal Taejon speaking to her.

"—understand, right?" Taejon said. "Tell me you understand, Dr. Durand."

Sophie stared at him. "Understand what?"

"We didn't have a choice," the soldier said. "They came at us, would've killed us."

A burst of laughter came from the shadows between two columns off to her left. Sophie turned to stare at Private Carson. He wore a T-shirt and army-issue trousers and boots, but the filtration mask Dr. Tang had given him had been torn apart, and there were no more.

"What's funny?" Dunlap said, cradling his weapon, steel in his spine, a calm presence in the midst of disaster.

Carson looked up. "Taejon says they would've killed us. But come on, Sarge. They did kill me. My clock's ticking down to zero."

"You don't know that," Sophie said.

Dr. Tang shot her a hard look, and she realized how foolish the statement had been, given the dead people on the floor. This infection happened fast. The team from the World Health Organization might be able to help, but would they get there in time to help Private Carson?

Martin sighed and slid down the wall. "You're not alone, Carson."

Sophie stared at him. "What do you mean? You have a mask. We're all sick, but not like the others."

Behind his mask, Martin might have smiled, but his eyes were full of dour wisdom, all the youthful exuberance burned out of him. "I have a rash," he said. "It itches like hell."

"When we found him, he'd taken his mask off," Beyza explained, with a baleful glance at Martin. "I'm not sure for how long. And there were . . ."

She faltered.

"Ghosts," Dunlap put in. "You can say it. You have to say it."

Sophie exhaled and turned away from them. Again, she leaned on the column, trying to figure out what to do next. Lamar had been her conscience in a crisis, and that felt like a bad joke. Beyza would be the closest to her now, and she knew the two of them ought to discuss this in private, but when she considered what to do, it seemed clear that there were zero good options. If Lou Redfearn and the others had become so sick so quickly, her first obligation was to keep the sickness contained, no matter the cost. Whatever the WHO investigators wanted to know, they might have to learn from the dead.

"Sophie," Dr. Tang said from her spot on the floor, barely looking up from Lamar's journal.

"What now?" Corporal Taejon asked as if Dr. Tang had not spoken. "Seriously, all you fucking smart people had better have an answer, because I'm on the verge of losing my shit. What do we do, man? I am not just sitting here and waiting—"

"Get it together, Corporal," Dunlap growled. "I didn't sign up for this either, but it is what it is."

Private Carson laughed again. "It is what it is," he echoed.

Dunlap ignored him but kept his gaze locked on Taejon. "I need you to rein it in."

Taejon nodded slowly, thoughtfully, getting a firmer grip on his weapon.

"Sophie," Dr. Tang said again, a bit louder. "You need to hear this. You *all* need to hear this."

Her tone silenced them. Everyone turned toward her. Sophie knitted her brows, unsettled by the expression on Dr. Tang's face.

"What is that, anyway?" Dunlap asked. "What you're reading."

"It's Lamar's journal," Sophie said, glancing at Beyza and Martin. "From the second he entered the Pandora Room. It's mostly translations, but some notes as well. The writing . . . changes. Something was happening to him."

"Yeah," Martin said. "He was selling us out to the jihadi maniacs who are going to kill us all."

Dr. Tang stood up, the journal open in her hands like a priest about to give a sermon. "Sophie, tell them about Locri."

A shiver went through Sophie then, a feeling of foreboding that had nothing to do with the illness inside her.

"What's a Locri?" Dunlap asked.

Sophie glanced at him, then scanned the others in the room. Beyza, Martin, Taejon, Carson, and Dr. Tang, who had been bored with her historical explanation of Locri not half an hour ago.

"According to Lamar," she said, gesturing toward the steps, "the walls downstairs include the story of a city at Akrotiri called Locri. A Minoan offshoot, an advanced society. They're the ones who made the jar."

Beyza started asking questions immediately, but Dr. Tang shushed her.

"I'm sorry, Professor," Dr. Tang said. "You can read it for yourself afterward. Sophie was reading it, explaining it to me, when Sergeant Dunlap came to get us. She didn't get very far, but I've read more of what Lamar had to say, and we have to consider the possibility there is truth in it."

Sophie took two steps toward her, but stopped at the edge of a drying puddle of blood. They were separated by a gulf of disease-ridden corpses.

"Go on," Beyza said.

Dr. Tang glanced down at the journal. "If you open that jar, you're going to find flowers inside."

"Flowers?" Private Carson said, barking a laugh. "Oh, that's beautiful. Flowers are killing us."

"Not only flowers," Dr. Tang went on. "There are definitely contagious bacteria in there. More than one type, considering that we're sick, but those who were exposed after the seal on the jar was cracked have contracted a virus whose symptoms haven't affected the rest of us. The rash, the lesions, swelling, the burst blood vessels in the eyes, massive hallucinations—"

"We're all hallucinating!" Martin blurted before hanging his head and repeating it quietly. "We're all fucking hallucinating."

"Maybe," Dr. Tang said. "Lamar's notes say the elders of Locri were frustrated with the failings of human nature. They had achieved great things as a society but felt themselves hampered by savage urges. Theft, murder, jealousy . . . Lamar translated one phrase simply as 'animosity.'"

"Sins," Taejon said.

"Offenses against the gods," Beyza said. "Maybe you could call them crimes. They wouldn't have used the concept of 'sin,' I don't think."

"Evil," Sophie muttered. "Human frailty."

Dr. Tang waved Lamar's journal at them. "The Locritians, as Sophie called them, had some kind of priesthood, men who were said to forge the spirit and the flesh and guide the people to their potential."

"Self-help guru bullshit," Carson muttered.

"These priests—Lamar uses the term *Forgers*—created a ritual. They promised they could draw out the worst parts of themselves and the people of Locri. They wanted to extract people's most horrific urges, as well as the guilt they felt for the evil they'd done in the past. But there's more to it than that. A plague had struck Locri, and the Forgers told the elders that their worst fears were true, that these urges and crimes were the root of the plague, and that this ritual could draw out the sickness of body and spirit together."

Sophie felt a numbness spreading inside her. With the thudding in her temples and the stinging pain in her throat, it came almost as a relief. She felt detached from herself, looking down on the room from afar as if reality had shifted away from her.

"Are you really suggesting what I think you're suggesting?" she asked.

Dr. Tang shot her a withering look. "I'm not suggesting it, Sophie. Lamar translated this story from the Pandora Room. You can read the journal yourself. You all can. Do you honestly think that as the one doctor here, as a woman who has spent her life studying disease, that I want to admit I'm even considering the idea that any of this . . ."

She opened the journal and stabbed a random page with a finger. "*Any of this is true?* That's the last thing I want. But I saw ghosts, whatever they were. I saw one spirit murder another. And I know some of you have seen things, too."

Taejon raised his hand like he was still in middle school. They all turned toward him.

"I saw some, down in the Pandora Room. A bunch of them," he said. "Doing all kinds of heinous shit. But let's say for a second that any of that crazy stuff is true. If these priests found a way to leech out the sickness in people and trap it inside the jar—"

"In the flowers," Dr. Tang said. "They were poisonous to begin with, but—"

Taejon held up one hand. "Yeah. I got that. I'm saying, some of those ghost stories go back before Lamar tried to steal the damn jar. Before the seal cracked. And people were getting sick before that."

"But not with plague," Sophie said quietly. She went to the top of the thirteen steps, careful to avoid the dead and their drying blood, and she stared down the garishly lit stairwell into the entrance of the Pandora Room. The strange light seemed to shift and breathe below. "The malice in there, the dark urges, started leaking out early on, I think. Alexander's warning hinted at the dangers. Maybe the ghosts were here, even then."

She turned to face the others. "If this is true, they're not ghosts at all. Just the echoes of the guilt and temptations of the people of Locri, locked inside the jar with all their physical ailments. Let's say the mortar used to seal the jar was porous and some of that sickness leaked out . . ."

Beyza nodded. "Okay. I see where you're going. So the seal cracks, those flowers are exposed to the air for the first time in thousands of years, and they crumble to dust. Microbes seep out through the crack, and some of our team breathes it in, and then it starts to spread person to person, just like it did in Locri."

"Rapid contagion," Dr. Tang said. "Rapid progression."

Sergeant Dunlap stared at Sophie as if the two of them were alone in the room. "You're talking about magic."

"Am I?" Sophie replied. "A way to draw out disease and transfer it to some other object, some other organic matter . . . is that magic just because we don't understand it?"

Dunlap shook his head. "Did you forget we're talking about ghosts?"

A debate ensued. Beyza and Sophie attempted to discuss the possible contents of the jar and what else might have been inside it, what sort of infections might have bloomed from within it when the seal cracked, while Dunlap challenged their assumptions and Taejon described the ghosts he'd seen downstairs.

Martin Jungling shouted them into silence.

Sophie stared at him. For the first time, she saw the rash that had begun to blister the left side of his face. She wondered how long he had been without the mask and how long the masks would protect the rest of them if Martin hadn't needed to be in close contact with someone already infected. There were three hazmat suits. Someone would have to decide who would get to wear those suits.

"Martin," she said, wondering if he knew. If he felt it.

"I just want to know how much time I have," he told them. "You can argue about ancient rituals all you like. You can dispute the ghosts I saw with my own eyes and whether they're echoes of past events or actual lost souls, and how these Minoan priests put crimes and plague and sickness inside fucking flowers. A day ago, they would be the most fascinating arguments I had ever heard. But right now, all I care about is how long I have to live and how much it will hurt when I die."

Sophie's heart broke. Martin had been such a part of her daily life for a year, had made her laugh a thousand times, had worked hard and made himself invaluable enough that she had promoted him, and yet still she had taken his friendship for granted. Maybe it had been because he was only a graduate student or because of his crush on her. Perhaps it had been because she had relied so much on Lamar's company that she had never fully appreciated Martin's. Even now, in the midst of her own pain and confusion, she had barely recognized the truth of his situation. Upstairs, her friends and colleagues, her team, were sick with plague, even dying, and others lay dead on the ground before her. In the midst of that urgency, she had not stopped to focus on loyal Martin.

"I'm sorry," she said, moving toward him, dropping to one knee. The words sounded so weak coming from her lips that once again she wished her tears would fall, but her eyes remained dry. "I don't know the answer, Martin."

Sophie turned to Dr. Tang, silently imploring her to respond.

"We don't know this sickness will kill you," Dr. Tang said. "I promise you, Martin. As soon as we're out of here—"

"Then let's *get* out of here!" Martin shouted, climbing to his feet too quickly, swaying a bit before he managed to steady himself. "Let's go!"

He looked from one face to another, and Sophie knew what he saw on each of those faces because she saw it herself. The quarantine had to stay in place. The stakes were too high. If Martin were to attempt to leave, Dunlap and Taejon would help stop him. And with the battle being waged overhead, they had nowhere to go.

Carson sighed, the last of his amusement abating. He spat a wad of black phlegm on the ground, the sickness moving more swiftly in him for some reason they might never understand. Or symptoms arriving differently. Sophie didn't know anything, and it made her want to scream with helplessness.

"Brother," Carson said to Martin, "we're not going anywhere."

As if in reply, the whole room trembled. A crack ran along the ceiling and through one of the columns, and dust sifted down from above. An echo seemed to travel through the floor, and Sophie felt it in her bones.

Beyza swore in Turkish.

"What the hell?" Martin asked. "That was a direct fucking hit."

Another boom shook through the chamber, through all of Derveyî.

Dunlap stared up at the ceiling, taking a tighter grip on his gun. "Which means if reinforcements are here . . . they're not ours."

TWENTY

By the time Walker reached the column chamber, he had already decided he wouldn't be staying. All he wanted was to make certain that Kim had been safely reunited with the others. He didn't say that, of course—they didn't have time to argue about her ability to defend herself, or for him to remind her of his training and how many times he'd had to fight for his life. Kim Seong might be an eminently capable woman, but her firearms skills were lacking, and Walker had a feeling he would shortly have to shoot a lot of gun-toting jihadi motherfuckers.

Lights flickered in the corridor as Walker, Kim, and Ruiz ran into the column chamber. The whole labyrinth shook around them with another explosion, and he ducked his head. Motion among the columns made him whip around just in time to see guns pointed at them, and Walker threw up his hands.

"It's us!" he shouted. "It's Walker!"

Dunlap moved into the light, sweeping the barrel of his weapon left to right—Walker, Ruiz, Kim. "Come ahead. Let me see your skin and your eyes."

Walker grunted. "Jesus, Dunlap, we're not—"

"Come into the fucking light!"

Ruiz went first. He hoisted his weapon over his head and walked slowly into the lights beyond the columns. Walker heard other voices, people calling out to them, but then they were drowned out by the thunder of another mortar round striking aboveground.

Kim followed Ruiz. She pulled up the sleeves of her shirt, trying to show as much skin as possible. Walker followed her, stuffed his M17 into his rear waistband, and widened his eyes.

"I guess you're all right," Dunlap said, backing up to join the others.

"None of us is all right," Walker replied.

The whole chamber shook. Walker scanned the room—Sophie, Dr. Tang, Taejon, a handful of others. Martin Jungling looked like shit, and he wasn't the only one. Ruiz took up a post between two columns, anxiously watching the shadows, almost as if the corpses on the floor weren't there at all.

"Do I ask?" he said to Sophie, gesturing to the dead, most of whom were covered with welts and blemishes and ugly pustules of rash.

"Why don't we focus on what's happening topside?" she replied.

"I'm on it. Meanwhile, you all figure out the safest spot to shelter down here. A hiding place would be nice." Walker pointed to Dunlap. "You're with me. Ruiz can help protect everyone else."

"Make it fast," Kim told them, eyes alight with fear and courage. "Evaluate, but don't engage. Report back as quickly as you can. We need information more than anything."

Walker snapped off a crisp salute, only halfway ironic. Urgent conversation kicked off again in the column chamber, but he had stopped listening. Dunlap fell into step beside him, and the two of them hustled back through the stairs and twists and corridors that led toward the atrium.

"Can I ask you a question?" Dunlap said as their footfalls echoed off the walls.

"I can't tell you more about myself than I already have."

"Figured as much. I just wanted to ask if you think we're going to die tonight."

Walker did not reply. They hurried up the last stairwell and then into the atrium. A crack had appeared in the floor. Walker pulled his gun from his waistband and shone his flashlight through the archways that led toward the residential wings. The lights strung about the atrium seemed to burn brighter than before, but that only deepened the shadows.

Nothing moved in the darkest parts of the cave. They hurried on through the atrium, up the sloping floor toward the exit. Walker felt every step in his back and leg, spiking pain in his old injuries, but he refused to let it slow him down. They reached the exit and started through and then up the spiral stairs that led to the surface.

"You going to answer my question?" Dunlap asked.

"About us dying tonight? Between what's happening upstairs and what's happening downstairs, I guess we'll know soon enough."

"Fuck that," Dunlap said as they reached the top of the stairs and raced toward the outside. "I just wanted to see where you stood on the subject. I've got no intention of laying my head down."

Walker appreciated the sentiment and would have said so, but voices were shouting ahead. Smoke billowed outside the mouth of the cave— the entrance to Derveyî—and in the midst of bursts of gunfire, at least two languages could be heard. Figures loomed in the smoke, and he realized the volunteer lookouts were gone. They had either run off or been killed.

"Incoming," Dunlap said, and he put his back against the wall, just inside the cave mouth.

Walker did the same, both of them with their guns aimed toward the silhouettes emerging through the smoke. A lumbering shadow revealed itself, and Walker realized he had judged the volunteers too harshly. Two of them—a man and a woman—were helping injured soldiers limp through the entrance to Derveyî. Other soldiers flowed in after them, a stream of desperate, dirty faces, many of them wounded. They barely took notice of Walker or Dunlap, hustling into the gloomily lit cave mouth and smashing the lighting arrays one bulb at a time, throwing the space into darkness.

A dozen men and women. Two dozen. Walker lost the head count when he'd nearly reached forty soldiers, and then he spotted the towering form of Lieutenant Cobb. The expression on Cobb's face, the cornered-animal glint of his eyes, told Walker all he needed to know, but Dunlap grabbed the lieutenant's arm.

"Is this a retreat, Lieutenant?" Dunlap asked.

"Bet your ass it is, Sarge."

"Where's Major Bernstein?" Walker said, scanning the smoke outside as he listened to the constant percussion of gunfire coming nearer in the camp.

Cobb shot him a dark look. "Not going to be joining us." He shouted orders at his remaining troops to form up inside the cave mouth, to prepare for an assault on Derveyî itself, and the soldiers rushed to obey, even those who already sported bandaged wounds. Even those whose wounds were still bleeding, untended.

Walker shouted for Cobb's attention, and when he didn't get it, he grabbed the man by both wrists.

"Listen to me, Lieutenant. There's contagion from the jar down below. It's bad. You take your people down there and most of you are going to die."

Cobb scowled, towering over him. "Brother, we stay out there, none of us makes it out. If we're lucky, we'll be able to hold these fuckers off from cover. If we have to, we'll withdraw to the stairs and pick them off one at a time. Ambush after ambush. There's only one way into this goddamn hole, which'll make it hard for them to smoke us out."

He barked other orders. Some of the smoke rolled through the open entrance.

Lieutenant Cobb turned to Dunlap. "Whatever happens, these New Caliphate assholes cannot get their hands on that jar." He glanced at Walker. "You hide it, you protect it, you die for it, but you do not surrender it under any circumstances. Do whatever you have to."

Dunlap snapped off a salute and headed down the slope toward the stairs at a hustle. Walker glanced out into the smoke, heard the thump of artillery hitting the camp. Something exploded out there, and a spark ignited in his thoughts. Lieutenant Cobb and his troops had gotten back to doing their job, and the volunteers from Sophie's team were helping tend to the wounded. Walker turned and raced after Dunlap, catching up to him on the stairs.

He grabbed Dunlap by the shoulder and spun him around.

"What?" Dunlap barked. "You heard him!"

Walker let go of him but pinned him instead with a look. "The backpack you took off that jihadi. Where is it?"

Dunlap stared at him. "Jesus Christ, Walker."

"You're focused on Lieutenant Cobb's orders. *You* heard him. We don't surrender the jar under any circumstances. We do what we have to."

The sergeant hesitated.

"We do what we have to," Walker said again, slower this time, his stare unwavering.

Another artillery shell hit the hill above their heads, and dust sifted down from the ceiling. Dunlap swore.

"It's in a footlocker in my quarters, under the bed," Dunlap said, then he poked Walker in the chest. "But this is for when we have no alternative, man. I'm gonna need you to promise me—"

Walker struck him hard, so fast that Dunlap didn't have time to defend himself. With the second blow, he saw Dunlap's eyes roll back to white, and the man staggered and went down on one knee.

He knew Dunlap might hurt him for this, even shoot him, so he punched him a third time to keep him down for a while. If they were extremely lucky, he would have a chance to apologize later, but he couldn't worry about anyone inside Derveyî anymore. Not Dunlap, not Sophie, not even Kim.

Cobb had been right. All that mattered was the jar.

As a boy, Elio Cortez had been in dozens of fistfights—in the schoolyard, in a parking lot, at beach parties. He had never won such a fight, but that history of defeats had never impacted his willingness to stand up for himself. Cortez had courage and determination, and he could take a brutal pummeling and stay on his feet. But he couldn't fight ghosts, and he couldn't fight contagion, so as the long minutes alone in Beyza's quarters stretched even longer, he paced the floor with the anxious purpose of a man used to settling things with direct action— settling them one way or the other.

Patience had never been his forte.

He had tried to sleep, even drifted off for a few minutes, but no matter how exhaustion had frayed his nerves and clouded his thoughts, the need to act overwhelmed him. Cortez paced, fists opening and closing at his sides. Occasionally, he muttered to himself. There were books on a shelf, but even if he had shared Beyza's tastes, he would not have been able to calm his mind enough to focus. Instead, he went to the curtain and glanced into the corridor. He listened to the distant voices in the gloom. There had been screams, muffled and anguished. Lonely. Helpless. But there had been other cries as well, and he thought of tales he had read of Bethlehem Royal Hospital in England, the asylum that gave the word "bedlam" its origin. Derveyî had become an asylum of a different kind.

"Come on, Beyza," Cortez whispered.

He sat on the edge of her cot, hands clasped, fingers interlaced as if he might be praying, but there were no gods he trusted. Cortez was done with waiting, done with attempting patience or faith in anything but himself. Beyza had a husband at home, but Cortez had taken the foolish step of falling in love with her, so he would wait here in this chamber with its still, suffocating air until she returned, and he would tell her that he was leaving and implore her to come with him.

The cave trembled with the impact of the battle going on overhead, but only once. Whatever had been falling on them—bombs or shells or fucking mini-nukes—had abated almost entirely. That might be a good sign, or a very bad one.

Don't think about it. Just breathe. Just wait for her.

Beyza would come back. Her dark eyes would shine in the dim, golden light of her quarters, and he would tell her that he was getting out of here, that he was leaving no matter how dangerous it might be. Cortez had never suffered from claustrophobia, but now the knowledge of the plague spreading down in Derveyî made his skin crawl. A scream lodged in his chest, just waiting for its moment.

He would tell Beyza she ought to come with him, that she never needed to return to her husband. If she refused to go, Cortez would leave her there. He would see the answer gleaming in those dark eyes, and he would know.

Either the coalition forces aboveground had driven the jihadis away or the jihadis had killed them all. No matter who might be winning up there, people would try to stop him from leaving, but he didn't care. In the darkness, in the chaos, one man alone might slip out unnoticed. Even two people might. A man and a woman. Lovers whose meeting had seemed perfect out here, far from the complications of the world, but whose bond had never been tested.

To hell with that. It's being tested now.

Someone coughed out in the corridor. Cortez stood up, took a step toward the curtain, a spark igniting in his chest as he thought, *Finally. Finally, Beyza. We're getting out of here.*

But the cough came again, and then a guttural stream of profanity followed by weeping. A choking sob, a man's voice.

Riveted to the floor, Cortez stared at the curtain. The lights in the corridor flickered, dimmed, brightened, went dark, and flared again. The generators had always been imperfect, but now they were sputtering as if they'd become ill in their own right.

He watched a shadow move past the curtain and held his breath, staring at that silhouette. The figure lurched, dragged its feet, head hunched over. For a moment, he thought there were two people out there, the man with the hacking cough and a second person walking beside him, though its shadowy silhouette seemed merely a suggestion.

Cortez had gone so still that he could not even feel his heart beat, but then the shadow passed by the curtain and his chest thundered with rhythm as if his heart rushed to make up for the beats it had skipped. Padding in near silence to the curtain, he drew back the edge, wary of any noise he might make.

The voice cried out, "Just stop! Let me die! I don't want to see anymore. Show someone else your . . ." The coughing erupted, wet and thick and sickly. "Show someone else your sins."

With a grunt, the man in the hall collapsed to the floor. Cortez bent forward and peered around the edge of the curtain. In the flickering lights in the corridor, he saw one of the workers—a digger named Yorkin—on hands and knees. Even at this angle, Cortez could make out the left side of his face and neck, could see the way his throat had swelled and blackened. Purple, weeping lesions marked his face. Yet as hideous as these plague sores were, the thing that froze Cortez with a fear he had never known was the thing standing just behind Yorkin.

The ghost—for as translucent as it was, it could only be a ghost—carried a ragged-stumped human head in its right hand, dangling from a tangle of filthy, matted hair. With its left hand, the phantom held a slim, curved dagger, but it did not aim the blade at Yorkin. Instead, the ghost clutched the blade in its fist and drove it once, twice, a third time into its own face. Into its own eyes.

Yorkin tried to scream but only choked on whatever bloody mucus lodged in his throat. He whimpered and pleaded. "Please," he managed to say. "I can't watch it again."

Weeping, Yorkin slumped to the floor.

The ghost knelt by him, lay down beside him, the severed head vanishing from its grip. It slid closer, like a lover seeking intimacy and comfort, and then it began to vanish inside Yorkin, as if the dying man's flesh absorbed its spectral body.

Yorkin went rigid. The coughing ceased. In a moment, back still toward Cortez, he began to stand. Somehow that wicked dagger remained in his hand, still a transparent wisp of a blade, but real enough that when Yorkin raised it and drove it into his left eye, blood and fluid sprayed out. This time, the digger did not scream.

Instead, he began to turn.

Cortez allowed the curtain to drop. Fearful of making a sound, he managed to move just to one side so that he would cast no shadow of his own—nothing that Yorkin, or the malice in residence within the digger, might notice. Not breathing, barely allowing his heart to beat, he waited for Yorkin to shuffle past and then another two full minutes of silence went by before he exhaled.

All thoughts of escape fled his mind. He went to Beyza's cot, lay on the floor, and slid himself beneath the frame. There in the darkness under the bed, he waited for her to return. In his entire life, he had never avoided a fight, even when he knew he would face defeat. This was different. Blood and broken bones held no fear for him, but evil had just strolled by, and Elio Cortez decided there was no shame in hiding now.

So he hid, and he waited.

A tickle began in his chest, the beginnings of a cough, and he told himself it was just the dust. It had to be just the dust.

He would wait for Beyza, and together they would decide what to do.

"There may be a way out," Dr. Tang said.

Sophie studied her, irritated and hopeful and high on adrenaline. "All due respect, Doc, but I've been here a very long time. There are other entrances we never excavated, but we'd need earthmovers to clear a path, and we don't have the time or the equipment."

"The Pandora Room was hidden," Dr. Tang replied. "Isn't it possible there were other hidden rooms? Other hidden passages?"

Propped against a column, Martin coughed. "We'd have found them. We've been over every inch of this place."

Ruiz had barely torn his gaze from the shadows of the column chamber, but now he glanced over at them. The barrel of his weapon remained pointed at the darkness as he spoke. "I don't know about you folks, but I'm happy to listen to any idea that doesn't end in us dying down here."

Sophie nodded, shuddering with tension. "Of course. I'm sorry, Dr. Tang. If you've seen something that suggests—"

"A draft," Dr. Tang said quickly. She held Lamar's journal at her side and walked away from the steps into the half-lit space among the columns. "Back that way, toward the worship chamber. I snuck a cigarette and watched the smoke whirl in a draft that came from a crack in the wall. I knocked a bit on the stone, and I was sure there was a hollow area behind it."

"A ventilation shaft," Martin rasped.

"Maybe," Dr. Tang admitted.

Beyza pushed her hands through her hair, yanking it back as if she wanted to tear it out by the roots. "Maybe not."

Sophie turned to her. "What are you saying?"

Beyza glanced up. "I saw a ghost along that hallway. Just a flicker, not much. I thought it might be imagination then. But it went through the wall, and I don't mean passed through it . . . I mean it slid through a crack like it was made of smoke."

Taejon had been kneeling by the weakening Carson, but now he stood. "Going where?"

Sophie exhaled, making a decision. "Wherever it went, I'd rather be finding the answer than standing here waiting." She glanced at Kim. "You have thoughts on this?"

Kim shook her head. "I'm going to wait for Walker and Sergeant Dunlap, and someone needs to make sure nobody else comes after the jar. I'll stay with Martin and Private Carson."

The decision made sense. Over the past fifteen minutes or so, as the sounds of battle topside had begun to diminish, Sophie had realized that their fate would not wait until morning. If they were going to take action, it had to be now.

"All right," she said. "Beyza, you and Taejon are with me. You can show us where you saw that crack. There are some tools still in the Alexander Room. If there's something on the other side of the wall, we'll find it."

She turned to Dr. Tang. "How many hazmat suits are there?"

"Three."

Sophie pointed to Ruiz. "Accompany Dr. Tang to retrieve those suits."

"And who *gets* those suits?" Ruiz asked. "I mean, I'm not ungrateful for this mask I got. So far, it seems to be doing the job. But a goddamn hazmat suit would make me feel a lot safer."

Taejon scoffed. "Not gonna happen. Three suits, that's it. Sophie and Kim are in charge, and Dr. Tang is the best chance any of us have of living through this. That's three. The rest of us will just have to stay lucky."

Martin laughed wetly, coughed a bit of blood into his palm, and smiled red-stained teeth at them. "More than one kind of luck."

Carson shot him a thumbs-up. Both men had begun to develop darker lesions on their skin. As Sophie looked at Martin, she saw his eyes begin to shift, following something she couldn't see, and with a shiver she wondered if there were ghosts in the room with them even now, like the grim reaper waiting for these men to breathe their last.

"All right, let's move our asses," Sophie said, thinking of Paris, of her parents. Thinking that maybe there would be one more day that her father would see her face and know her name. "If there's a way out of here, let's find it."

TWENTY-ONE

Dr. Tang kept silent as she and Ruiz moved through Derveyî. It felt as if the walls were closing around them, the ceiling lower, the air thinner. Though a cough built in her chest, she fought it, breathing evenly through her filtration mask. She padded along the stone corridors and up stone steps. Ahead of her, Ruiz did the same. He swept the barrel of his rifle in small arcs, careful with every corner they encountered. The thunder aboveground seemed to have ceased, but moving so quietly, they could not fail to hear distant shouts and cries from some of the Beneath Project's staff.

Gunfire, too, Dr. Tang thought. For what else could that sound be, the muffled, barely audible crackling noise that kept repeating itself?

She watched Ruiz's back, unsure what they would do if they encountered anyone. Most of their colleagues had been infected by now. Dr. Tang tried not to think about how many were dead. The walls seemed to breathe and flex, cold and dry and constricting. The tuffeau appeared to have darkened, the yellow turning sickly, but she told herself the effect was only her imagination.

Lamar's journal felt warm against her skin. She had tucked it into the waistband of her pants, and the cover scraped roughly on her abdomen as she walked. Why hadn't Sophie taken it back? Had her mind been so distracted, or did she simply not want to hold it again so soon, this book full of secrets and ugliness?

Quiet footsteps echoed off the stone, and Dr. Tang frowned, intending to admonish Ruiz before she realized they were not his steps at all.

Her breath gave a small hitch, and she froze in the passageway, even as Ruiz halted and took aim at the dimly lit corner ahead. One of the lightbulbs strung along the hall had gone out, and the rest flickered as if the generator had lost its motivation.

Dr. Tang stared at that corner long enough to begin wondering if she'd imagined the sound, but just when she might have spoken aloud, a dark figure slid into view, arm extended, pistol aimed at Ruiz's chest. Ruiz juked to one side, and then both men were moving in some strange interpretive dance as they tried to find a kill shot.

"Don't shoot, you idiots!" Dr. Tang snapped.

Ruiz took an audible breath, hesitated, and lowered his weapon. "Dr. Walker?"

Walker let his pistol hang at his side. "Sorry. I'm in a hurry, and there's no telling who's a threat now." He glanced at Dr. Tang. "Are we going to go through a whole health check? 'Cause I've got to tell you, the clock's ticking. Our guardian angels have taken shelter in the entrance, and it's not looking good. They can hold the jihadis off for a while, but not forever."

"Long enough?" Dr. Tang asked.

Walker frowned. "Maybe," he said, but what she heard was, *Maybe not.*

"Get moving, then. Kim is down by the Pandora Room. We've all got work to do."

Walker shifted the backpack he'd acquired—Dr. Tang did not remember him having it before—and hurried past them. It occurred to her that she ought to have told him what Sophie and the others were up to, but if he was heading toward the Pandora Room, he would pass them on the way.

"Come on," she said, taking the lead.

Ruiz picked up his pace. "How badly do we need these suits? If Walker's right, we could be overrun anytime. I don't want to be caught in the atrium if our only way out is behind us."

Dr. Tang broke into a light run.

Ruiz swore quietly and matched her pace. "I guess that's my answer."

When they reached the worship chamber, they paused to listen to the muffled gunfire and the howl of the voices of the sick and mad. Dr. Tang did not want Ruiz to have to kill anyone, but those who were already infected were going to die no matter what they did, and she wanted to live. It felt savagely simple.

"This way," she said, leading him into a narrow hall and then up the curving staircase into the wing where Sophie and her senior staff had their quarters and where Walker, Kim, and Dr. Tang herself had been placed.

As they went up the stairs, Ruiz moved in front again. The lighting had worsened. Half of the bulbs were burned out, and the rest flickered into darkness and then seemed to hesitate before brightening again.

Something shifted in the shadows at the top of the stairs, and then the lights snapped on and she saw the landing was empty. *Nothing there in the dark that isn't there in the light,* her father had always told her.

Dr. Tang had never believed it, not even then.

At the landing, they paused. Ruiz kept his gaze and his aim pointed along the hallway.

"Two of the suits are vacuum-sealed, and one is open. They're all in a bag under my cot," she said. "But understand something, Ruiz. We can't leave without the jar, and that means someone has to carry it. I don't mind doing the carrying, but I'm not doing it without one of those suits. If you feel like holding the jar in your own hands, you're welcome to my gear."

Ruiz gave her a lopsided grin. "I think I'm good."

Something laughed in the darkness. The sound moved in the shadows, a wet hiss of amusement, and then it cut off. No more laughter, and no echo.

Dr. Tang stared at Ruiz, but he ignored her, stepping along the corridor with his gun leading the way. The voice had not echoed, but it did linger in her head, and Dr. Tang had the unsettling certainty that whoever owned that voice had no fear of guns.

Stop, she told herself.

She stood and watched Ruiz advance through the flickering light.

"Who's there?" he asked. "Sing out now. I wouldn't want to shoot you by accident."

When no one replied, Dr. Tang hurried to follow Ruiz. Better she be close to the man with the gun than left alone at the top of the stairs with unreliable lighting and bulbs dying like ancient stars.

A bit of information floated up in the back of her mind. Her brows knitted as she forced this puzzle piece into place.

"It's Cortez," she said quietly.

Ruiz pushed back a curtain and aimed his weapon into the room Walker had been using. He scanned the cave and then backed out, glancing farther along the hall.

"Who's that?" he asked.

"Cortez. He's on staff. Professor Solak left him waiting in her room."

"Is he sick?"

Dr. Tang wiped sweat from beneath her eyes, careful not to shift the mask that still covered the lower half of her face. Sometimes she felt suffocated by it, but she'd be damned if she took it off.

She pointed at the right doorway. "Be careful."

Ruiz first checked the room across the hall from Walker's and then kept moving, checking a third. Finally, he stood outside the last room on the corridor and aimed his gun at the thick fabric curtain. Beyza's room.

Dr. Tang listened for that laughter. She felt the sweat trickling on her face again and the cough that lodged in her chest, ready to burst free. The lights dimmed and buzzed, and a bulb just over the doorway winked out. It felt to her now as if she had begun to suffocate, as if at any moment they might all be buried alive.

Ruiz nodded to her and gestured to the curtain. Dr. Tang took a deep breath and then yanked it back, and Ruiz stepped into the room, gun barrel shifting back and forth. She narrowed her eyes, tensed up, waiting for violence.

"Nothing," Ruiz said. "Whoever this Cortez is, he's gone."

Dr. Tang wondered what had happened to the man, but it was really Beyza's problem.

"This room is mine," she said, pointing to one of the curtains Ruiz had already checked. "Let's grab those suits and get back to the others."

The corridor lights dimmed again. Something whispered in the dark, and when she turned to Ruiz, for just a moment it seemed as if someone stood behind him, as if she were seeing double. The lights flared brightly, and the illusion disappeared—if it had been an illusion.

"You really think there's a way out of here?" Ruiz asked, following her into the room and dropping to his knees to help her drag the hazmat suits from beneath the bed.

Dr. Tang grabbed hold of the binding of Lamar's journal, which still jutted from her waistband. It had shifted around and nearly fallen out, and she didn't want to lose it while carrying the suits.

"I'm sure there is."

They might find a new exit, but her confidence came from a darker place. No matter what happened, there would always be a way out. Dr. Tang did not tell Ruiz that their only exit might be through death.

The man was a soldier. She figured he already knew.

Sophie stared at the crack in the wall. They had found it easily enough, though Beyza said she thought the crack had gotten bigger since the last time she had noticed it. Now they stood in the tunnel that connected the Alexander Room to the stairway down to the column chamber. For some reason this space had always felt cold to Sophie, even that first day when she had crawled through the hole in the wall and discovered the Alexander Room, then gone on to discover the Pandora Room and the jar.

"You want me to do the honors?" Taejon asked, voice muffled by his filtration mask.

Sophie glanced down at the sledgehammer in her hands, felt the strain in her biceps. She could swing a goddamn sledgehammer without anyone's help, had worked to build her core and the muscles in her upper body. For a few seconds, she allowed herself the luxury of being offended by the question, and then she relented. Corporal Taejon hadn't offered because he didn't think she was capable.

Taejon had wanted to lift the burden from her. She was an archae-ologist. Her job usually required meticulous work. It called for brushes and shovels and adzes. Hand tools. Archaeologists moved soil, used mattocks to break up dirt and rock, but carefully. A sledgehammer wasn't a careful tool.

Sophie lifted the sledge, backed up, gestured for the others to stand clear. Beyza had a pickax, but Sophie hadn't let her anywhere near the crack except to feel for the draft they all agreed was there.

"Thank you, Corporal, but just watch our asses. You use your weapon," she said, listening to the dull crack of intermittent gunfire. "I'll use mine."

She swung the hammer at the crack. Stone chipped away. The tuffeau had hardened, of course, but still it gave way in chunks and clods. Sophie swung the hammer again and again, widening a foot-long section of the crack, breaking away bits of the wall.

On the fifth strike, she knocked a hole into hollow darkness.

"Oh, my God," Beyza said, and Sophie could hear the hope in her voice.

She bent and felt the draft slipping from that hole. It was big enough to put her fist through, and she let the sledgehammer hang from her left hand as she pushed her right into the hollow.

"A vent?" Taejon asked.

"I don't know," Sophie said. "It's dark as hell."

Beyza nudged her away from the hole. "Let's not worry how many flashlights we have until we're sure there's more back there than a gap. Come on."

She swung the pick. Sophie followed it with a blow from the sledge, and then Beyza struck again. Both of them were wheezing behind their masks.

When they heard a voice, at first Sophie thought it came from the hole, but then they turned and saw Walker hurrying toward them, holding the straps of a backpack that hung heavily over his shoulders.

"What's happening up top?" Sophie asked, eyeing that backpack. "You look like you're ready to go."

Walker gestured to the hole they had made. "You find us an exit?"

"Working on it. Too soon to tell."

Beyza swung the pick, smashing away another chunk of stone around the widening crack. "I've got a good feeling about it," she said, and then she started to cough, turning away from them.

Walker stared at Beyza a moment, his expression dark, as if he wanted to dispute her good feeling. Then he seemed to shake it off and turned to Sophie.

"I'll be down in the Pandora Room with Kim. Let us know if you find anything."

Sophie nearly stopped him—Walker hadn't answered her question about what was happening topside, and she wondered where Dunlap had gotten off to—but he jogged down the corridor, and then Beyza swung her pick again and a ten-inch square section of the wall gave way. The darkness on the other side felt deep and yawning, and hope again flared within her.

She swung the sledgehammer and smashed in another big chunk of wall, so that the crack had been almost completely obliterated and replaced by a black void. Bits of rubble tumbled into that darkness, and she could hear an echo.

"This is promising," Taejon said.

Sophie heard a bustling off to her left and turned to see Dr. Tang and Private Ruiz striding down the corridor toward them. Dr. Tang had put on a hazmat suit. Ruiz carried sealed plastic bags that must have been the other two, but if his bitterness about not getting one of those suits for himself remained, it had been overrun by urgency.

"We ready to go?" Ruiz asked as he rushed up to them.

"Getting there, I hope," she replied.

Beyza had stopped working and turned to Dr. Tang. "Did you talk to Cortez? Is he all right? I need to go and get him. I should have—"

"He's not there," Ruiz interrupted.

Dr. Tang scorched him with a glance. "We didn't see him."

"He was in my quarters," Beyza said. "Maybe he's sick. He could've been sleeping, I guess."

"No, Professor Solak," Ruiz said. "That's what I'm saying. We checked your room, and most of the west wing as well. No sign of Cortez at all."

Sophie watched Beyza's expression go slack. First her friend and colleague had kept this affair with Cortez from her, and now it seemed that Beyza had deeper feelings for Cortez than she'd let on.

Beyza handed Taejon the pick she'd been wielding and turned to Sophie. "I'm sorry. I need to . . ."

"Go," Sophie told her. "But hurry. If there's a tunnel through this wall, we're taking it no matter where it leads."

Beyza frowned and cast a dark look at the hole as if she didn't quite trust it. Then she started back the way Dr. Tang and Ruiz had come.

"You want me to go with her?" Ruiz asked.

Sophie handed him her sledgehammer and took the two vacuum-sealed hazmat suits from him. "No. Help us here."

As Taejon and Ruiz smashed away at the wall, Martin Jungling walked up. He had no mask at all, not a filtration mask and certainly no hazmat suit. He coughed as he approached, a wet, rough sound in his chest.

"Christ," Taejon said. "Place is like Grand Central Station."

Martin coughed again.

"What are you doing up here?" Sophie asked, but gently, with a kindness she would not have afforded him before today.

Martin took the moment to lean gratefully against the wall. "I want to check on the south wing. If we're going to leave, we should see if anyone there is still healthy."

"I'm afraid that's not likely, Martin," Dr. Tang said.

"But we can't be sure unless someone goes up there," Martin argued, stopping to cough again, wheezing in a few breaths to calm himself. "Carson told me I was crazy, but someone has to do it, and I'm already infected. I can't catch this thing twice. If there's a chance some of them are healthy enough to leave with us, I'm not abandoning them."

"We're not waiting for you, man," Ruiz said.

Martin nodded.

Sophie put a hand on his arm. Her hazmat suit crinkled loudly. "Be safe, please."

As Martin went up the corridor in the same direction Beyza had gone, Sophie noticed Dr. Tang staring at her.

"What?"

Dr. Tang shrugged, her own hazmat suit crinkling. "I just can't believe you let him go, as sick as he is. This will kill him if we can't get him help soon enough. His mind may unravel. But you just let him—"

"Don't you think he knows that?" Sophie asked bitterly. "He wants to feel useful. If he dies, he doesn't want to just wait around for it to happen. And neither do I."

Taejon swung the sledgehammer, and this time a whole section of the wall collapsed, huge chunks of rubble piling up between the corridor and the gaping blackness beyond.

Ruiz bent and picked up a chunk of rock, then hurled it into the darkness. It struck stone and then skittered and rolled to a stop.

"I want flashlights," Sophie said. "We're going in."

Dunlap wanted to strangle the fucking guy.

He had trusted Walker, and the asshole sucker punched him. Lieutenant Cobb had retreated into the entrance with what remained of the coalition troops who had been guarding the Beneath Project, and those were some tough soldiers, men and women who had survived the night thus far and were going to do everything they could to make it through until help arrived. Dunlap had faith in them, but Walker had none.

Groaning, Dunlap knelt in the tunnel that led from the surface into the atrium. He took deep breaths, trying to clear his thoughts. His fists opened and closed.

"Son of a bitch," he muttered.

Tasting copper, he spit a wad of phlegm onto the stone floor, then wiped blood from his nose and mouth.

Then he remembered the explosives. He doubted he had been unconscious for more than a minute or two, but Walker had rattled him. Dunlap figured he had a concussion, which pissed him off even more. His head throbbed with a deep ache, like it went all the way to the center of his brain, and his vision blurred as he leaned on the wall and forced himself to stand.

Yeah, he had only been out for a couple of minutes, but he had been lying there for longer.

Unsteady on his feet, he started down into the atrium. If Walker intended to set off explosives in the Pandora Room, Dunlap would stop him.

And he had no intention of being gentle about it.

The moment Kim saw Walker's face, she knew he was about to piss her off. She sat on the floor of the column chamber, about ten feet to the left of the entrance to the thirteen steps. There were too many places on this floor where people had been killed in the past twenty-four hours, and many still had smears and stains from the blood of the dying. It chilled her and made her slightly queasy. For a while, she had been able to fight off those feelings by talking to Carson, but now Private Carson had fallen asleep. He lay on the floor on the other side of the entrance to the steps. In the gloom of the poorly lit space, with the generators causing the lights to flicker, the lesions on his skin were so dark they seemed almost black. In that gloom, it was also difficult to make out whether Carson was still breathing, but every minute or two she heard him snort or exhale loudly, and he rustled a bit and turned over once or twice, so she left him to his rest, wondering if he would die.

Now, though, she barely remembered Carson's presence.

Walker stood just at the edge of the illumination. He'd emerged from the darker part of the room, among the columns, wearing a backpack that hung heavy on him, straps digging into his shoulders.

Kim had seen that backpack before. She held her breath but did not rise to her feet.

"So here you are," she said quietly.

"He alive?" Walker replied, gesturing toward Carson.

"I think so. Did you see Sophie? Are they having any luck?"

"Some. They made a hole in the wall, so maybe that's a start."

Walker took a step toward the stairs, almost as if she weren't there. Almost as if he didn't think she would try to stop him.

Kim stood up and walked to meet him. Walker could have picked up his pace, could have held up a hand and brushed her aside and headed down into the Pandora Room without having to face her. She had wanted to fall in love with him, but something had prevented that from happening. Kim cared for him, admired him, even loved him, but as many times as they had made love, she had never felt *in* love with Walker. She saw it now, looking at him, the hard edge that created the invisible, unspoken distance between them. She understood why his marriage had ended in divorce and why, try as he might, he struggled to be the father he wished he could be. This was a man who knew his life would include ugly choices that the people he loved would never understand, and all his love came weighted with that knowledge. A gulf that could never be bridged.

"Where are you going?" Kim asked.

To make sure the jar is ready to move, he would say. Or there would be a different lie, something about Sophie asking him to retrieve a tool. But Kim recognized that backpack, and he must have seen the clarity of knowledge in her eyes, because he stuck to the truth.

"Things topside have gone pear-shaped. Our guns are way outnumbered. Cobb and the survivors retreated into Derveyî, and they can hold off for a little while, but not for long. The jihadis have to know help is coming. Choppers first, probably, and then troops. I don't know how it'll go, but once our help arrives, they are done, so they're going to do whatever it takes to get into this place and get their hands on that."

He pointed down the steps.

"They'll do whatever it takes. And so will I."

Kim felt sick. She breathed deeply and shifted herself further, interposing herself between Walker and the steps.

"You're not thinking clearly," she said.

"Don't make this harder than it is."

"Walker, I don't know exactly what your orders were on this trip, but I'm very sure they did not involve destroying the jar. Your bosses want this thing, and they want it badly. Even more than my bosses do, and that's saying something."

His expression crumbled, but only for a moment. When he recovered, he gazed at her with loving sadness and reached out to take her hands.

"It wouldn't matter what my orders were. No way can I let a bunch of psychotic jihadi pricks get their hands on this thing. Look what it's already done. Most of the people in Derveyî are crazy or dying or both. If any of us survive this, it'll be a miracle—"

"Sophie and the others are making us an exit," Kim interrupted.

"It's a Hail Mary, and you know it. We can't rely on that," Walker told her. "As for my job, it has two parts. First is to acquire the jar. Second is to make goddamn sure lunatics don't get it. So my bosses may not be happy, but they'll live with it. And to be honest, after seeing what I've seen here, I don't really want *them* to have it, either."

Kim lifted her chin. Walker had been trained to fight, trained for combat. He had her in size and strength and weight. But she met his gaze without wavering.

"I'm not going to let you do this."

Walker stared at her, brow furrowing. "Don't make me choose, Seong."

She felt an icy certainty in her chest. "I've already chosen. It's your turn."

Walker closed his eyes, exhaling slowly. "Fine . . ."

A hand grabbed hold of Kim's ankle.

She let out a tiny scream as she jerked her leg away, staring down to see Carson had woken and reached for her. Even now he stretched his hand out. His eyes were red, and a lesion had opened on his left cheek that looked to be eating through the skin, but he had the strength to get to his knees.

"Get back," Walker said.

As if she needed him to tell her.

Carson pointed deeper into the column chamber, but not into darkness. He gestured toward a well-lit corner, where the flickering of the lights seemed less significant.

"Don't you . . . see them?" the ailing soldier asked.

Kim and Walker stared where he was pointing.

"What are we looking at?" Walker said.

"The man . . . he keeps kicking that boy. Over and over. The pain . . . in the boy's face . . ."

Kim glanced at Walker. "Ghosts. He sees them now."

"I don't see anything," Walker said.

But as Kim stared at that flickering corner and listened to Carson, she started to think she might be able to make out the silhouettes of the figures that had so disturbed him. A man in a robe, with a cloth wrapped around his chest and a tall headpiece. A small boy on the ground, curled into a fetal ball and barely moving. It was just the suggestion of figures in the light, but the more she stared, the more she felt sure it wasn't just her mind reacting to Carson's words. They were there.

The evils of humanity. The cruelties.

Carson began to struggle to his feet.

Kim turned to look at Walker, to stare at the pack full of explosives that hung on his back, and she wondered if maybe his solution was the only way this could all end.

TWENTY-TWO

Beyza stumbled and turned to look at the tunnel floor, but if she had caught the toe of her shoe on something, she couldn't see what it had been. When she glanced up again, the motion of moving her head made her sway, and she had to put out her hand to keep from losing her balance.

She dragged in a sluggish breath, suddenly hating the filtration mask. The urge to tear it aside, to get a full, clear breath, tempted her. Instead, she stood for a few seconds and forced herself to inhale slowly. The wall felt slick, almost spongy, which she knew had to be impossible. The tuffeau might be soft enough to carve, but it didn't stay that way. The walls were solid and permanent. Like the floor beneath her feet, they remained stable and reliable. Beyza thought of her marriage and nearly laughed at herself for the unintentional metaphor—or whatever the opposite of a metaphor might be. It wasn't the reliability of stone walls that had her thinking about her husband but the fact that her lover had vanished. Here she was, risking her own self for a man with whom she could never forge a life.

And yet . . .

Despite what Dr. Tang and Ruiz had said, she went to the west wing first. She looked in every room, but there was no sign of Cortez. She whispered his name because, alone in those strange caves and tunnels, it did not feel right—or safe—to speak in full voice. The walls were striated with wan yellow light from modern bulbs and stripes of ancient shadow.

When Beyza had not been alone, Derveyî had seemed rich with the promise of discovery, but now she felt the age of the place and the long-concluded lives of its people. Others had walked here, lived here, died here even after those original residents, and some of them had been infected, too.

At the top of the steps that would lead her out of the west wing, Beyza leaned against the wall again. She coughed, choking up something bitter and bloody, but she swallowed it back down for fear of removing her mask.

"What are you doing, woman?" she asked, her own muffled voice sounding deep and rasping and alien beneath her mask.

This man is not your husband. If he is not here, he is gone. He is sick. You cannot stay behind. You cannot die for him.

Panic rushed into her heart. What if the others found the way out and left her behind? She told herself that Sophie would never do that, but they were leaving so many colleagues behind, and after Lamar betrayed her, there would be no telling who Sophie might trust enough to risk her life for. If they had the jar and they were ready to leave, wouldn't their need to get it out of here and away from the jihadis override any concern for Beyza?

Shit, she thought. A loud voice at the back of her head kept repeating that Sophie would never abandon her, but what streamed from her lips was nothing but self-abuse and profanity.

She started down the steps, still unsteady but determined. At the bottom, she turned into a curved corridor, off which there were several balconies that overlooked the atrium. The sounds of chaos had abated, but now she heard cries of anguish that echoed off the walls as if they came from the shadows instead of from the south wing. Her heart broke. She wanted to go to her friends there, to see if anyone could be helped, but that other voice in her head reminded her that she did not want to be left behind with them.

Gunfire cracked and resounded, and she hurried faster, turning down a narrow set of steps that brought her to a small room. One more short corridor and she would arrive at the stairs that led to the worship chamber, and then the Alexander Room, and the path to the Pandora Room.

Get the jar, she thought. *And get out.*

The lights were out in this corridor. Not flickering as in other places. This was not the result of trouble with the generator. Beyza slipped the small flashlight from her pocket and clicked it on. Her pulse quickened as she saw the scattering of broken glass that littered the floor. The lightbulbs had been removed and smashed, one by one, all in the few minutes she had been up in the west wing. A deliberate act, and weighted with malice she could feel. The shards of glass were like eggshells all across the floor. Claustrophobia had been infiltrating her mind, insidious and suffocating, and with every breath, every step, the walls felt closer.

Beyza had to get down to the worship chamber, had to get back to the others. She thought of her students and her friends back in Istanbul, and the safety of home. An image rose in her mind of Dorothy clicking her heels three times and saying those magic words—*There's no place like home.* The girl had transported herself back to Kansas.

But Beyza had never owned a pair of ruby slippers.

As she hurried through the dark, she heard Cortez say her name.

Beyza jumped, swung the flashlight toward him. Its beam turned him gray and pale. His eyes were wide and pleading, and his shoulders were slumped, his head lolling slightly to one side. A rash had spread up the left side of his face, and his lips were swollen with it. When he spoke, the words came out stunted and soft, their edges rounded.

"Elio," she said. "Oh, my God."

"Stay with me," he said, his eyes full of sorrow. "We'll hide together. In the dark, we can be safe."

He shifted backward into the grotto where Beyza and Sophie had argued only days before. Days that seemed like months, like years. So many of their colleagues had been alive then and were dead or dying now, and Beyza felt the weight of their suffering. Felt the blame.

"I'm sorry," she said, wanting to reach out to him but unable to force her hands to do so. "I'm sorry you're sick—"

"If I'm sick, so are you," Cortez said, words muffled by the swelling of his mouth. He smiled, and his lower lip cracked, dark blood trickling down his chin. "You fucked me good. Bet you never fucked your husband like that."

Beyza winced. He'd never talked this way to her, not even in the midst of sex.

"Stay with me," he said again, demeanor shifting like a weather vane. The pain in his expression made her forgive him. "We'll hide. We'll be together."

"It's not safe here," she said, moving toward him, trusting her filtration mask. She held up her hands to ward him off as if she'd stepped into the lion's den. "We need to go with Sophie and the others. I told you I'd be back. You were supposed to—"

"Wait for you. I did wait, but you never came."

"I'm here now."

Tears spilled from Cortez's eyes. He hung his head and turned to lean against the wall, almost as if he'd forgotten he was not alone. Her flashlight beam lost him a moment, illuminating his denim-clad legs.

"You're too late," he said. "I waited, but someone found me before you came looking."

"Someone . . . ," she began.

Cortez raised a hand to dab at his eyes, and she saw something shift and resettle on his back. Something that moved independently of him, a pale gray thing the same color his skin had become, almost invisible in the darkness thanks to those shattered bulbs.

"Elio." Her face flushed with heat, her skin prickling with fear. "What is that?"

He shuddered as he exhaled. His shoulders slumped farther, and he put more of his weight on the wall as if the burden he carried might crush him. As he turned, Beyza saw the eyes of the gray thing behind him, only now she saw that it had a bluish cast to it, and a blue mist seemed to smoke from its eyes, like her breath in the dead of winter.

The ghost on his back stabbed a long finger into his spine, then sank its teeth into the fleshy lobe of his right ear. Cortez whimpered and stood straighter, the ghost yanking his strings as if he were its puppet. Attached to his back, using him, whispering to him words that Beyza could not hear. Words that made him cry all the harder.

When Cortez glanced at her again, wisps of that same blue light puffed from his eyes, and he took a step toward her.

Beyza backed away. Her boot heels crunched broken lightbulb glass underfoot.

"It's only a matter of time," Cortez said through swollen lips, in a voice that might not have belonged to him after all. "You're infected, and you know it. Stay with me, Beyza."

She turned and ran for the atrium, knowing there was no safety there.

Behind her, the thing clinging to Cortez laughed and laughed.

Jihadis were piled up outside the entrance to Derveyî. The stink of blood and shit and fear filled the tunnel. Lieutenant Cobb had lost only two men in the ten-minute eternity since the New Caliphate fuckers had started their assault on this hole in the mountain, this ant-hill, this tomb to which they had all retreated. Jihadi terrorists—he didn't want to think of them as soldiers—crouched or lay on the ground outside, using their dead comrades as cover, and fired indiscriminately into the darkened entrance. Bullets pinged off the stone walls and sent shards raining down on Cobb and his surviving troops.

His people kept silent. Cobb had beads of sweat trickling down his face and neck, and his throat had nearly closed with all the dust he'd inhaled out in the camp while they'd been under attack, but he breathed through his nose and sighted along the barrel and squeezed the trigger. Bullets sprayed from the muzzle, and two of the jihadis sheltering behind their dead were knocked backward, blood spraying, and they fell into the spreading pile.

One of the corpses moved.

Cobb frowned. The woman beside him, Karnacki, shouted something to the others, so he knew they saw it, too. The dead man seemed to jerk and twitch, and then he slid backward out of the pile, and Lieutenant Cobb saw the top of a head on the other side and realized that the jihadis were starting to drag their dead away from the entrance.

"Son of a bitch!" he shouted as he opened fire.

He took two steps forward. Karnacki barked at him to stay in formation, despite his rank, and she was right, but he winged the bastard who had dragged the body out of the pile. Then three or four other bodies were dragged away, and Cobb shouted to his troops to rip them apart.

Everyone opened fire, trying to kill as many of the assault force as they could. One jihadi went down, but another grabbed him by the collar and hauled him away. Most of Cobb's troops were firing into the pile of bodies, hoping to kill anyone who might be trying to clear the hellish barrier that had built up there.

"Stop!" Karnacki shouted. She grabbed his shoulder and shook him. "Lieutenant, stop firing!"

Cobb released the trigger and glared at her. "What the fuck do you think you're doing, Corporal? We need every advantage we can get. A clear path benefits the enemy, not us!"

Karnacki nodded grimly. "Yes, sir! But nothing benefits them more than us using our ammo. We can't hold them off if we've got nothing to kill them with but our hands, sir!"

Cobb swore, dropping back in line. He lowered his weapon and shouted for them all to cease fire.

The moment the echoes stopped, the jihadis charged in, sweeping toward the entrance in numbers that blotted out the indigo glow of nighttime outside Derveyî. They ran over the bodies of the dead, climbed onto them, leaped down from them, shooting all the while. Bullets strafed the tunnel inside the entrance. Two of Cobb's soldiers went down. Karnacki and Ellison roared at the others to stay low and keep firing, and they did so. Jihadis died and fell, and their comrades stepped over them.

A bullet struck Cobb in the left side, punched through his body, and exited out the back. His blood spattered Karnacki, but he let the wound spin him around.

"Fall back!" he ordered.

They'd been ready. They hustled back down the curving stairs, just a dozen steps. The wounded had already been moved to the bottom, but those who could still hold and aim a gun waited. The jihadis had to proceed two at a time now, perhaps four or five able to fire at once, ganged up on the steps.

Cobb had the stink of blood in his nostrils and knew this time it was his own.

He took aim and fired and kept shooting.

It was the only choice they had.

Martin had lived what he had always considered an ordinary life. Growing up on a dairy farm had been idyllic some days, boring on others, but there had always been peace and beauty and fresh air. He knew he'd had good fortune to have two parents who were willing to strive and sacrifice for his education and to push him to pursue his passions. Before he had gone off to university and begun studying archaeology, he had never been farther from Belgium than the train could take him. Working with people from around the world, learning from brilliant, determined examples like Sophie Durand, had been for Martin like entering a wardrobe and finding himself in Narnia.

Now he yearned for the farm, wished he could walk the fields and talk to the cows and get his hands dirty fixing the machines when they broke down. He missed his parents more than he ever had. His ordinary life had become extraordinary, and he had always thought he'd wanted that, but now extraordinary had killed him.

Not yet, he thought. *It hasn't killed you yet.*

But it had, really. He felt the itch of his rash spreading, felt the thick mucus building up in his lungs, tasted blood and bitter bile on his tongue. And he saw ghosts now. The people from the east wing had gone mad, more or less, and were dead or dying. Worst of all, though, had been the look in Sophie's eyes. She had sparred with him in the past, teased him and bossed him about, laughed with him and sometimes outright dismissed him, but he'd seen the way she had looked at him when she realized he had been infected, like she had really noticed him for the first time, as if maybe she felt something for him.

He had wished to see such a thing in her eyes for months, but now it came with something more—pity, sorrow, grief, mourning for a friend who still lived but whose clock was winding down.

That look in Sophie's eyes had galvanized him. Martin wasn't dead yet, and that meant there was still a chance for him if they could get out of this place. It also meant that their colleagues who were infected but still alive, who were not so far gone that they had turned violent, might be brought along if an exit could be found. Martin was determined to find those people, and he was furious with Sophie and Beyza and the rest for not having thought of it themselves. If he had been up in the south wing, would they have left him there, not even tried to get him out? He thought he knew the answer, and it drove him onward.

Coughing, he spit a disgusting wad on the steps as he climbed up into the south wing. He wanted to be quiet, tried to stifle his coughing and muffle his footsteps, but he had to pause halfway up just to rest, and there was only so much he could focus when he felt as awful as he did now. At the top of the steps, he paused to scratch through his shirt, and his fingers came away damp with whatever fluid leaked out of the lesions on his skin.

"Fuck it," he whispered.

He stepped into the south wing corridor. On the verge of calling out to see who was still in their right mind enough to answer, he froze.

There were at least three people dead on the floor in the corridor, one of them Zehra, who'd been his friend and who had been guarding Dr. Tang's makeshift morgue the last time he'd seen her. Blood smeared the walls. A big, bearded man with lesions and deep scratches all over his body knelt, naked, as he defiled Zehra's corpse. Any other day and Martin would have recognized the man instantly as Ed Pellegrino, whom they'd taken to calling Pelican, but it took him long seconds to reconcile this abomination with the man he'd known.

In a doorway, the curtain half torn down, Delia French knelt and wept, leaning against the smooth stone of the doorway. Her clothes were stained red and black, and she picked at a lesion on her face that seemed deep and growing. But it wasn't the sight of Pelican or Delia that had silenced him. It was the ghosts.

There were so many of them—at least eight or nine in the corridor, each committing unspeakable acts of violence and depravity.

Or, at least, they had been doing so until Martin had walked in.

Now, one by one, the ghosts paused in their perversity and turned to stare at him, their eyes little more than ice-blue mist. Martin's breath caught in his throat. He began to tremble as he took a step backward. His whole body seemed to go numb as he took another step back, moving to the top of the stairs. The ghosts had gone impossibly still, but their eyes tracked him with the dire focus of a wolf pack.

Martin felt that awful tickle in his chest, the clogging in his lungs, and the urge to cough overcame him. He fought it, but his throat betrayed him, and involuntarily he cleared it.

Pelican whipped his upper body around to stare. His left eye had been gouged out. He grinned and stood, his cock erect and bobbing and slick with blood. In her doorway, Delia started to slide her back up the wall, rising to her feet, staring at Martin with a malice he had never seen before.

The first ghost moved, and then all of them together, like murderous birds taking flight. In pursuit of Martin.

He turned and fled down the stairs, chest burning, head thundering, coughing as he ran. Behind him came the ghosts, and Pelican and Delia shouting wordless rage, and others of the infected who were further along the road to madness and death.

Martin sobbed as he ran.

He prayed.

The ground hadn't shaken in a while. Down in the corridor where they had made a new hole in the wall, Sophie worried that things had gotten quiet. A voice in the back of her head told her not to worry, that quiet might mean good things. Quiet might mean rescue or victory, or both. But she thought that if quiet meant survival, someone would have come running to tell her that by now. Instead, she thought quiet meant the calm before the storm. The screaming people had likely died or were too weak to scream. The jihadis had stopped shelling because they didn't need to do so anymore. As for the gunfire . . . it had been so muffled down here that it was impossible to know what she was hearing, and now it was hard to make out any sound louder than her booming heartbeat.

Sophie tore open the package with her hazmat suit, and Dr. Tang showed her how to put it on. Inside the suit, she wouldn't need the filtration mask she'd been wearing, but she kept it on for fear of exposure during the transition from one mask to the next.

Dr. Tang latched the headpiece into place, the two women staring at each other through layers of clear plastic face shield.

"Wait. You should have this." Dr. Tang held out Lamar's journal. "And there's something you should know."

Sophie took the journal. A few feet away, Taejon and Ruiz were smashing away bits of the wall, and the hole had been widened enough for them to step through, but Sophie didn't yet know if the breach would lead them anywhere. It was time to find out.

"It's going to have to wait," she said, sliding the journal into the wide, deep pocket on her left thigh before zipping up the hazmat suit.

Dr. Tang helped her seal the suit and then aided her in securing the headpiece. "You can read it when we're out of here. I just thought you'd want to know that, toward the end, Lamar described the ghosts he saw in more detail . . . and that one of them touched him. He had some pretty disgusting urges, and he understood that whatever this was, it would infect others."

Sophie breathed deeply, trying to get used to wearing both the filtration mask and the hazmat headpiece. She stared at Dr. Tang.

"Are you suggesting Lamar stole the jar to . . . what . . . protect us?"

Dr. Tang shrugged, her hazmat suit crinkling loudly. "I don't know. I never got to finish reading, and some of what's at the end is either gibberish or some language I've never seen before."

Sophie lowered her head, staring at the stone floor of the corridor and the debris gathered there. "I wish I could believe that. But the officer up top, Cobb . . . he told Walker and Dunlap the New Caliphate had someone on the inside. If it wasn't Lamar, who was it?"

"I don't have any answers."

"It doesn't make sense," Sophie replied, but her thoughts were churning.

Which was when Ruiz smashed a three-foot section out of the wall with one blow. Taejon unleashed a string of shocking profanity and leaped aside as a huge chunk of stone crashed onto the place his feet had been a moment before. He snapped at Ruiz and punched him on the shoulder, but Sophie barely noticed their squabble.

She clicked on the powerful light attached to her suit's headpiece. Ruiz shielded his eyes from the glare and moved aside as Sophie stepped forward, climbed onto the fallen rock, and entered the hole. For the moment, Dr. Tang and Lamar and the journal were forgotten.

"So, what do you see?" Taejon asked. "We wasting our time?"

Sophie held out her hands for balance, but as soon as she was away from the debris of their breakthrough, the ground beneath her feet was rough, natural stone. Inside the hazmat suit, she couldn't feel the breeze anymore, but when she glanced upward, her headlamp showed a wide ventilation shaft that turned at a slight angle as it shot toward the surface. No light was visible above, but it was still dark outside so she did not expect sunshine.

The words stuck in her throat. She ought to tell them that their efforts had been for nothing, that the time had come for them all to hide. This was just a ventilation shaft.

Then she glanced to the right and saw that the floor sloped downward and that the wall in front of her seemed darker in that direction, that the chamber she had entered seemed to widen. The thought of escaping, of fresh air, of leaving the plague and sickness behind, made her almost giddy.

Noise of running footfalls echoed to her from out in the corridor, and she paused. Voices reached her, a quick question and answer, muffled.

"What's going on?" she called back to the others.

"Sergeant Dunlap," Ruiz replied. "In a hurry. Didn't slow down to explain. Kind of a prick, if you ask—"

Sophie shut him out. She didn't have time for petty squabbles.

One hand on the wall ahead of her, she started down the slope. Though she knew it was for the best, she wished she had never put on the hazmat suit. She wanted to feel the stone, wanted to be more confident of her footing. The footgear that went with the suit didn't have the tread of her own boots, which were underneath. Sophie tried to calm herself, breathing evenly despite being buried beneath the filtration mask and the hazmat suit. She felt sure her anxiety was mostly self-inflicted. She wished she had let someone go ahead of her, but whatever remained of the Beneath Project was still her responsibility.

She felt sweat on the back of her neck, felt a chill, and a flicker of claustrophobia that had not touched her in all the many months she had been down here.

"Come on, boss!" Ruiz called.

Sophie wanted to cuss him out, but then her left hand reached the end of the wall, and she stumbled and nearly fell over. With a glance, she turned her headlamp into the darkness, and a smile blossomed on her face.

"Beautiful," she whispered.

"What did you say?" Dr. Tang called. "What's going on?"

"Hang on!" she replied, wending her way carefully down a roughly hewn set of stairs.

They had been carved, but not adeptly, as if whoever had done the job had been in a hurry or simply never imagined a regular use for them. Or, as if the work had been abandoned partway through, as she now saw seemed to have been the case. There were no more than a dozen steps before the rift in the stone narrowed dramatically, barely wide enough for her to squeeze through, the height of the passage so low she would have to crouch if she meant to shuffle onward.

For a moment, the spark of hope in her dimmed. Then Sophie crouched to peer through the fissure, and her headlamp illuminated the way forward. Beyond the short, narrow crevice, the fissure slanted at an angle, but she could see that it widened. There, down on one knee, the draft picked up enough that it puffed against her hazmat suit. Sophie knew it would be impossible to tell if the wind came through a narrow gap in the mountain or if they would find a true exit, but she also knew they had little choice.

"Someone run and tell Kim and Walker we're getting out of here," she said. "I'm giving it about five minutes, and then we're going."

She heard whooping back in the corridor, but Sophie paid little attention to that celebration. Ahead of her, in the narrow crevice, she heard the whisper of something strange, the sort of susurrus that she thought she had heard elsewhere in Derveyî.

Ghosts, she thought, and she put a hand on her thigh, feeling the outline of Lamar's journal through two layers of clothing. A shiver went through her, and she wondered just how old these spirits were, how entwined with the mountain. Entombed with the ancients.

Then the whisper took on a gentle tone, a musical note, almost a burble, and Sophie laughed softly to herself and leaned her plastic-encased head against the wall. What she heard issuing from deep within the mountain, beyond that crevice, had nothing to do with ghosts. It was the whisper of running water. A stream or an underground river.

It had to come out somewhere.

She stood, a fresh strength flowing through her, and turned her headlamp back toward the hole they'd made in the wall, but there was no one there to celebrate her discovery with her.

"Come on," she whispered to herself. "Hurry."

Sophie waited in the dark, and when she began to hear again the distant muffled sounds of gunfire and screams, she told herself to focus on the draft and the running water and the promise of getting out from underground and seeing her parents again.

TWENTY-THREE

Walker didn't see any ghosts. The corner where Carson stared was so brightly lit that nothing could have been hiding there. If the infected soldier had pointed into the shadows of the dark part of the column chamber, he might have thought someone had been spying on them, but the lights were so bright where the ghosts were supposed to be that only someone suffering from hallucinations or madness could have seen anyone there.

The trouble was that Kim saw something, too, and she didn't look sick.

"We don't have time for this," Walker said. "Get out of here, both of you."

Kim glared at him. "Private Carson can barely stand."

"If you want to carry him, go right ahead," Walker replied. "But you need to go and join Sophie and the rest of them."

"Walker—"

She touched his arm, and he shot her a withering glance, hoping she didn't see how much it pained him. "Get the fuck out of here, Kim. It's not safe for any of us."

Her eyes narrowed, and she gripped the strap of his backpack. "You promised you would talk to me before you took any action."

"I promised I would tell you, not that I'd abandon my mission for you." He glared at her hand, but she didn't release him.

"What if you make it worse?" she demanded. "What if the contagion spreads farther because of you instead of getting trapped down here?"

Walker grabbed her wrist, pushed her roughly away, and held her at a distance. "Better a risk of contagion than the certainty of it. I don't have time to debate."

Carson swore and dragged himself to his feet. He reached for Walker, who stepped aside, causing Carson to stumble and nearly fall. The man bent over, coughing, hands on his knees.

"Just go," Walker said. "And fast."

Before Kim could try to talk him out of it, he started down the thirteen steps to the Pandora Room. He had seen the fury and disappointment in her gaze but now he pushed it from his mind. No matter what it cost him personally, he had a job to do.

In the Pandora Room, he glanced at the jar but did not allow himself to be distracted. The room felt cold, and many of the lights had been broken and not replaced, so the jar sat on its altar half-cloaked in shadow. If there were ghosts down here in this room, he was determined not to see them.

Walker slipped off the backpack and set it gently on the floor in front of the altar. He opened it and looked inside. As he'd expected, the jihadis had put together an IED—an improvised explosive device of the sort used for roadside bombs, designed to obliterate everything in its vicinity. It wouldn't just destroy the jar and the altar and scour away the ancient writing; it would bring down the roof and many tons of stone and earth.

He held his breath. This was an irrevocable action, what some would call the nuclear option. He had just set fire to his relationship with Kim, and it had cost a little piece of himself to do that, but it wouldn't just be Kim he would infuriate. Walker knew what he was about to do would save lives—thousands, maybe millions—but nobody would thank him for his actions, at least not publicly. The U.S. Department of Defense would never admit he worked for them. The United Nations would condemn him. Sophie Durand and her employers—hell, anyone with an interest in history or archaeology— would want him in front of a firing squad.

His only comfort was the knowledge that he probably wouldn't live long enough to suffer any of those consequences. Even if he got clear of the explosives before a cave-in could bury him, the jihadis would surely kill him once they'd scythed through Cobb and his troops. He would be fortunate if they didn't decide to punish him for his actions by keeping him alive to suffer. His thoughts strayed to Charlie and what his death would mean to his son, but he cut off that thread instantly. Hesitation would not save him, but it might mean he would die for nothing, and he would not allow that.

Walker knelt in front of the backpack. He had unzipped it all the way and gotten a good look at the IED. It had a cell phone attached, so it could be set off that way if a signal got through, but it also had a timer—presumably in case no cell phone signal was available in the caves.

He set the timer to ten minutes, then reconsidered and shaved off two. There was no telling how long it would take the jihadis to get past the remaining coalition soldiers, and he needed to make this happen. Eight minutes ought to have been plenty of time to get people far enough away from the Pandora Room. They could retreat to the west wing, or through the hole Sophie and the others had opened up, if the tunnel on the other side actually went somewhere and didn't trap them too close to the explosion.

Walker took a breath. Despite his efforts to put Charlie out of his mind, he thought of his son and the promises he had made to the boy—that he'd be safe, that he would come home, that they would have more time together. He had not been a great father when Charlie was small, but he remembered holding the boy, the smell of his head, the vulnerability of that tiny baby, and all the ways he had wanted to make himself a better father. Now, like he had so many times before, he had to pack away his love for his son into a compartment inside his brain. Charlie would be safer because of the actions he took today, but Walker doubted the boy would ever understand.

Eight minutes.

He pressed the timer, and it began ticking down.

"Back the fuck away from that right now."

Walker put up his hands. The skin on his back prickled. He knew that voice and didn't have to turn to know Dunlap had a gun aimed at his spine.

"You're light on your feet," Walker said.

"I put my training to use when I'm sneaking up on motherfuckers who get the drop on me and knock me the fuck out."

Walker turned slowly, hands still up. Dunlap glared at him over the top of his filtration mask. Beyond him, Kim Seong had just reached the bottom of the steps, but she definitely wasn't there to help him. She crossed her arms, her own eyes narrowed with fury. Her anger had apparently overridden her claustrophobia—though how would he have known? She had been so expert at hiding it before.

There they were, the three of them with their masks, yet to succumb to the poison and madness seeping out of the jar. How could the others not see that this was the only choice?

"This needs to happen," Walker said.

"Not if we can get out of here," Kim said.

"It's leaking, anyway. Whatever it is, we've all been touched by it." Walker lowered his hands but made no move to grab his gun. He stared at Dunlap. "Our government isn't known for using its powers for good."

"There are worse," Dunlap said.

"I work for them, too, remember? I've been helping the DOD get their hands on dangerous shit for years, mostly making sure the folks with blacker hats don't get that dangerous shit first. But this . . . no one wins. It's death."

"If it's handled publicly," Kim said. "The U.N. will do it right."

"Maybe, but the jihadis have taken that choice away from us. I can't risk letting them—"

Dunlap had been shifting closer to the backpack, gun still trained on Walker. Now he scuffed his boot heels even nearer and took a glance in through the open zipper. His forehead creased with anger.

"Is that thing counting down?" He shot a look at Kim, then back at Walker. "You're wasting our time, and we're about to get our asses blown up?"

"We've got at least seven minutes to get clear. We should get going," Walker replied.

Kim swore and marched over to Dunlap's side, staring into the bag. Walker admired her fearlessness as she reached into the backpack, but he didn't want it to get them all killed.

"Don't do that," he said. "It's not safe. Best to just leave it now."

Kim cursed at him in Korean. She had done so before, but always with a half smile or a loving glint in her eye. Tonight she had neither. She stared at the backpack, then turned to look at the contagion box—the cracked Pandora jar remained inside, exerting its sickening influence.

"Screw it," she said, reverting to English, and she crossed the four feet to the altar.

"Kim, no!" Walker shouted, too late.

She picked up the contagion box, slung its strap over her shoulder, and turned toward Dunlap.

"Sergeant, we're leaving."

Dunlap nodded, keeping his gun aimed at Walker.

A grunt and a cough came from the stairwell, then someone called Kim's name. They all turned to see Private Carson, weeping lesions all over his face and hands, stumble into the Pandora Room. Walker's fingers twitched with the urge to reach for his gun, but Carson made no move to attack them.

"Give me the box, Miss Kim," Carson wheezed. "It can't do me any more harm than it already has."

Kim seemed to be considering it.

Dunlap's gun hand twitched toward Carson, which was the opening Walker needed. He launched himself at Dunlap, trying to wrest his gun away. Dunlap headbutted him in the jaw, and Walker tasted blood in his mouth.

Out of the corner of his eye, he caught a glimpse of someone in the shadows, watching the violence with eager eyes. Not Kim, and not Carson, but a ghost of ancient sins, ancient hungers.

Kim shouted at them both, holding the contagion box against her abdomen.

Inside the backpack, the countdown continued.

Beyza stood frozen in the atrium. Her breath came in such tiny, panicked sips that she feared her filtration mask had somehow become blocked.

"Where you running now?" Cortez asked, in a voice not his own. "Where you going?"

He'd chased her into the atrium, hands reaching out for her with hooked fingers. The ghost clinging to his back peered over his shoulder at her, its hateful eyes trailing mist. For a moment, his fingers had caught her hair and she'd turned left instead of right, lurching away from him. Cortez took the moment to cut off her path.

Now he stood between her and the dark, yawning entrance to the deeper tunnels, to the chambers and steps that led back to where Sophie and the others were making a last-ditch attempt to find them a way out.

Up the slope of the atrium floor, the echo of gunfire grew louder and louder. It might have been a trick of the ear, the sound reverberating off the walls, but she thought the gunfight must be coming nearer, sliding down Derveyî's throat. She wanted to run, to scream, to do anything, but the only way out or back to her friends was past the dying man in front of her.

"You can feel it. The itch under your skin," Cortez said in that other voice.

The hell of it was that she could. Beyza scratched at her throat, and the tip of her finger punched through a wet, scabby patch of skin. Her breath caught, and she wanted to collapse right there. The contagion was in her—Cortez had been right. He had been infected when they'd made love, and now the sickness had taken root. She felt the black bile in her throat and tried to cough it up, despite her filtration mask—a mask which now seemed useless to her.

"Let me pass," Beyza said. She wanted it to sound dangerous, like a warning, but instead the words came out as a plea.

Cortez's face went slack and his eyes rolled back to white, but on his back, the ghost laughed. It seemed to slide deeper inside him as if stepping inside a sweating, bleeding costume that looked something like her lover.

A fresh round of gunfire echoed through the atrium, closer still. Panic clawed at her chest, and Beyza slapped her hands over her ears. She wanted to scream, but before she could, she heard other voices screaming.

She turned, but not up toward the exit. The screaming came from her left, from a passage that led to the south wing. Martin Jungling burst from the shadows, bloody tears on his cheeks. His scream turned into an eruption of coughing, but instead of letting that stop him, he barreled forward, and Beyza saw why.

Behind him came some of their friends. Their colleagues. So sick they looked near death, so twisted by the hate and cruelty inside them that they pursued him nevertheless, bodies riddled with plague and rot. In a moment between heartbeats, Beyza saw what she would become, what Martin would become, and she wondered why they bothered trying to escape the fate that had already claimed them.

Then the ghosts came screaming out of the passage in pursuit of the dying and in pursuit of Martin, and she wept . . . but she turned to run, the will to live more powerful than her despair.

Cortez still blocked her path. He lunged at her.

Martin used his momentum, shifted course, and barreled into Cortez. The two of them crashed to the stone floor, and then Martin rose and kicked him in the skull once, twice, a third time. Something soft gave way, even as the sick and the spectral sins caught up to both Martin and Beyza, only a dozen feet away.

Their screams were drowned out by a fresh eruption of gunfire, louder than ever. New shouts joined the hellish chorus, and Beyza whipped around to see American and Kurdish soldiers falling back into the atrium, firing their weapons at the dark passage toward the surface. There were perhaps twenty of them left, and in that frozen moment, two of them were ripped apart by gunfire from the exit.

The jihadis rushed in. The gunfire seemed deafening. Bullets flew indiscriminately as they shot not only at the soldiers but at anyone inside the atrium. Several of the plague-ridden victims jittered as bullets punched through them, and the others turned toward the soldiers and rushed in that direction.

Beyza blinked once, but she would not freeze again. She bent and grabbed Martin's wrist, yanked him away from Cortez, who lay twitching and seizing on the floor.

"Let's go!" she shouted, and she gave him a shove to get him moving.

Together, they rushed to the base of the slope and through the doorway into the half darkness of the passage that led deeper into Derveyî. Once this would have seemed like suicide. Now it was their only hope.

Lieutenant Cobb died because his mother had taught him not to slouch. He had been five foot eight by the fifth grade, so much taller than the other kids that he felt constantly self-conscious. His mom, Rita, had noticed that he had begun to duck his head or drop his shoulders so that he would not be so conspicuous, and from then on she had reminded him many times each day to stand up straight. To be proud. When Cobb had told his mom that he was embarrassed, she had fixed him with a soul-deep stare and said, "Live a life you can be proud of and you won't need to slouch." He had often credited this advice with his rapid advancement in the U.S. Army.

The bullet struck him in the right temple.

Cobb spun around, went down on one knee, and then pitched onto his chest. He heard Karnacki shouting, immediately barking orders at the rest of them to fall back, to keep firing. The gunfire went quiet somehow—still there but muffled, as if Cobb had sunken into a tub of water and the battle went on without him.

Someone put a hand on the back of his neck. *Lieutenant! Are you . . .*

The voice cut off. The hand touched his throat, searching for a pulse. Cobb could feel his pulse slowing, could feel the blood surging in his head. Someone knelt beside him, and he saw it was Ellison. Her eyes were sad, and he wanted to tell her not to be fucking stupid, to run, to fall back, to take care of what remained of their unit.

He saw Ellison twist her head to one side, watched her face contort with fear as she raised her gun. She stood, nothing but her legs remaining in his field of vision, and then she fell backward as her blood showered down around him.

The stone felt cold beneath him. The crack of gunshots and the voices shouting in two languages became nothing but white noise, like the burr of the fan he had used every night as a child, summer and winter.

Boots tromped past his face.

Cobb exhaled. He had lived a life he could be proud of, and he had stood tall.

Kim held the contagion box in her hands and wondered how she could have been so foolish. It had been dumb enough to be surprised that Walker had acted without consulting her—this was his job, after all, and he had made no secret of that. But a plague had spread underground, sickened people and driven them mad. Many had died, and many more would follow. An army of religious zealots who would sacrifice their lives for their hatred was attacking from above, just to get their hands on the horror inside the contagion box. And she, Kim Seong, had been crazy enough to pick the box up in her bare hands.

She still wore a filtration mask, and the box itself was meant to keep contagion inside, but she couldn't escape the certainty that she had made a terrible mistake.

"Walker!" She strode across the Pandora Room with the box clutched between her hands, and she kicked Walker in the ribs.

Sergeant Dunlap got his hands around Walker's throat and slammed him to the floor. Over in the corner, the moaning Private Carson pleaded with them to stop.

"Don't be . . . assholes . . . ," Carson croaked.

Which summed it up pretty well for Kim. She swept her leg back to kick Walker again, and despite Dunlap on top of him, he managed to reach out, grab her booted foot, and shove her backward. She pinwheeled until she collided with the wall but managed to keep from falling. The hurt in his eyes at that moment shocked her. It had seemed that he had moved beyond their intimacy, beyond recrimination or trust, but somehow he still thought they had a personal connection, unable to see what he had done to shatter that relationship.

Dunlap smashed Walker against the floor again. This time Walker shot a hard punch into Dunlap's solar plexus and, in the moment the sergeant was stunned, tossed him aside. Bloody-faced, their filtration masks dangerously askew, the two men faced off against one another.

"The countdown is on!" Walker shouted. "If we stay here, we're going to be obliterated. We have to get out of here!"

On the floor in front of the altar, the backpack sat inert. If Kim had any suspicion he might be bluffing, the look on his face would have erased it.

Dunlap lunged for him. Walker snatched his wrist, twisted, and slammed a knee into the sergeant's abdomen. As Dunlap grunted, doubled over, Walker hooked one foot behind him and shoved the man backward. With both of them reeling, it came down to training and experience now, and Walker had more of each. If he had wanted to damage Dunlap further, he could have. Instead, he spun to glare at Kim again.

"Put that fucking thing back on the altar and let's go! We don't have another choice!"

Kim hesitated, wondering if he was right after all. Wouldn't it be better for all of them to die here than for her to risk the jihadis getting their hands on the jar? The logic seemed so clear suddenly. The things that shifted in her peripheral vision, the twist of sickness in her gut, made her want to run, but what kind of solution was that?

"We'll never make it," Kim said, not sure if she meant they would never escape the plague or the explosives. Maybe both.

Dunlap staggered to his feet.

Walker stared at Kim. "Seong . . . there is no other option."

The quiet, terrible moment of realization that followed was interrupted by a shuffling thump and a plastic crinkling, and they all turned to see Dr. Tang step out of the stairwell in a blue hazmat suit.

"Erika, no," Kim said. "You can't be here—"

Dr. Tang pointed at the contagion box in Kim's hands. "I don't know what you think you're doing with that," she said, her voice muffled inside the hazmat suit, "but you'd better hand it over to me."

Walker started to argue with her.

"Hush," Dr. Tang said. She glanced at Dunlap, then back at Walker, and finally at the backpack in front of the altar. "Idiots. Listen up. They've broken through the wall, and there is definitely a tunnel there, including an underground river."

"There's no time," Walker said. "The jihadis are going to get through."

Dunlap eyed him warily. "You don't know that."

Kim faced Dr. Tang. "There are explosives in the backpack. It's on a timer. We need to go."

"Agreed," Dr. Tang replied.

Carson coughed, leaning against the wall. "What difference does it make? Nobody's making it out of here."

Dr. Tang put a hand on his arm, helping to steady him. The hazmat suit crinkled with her movement as she turned quickly to stare at Walker.

"I understand the temptation," she said. "But there are already enough people infected, and we need to study the jar if there's any hope of creating an antidote to its effects. Never mind that if you blow up the jar, you could cause a cloud of this stuff to shoot out through the vents aboveground, infecting the jihadis. They take that contagion home and it is going to get ugly very fast."

"Why the hell are you worried about them?" Dunlap growled.

"Because it won't end with them," Kim said.

Dr. Tang nodded.

"You sure this new tunnel is a way out?" Walker asked, glancing nervously at the backpack. He reached up to adjust his filtration mask, making sure it was tight on his face.

"How could we be?" Dr. Tang replied. "But there's a draft and water, and it beats dying in this room or being murdered by jihadis."

"Walker," Kim said, sliding the strap of the contagion box over her shoulder. "I'm going. You want to stop me—"

He threw up his hands. "Hell, no. If we've got an exit, let's take it."

Dunlap looked as if he might want to pick up where the fight left off, if they lived long enough, but instead he pointed at the backpack. "What about that?"

Walker rushed over to Carson and helped the man to stand up straight. "You want to bring it along, be my guest, but I have no idea how to stop the countdown."

Dunlap took one more look at the backpack, then hurried for the thirteen steps. Dr. Tang went up ahead of him, hazmat suit whickering noisily.

Kim followed them, with Walker and Carson coming up behind her.

"Sophie's going to kill you for destroying this room," she said, glancing over her shoulder. "If I don't kill you first."

"Sorry, honey. A leopard can't change his spots."

"You're not a leopard. You're an asshole."

Walker didn't argue.

TWENTY-FOUR

Heart thrumming in panic, struggling to breathe, Sophie wanted to rip the hazmat suit off. Being underground all these months hadn't bothered her as much as she had feared, but that had changed. The mountain pressed down on her from above. The tunnels were filled with human frailties, the air choked with them, and sickness gusted along the corridors and through the vents. She wore a filtration mask, and the hazmat suit over that, and her chest ached with a congestion she tried to ignore because she knew what it signified. The tickle there, and the wheeze in her throat, told her the mask hadn't been enough and the suit had been too late.

Maybe she wouldn't get any sicker, maybe it would be slowed by her limited exposure, but she had been infected. She imagined they all had. The knowledge made her want to rip off her skin along with her suit, to rush out of the caves and across the desert, to pump her legs until she reached her mother and father in France.

Yes, she thought. *Bring them more disease. That's all they need.*

Sophie shifted her weight from one leg to the other and tried not to shout out her frustration and fear. She glanced at Taejon and Ruiz. "What's taking them so long?"

"No idea," Taejon said. "But you're the boss. How long do we wait?"

"You think we should leave them all behind?"

Taejon cast her a sidelong glance, a sad wisdom in his eyes. "I'm a soldier, Dr. Durand. I'm not inclined to leave anyone behind. But a lot of people down here are past saving, and I don't want to be one of them. I figure we give them a few minutes longer, and then we get out of here."

Sophie looked at him. Her heart pounded in her chest. Abandoning the others did not sit well with her, especially Beyza and Dr. Tang, but neither did standing around waiting to die. She replied to Taejon only in her head, knowing what she intended but unwilling to admit it out loud.

Come on, she thought, glancing both ways along the tunnel. *Come on.*

A draft issued from the hole in the wall behind them, and she nodded slowly. It felt almost like the spirits were trying to tell her something.

"Two minutes," she said. "Then we go."

She'd barely uttered the words when the group of them came up the corridor from the direction of the column chamber. Kim led the way, moving fast with the contagion box slung over her shoulder and clasped between her hands. Dr. Tang and Walker hurried after her, but behind them, Dunlap helped a visibly sickened Carson. A wave of revulsion swept through Sophie, and she wished they could leave Carson behind, then hated herself for that wish. Bad enough they weren't going back for the others, not knowing if they were alive or dead. Carson was right there with him, and they couldn't just abandon him.

"Jesus, man," Ruiz said, moving to help Dunlap with Carson. "You look like shit warmed over."

"Feels about right," Carson wheezed.

Sophie tore her gaze from the men. She turned and picked up the plastic package from the floor and handed it to Kim. "Your hazmat suit."

From down the corridor, they heard the muffled sound of gunshots, and Sophie glanced in that direction. With the stairs and the worship chamber and the Alexander Room, they should have been barely able to hear such sounds except through the vents, but this wasn't from the vents. The noise didn't come from outside but from there underground with them, and it was getting closer.

"Make it fast," Sophie said, even as Kim tore open the package.

Walker strode to the opening they had smashed through the wall. He picked up the pickax and ducked his head through the hole, glancing around a moment before turning back to her.

"This for real?"

Sophie cocked her head. "Looks real to me. It's the best we've got."

Walker turned toward Kim and stared at the contagion box in her clutches. It looked as if he meant to say something, but then he stepped through the hole and into the darkness. The hazmat suits had their own headlamps, and they had an additional two or three flashlights, but Walker didn't wait for a light.

"You know this is a terrible idea," he said.

"So is staying."

He nodded. No arguing with that.

Just as Sophie attached the headpiece on Kim's hazmat suit, they heard running and shouting and turned to see Beyza racing toward them from the direction of the atrium, desperate and broken and more human-seeming than Sophie had ever seen her.

Eyes wide, Beyza pointed at the hole in the wall. "Does that go anywhere?"

"We don't know if it's an exit—" Sophie began.

"Does it go *anywhere?*"

Now Sophie spotted Martin farther up the corridor, stumbling and pale, following in Beyza's wake.

"There's a river," Dr. Tang said.

"Then fucking go!" Sophie shouted.

They went.

Through the new hole in the wall, one by one, the sick helping the sicker, they scrambled in desperation and determination. Sophie, Dr. Tang, and Kim were less agile in their hazmat suits, but their headlamps were vital sources of light. Walker took Martin's flashlight and Beyza had her own, and yet the new tunnel seemed to swallow them all. As they stumbled and shuffled swiftly along the rough stone floor, descending a seemingly natural ridgeline within the cavern, the sound of gunfire vanished as if they had stepped into another world.

Even with her hazmat suit on, Sophie could feel a pressure shift in the air, like a storm was coming in. But this wasn't humidity. It felt like malice, like the quiet minutes in the midst of a couple's worst fight when words have proven useless. It felt like the eye of the storm.

"Sophie," Walker said, coming up beside her. He found his footing easily as if their exodus did not frighten him, and she wanted to punch him for it.

"Not now," she said.

"Something you should know."

She snapped a withering glance in his direction. "Walker—"

The explosion rocked the mountain overhead and shook the floor beneath their feet, and Sophie came to a halt. Beyza and Martin froze as well, staring back the way they'd come.

"That wasn't topside," Beyza said.

Only then did Sophie notice the others had paused only a moment before they'd kept moving, as if the explosion hadn't surprised them at all.

"What the fuck *was* that?" she asked.

Walker glanced over his shoulder, and he told her.

Rage swept through her. "You just blew up the Pandora Room? Are you—"

Beyza grabbed her arm and propelled her forward, hazmat suit crinkling. "They would have destroyed it, anyway. And we need to keep moving."

"What did you see?" Kim asked, stumbling along with the contagion box in her hands.

"Infected people," Beyza replied. "Jihadis. Ghosts."

"They're not ghosts," Sophie snapped. "They're just . . . manifestations."

"Call them what you want," Beyza said.

"They're everywhere," Carson rasped, and he caught his foot on a stone and nearly collapsed. Without Dunlap and Ruiz, he would have. "All around us. Killing each other. Beating and raping and stabbing and crying . . ."

Carson himself was crying bloody tears, and for the first time Sophie realized it wasn't because of his sickness but because of what he was witnessing there in the tunnel as they fled.

The chill along her spine took root and did not go away.

Sophie heard the river ahead, and a moment later she saw the glow of her headlamp shining on the water. It was wider than she'd expected—perhaps fifteen feet across—and it rushed along swiftly. She wondered at its source, but there were hills and even mountains nearby, and she was more grateful than curious.

"Just follow the edge," Kim said.

Sophie didn't need to be told, but she wasn't about to argue. The time for butting heads over who was in charge had long passed. The tunnel had a shelf on either side of the river, more than wide enough. On the near side, the rough stone bank ranged in width from just a couple of feet to perhaps a dozen. It might narrow dramatically as they went deeper, or vanish entirely and force them to swim, but they had no choice, and so they forged ahead. As the cave closed around them, every animal instinct told her to turn back, that going deeper led only to death, but she knew going back was no better.

"Let me take that."

With a glance back, Sophie saw that Martin had come up beside Kim, gesturing toward the contagion box.

"You're sick," Kim said.

She was right, but Martin seemed to still be able to take care of himself. His skin showed a terrible rash and weeping lesions, and his cough had grown worse, but his eyes were clear in the flashlight beam, and he remained steady on his feet. Carson, on the other hand, looked like hell. He and Dunlap had already fallen behind a ways.

"Let him take it," Sophie said.

"What if he drops it?" Walker asked. "Smashes it open?"

"You were going to blow it up," Kim reminded him. "You don't get a say."

The tension between them thickened a moment, and then Kim slipped the box's strap off her shoulder and handed it over to Martin. Sophie felt her heart break all over again, looking at this kind man. She would never have predicted the kind of courage he had shown her tonight, and she wished she could tell him how sorry she was for under-estimating him.

"Go," Dunlap called from behind them.

Sophie spotted something behind him and Carson, and for a

moment she thought it might be the jihadis sneaking up on them, but it was only a shadow. Or a ghost. Her chest ached, and she rattled out a terrible cough and wondered how sick she was.

The river carried on, and so did they, but there was no way to know how long before the river brought them to the surface—or if it ever would.

Martin tried to keep his eyes down, watching the ruts and ridges in the rough stone ledge, with an occasional glance at the dark water running past. If he looked up, glanced around, he would see ghosts in the shadows. Their presence no longer frightened him; what he feared was their attention. Even his disgust at their actions had dulled. As long as they continued to reenact the crimes and horrors of the past, they would not be focused on him. He knew they were not the spirits of the actual dead, only memories of sins and hideous urges siphoned from the ancients, but whatever these things might be, they had a level of awareness and malice. He would do anything to avoid them noticing him.

The strap of the contagion box chafed his shoulder. It had been light when he had first taken it from Kim, but now it grew heavier and heavier. He felt the sting of the lesions on his skin, felt little liquid rivulets drooling down his skin and couldn't be sure if they were sweat or some kind of bloody rot leaking out of him. The idea made him nauseous, but he kept putting one foot in front of the other because he had no other choice. He could walk forward or he could sit and wait to die, killed by the plague or by ghosts or jihadis.

Ruiz walked beside him, constantly glancing around, jittery and urgent.

"Don't you see them?" Carson muttered.

Martin glanced over his shoulder and immediately regretted it. In the glow from Dunlap's flashlight, Carson had the waxy yellow pallor of a melted candle. The shadows behind the two men shifted and came alive. Martin caught a glimpse of two ghosts, both women, one on the ground and the other laughing and pointing at her misfortune, then sneering and spitting on her. Harmless in comparison to some of the others, but then the ghost who was the subject of that humiliation began to turn her head as if to look at him, feeling his attention, and he whipped his head around to face forward. He nearly stumbled into Walker's back but then lowered his gaze.

"What?" Ruiz whispered. "What'd you see?"

Martin didn't answer. Looking at the stone beneath his feet felt safe, and if it wasn't, at least he wouldn't see the horror coming.

Carson kept mumbling about the ghosts. Martin wanted to ask Sergeant Dunlap why he didn't just sit the man down, since there seemed no chance of Carson surviving. But the two men were soldiers, and Martin understood. There had been very few people in Martin's life for whom he would have taken the risks that Sergeant Dunlap was taking. His parents, his little sister, maybe Sophie.

The moment this thought occurred to him, he realized how ridiculous it was. Dunlap wore a filtration mask, but he had Carson's arm around him, which heightened the sergeant's risk of exposure. Martin was carrying the contagion box on his hip, the Pandora jar inside it, and it was killing him.

Be honest, he thought. *It had already killed you before you picked it up.* And that was true. At this point, he had nothing left to lose, but he could help his friends. Help Sophie.

"Oh, God . . . please keep them away . . . their eyes," Private Carson rasped.

Martin shuddered. Instinctively, he began to glance over his shoulder again, but then he stumbled over a jutting bit of stone. Weak and weary, he pitched forward and crashed into Walker's back. His hands closed tightly on the contagion box, but he tripped again and began to fall. Walker turned and caught him by the elbows. Martin went down on one knee and cried out as his kneecap struck the rough stone, but the rest of him stayed upright.

"Watch it, Martin!" Walker snapped. "If you drop that thing—"

"I'm sorry. I tripped over—" Martin began, and then his chest erupted in a cough so deep and ragged that it left him exhausted. He remained on one knee, sagging as Walker stepped away from him with wide eyes.

"Shit," Walker muttered. He reached over and lifted the strap from around Martin's neck and removed the contagion box from his possession. "Let me take this. It was stupid of me to let you carry it. We can't take the chance."

"Someone who's already sick should carry it," Martin argued.

Walker glanced at Taejon and Ruiz, then shot him a hard look. "We're all sick, kid."

Martin relinquished the contagion box. He was right. Even if some of them showed more symptoms than others, there seemed no way to avoid this plague and the ghosts that came with it. Walker had Carson's assault rifle over his shoulder already—he had taken it when it became clear Private Carson was too ill to be much use with a gun—but while he let the gun hang at his back, he clutched the contagion box close to his abdomen to keep it from jostling too much.

Walker caught up to Dr. Tang and Beyza but stayed well behind Kim. Whatever their tension sprang from, they weren't going to resolve it today.

Whispers came from the river—not from the water, not the rush of the current, but from the other side. Martin took a rattling breath and kept his gaze downcast. But the muttering from behind him grew.

"Shut up, Carson," Dunlap growled.

Still, Martin did not look back. He felt the two men behind him, the dying private and the grim sergeant. Their presence seemed too close, as if they dogged his heels, and Martin wanted to run ahead to catch the others, although he knew his own progressing illness would make him unwelcome among them.

"Don't you see it, Sarge?" Carson muttered. "The blade . . . his blade is sharp. It's right here with us. It's looking at you."

Martin began to cry. He didn't want to listen to Carson anymore, didn't want to be underground. He wanted to be back on the dairy farm with his family and never go underground again, maybe never be inside. He could sleep under the stars and breathe the fresh air, he could have music and laughter.

When Carson whimpered, Martin could not help but turn around and look. He saw the ghost with its strange headdress and the rough cloth wrapped around it, saw the curved dagger in its left hand as it reached for Carson. The blade sank into Carson's chest, but it did not cut him, did not stop there . . . the ghost sank into him, and Carson stood up straight and rigid as if electricity had just surged through him.

"Hey, man," Dunlap began, reaching out to him. He hadn't seen the ghost.

"Sergeant, don't!" Martin shouted.

Carson turned on Dunlap. The frailty of illness had fled his body, and he grinned as he grabbed a fistful of Dunlap's shirt with one hand and tore away the man's filtration mask with the other. Dunlap twisted, trying to escape his grasp, and smashed a fist into Carson's jaw. Lesions split into fissures in the man's face, but Carson seemed not to feel it. He grabbed hold of Dunlap with both hands and hurled him aside with such force that Dunlap struck the tunnel wall.

With a gleeful whooping, Carson barreled at Martin. Wheezing, Martin raised his hands to defend himself but was seized with a fit of coughing that doubled him over. Carson laughed and shoved him aside.

Martin wheeled, trying to grasp at him but missing. He fell on his ass, helpless as Carson lunged at Walker, reaching for the contagion box. In that moment, Martin knew it had all been for nothing—the Pandora jar would be shattered, the plague released in its full potency, along with the darkest parts of an entire civilization's human nature . . . those that were not already loose in Derveyî.

Walker turned his back and dropped to one knee, using his body to protect the contagion box and its contents the way a man might defend his own child. Carson whooped again, but before he could reach Walker, Taejon was there. Martin felt a flicker of relief as Dr. Tang, Sophie, and Kim all started shouting and Beyza followed Taejon, ready to fight with her bare hands, ferocity lighting her face.

Taejon aimed his gun at Carson's chest, finger on the trigger. "Get it together, man. Don't make me—"

Carson ripped the weapon from Taejon's hands with such strength that the sound of his fingers breaking echoed off the wall. Whatever was inside him had only one use for that gun; Carson turned it around and smashed Taejon in the skull with it, then followed him to the ground and began to club him in the head with the butt of the rifle, again and again.

"Fucking bastard," Martin rasped, not knowing to whom or to what his own words were directed. He staggered toward Carson.

Beyza and now Sophie tried to go around Walker, but he blocked them, shouting at them to stay back.

Martin knew why. Taejon's skull lay open, cracked apart like an eggshell, a pool of blood matting his hair, gray brain visible in the strange glow from the flashlights and headlamps.

Ruiz shoved Martin aside. Sergeant Dunlap took three strides, raised his gun, and shot Carson in the back of the head. He whirled and pointed his gun at Martin.

"Kim, I need your goddamn flashlight over here!" he snapped.

With the crinkle of her hazmat suit, Kim lumbered past Walker. Through the plastic face mask, the pain in her face showed clearly as she avoided looking at the two dead men at her feet.

Martin narrowed his eyes when her headlamp pointed directly at his face. Dunlap's weapon remained steady for several long seconds.

"I'm fine!" Martin protested. "Jesus, Sergeant, I swear I'm . . ." He burst into a fit of coughing.

"You're far from fine," Ruiz said.

Martin wanted to disagree. Instead, he launched into another fit of coughing and fell to his knees, pain shooting through him as he struck the stone ledge.

"Shit," he groaned. His gaze turned toward Carson's corpse. "I don't want to be . . . I can't be that."

Walker and Kim stood over him, backlit by the headlamps on Sophie and Dr. Tang's hazmat suits. Beyza lingered in the shadows, her half-darkened face etched with pity. Then she began to cough as well, and they all looked at her.

"I'm fine for a while yet," she said. "Can we get out of—"

Sergeant Dunlap hushed them. They glanced at him sharply, and he held up a hand for silence. Martin craned his neck to listen and realized that beneath the hiss and burble of the river beside them, he could hear the punch and crack of gunfire.

"They've found our exit," Walker said. "They'll be after us now."

The jihadis, Martin thought. And they'd be moving faster than any-one infected with this contagion or wearing a hazmat suit.

He struggled to stand and reached out to Walker. "Give me Carson's weapon."

Sophie stepped forward. "Martin, no."

She didn't come within eight feet of him, but even with the light and shadow bouncing around the cave, even with the ghosts darting in and out of his peripheral vision while committing horrors Dante had only imagined, he could see the emotion on her face. The fear for him, the fondness, even love of a sort.

"I'm not getting out of here," he said. "I might as well be useful."

Behind the mask of her hazmat suit, tears welled in her eyes. "I'm sorry I wasn't . . . better."

Martin studied those eyes. "We were friends, weren't we? In the end."

"We were. We are," she promised.

He nodded. "That's all right, then."

A few seconds passed in silence, all of them watching him, and then more gunfire could be heard. The infected were being killed—that was the only explanation he could think of for those shots—but the jihadis would not be stopped by them.

Walker set down the contagion box, working quickly, and then handed over Carson's weapon. "You know how to use this?"

"I can aim and pull a trigger."

Walker nodded, then picked up the contagion box again.

Dunlap moved up next to Martin. "I'll keep him company. We'll buy you as much time as we can. Just get that goddamned jar away from here, and don't put it in the hands of anyone who'll use it. This can't go farther than Derveyî."

Martin expected the others to argue, but the world had made them pragmatists. Even Ruiz just looked down at Taejon's corpse and turned away.

"Thank you," Kim said, her voice muffled inside the suit.

Dunlap gave a single nod and turned his back to the others, then walked to an outcropping of rock and took up a defensive position.

Sophie raised a gloved hand in a tentative wave. Martin waved back and then turned to join Dunlap. He kept his back turned, watching the darkness he thought he had left behind, and listened to their receding footsteps.

He would have liked to see the sun again. To see the farm. To hug his parents.

He hoped they would be proud of him.

TWENTY-FIVE

Walker did his best to hide the swiftness with which the plague had taken root in him. During his fight with Dunlap in the Pandora Room, his mask had come askew. It had only been seconds, but in such proximity to the jar—or perhaps simply in the atmosphere of that room— seconds had been enough. He assumed Dunlap had also been infected, so Carson tearing off his filtration mask would only hasten things.

As for Walker, he figured carrying the fucking contagion box probably wasn't helping.

He had a sidearm still, but he planned to hand it over to Kim the moment he felt he might lose control. A slurry had built up in his chest and throat, and his breath came only thinly, but he managed to keep his coughing to a minimum, and by walking behind the rest of them, he had covered up just how weary he had grown. The noise of the river helped, its weird echo filling the tunnel.

There were only six of them now—himself and Kim, Beyza and Ruiz, Dr. Tang, and Sophie Durand. He figured they must all be sick, though he guessed Dr. Tang must be the worst of all. Like him, she had been fighting to hide just how ill she was, but Dr. Tang was doing a poor job of it. During the violence that had left Carson and Taejon dead, Walker had seen the rash on her face and several lesions. Ruiz had gone silent, either in sickness or in shock, and his gait had become a shuffling. He coughed frequently, and he never lifted his gaze from the ledge in front of him.

Walker's own neck itched, and he knew there were painful lesions on his chest and arms, but he had no flashlight and all their headlamps were aimed forward. He huffed, shifted the contagion box where it hung over his shoulder, and kept marching along the ledge.

At the front of their little dying parade, Sophie coughed wetly. She swore, coughed again, and then picked up her pace. Beyza took up the cough as if it were a song stuck in her head, and she kept it going.

Kim seemed the least sick among them. Walker figured if he had to hand over his burden, he would give it to her. She might be furious with him, might feel he had betrayed her, but they had moved beyond the tug-of-war over the jar now. If Walker could not make it out of Derveyî, then Kim would have to do it, and whatever happened with the jar then would be up to her.

And yet . . .

Sergeant Dunlap had chosen to stay behind, to sacrifice himself to help them escape with the jar. He had extracted a promise from Walker not to put it in the hands of someone who would put the death it contained to use. Which meant that if Walker intended to keep that promise, he had to live long enough to do so.

I should have blown it up, he thought. The passage ahead grew ever smaller. The tunnel remained dark, except for the glow of flashlights, which meant that if the river ever led to the surface, they were nowhere near that exit.

But destroying the jar was no longer an option, and neither was dying, as sick as he was. Walker trudged ahead, careful not to trip. When he heard whispers from the shadows—whispers he knew were not the voice of the rushing river—he refused to do more than glance toward them. He had heard enough about the living bits of cruelty they had taken to calling ghosts. By now, he had even seen some of the wispy silhouettes that seemed to grow more solid as time passed.

His eyes felt heavy. There must have been a hundred times when he had been driving home late at night, fighting the lull of the engine, head bobbing as he tried not to fall asleep. This feeling echoed that one.

The six of them had fallen silent now, each alone with their thoughts and the plague that had taken root in them.

Dr. Tang tripped and fell, tearing open the right leg of her hazmat suit. Beyza offered her hand, helping Dr. Tang to her feet, but none of them addressed the exposure Dr. Tang would experience now that her suit had been breached. They all knew she had been sick already.

Several minutes later, Walker realized there were only four people in front of him. Ruiz had vanished, either into the river, running ahead, or dropping back. Walker could not have sworn that he had not passed right by the young soldier without noticing the man. None of the others seemed to have noticed his absence, all withdrawn into their illness, haunted by the ghosts around them, focused on survival.

Sophia, Beyza, and Kim had paused only a moment to make sure she was all right, but then they had hurried on. Nobody wanted to waste the sacrifice that Dunlap and Martin were making.

Without the headlamp from her suit, Dr. Tang pulled a thin flashlight from her pocket and clicked it on, shining it at the floor. In its yellow glow, she took a good look at Walker's face. They gazed at each other for a moment. Walker realized only then how sick she really was, and he saw the moment in Dr. Tang's eyes when she had the same epiphany about him.

"We'll get out of here," she said, falling into step beside him.

Walker coughed. His bones ached.

"Yeah," he agreed. "I have faith."

He lied to her.

Dunlap exhaled slowly, soundlessly, as he watched a small squad of jihadis come around a corner in the tunnel. Beside him, Martin managed to stifle a cough. The lanky young guy looked almost absurd with an assault rifle in his hands. One look at him and you had to know he was an academic. His identity as a graduate student practically radiated out of him; with that scruffy almost-beard and spectacles, destiny would demand people call him *Professor* someday. But nobody would be calling Martin anything ever again. Nor would Dunlap himself be rising above the rank of sergeant. Their road ended here.

The river churned, fast and deep as it swept by, and the plink and shush of its voice masked the sounds of Dunlap and Martin shifting behind the stone ridge in the darkness, the wall on their left and the river on their right. The jihadis looked better organized than Dunlap would have expected. They swept their gun barrels left and right, most of them equipped with flashlights strapped to the barrels, but Dunlap got a good look before he had to duck out of sight. Most of them wore black or tan fatigues, some with body armor and some without. They were coated with dirt and dust from the rugged terrain and the firefight, and they had thick, unruly beards, but they moved with determination and silent menace. This was not some ragtag group of desert warriors.

A quiet shuffling came from behind him. Dunlap assumed it would be a ghost as he turned, but he saw Ruiz approaching on his hands and knees, weapon hanging beneath him like an infant in a sling.

Dunlap would have asked him what he thought he was doing, why he had backtracked to join them, but then he saw the look in Ruiz's eyes and he understood. None of them were getting out of here, and Ruiz preferred to die in combat.

Ruiz gave Martin a nod. Martin returned it. Nothing more needed to be said.

One of the jihadis started coughing, staggered into the wall, and went to his knees. Another shushed him, grabbed him by the shoulder, and shook him. Dunlap waited until a flashlight beam swept by and peered above the ridge. Several of the jihadis looked unwell, one with lesions already blossoming on his face. Whatever they had been exposed to when they had come underground, it had sickened them much faster. Perhaps it had been the ghosts Martin had described as swarming in the atrium, but regardless, they were infected.

Dunlap bared his teeth in something like a smile. At least he and Martin and Ruiz weren't dying alone.

Martin muttered something about ghosts. Dunlap tapped his arm to hush him, freezing there behind the ridge to make sure they hadn't drawn the jihadis' attention. He lay on his belly on ragged stone and studied Martin in the dim illumination of the roving flashlights. Pale and sweating, gaze flitting around with fear and paranoia, he nodded as if having listened to some great revelation. Martin glanced around with a peculiar attention, flinching and shivering at nothing.

Yet it wasn't nothing. Dunlap could see the ghosts now, or at least the hint of some coalescing darkness, some blue-gleaming mist that seemed to drift along the surface of the river and to creep over the rocks and ledge as if full of its own sinister purpose.

And now that he could see them, he could see that they were everywhere.

Sophie felt the most sadness for her mother. If she died before her father—something she never could have imagined—at least he would never have to know, but her mother would learn soon enough, and she would have to live with her mind's horrible imaginings. Sophie feared dying, grieved so much that she would leave behind so many loving words unsaid and questions unresolved, but she would not have to endure the pain that would come after, and her mother would live through all of that. Alone. Even if her father had a lucid hour, Sophie felt sure her mother would never tell him what had become of their daughter.

I'm sorry, Mom, she thought.

She caught the toe of her boot, stumbled a bit, but managed to keep her feet beneath her. They were trudging now, barely acknowledging one another. If she glanced at Dr. Tang or Walker, or worst of all Beyza, she would see that they were all sick. Looking ahead, the headlamp of her hazmat suit illuminating their path along the river, all it showed her was the narrowing passage and the darkness and the ghosts that now seemed to take shape in every crevice, clawing and stabbing and fucking one another, smashing with clubs and laughing at pain and pissing on the dying and the poor.

Sophie kept her gaze forward, waiting for a glimpse of light, for a stronger breeze, for some hint of the outside world. The more she allowed herself to sink into contemplation, the more she understood that all she desired now was to see the sky. The hazmat suit had not saved her. She had been exposed before slipping into the suit, and it had only delayed the inevitable. Now the sickness came on quickly, and the ghosts had come to stay. Even if they found their exit, made their way into the open air, they would doubtless be in some valley, hidden by surrounding hills, with no time for a rescue.

Yet they had to keep going. They had to do whatever they could to keep the jar out of the hands of the New Caliphate. Her mind drifted to the thought of her mother enduring this plague, to little children being infected, to infants being clawed at by the ghosts of humanity's most hideous impulses.

She would keep going.

Something touched her arm. Sophie whipped around, heart lurching, only to find Beyza had come up beside her. The stone ledge alongside the river barely allowed them to walk together here, but Sophie saw the lonely sorrow in her friend's eyes, and they linked arms. Beyza's left eye had begun to turn red. That side of her face had swollen with purple-black plague blossoms. Sophie wished that she could save Beyza, almost more than she wished she could save herself.

In silence, they walked along together, careful not to trip. The river swept along only inches away from Sophie now, a constant companion. Dr. Tang, Walker, and Kim were behind them, but they vanished almost completely from her mind. Only she and Beyza existed now. She and Beyza and the ghosts who were coming clearer, these phantoms of ancient cruelties, manifestations of the ugly roots of humankind.

Sophie did not want to die here among such horrors. She wanted a moment of beauty, at least. Beyza sagged against her, and Sophie wished she had not ever put on the hazmat suit. It had not saved her, and it created a barrier between herself and her friend. If she had not needed the headlamp to light their way, she would have torn it off in that moment.

"We'll be all right," she told Beyza, knowing neither of them were foolish enough to believe it.

Off to her left, above the water, one ghost caught her eye. It had manifested more clearly than any she had seen thus far, and though Sophie knew this meant the plague had rooted deeper inside her, she could not tear her gaze away. He seemed to kneel just above the churning current. With a blade held in both hands, he stabbed himself in the abdomen again and again.

In profile, he reminded her so much of Lamar that she forgot to breathe. Already coughing, already suffocating inside her suit and mask, she saw small black spots form in front of her eyes and took in a long breath, gasping, faltering. Knowing she would die here. This time it was Beyza who aided her, compelling her to keep moving, but Sophie glanced back at that ghost so full of self-hatred. She knew it was no lost soul, just as she knew it only reminded her of Lamar, that it wasn't truly him, yet her heart ached.

I miss you, she thought.

And she whispered, "I forgive you."

Kim wanted to take the lead. Sophie and Beyza were ahead of her, blocking the ledge, but they had both slowed down. Walker and Dr. Tang had dropped behind her, and they, too, seemed to be running out of steam. All this time she had been fighting her claustrophobia, but as they kept walking with no sign that the tunnel would ever end, she felt the stone closing around her, as if the space kept narrowing. The urge to scream built up inside her as she put one hand on Sophie's back and the other on Beyza's and quietly encouraged them to hurry.

"I'm doing the best I can," Sophie said, voice as cold as a blade.

The unfairness of her tone stung, but only for a moment. Kim could not allow herself to care about small courtesies now. The gunfire had died off in the tunnel behind them, but instead of reassuring her, that silence only stoked her fear. The odds that Dunlap and the dying Carson had been able to ambush and kill the jihadis pursuing them seemed slim. Instead, Kim could practically feel the swift approach of the men who wanted the jar and who wanted the rest of them dead. The temptation to take the jar out of the contagion box and just leave it behind, to give to these monstrous men the ability to murder who knew how many people, grew strong. She glanced back at Walker, remembering that he'd been willing to blow up the Pandora Room and himself along with it, as long as the New Caliphate did not get this jar, and that she had fought him on it.

It might have been better if they had all been down in the room when the bomb had gone off, but she would never say those words out loud. Which meant that turning back now, surrendering the jar, was out of the question.

Kim turned to glare at Walker and Dr. Tang. "You must go faster. Move!"

Dr. Tang replied with a burst of coughing that sprayed the inside of her hazmat suit's headpiece with black and yellow bile. She bent, dragging in a ragged breath and then another, until at last she stood upright again. Her features were obscured by the flecks of mucous liquid inside the plastic face screen, but she only nodded and kept walking.

Walker did not acknowledge any of it except to pause and put a hand on Dr. Tang's arm. When she seemed ready to continue, he let her go ahead of him. Kim stood and waited as Dr. Tang passed her on the river's edge.

She stared at Walker. "They're coming. Don't you feel it?"

"There are worse things," Walker replied, his gaze shifting left and right, twitching over to peer into darkness like some barely competent Cold War spy.

The ghosts, Kim thought. It was obvious that the others had all seen them, but Kim had not. A few shimmerings and shadows, but nothing solid, nothing that overrode the rational part of her mind. Of the five of them, she had thus far been least affected by the plague, and now she realized she had also kept more of her wits about her.

Her heart pounded in her chest. She could feel it in her throat and her temples, thumping in her skull. The urgency swept her along with a current stronger than the river, but the others were so sick now that they were unable to feel that urgency, or if they felt it, they were too weary or brain-fogged to act on it.

"Oh, my God," Dr. Tang said, and she turned her face away from something she had seen, so disgusted or frightened of the ghosts that she stumbled to her left, nearly falling into the river.

Kim turned to look back the way they'd come. The glow from her headlamp illuminated the ledge and the edge of the river. The water seemed deep and black and unforgiving, but the tunnel swallowed her light. Farther back, it curved around a corner, and she imagined the jihadis were already there, nearly upon them.

Above the shush of the river, had she heard the bark of a voice? A rough, guttural language? Or had that been the first of the ghosts to visit her?

Time had run out.

Fear overcame her.

Kim swore and caught up with Walker, whom she'd allowed to pass her by. She took hold of his arm, and in his illness he did not resist.

"Give it to me," she said.

Walker frowned. He stood straighter, blinked as if waking up, mustering as much of his training and courage as he could manage. "Keep going. I'm all right. We have to move."

He tried to turn away. Kim snatched the strap of the contagion box, yanking him toward her. Walker rocked back, unsteady on his feet, and snapped around to glare at her.

"Don't be a stubborn ass. You're all moving too slowly. If we can't stay ahead of them, we're dead before we ever find a way out of here."

Walker squinted and shook his head as if to clear it. She saw the change in him, as if he had woken from some enchantment. Kim had fallen for this man not merely for his strength and courage but for his clarity of purpose, the kindness at his core, and his way of putting others before himself. There were times she could not understand how he could cleave to such beliefs and continue in his job, but she had never doubted the man himself.

He slid off the strap and carefully put it over her head, resting it on her shoulder. Kim took the contagion box from him. The moment its weight fell fully upon her, she wished she could give it back.

They hurried to catch up to Sophie, Beyza, and Dr. Tang, cautious with their footing. The spray from the river wet the ledge, and here and there were places where the stone had become slick.

"Sophie," Walker said. "You awake up there? Because Kim is right. We need to get our asses in gear."

Beyza and Sophie were practically holding each other up like a pair of drunk women on some bachelorette weekend in Las Vegas. As Sophie turned to respond, Beyza sagged forward. Without her friend to lean on, she tripped on her own feet and spilled to the ground. Beyza slid across the ledge, rolled over twice, and came to rest with her left arm dangling down into the river, the current tugging at her.

Sophie nearly fell trying to reach her, but Walker managed to catch her.

"All right, everyone just sit down for a minute," Kim said sharply. "Just sit and catch your breath."

Dr. Tang knelt beside Beyza and helped her sit up, examining the scrapes she had suffered in the fall.

"You're the one telling us we're not moving fast enough," Sophie said, sinking to the ground.

Walker coughed wetly. He scratched at the rash that had begun to spread on his neck. "And she's right. But if we don't take a minute to rest, we're only going to keep slowing down."

Kim hated to lose even a moment, but her chest hurt, and she felt an ache in her throat as if everything had swollen. Even her eyes ached, but if she kept going, as long as there was an exit, she knew she could find it.

But maybe not with the others.

Staring at Sophie and Beyza, at Dr. Tang and Walker, she blinked in shock to discover she had just considered leaving them behind. Sickness had crept into her, but she had been exposed the least and so her infection had not planted its roots too deeply into her body yet. She could run, just get the hell out of there. Guilt flashed through her, but then she began to rationalize. She could get the contagion box out, get the jar and its dangers out. She could take Lamar's journal from Sophie, so the information there would not be completely lost. Wasn't that the whole point? To keep the jar and its story away from the hands of the jihadis?

Could she do that? Leave the others behind? Could she leave Walker behind? It seemed dreadful to contemplate, and yet the logic resonated within her.

A light flashed from the curve of the tunnel, back the way they'd come.

Kim flinched as the cone of illumination struck her, and she raised her hand to shield her eyes. A voice shouted in Arabic. Kim looked down and saw that the light had settled on the contagion box, and instinctively she turned her back to protect it. A burst of gunfire sprayed the ledge and the wall to her right, sending shards flying. Some impacted her hazmat suit, and she felt the sting as something sharp jabbed her arm.

Then Walker had risen up between her and the flashlight beam . . . between her and the jihadi soldier, the terrorist who had been scouting ahead for his group. He had to be a scout, because now he turned to scream back along the tunnel for help.

Walker took aim and shot the man three times in the chest, one of the bullets taking out his flashlight, as if Walker had used that as his target. Then he turned and grabbed Kim's elbow, running with her along the narrow ledge. Whatever exhaustion had struck him, whatever fog had drawn around his mind, adrenaline had woken him.

Dr. Tang and Sophie grabbed Beyza and they ran, all five of them, no matter how deeply the plague had struck them. It was better to be sick than dead.

TWENTY-SIX

When the ghost came at Walker, he thought he could defend himself. They had been running and stumbling through the winding tunnel. Beyza had fallen again, and this time only Dr. Tang could drag her to her feet. Sophie careened forward with her arms outstretched as if she had been struck blind, but somehow she followed the light of her suit's headlamp. Walker and Kim stayed together, leading the way, Kim's light picking out the shadows and crevices.

The river. Always the river by their side. It echoed and burbled. In places its level dropped, and Walker tried not to think about the fact that they had been going deeper underground instead of climbing toward the surface. With all the hills and valleys in this region, who was to say where the surface might be found?

Shouts followed them and a few bursts of gunfire as if to frighten rabbits from the underbrush, but there were no rabbits here and no brush to hide in. Only the tunnel and the river that must have carved it over centuries. The jihadis went quiet again, perhaps not wanting to let their quarry know how much closer they had come, but Walker felt them gaining ground. The next shots that were fired would be at their backs.

The ledge grew narrower, wide enough for only one of them in some places, and then it broadened again, and here he launched into the closest approximation of a run he could manage with the plague settling into his bones. He felt the fire of lesions opening on his throat and saw them on his arms, and he ignored them and what they meant. And he ignored the ghosts . . .

But the one directly ahead of him, the one standing on the ledge as if it waited for them, could not be ignored. It stared straight at Walker, head cocked to one side as if its neck had been broken. Where the light from Kim's headlamp touched it directly, the thing vanished, but in the gloom of light reflected off the tunnel wall and ceiling, it seemed alive with malice, wisps of blue mist rising from its eyes, though the eyes themselves were oil-black pinpoints.

When it lunged toward him, its lower body lost in shadow, flickering in and out of existence as it passed through Kim's light, its head still canted at that awful angle, yet its eyes remained locked on Walker's. He had been in a hundred fights, had faced would-be killers before, and though he knew this thing existed only as the waste that had been flushed from a human soul, still he charged to meet it. Feverish with plague, all he knew was that it reached for him, and if it could touch him, then surely he could do the same.

Walker had never been so mistaken.

It entered him with the force of a punch to the chest, staggered him backward. Blinking, he bent double and tried to vomit. Something filled him now, like nausea churning in his gut, and the only connection he could make in his mind was to times he had needed to be sick. He heaved, wanting it out of him.

Walker felt it snaking through him, spreading faster than any poison. Images flickered through his mind of hands that were not his own, hands around throats, fingers clenched on the hilts of daggers, palms stained with blood. A jubilation rose in him unlike any he had ever known, a joyfulness that matched the day his son Charlie had been born, the day of his wedding, the moment of his high school graduation, the night he had discovered Sheila McTeague naked in his bedroom, a bow around her waist to celebrate his seventeenth birthday.

No, not matched. This happiness suffused him so that he cried out and thrust his fists toward the ceiling of the tunnel in ecstasy. His hands flexed and opened, and he laughed with the freedom of it.

Then he turned toward Kim, tore open her hazmat suit, and ripped off the headpiece. He grabbed a fistful of her hair and punched her in the side of the face with such force that she spun out of his grip. Locks of black hair hung from his fingers, dancing in the breeze that swept along the tunnel, and he laughed again as she spun on him, eyes wide, and screamed his name, not in fear for herself but in horror at what had become of him.

Even trapped in the little space at the back of his mind where he'd been banished, where he now suffocated as the humming lust for cruelty filled his body, Walker could read Kim's face and her intentions.

"Fight it, Walker!" she said, cradling the contagion box against her ruined hazmat suit. Blue plastic hung around her, and she began to tear it away, keeping the strap of the box over her shoulder. "Don't make me leave you here."

The cruelty inside Walker glanced over his shoulder at the darkness of the tunnel—their only way forward—and then faced the four women again. Beyza wilted to the ground. Sophie tried to make her stand, and she only shook her head, unable or unwilling to rise again. Dr. Tang hung back.

Walker smiled so wide that he felt the corners of his mouth split and tasted his own blood.

Again, Kim said his name. She did not turn away, did not try to run. Instead, she reached out a hand, her eyes pleading with him.

He knew he loved her then, but only in that little space in the back of his mind. The rest of him wanted to rip out her throat with his fingers and paint his entire body with her blood. There was power in that, and he wanted every drop.

The Walker inside wanted to cry out in grief and sorrow, but the outside Walker spat a mouthful of his own blood and lunged for Kim.

Sophie watched it happen—the moment the light went out in Walker's eyes and some other, darker thing gleamed there. She had seen the ghost as it raced toward him, seen it vanish within him, and now she understood. Horror settled into her gut, driving out the terror she had felt only seconds before, and she found herself moving before she had made a conscious decision to do so. All thoughts of herself and her parents disappeared, and she found herself trapped in this single instant, this singular choice. The jar had sat on its altar down in the Pandora Room for so many centuries, an unexploded bomb full of malice and cruelty and disease, and her entire team had been in the midst of a slow-motion explosion ever since she had first set foot in that room. Frustration and anger, guilt and fear all swept up together and drove her to action.

She heard the jihadis shouting farther along the tunnel, but those voices seemed far away as she threw herself at Walker. As he reached for Kim, Sophie tackled him, drove him against the wall, and the two of them fell onto the rough stone ledge. Her left shoulder struck a jutting rock, and she felt her hazmat suit tear. It didn't matter—nothing mattered now. Pain shot through her shoulder, but Walker had landed harder, whacking the side of his head on the ledge.

Sophie hauled back and punched him. Blood and dark spittle flew from his lips. His eyes had begun to turn red as she hit him again, and then a third time, breaking two fingers. The hatred slipped from his face, just a little, and she saw he was in a daze. Sophie leaped up, hauled back, and kicked him hard in the side.

Kim called her name, voice full of fear and concern, maybe for her or maybe for Walker, despite that he'd reached the last stage of this impossible contagion.

"Go!" Sophie shouted at her and Tang and Beyza.

The others started past her on the ledge, teetering on the edge of the river, Dr. Tang holding on to Beyza and almost forcing her to move. Beyza looked so sick now that she would have to be carried if they went much farther.

Kim hesitated, clutching the contagion box against her.

Then the rest of the jihadis came around a corner of the tunnel, back where their advance scout lay dead. They shouted in fury and opened fire. Bullets chipped holes in the tunnel wall and the ledge, some plinking into the water. Sophie whipped her head around to stare for a heartbeat, and she saw them—saw in the light from her headlamp that some were already badly infected, saw the ghosts swarming around them.

Kim ran past her, bullets whining around them.

Sophie turned to follow her, but a sneering Walker reached out and grabbed at her ankle. He used her struggle to drag himself to his feet, took a fistful of her clothing, and spun her around to face him, his grin tearing farther at the corners of his mouth. Red tears slid down his face. He grabbed her throat and squeezed.

She tried to appeal to whatever part of him remained behind those eyes, tried to get him to see the jihadis coming for them. She twisted, tried to get his body between her and the terrorists, but too late.

Bullets struck them both. Sophie felt one punch through her side, then another hit her from behind, exiting out through her left shoulder, and she stepped right off the ledge and into the river.

The last thing she saw as the black water swept her away was Walker tumbling in after her, bullets zipping into the current in pursuit.

TWENTY-SEVEN

Walker thrashed in the water, unable to control his own body. He twisted and began to swim with the current, lit up with the desire to inflict pain. The lust for it kept his eyes open in the darkness, seeking Sophie. A glimpse of the glow of her headlamp reached him, but it winked out, and the current dragged him deeper. He struck a rocky outcropping, twisted around again, and much of the strength left him. On his lips, he tasted the blood streaming from his bullet wounds. He coughed underwater and swallowed a lungful.

Only then did the hate begin to seep from him. Fear became his new infection.

When he kicked his legs and tried to swim for the surface for air, he could not tell if it was his own desire to live driving him or the fear of this ancient cruelty, the horrid relic that had settled into his flesh.

He burst into darkness, no sign of any light. The echoes of gunshots danced from the ceiling overhead, but they were dim and muffled. Walker choked up water, gasped at air, and the last of his strength left him as the pain of his wounds dug in deep.

He sank into the river, and it carried him away.

Dr. Tang saw Sophie floating by, and she knew what they had to do. The gunshots were so loud in the tunnel that she wanted to do nothing but duck her head and scream. But Beyza could not go on without her. She glanced back, expecting to see the jihadis appear behind them in the tunnel any second. Instead, her light found gray figures staggering and floating toward them, blue mist in their eyes. Whatever violence and perversions these ghosts had been perpetrating on one another moments before, they had new targets. The sickness had rooted deep now, and however these ancient sins had grown awareness, they yearned to fill the space inside human flesh again, to infect again.

More gunshots rang out, but the eyes of those cruelties chilled Dr. Tang more than fear of bullets ever would.

Beyza stumbled again, went down on one knee, and from the pure weight of her, Dr. Tang knew they would not make it another step.

Kim had gone ahead a few paces, but she turned and came back for them, reached for Beyza's arm with one hand while holding the strap of the contagion box with the other.

"No," Dr. Tang said, half glancing at the ghosts as she dragged Beyza off the ledge. "Hold on to the box; don't let the jar break. And for God's sake, hold your breath."

Lugging Beyza with both arms, she fell into the river.

Whether or not Kim followed, she could not be sure. Only in that moment did she realize that she should have made the other woman go first. After all, Kim had the jar. If she didn't survive this, it wouldn't matter if the rest of them got out.

Not for long, anyway.

TWENTY-EIGHT

Sunlight.

Walker slit his eyes against the glare. His head pounded, and his body felt empty. Pain clawed at his right thigh and at the left side of his chest. Screams crawled around in his throat and lungs, churning, lurching to find a way to be heard.

A shadow loomed over him. His eyes opened slightly, lids and lashes tacky with dried blood. The sun had been blocked by a man in a uniform. The man's mouth moved, but in Walker's mind, the words were the wretched wail of microphone feedback. Sunlight haloed the man's head.

Walker grabbed his jacket, dragged himself up onto his knees, wrapped his hands around the man's throat, and started to squeeze, baring his teeth with a snarl.

The man used the butt of his gun to knock Walker the fuck out.

TWENTY-NINE

Dr. Durand . . .

Sophie came slowly to wakefulness and wanted nothing more than for sleep to claim her again. Her eyes had yet to open, but she felt the sound begin in her chest, a low moan, the saddest sound she had ever heard—and it came from her.

"Dr. Durand?" the voice said again.

Her entire body hurt. Bright, vivid pain radiated from her shoulder and her side, and she recalled the impact of the bullets punching into her flesh. The smell of her own blood filled her nose, but not only blood . . . fumes.

A sound raged behind the moaning in her chest and the person calling her name, white noise that blanketed everything, so that whoever it was might be beside her or blocks away. Her body swayed, the hard surface beneath her swayed. Vibration came up through that surface and rattled her.

Sophie opened her eyes. She had a mask on, but as she inhaled, she realized this was not the filtration mask. The man kneeling beside her wore a hazmat suit, but the face she saw through the plastic shield was unfamiliar to her. He leaned a bit closer to her.

"Dr. Durand—"

"Sophie," she rasped. "Anyone . . . trying to save my life . . . gets to call me Sophie."

She started to cough. The man glanced up, and only then did

Sophie realize someone else knelt on her other side. A woman in a hazmat suit, also a stranger, injected her with something.

The fear in the woman's eyes woke Sophie's own fear, which rose above the pain. She stared at the woman.

"Am I . . . gonna die?"

"We're doing everything we can," the woman said, but the words sounded hollow, like a blessing from a priest who'd lost his faith. She had obviously said these same words a thousand times and expected to say them thousands more.

"My journal," she rasped.

"It's right here. You haven't lost it," the man said, plucking Lamar's journal from where it had apparently been left, tucked beside her. He pressed it into her hands, and she held it to her chest, wondering how much water damage it had sustained, wondering if it would still be readable, and if she would ever understand Lamar's choices.

"Rest, Dr. Durand," the woman said, taking her hand, her own sheathed in latex. "We've given you something to help with the pain. Everything else we're working on."

Sophie wanted to thank them, but a numbness slipped through her body that felt wonderful and terrifying at the same time. She wanted to be awake and aware, but she would trade those wishes for whatever pain relief these people could provide.

The journal clutched against her breast, she slid into shadow with only a sliver of hope. As the last of her awareness blinked out, one thought followed her down into unconsciousness—the people treating her were alive and well. Wherever they were taking her, there were no ghosts here.

Later—she did not know how much later—her eyes fluttered briefly open, and she saw people rushing around her, medical personnel in hazmat suits shifting her to a gurney and rushing her away from the helicopter. For a moment, she thought they had arrived at a medical center, but she could smell the ocean and could see the ropes and the markings, and she realized they were on some kind of hospital ship.

The helicopter rotors whined, the sound diminishing enough that she heard someone shouting at others to keep back, to clear a path. Sophie's head lolled to one side, and she spotted a group of personnel in white hazmat suits surrounding a single figure in blue. They rushed the blue hazmat suit across the deck toward a door marked with a massive red cross. Someone opened the door, and as the crowd thinned to pass through the door, Sophie saw that the figure in blue still wore the contagion box strapped across her back, the box itself still clutched against her abdomen.

Kim, she thought.

If the doctors on board could find a way to help them, at least Kim might come out of this alive. That was something. Someone would live to tell the story so that Sophie's mother would know how and why she had died and what she had died for.

She found strange comfort in the thought.

THIRTY

When Walker awoke and heard the beep and hiss of medical machinery, he lay frozen on the painfully hard bed and held his breath, waiting. Just waiting. Seconds ticked by as he lay there with his eyes open, staring at the ceiling, listening to the beeping, knowing that his limbs were not his own and expecting that giddy violence to seize him again.

Half a minute went by with him waiting, barely breathing.

Walker blinked. He flexed his fingers and discovered that they were his to control. Drug-dulled pain throbbed in the places he'd been shot and in other places he didn't remember injuring, but when he tried to shift his legs, they moved for him. Spikes of pain rushed through him, but it was his pain. His body. And that counted for a great deal.

Charlie, he thought. If he'd had the strength for tears, he would have been crying. He could see his son's face in his mind. As hope surged within him that he might get home alive, he felt a determination unlike any he had ever known. He would see his son again.

"Charlie," he said aloud, his voice little more than a croak.

Something shifted to his left, in shadow, the creak of weight moving on the adjacent bed. He shifted his head, inviting a spike of pain in his chest, but it was enough to see Dr. Tang sitting on the edge of another hospital bed. The figure lying in that bed did not move, but just from the braids, he recognized the back of Sophie Durand's head.

"Well, well," Dr. Tang said. "I wondered which of you would come around first."

Walker tried to speak, but he coughed instead. Lightly, but enough to light up his chest with pain. He put a hand gently on top of the thick bandages over his chest, wincing.

Dr. Tang hesitated, watching him with concern. After a moment, she exhaled.

"Just a dry throat," she said. "Maybe a residual cough. But you're getting better. We all are."

Walker frowned and groaned as he turned his head the other direction. This ward had eight beds, but only two were full—three, assuming that Dr. Tang had been sleeping in one of them.

"What about—"

"Kim's fine, or she will be," Dr. Tang said. "She was the least affected. Unfortunately, I can't say the same for Beyza. She's isolated in an intensive care infectious disease unit down the hall. It's touch and go, at least from what I've been able to get them to tell me."

Walker laid his head back, stared up at the ceiling. Kim was fine.

"No ghosts?" he rasped.

"No sign in any of us. Beyza hasn't regained consciousness at all since they dredged her out of the river, so there's no way of knowing."

Walker turned his head, frowning at her. "In your medical opinion, Doctor."

"In my medical opinion? We're damned lucky to have gotten out of there alive. Even luckier that the navy had a hospital ship in the Strait of Hormuz. Beyza would be dead if rescue had taken any longer, and you and Sophie would certainly be dead if we had spent any more time underwater. They won't even tell me what they're treating us with, but I'm going to get to the bottom of it. I'd like to know where they've encountered a plague like this in the past, how they recognized its signature so quickly that they knew how to treat us."

They were good questions, but not what Walker wanted to talk about.

"The ghosts," he said again.

Dr. Tang shook her head. "No sign of anything since they dragged me out of the river. I saw something then, but with the sun so bright it might have been dust or just the glare. That was it."

"They haven't done anything . . . like bring in a priest or something?"

"No priest." She smiled, though she seemed more haunted than amused. "No exorcist. The only treatment that I've seen has been medical, but that's been enough to scare the shit out of them."

"They're right to be scared," he rasped.

The pain throbbed in his wounds, but Walker allowed himself a flicker of a smile as he thought of Charlie, of going home. Maybe the time had come to quit this life. He owed that to his son, owed it to himself. But he wasn't going anywhere until he was absolutely certain nothing remained in him from this mission—no trace of anything that had come from that jar, be it illness or the seed of malice.

He glanced down at his body, saw that his clothes had been removed—likely burned—and now he wore only a hospital gown. Walker flexed his hands again, feeling no trace of the cruelty and lust for violence that had possessed him, though the scars of that memory would always remain.

"What about the jar?" he asked.

When the answer came, it wasn't Dr. Tang who provided it.

"Mission accomplished, I guess," the voice said, and Walker craned his neck to see that Kim had entered the room. She wore a hazmat suit, this one white instead of the blue they'd had before. Behind the plastic face shield, her eyes held an unfamiliar hardness, as if they were strangers.

"My mission or yours?" Walker asked.

Kim walked only as far as the bed where Sophie lay unconscious and upon which Dr. Tang still perched.

"Want to hazard a guess? The United States has decided the events of the past two days prove the jar presents a clear and present danger to their own security. Your government might be a three-ring circus of ineptitude these days, but there are still enough strings and levers in place for them to pressure the U.N. to capitulate. The jar is on board this, an American vessel. The second we're out in the open ocean, expect a special ops team to land a helicopter on the deck and make the jar vanish."

Walker felt the anger rising inside him. "How long?"

"An hour or two at most." Kim cocked her head, hazmat suit crinkling crisply. "You should be happy, Walker. You've done your job. Your bosses will be very pleased."

It required no special skill for him to intuit the rest of her thoughts. If and when the contents of the jar were used to kill someone, possibly many someones, Walker would share the blame.

He reached up and ripped the IV out of his arm, then forced himself to sit upright, turning to let his legs hang over the side of the bed. Heat flushed his cheeks, and a wave of nausea struck him, driven by the sting of pain that overrode whatever drugs they'd given him. He ripped off the little pads that had been stuck to his skin to monitor his condition, and the machines began to beep angrily, one producing a low but antagonistic alarm.

"Jesus, Walker, lie down!" Dr. Tang said, jumping up and rushing to take hold of him.

Walker grabbed her wrist and pushed her back. "Not now, Erika."

He groaned as he rose to his feet. Something shifted in his shoulder, grinding bone against bone, as if the bullet might still be in there, but he didn't care. For a moment, he wavered and thought his legs would go out from beneath him, but he took a deep breath and forced himself to walk stiff-legged, a Frankenstein's monster of a man.

Dr. Tang kept talking to him, but Walker ignored her, heading for Kim.

"Where is it?" he asked, staring at Kim.

"What's the point?" she said. "Your work is done, Walker. You did your job."

One hand over the bandaged wound at his side, he glared at her. "Where is it, Kim?"

"Three doors down. This whole corridor is quarantined."

Walker slid past her. Kim grabbed his arm, but he twisted free of her grasp and yanked open the door. It probably should have been locked—probably would have been locked if Kim hadn't just come in. In the corridor outside the door, a hazmat-suited guard glanced up at him, and his bored expression vanished as he realized it wasn't Kim leaving.

"Sir, you can't—" the guard began, not bothering to reach for his sidearm.

Walker reached up with both hands and twisted the headpiece of his hazmat suit halfway around so the guy couldn't see a thing. The guard scrabbled for his sidearm, but Walker had already snatched it from its holster. He shoved the guy against the wall, poked him in the head with the gun's barrel, and then shoved him again.

"Do not test me."

Even blinded, the guard tried to wrest the gun from his hand. Walker smashed him in the skull with the butt of the weapon, then did it again. The guard began to slump, but Walker did not wait to see if he fell. Instead, he turned to run to his left, down the long corridor.

He should have expected the other guard to be there.

Gun pointing at Walker.

"On your knees, right now!" the guard shouted.

Walker obeyed. The man was armed, nervous, and pointing a weapon at his chest, so he followed further instructions as well. He set his stolen gun on the floor, slid it away from him, laced his hands behind his head. The guard he'd attacked groaned and shifted on the floor, but Walker ignored him, focused on the other one—the man walking toward him now.

The guard came an inch too close. Suffused with bright pain, heart galloping, Walker grabbed the barrel of the guard's gun, twisted it sideways, and as the man pulled the trigger, Walker punched him in the crotch. The guard let out a terrible cry as Walker rose, stripped him of his weapon, and raced along the corridor. Bones ground together. A suture at his shoulder tore and began to bleed again.

The whole corridor was under quarantine. There were only patients here, and not an endless supply of hazmat suits, so these were the only two guards. Walker winced as he ran, beginning to limp.

He fired three shots into the locking mechanism of the door Kim had named—the door the guy he'd dick-punched had been guarding—and kicked it in.

The jar had been left inside the contagion box, but the box had been put inside a portable isolation chamber. To Walker, it looked like the sort of thing a sickly newborn would be placed inside at a natal ICU, but this one had the contagion box within its transparent walls. The same dirty cooler with its tangled strap, much the worse for their trip through the tunnel and the river, but still somehow intact.

Walker left the stolen gun on a table. In his hospital gown, he had nowhere to hide it. He unzipped the isolation chamber, reached inside and hoisted the contagion box out by its strap, then slid the strap around his neck and over his right shoulder.

Rushing from the room, he heard shouts from the guards he had assaulted, but they weren't talking to him. They were calling to others who had heard the gunshots and were responding. As Walker came out of the room with the box, he saw the two newcomers stepping through the plastic sheeting at the end of the corridor, where the quarantine zone ended.

Before the second guard had come through the plastic sheeting, Walker was on them both. Cold sweat beaded on his forehead as he struck the first man in the throat, took his gun, and kneed him in the gut. He turned the gun on the second guard as he entered the corridor, and the man raised both hands.

Walker punched him twice in the ribs and shoved him aside. The man grunted, swore, and drew his gun. Walker slammed his foot down, trapping the gun and breaking the guard's fingers, possibly his wrist.

Down the corridor, Kim and Dr. Tang emerged from Walker's own hospital room.

"Ben!" Kim called. "There's nowhere to go!"

Walker heard more guards about to enter the quarantined area, and he realized that he would never fight his way out of here. Hands trembling, he discarded the gun and unzipped the contagion box. Fishing one hand inside, he drew out the jar, tilting it against his chest to keep it from falling. It no longer mattered to him—if it ever had—whether the jar had belonged to Pandora or Anesidora, or whether it was the box of legend in the first place.

"What the fuck are you doing?" Dr. Tang shouted, starting along the corridor toward him.

He held the jar against his chest with both hands. Warm, fresh blood soaked through his hospital gown, a stain spreading at his side and another at his shoulder. Shadows played at the edges of his mind, and he felt the strength leeching out of him. The initial surge of adrenaline had gotten him this far, and now he forced himself to put one foot in front of the other, practically crashing forward.

He purposefully did not hold the jar up to see if the crack in the seal had grown larger in the aftermath of all this jostling. Lurching toward the end of the quarantined corridor, he pushed through the plastic sheeting. On the other side, he found the Plexiglas door to a decontamination chamber.

Walker entered the chamber, yanked the door shut behind him, and hit the red button for decon. He slumped against the wall inside the chamber as jets sprayed him with chemicals and hot water. For long seconds, his mind went dark, nodding off while standing, and then he snapped awake and alert with the pain singing through his body.

A light turned green, and he heard the door unlock.

Walker shoved through it, expecting a dozen guards on the other side, summoned by the gunshots in the corridor. Instead he saw one tech, sitting in a booth where he ought to have been monitoring the decon chamber but was instead reading some kind of textbook. Doing homework for something.

The urge to attack prodded him forward, but Walker shook it off.

As he reached a metal staircase, he heard the tech shout at him, and he did his best to run up the steps. The guards in the quarantine area would be after him now, and this guy he should have knocked out would be raising an alarm, but the best Walker could manage was a fast limp.

The jar felt warm against his chest. A smell rose from it, the dry, powdery scent of old paper. The shadows at the edges of his mind began to swallow his thoughts, and he felt himself falling. Turning, he protected the jar, and he crashed his good shoulder against the stairs. The pain seared through him, could have blacked him out but instead woke him up with a fresh spike of adrenaline.

Jaw clenched against the pain, Walker snarled as he rose. Only three more steps, and he stumbled up them to a landing, a door just ahead.

He heard the stomping of the guards on the metal stairs even as he opened the door and burst out into the hot, humid night under a moonlit sky on the Strait of Hormuz. More voices shouted, not from behind but from either side. An alarm began to sound, the clangor of panic and urgency as news of his theft spread.

Threats were shouted. Guns were raised. Lights were brought to bear on him.

But Walker had the jar, and nobody would dare to shoot him now. They didn't want to breathe whatever it contained.

He shook his head to clear it, unconsciousness threatening, darkness dragging at him.

The railing caught him as he stumbled forward. His forearm cracked against the metal, and he wondered if the bone had broken but knew it was better his bones than the jar.

Drowning in voices and warnings, he hefted the jar over the railing and gave it a shove. Walker collapsed onto the railing, hung draped over it as he watched the jar tumble down through the dark. When it hit the waves, it went straight down as if it held something far heavier than herbs and spells and sins.

It vanished with the tiniest of ripples.

Sailors grabbed him by his hospital gown, twisted him around, and slammed him to the deck. Guards had recovered their weapons, and now they and others took aim, waiting for an order, practically begging for that order.

An officer shoved one sailor aside and grabbed Walker by the throat.

"What the fuck is wrong with you? Do you have any idea what you've done?" he screamed.

Walker smiled.

Kim appeared then, forcing her way among the sailors. "It's not him! I told you already, and Dr. Tang told you, he's not the one doing this."

The Strait of Hormuz was one of the most disputed maritime territories on earth. A U.S. Navy officer sneezed wrong and it could start another Gulf War or worse. An Iranian vessel grew too ambitious, misjudged a moment of hostility, and the result might be just as catastrophic. Simply bringing a navy hospital ship into these waters would have the region on high alert. The United States could never tell anyone what had just happened, never reveal that the jar was at the bottom of the Strait of Hormuz, or a war would erupt before anyone managed to dredge it up from the bottom. If Walker's employers wanted to get their hands on it, they would have to be 100 percent certain they could do so in secrecy. That wasn't likely to happen soon.

By the time they managed to search for it, the currents might have shifted it anywhere. The jar might never be found.

The officer swore at Walker, slammed his head against the deck.

Kim grabbed him by the arm. "Listen to me! Whatever got inside him still hasn't completely burned itself out. This isn't him."

Dr. Tang's voice lifted over the crowd of sailors and guards. "You've also just exposed yourself, Commander. You'll need to be quarantined."

The commander threw up his hands and swore, then turned and started cursing out the guards for letting this happen.

Walker's smile grew wider.

He knew exactly what he'd done.

THIRTY-ONE

When she awoke, but long before she cleared quarantine, Sophie at last found the time to read through Lamar's journal from beginning to end. Some of the pages had been damaged or stuck together, some of the ink blurred, but Sophie could make out enough to fill in the rest. Dr. Tang had told her that Lamar's decline could be traced through his writings, yet still his translations and interpretations were invaluable. It had been his greatest achievement, up until the moment he had begun to unravel.

But the pages she kept coming back to were at the end, where he had scribbled what had look like gibberish to Dr. Tang. They were written in biblical Hebrew, which both Sophie and Lamar had studied. The scrawl had been difficult for her to decipher, but Sophie was sure she had translated it correctly now, after much effort, and the message both healed her and broke her heart. No matter how lost his mind had been there, in the end, he had meant this entry as a message to her. She could interpret it no other way.

I stabbed you in the back, Lamar had written. *Once I crossed that line, I knew I could not go back. If I can say anything in my defense, it is only that when I told them about the jar, I did not believe it was anything but a jar. Now, too late, I know better. The sickness is in me. I see obscenities acted out before me. I have seen so many phantoms here, and now there is a rash spreading on my skin. I think it is in my lungs, too.*

But there is something worse inside me now. It wants me to do terrible things. The caliphate will come for me and for the jar, but I realize now what a fool I have been. So many will die. Friends and strangers by the thousands. It was not supposed to be like this, and I cannot allow it to happen, which means I must become a thief now. I must reveal my ugliest secret to my dearest friend, and I know it will destroy her view of me forever. But if I am successful, you will live, and that is worth any cost.

I hear things. I see things. The urges inside me are repulsive, but I know this one is real. This one is right. I must do it now . . . this very minute. At any moment, the last of me could be erased, and there will be nothing left of me that you would recognize, nothing left of me that would recognize the right and the wrong.

Hate me if you must, my friend.

But live. Whatever you do, please live.

Sophie closed the book and set it aside, waiting for sleep to come again. Waiting for the day the doctors would release her and she could breathe fresh air and feel sunshine again. She would go to France and be with her parents and stay with them for as long as her father had left. Lamar had battled sickness of body and soul to concentrate enough to write her those final thoughts, and his last action in this world had been to try to save her and the rest of their team. Their friends and colleagues.

She would do as he'd asked for as long as she was able.

Sophie would live.

THIRTY-TWO

At the bottom of the sea, the jar rolled in the current, brushed against a bed of seagrass, where it caught for a time. A turtle hiding in the grass turned and swam away, and even when the ebb and flow of the current tugged the jar away, turning it 'round and tumbling it far from that bed of seagrass, the turtle never returned.

Fish began to follow the jar, to swim circles around it, languidly at first and keeping track of its movement across the bottom of the strait and out, in time, into the Arabian Sea. Far above, light glinted on the waves, but here in the depths was only darkness. Within that deep shadow were shadows deeper still. They appeared to be fish, but gray and translucent, with a blue gleam in their eyes that left a trail in the water as they swam.

The other fish—the ones who had always been here—began to rot and drift and die, but soon those spectral fish swam to them and vanished. The sick ones turned on each other then and tore each other apart.

If sound traveled down there, deep beneath the sea, you might have been able to hear them laugh.